Surviving Cyril

Ramsey Hootman

ISBN 978-0-9988070-0-3
ISBN 978-0-9988070-1-0 (ebook)

for Beowulf
my greatest challenge
Gawain
my extra measure
and
Ripley
my joy yet to come

Part One
Fall

1

ROBIN'S HAND CLOSED TIGHT around the bottle of pills when she saw him standing there, a big black thumbprint smudge on the fresh-cut field of green.

She probably wouldn't have gone through with it anyway. She'd survived the funeral, and the day after, and the day after that. Odds were, she wasn't going to work up the nerve.

Still. This was her place. Her time. His presence denied her even the small comfort of an imagined end.

She shoved the bottle into her low-slung canvas purse and started to get back in the truck, belatedly recognizing his geriatric gray Datsun at the other end of the lot. But then he glanced up and she knew he'd seen her there, in her ragged cutoffs and no bra and her hair sticking out at all angles in a huge, unkempt fro. There was no retreat, after that, because she wasn't a coward.

Cyril would have dwarfed her even if he hadn't tipped the scales somewhere in the neighborhood of five hundred pounds, but when she stopped next to him she found herself fully in his shadow. The armpits of his black t-shirt were ringed with sweat, and the flesh of his bare feet sagged over the edges of his ever-present flip flops.

He didn't look up. Didn't say anything, though he had to know she was there. The only sound was the distant drone of an air tanker and his heavy, labored breath. At his size, standing in one place for any period of time was an effort. And it was fire season in Camarillo. Even at eight on a September Sunday morning, the sun was scorching.

Let him stand, then. He was the one who owed her an explanation, not the other way around.

And so they stood, staring at a newly cut stone ringed with wilting flowers.

Tavis would have known exactly what to say.

Eventually Cyril shifted, letting out a heavy puff of air, and hiked up the waistband of his baggy black sweatpants. "Jesus," he muttered. "You couldn't've sprung for a spot under the trees?"

He excelled at nothing so much as getting under her skin. It was a sport, for him, even in the face of death. But he would not get the better of her. Not today. Not ever again. "Not if I wanted Seth to have a college fund," she said, with a kind of cool, dangerous calm.

That was a lie, mostly. Within twenty-four hours of delivering the news, ten interminable days ago now, the Casualty Assistance Calls Officer had handed her a check for a hundred thousand dollars. No strings attached. She could have blown every last cent on a spot back in the grove, with a proper headstone to match. Except that she had Seth. And a hundred grand would barely last them the year, here in California. So she couldn't just go crazy with grief. Couldn't down a bottle of pills and lay on the loamy sod they'd rolled out on top of her husband's body and breathe her last.

He grunted. "Where is he, anyway? School?"

"Why do you care?" Seth was staying with her mom, up in Santa Barbara, ostensibly until Robin pulled herself together. As if that were even possible. She looked at Cyril, her eyes level with the text on his stupid shirt that proclaimed, 'I read your email' in pixilated white letters. "What are you even doing here?"

He thrust a hand at the rectangle of granite on the ground. His skin was so pasty even the little half-moons under his fingernails were white. "What's it look like?"

"If you were here for him, you'd have shown up at the funeral."

"What, so I could watch a bunch of faceless drones shoot guns and play taps? Pass."

As if Robin had been eager to sit through three hours of ritualized mourning. Cyril's face made her want to punch him, but she thrust her clenched fist deep into her purse instead. Though she hadn't touched the pills, the sudden movement made them rattle.

Cyril looked down, eyes darting to her purse, and Robin could have sworn she saw the ghost of a smirk.

He knew.

Not only what she'd been contemplating, but that she'd never follow through.

She would have. In a heartbeat. If not for Seth. Parental love was the worst kind of impotence.

Robin imagined pulling out the pills—left over, ironically, from Seth's birth—and seeing how many she could choke down before Cyril stopped her. If he even bothered to try.

She turned and walked away.

"Hey. Wait."

"What? What do you want from me?" Whatever it was, she wanted it over, fast—so she could move on to never seeing him again.

He leaned to one side, fumbling in one baggy pocket, and held out a hand.

Robin didn't have to look to know her name was scrawled on the slightly-crumpled envelope, or that there was a handwritten letter inside. "Seriously?" Tavis knew how she felt about Cyril. He had about fifty best friends on the base. And still— "He left this with *you?*" Her voice whined upward at the end, threatening tears, but she choked down the golf ball in her throat.

"Yeah, *me*. Look, sorry, okay? Sorry for not—you know what? No, actually. I'm not fucking sorry." Cyril made a motion as if to fling the letter at her feet, but it didn't leave his hand. "Take it."

Robin looked at him, finally—really *looked* at him, and saw that maybe not all the glistening droplets on his face were the product of perspiration. She wanted to scream obscenities in his face. This was hers—her husband, her grief. Not his. And yet she couldn't deny that, partly, it was.

She snatched the envelope from his trembling hand and shoved it into her purse. "Okay. Duty fulfilled." She gave him a mock salute and turned once again for the truck.

"Are you—"

She whirled. "*What?*"

He drew in a breath. Pressed his lips together. "You're not gonna…"

She followed his eyes to her purse. "Oh, I'm sorry, did you want me to share? Read it out loud, maybe?"

"Depends," he shot back. "Got any popcorn?"

Didn't matter what she said; he could always one-up her for snark. "Screw you, Cyril." She started to turn away, for the last time, and abruptly changed her mind. She strode back to the fresh patch of grass, stepped into the ring of flowers, and seated herself on Tav's stone. This was her place. "Leave."

He opened his mouth, but she wasn't going to let him have the last word.

"*Leave.*"

Cyril made do with a sharp gesture, as if swatting an insect with the back of his hand. He said something else as he lumbered off—it might have been *bitch*—but a sudden breeze snatched the word away.

Robin followed him with a glare. Only when his car was out of sight did she dip a hand back into her purse. She traced her name with a finger, and then held the edge of the envelope against her upper lip. The paper didn't smell like Tavis.

She closed her eyes and sighed. "You jerk."

Cyril had been the one who brought them together, in his usual backhanded way, so having the final hand-off come from him was probably Tav's idea of a joke—at least, from the vantage point of planning for the worst without seriously considering it might happen.

"All of *a* sudden."

That's what he'd said to her. Spring in San Luis Obispo, her freshman year. She'd been in the big study hall on the bottom floor of the library, rehearsing her part of the philosophy presentation in front of her group—two guys and another girl, all jaded seniors just trying to get their last GE credits out of the way. She'd been fresh and new and trying too hard, but she couldn't help it that she cared.

Cyril? Cyril had been sitting a few empty chairs down, by himself, an honest-to-god astrophysics textbook propped open on the table as he dumped a snack-sized bag of Cheetos directly into his mouth. He'd been merely overweight then; cute, even, in a soft, baby-faced way. At least until he opened his mouth.

"I'm sorry?" she'd said, because it was quite clear to everyone that he'd been addressing her.

"Jesus, you've said it like five times. Goddamn nails on a chalkboard. It's not all of *the* sudden. It's all of *a* sudden. Don't you even read?"

Later—walking back to the dorms, in the shower, lying in bed that night—she'd composed a dozen scathing comebacks. But there, in the moment, she'd glanced at her group and seen that at least one of them had been thinking the same thing, just too polite to say. "None of your business," she'd snapped, or something like that, and managed to muster enough dignity to finish her speech.

Cyril had polished off his Cheetos and continued to flip through his textbook as the guy across from her took his turn presenting.

That was when Tavis had arrived: tall and slim and unquestionably *military* even in civilian clothes. He was fresh out of boot camp, quite literally having jumped on a northbound bus the moment graduation ended. The gaze of every girl within a hundred meters, and some guys too, swiveled to take in that sharp-cut flame of red hair. He dropped his canvas seabag on an empty chair and sat down. Next to Cyril.

Robin scowled.

Tavis cocked his head at her in a silent query as he clapped an arm around Cyril's shoulders. He was obviously the kind of guy who didn't get many scowls from women.

She'd turned her attention, pointedly, back to her group. Later, when she snuck another glance, he was hunched over next to Cyril, both of them talking fast and low.

"He's sorry."

That's what Tavis had said to her, when he'd caught up with her outside the library.

She snorted. "No he's not."

Tavis had opened his mouth, shut it again, and frowned. Clearly that was not the answer he'd expected. "How do you know... that?"

She'd thrust her palms toward him. "Because *you're* standing here.

Did he actually send you, or do you run around cleaning up his messes on your own initiative?"

He'd held the frown for another moment. Then the corner of his mouth quirked up, and he'd grinned—oh God, that grin—as he held his hands up in surrender. "He's not all bad, I swear. He just gets really into stuff—right now it's rockets—and forgets that people are, you know, *people*." He lifted his shoulders, a kind of helpless gesture, and let his arms drop. "Sorry. From me this time."

"Apology accepted." And without waiting for more, she'd turned on a heel and walked away.

As a first meeting, it wasn't much. Tavis had seemed nice enough, but no different from any of the other earnest, gung-ho squids she'd met over the course of her father's Naval career. No sparks had flown, and she'd mostly been irritated with Cyril.

And so, apparently, that was how it was to end.

She shifted, relieving the pressure on her tailbone, and slipped a thumb under the edge of the envelope seal.

As if. Who did she think she was kidding? She wasn't going to read it. Not today, not tomorrow. Maybe at some distant, hypothetical point in the future when even the thought of Tav's white-toothed grin didn't make her want to weep.

She put a hand on the tombstone. "I don't get it," she said. "You and him. I never have." And now she never would.

It was the first time she'd spoken to him. Tavis. Like this.

She knew her mother still spoke to her father, and found comfort in it. But Robin's words dropped from her lips like stones. What was the point, if there was no reply?

She stood—and only then discovered the two deep oval impressions Cyril had left in Tav's fresh blanket of sod. She used a toe to try to brush the grass back into place, but the damage had already been done.

2

ROBIN STRADDLED THE PIANO bench in the living room, staring at the envelope, until the half-finished Corona at her elbow grew warm.

The upright had been her paternal grandmother's, originally. When Robin was eight, her father had spent two weeks restoring it, sanding every inch by hand. When she asked why, he'd looked up, temples beaded with sweat, and said, "Honey, sometimes words just don't do shit." He'd patted the fallboard with one big, callused hand. "I need something real."

What Robin needed was his arms around her, strong and heavy and warm.

She couldn't have that, but... here, at the piano, was where the memory of him felt most real. Whenever she was feeling sad, she'd always been able to count on Tavis sitting down to pound out a few of her father's favorite ragtime tunes.

This was where she'd remember them both, now.

Robin couldn't play, but maybe when Seth got older, he—

No.

She finished off the beer, went into the kitchen, and spent the next twenty minutes in front of the fridge, staring at funeral leftovers. Having another beer seemed like the simplest solution, but she'd already done the get-drunk-and-pass-out-alone thing twice. Couldn't make it a habit. She wasn't *wife* anymore, but she was still Mom.

What was Seth doing, just now? Glennis had probably popped him into the car for her mid-morning Starbucks run. He'd be sitting in a big leather chair enjoying a cake pop and chatting with strangers while Glennis read the paper. Assuming they'd made it to the shop.

And why wouldn't they?

Robin dug her phone out of her purse and gave the power button a tap. Glennis had been sending a steady stream of photos since she had taken Seth home from the funeral on Thursday afternoon. Since Robin had gotten back from the cemetery this morning, however, there had been only one new notification, and it wasn't from her mother.

Andrews.

Lieutenant Commander Andrews, to be more precise, although he'd asked her to call him Bill. Didn't matter what she called him; he was still the guy who had appeared on her doorstep with his hat in his hands. She'd have preferred never to see that apologetic face ever again, but he was now her liaison in all things Navy.

I told the guys to lay low, the text read, *like you asked.* Because every single one of Tav's friends wanted to change her oil or fix her fence or accompany her to the DMV or contribute to Seth's college fund and she hated them all for the simple crime of being alive. Thank God she wasn't living on the base. *But there's an NCO who very much wants to speak with you. She served with Tavis last fall. Can I give her your number?*

Robin used both thumbs to punch out a reply: *What part of No Contact don't you understand?* She respected the service and the men and women who served. She could hardly do otherwise, as a Navy brat herself. The only reason she hadn't joined after high school was because her father had always said the military was not the same place for an enlisted woman as it was for a man. Go to college first, he'd said, and become an officer if she still had the bug. But then she'd met Tav, and now she was done. With all of it, with all of them. All that dignity and honor and strength and—what had it gotten her, in the end?

She opened the fridge again and grabbed a crystal bowl of fruit mixed with cool whip and coconut. The sink was overflowing and there wasn't a single clean plate in the cupboard, so she took the entire bowl back to the piano. There, she forced herself to eat a chunk of watermelon, a grape, and half a strawberry, ignoring the fact that her stomach had knotted itself into a little peach pit of dread.

Seth was fine. Her father had died at sixty. He'd had plenty of good years, even if she'd wanted more. Tavis—well, his death had been an anomaly, or at least significantly against the odds. And he'd been living in a war zone.

Still, just because she'd lost Tavis didn't mean she couldn't lose Seth. What was more common than death by traffic accident? Her mom was a good driver—but easily distracted, and there was no greater distraction than Seth in the back seat. It didn't even have to be her fault. Some other idiot in a rush might run a red, T-boning her mother's Prius on the passenger side. Seth could be injured fatally, bleeding out, wondering why his mommy wasn't there by his side as he took his last breaths, alone.

She couldn't do this. She *could not* do this. She needed—

Something real.

She retrieved her phone from the kitchen and thumbed to the last text from her mom, a photo of Seth at the park, and hit reply. *How's it going this morning? Haven't heard from you since—*

Robin clicked the screen off. She might be a basket case on the inside, but she refused to be the kind of widow who spent months curled up in bed, moaning. Her little boy deserved a functional parent.

Back to the piano.

Upstairs, under their—her—bed, there were boxes. Photo boxes, the roughly shoebox sized ones with the little metal frames on the end so you could slip in a label. You could trace Tav's deployments by looking down the rows: the neat, slightly yellowed envelopes he'd sent from Pendleton switched abruptly to typo-riddled emails from Afghanistan, which she'd printed out on the backs of returned homework at the nearest campus lab. After that came envelopes again, including all the extra wedding invitations he'd squirreled away somewhere and left, one by one, under her pillow on his way to work at Hueneme. That blissful two-year stretch bridged three boxes, ending with birth announcements and congratulations. The next deployment had been the hardest. He'd written every day, those long nine months, although he hadn't always been able to send them immediately. The backlog had run two or three weeks at times. But they were all there. And he had come home.

She'd held on through it all because she'd thought that would be the end of it: not his letters, but the need for them. His disillusionment with his service in Afghanistan had peaked, and he'd planned to come home, get his RN or train as an EMT. Except... he hadn't. He'd written the next series of letters on beautiful handmade stationery, lavender petals pressed into the fibers. As if the quality of the paper could soften the blow of his re-enlistment. His pigheaded conviction that he needed to go greenside again. Those pages were full of promises that he'd be much safer, as a senior line corpsman, than he had been the last time around.

Twenty-two emails more, after he'd hit the ground. One for each day. And now this one. This very last one.

She rested her hands, fists clenched, on either side of the envelope, and stared at her name written in Tav's hasty black scrawl. "Okay," she whispered. "Come on."

Like ripping off a Band-Aid.

The pills were in her purse, if she needed them.

Five minutes passed. Perhaps ten.

She couldn't. She wasn't ready for it to be the end.

Robin turned her back on the piano, the bench creaking as she scooted her legs around. She looked at her feet, and then the couch, and then the TV—Oh, God.

The cabinet beneath the television was packed with Seth's very favorite picture books and a big zippered canvas DVD caddy. Most of the discs corresponded to a book, all labeled in the same chicken-scratch permanent marker, although there were a few with Tavis singing silly songs and telling goofy made-up stories. He'd make one or two at Cyril's place whenever he went over, and by now there were probably about sixty recordings. Seth watched "Daddy Stories" every morning while Robin showered, and sometimes another one at night before bed. That's what he had been doing when Andrews rang the bell. And it would be the first thing he asked for when Glennis brought him home.

Robin hit the eject button. *Ladybug Girl* slid out of the player. She zipped the caddy open and tucked it inside. Maybe it made her the worst parent in the world, but she took the DVDs into the hall, opened the closet, and shoved them in between two winter blankets on the topmost shelf.

She wasn't trying to erase him. She wasn't. She couldn't. But she couldn't handle—she just couldn't. Not right now.

Right now, she needed to bury her nose in the sticky-sweaty crook of her son's neck and breathe his grubby little boy scent and know he was *alive*.

On her way back through the living room, she picked up the letter. She snagged her purse in the kitchen and tucked the envelope deep inside, into the zippered pocket she used for tissues and sanitary pads. By the time she crossed the threshold into the back yard, she was running. Out the back gate, hands shaking as she unlocked the cab. Forty-five minutes up the coast from Camarillo to Santa Barbara.

When Glennis opened the door of her bungalow and found her daughter on the porch, she spread her bony arms and pulled Robin into a hug.

"I need him," Robin said, stooping to return the gesture gently. Her mother had never been large, and she'd seemed to shrink a little more every year since her husband's passing. "I need him with me right now."

Seth sat on the living room floor, babbling to himself over a canister of tinker toys. When he was focused on something, the rest of the world simply ceased to exist. Rainbows from her mother's sun catchers and stained glass window hangings spiraled across the carpet. Robin stood in the entryway, watching, willing herself not to cry.

Glennis ran her fingers, rough and cracked from decades of handiwork, over Robin's ponytail, which stood out from the back of her head like a bottle brush. "Why don't you let me style this, sweetie? I have time." As the blindingly white mother of a biracial—ergo black—daughter, Glennis had received enough unsolicited criticism about the state of her child's hair that it was still a point of stress, even a decade after its care was no longer her responsibility. Even when it was just about the last thing in the world that mattered.

"It's okay, mom. I have an appointment." Well, she'd been meaning to make one, anyway. She'd pulled her hair out after the funeral and left it free since then. At this point, "untamed" was an understatement.

Glennis let her hand drop and sighed, heavily. "This… is a kind of pain I hoped you'd never have to experience."

"I know, Mom." The words came out sharper than Robin intended. Her mother meant nothing but the best, but her eyes flickered to the portrait on the mantle, Robin's father looming large as life in his service dress blues. Her mother's grief was not for Tavis so much as her husband. He'd died of heart disease, after thirty years of marriage. It was not the same.

Before Glennis had a chance to get all weepy, Robin knelt down on the carpet and rubbed Seth's shaggy head. No matter how old he got, she could never get over his hair—the genetically improbable cross between her tight coils and Tav's copper red. When she'd given birth, after that last great push, they'd popped him onto her suddenly gelatinous stomach and she'd laughed in surprise. Even now, it still seemed miraculous that her own body had produced this adorable little gremlin. "How you doing, bud? Having fun with grandma?"

Seth flashed his father's toothy grin and lunged into her arms. He was a big boy, barrel-chested like his grandfather; often mistaken for five or six even though he wouldn't even be four for another month.

A birthday party. Oh, God.

Not now. Right now she returned his vice-like squeeze and blew a raspberry into his neck, which made him flail with helpless laughter. One of his knees caught her in the ribs, but she was used to his exuberant battering. She sat him up again. "Whatcha makin?"

He lifted his creation and flashed a big grin. "A hoptacopter!"

"You mean a helicopter?"

"A *hopta*copter." He demonstrated what appeared to be some sort of gun attached to the wooden dowel fuselage.

"I see." Arguing with a three-year-old's linguistic authority was never wise. She pulled her knees up and rolled to her feet. "I'm gonna get your stuff together and then we'll head home, okay?"

She went to the guest room—which was mostly Seth's room, now— and collected his backpack, rumpled pajamas, and the stuffed penguin he'd loved into a lopsided parody of its namesake animal. Robin hugged it to her chest before tucking it into Seth's bag.

"Sweetie..." Glennis hovered in the doorway behind her.

"I know, Mom. Okay? I know." Robin ducked into the laundry room for the rest of Seth's clothes. She grabbed the potty seat and ran everything out to the truck, then came back and knelt next to him again.

"Hey Sethie." This time she interrupted him with a kiss on his hot little cheek. She wanted to squeeze him until he couldn't breathe. "You ready to go?"

Seth usually had to be wheedled out of grandma's house with a snack or a promise of a fun activity; this time, he dropped the tinker toys and bolted for the door.

"Whoa! Hold on, buddy! Go give grandma a hug and a kiss, okay? And tell her thank-you."

Robin used Seth to get out the door: That was a good hug, but did you kiss Grandma too? You love Grandma, don't you? All right, hop in your car seat. Wave good bye! Say thank-you, Grandma, see you soon! Her mother slipped in one last long, emotion-laden embrace, but Robin drew back, forcing a smile. "Okay, we better get going before Sethie has to pee again."

Glennis folded her arms and stepped back. "Are you sure you're okay to drive? I could—"

"I'm fine, Mom. Really." Robin shut the cab door and waved.

Glennis raised her voice as Robin backed out of the drive. "Text me when you get home, okay?" She pressed her lips together. "I worry."

Robin nodded an acknowledgement and headed for the freeway.

When she asked Seth, over one shoulder, what he'd done at Grandma's house, he claimed—as usual—that he "didn't know." Nor did he know what he'd eaten for breakfast, or lunch. Robin sighed and merged into traffic, settling in behind a big rig doing sixty. Seth busied himself playing with whatever toys had collected in the back seat, whispering explosive dialogue to himself. After a while he fell silent, and she wondered if the miracle of miracles had happened: naptime. The truck was the only place he ever nodded off, anymore.

She was angling the rearview mirror to check when there was a familiar click.

"Hey, Buddy," said the ghost of Tavis Matheson. "Daddy misses you."

She had forgotten the portable player.

"You wanna sing a song? I got a new one." There was a staticky rustle of clothing. Tavis clearing his throat. "Twinkle, twinkle, little Seth. Don't you know my kid's the best?"

"Sethie," she said, but it came out a whisper. Suddenly the semi in front of her was a blur. Robin fumbled for the emergency light before hitting the brakes and pulling onto the shoulder.

"Even though his daddy's far, his heart knows exactly where you are."

"Mommy? What's happen?"

"Sweetie—" she bit the inside of her cheek, hard. "Sweetie, can you please—"

"Twinkle, twinkle, little Seth, you're my kid and you're the best."

"What, Mommy?" Seth said loudly.

"Turn Daddy off!" she shouted. "Just turn him off, okay?" And she shoved the door open and tumbled out and slammed it behind her and put her hands over her mouth and screamed. The hot afternoon rush of traffic mostly drowned her out, and when her lungs were empty she turned around and kicked the tire as hard as she could. Her sneaker did nothing to blunt the impact, and her toe let her know she had made a mistake.

There was no switching Tavis off, no bottling up his memory for another day. His digital footprints were everywhere. Re-living those moments had been a comfort, when he was away—during his deployments, she'd watched the YouTube video of their first encounter twice a day at the very least. Not the one in the library, with Cyril; nobody had thought that incident worthy of record. That evening, however, when she'd been chatting with her roommate on their way back to the dorms—that was when Tavis had fallen out of the sky.

Robin had jumped back, letting out a shriek of surprise. The video, taken by one of the dozens of students who stopped to gawk at the encounter, caught the tail-end of her exclamation: "Where on earth did you come from?"

"Not earth at all—the moon!" He pointed upward through the maple tree branches—where, she realized, he must have been sitting. "And I don't mean that figuratively!"

His fervent delivery, marred slightly by the nervous waver in his tone, was completely disarming. She laughed, not unkindly.

"No, I'm serious! Look!" He brushed the shoulders of his white undershirt. "Stardust!"

She propped her hands on her hips. "And I suppose you rode there on your friend's rocket?"

"How'd you know? He was so ticked off at me he strapped me to the darn thing and shot it off. I'm lucky to be alive!"

She snorted. "Cute. Okay, what do you want?"

"Your ear."

"My *ear?*"

"For about five minutes." He reached into the back pocket of his crisply ironed khakis and pulled out a piece of paper. A flick of his wrist caused it to flutter open. "Dear Robin."

Robin groaned, embarrassed on his behalf. "Look, you seem like a nice guy, but please don't—"

He held up a hand. "Dear Robin," he insisted. "Forgive me for speaking like a fool today; it was only because I was so star-struck. Men have written poems about *la bella luna* since time began, but here I stand, with moon-dust on the soles of my shoes. I have trod upon its very face—and I tell you, Robin, that it is not more radiant than you."

"Oh my God," her roommate said. "This is the most romantic thing ever."

Robin wasn't so easily swept off her feet; her father had been stationed at NSA Naples for most of her high school career, and nobody beat Italians for over-the-top romantic gestures. But she smiled.

"Then you spoke," he continued, taking a step forward and lowering his voice. It was hard to hear his words in the video, but Robin had them memorized. The paper he gripped was the first entry in her collection— she'd read it so many times it was yellow from handling. "And I despaired. Because here is a woman both beautiful and eloquent, and I... have no voice. This stupid muscle, which some might generously call a tongue, is in every way the enemy of my brain. I know I have no more right to your presence, but please. Let me write."

And he had. Oh, he had.

Tires sounded on gravel. Robin looked up to see a brown Lincoln pull over in front of her. Of course—a good Samaritan. She gave the car a wave as the driver's door opened. "I'm fine!"

It was an older gentleman, graying hair slicked back over his skull. He wore a pair of snakeskin boots. "Estás bien?"

"Sí, sí, estoy bueno. Mi niño—" She hooked a thumb over her shoulder. "He was driving me a little crazy and I had to pull over before I killed someone." She fished her phone out of her pocket and held it up. "Don't worry, I can call if I need help. Thanks for stopping." What was the Spanish? *L'arresto* was Italian… "Gracias por pasar."

He nodded, mimed tipping a hat, and got back into the vehicle. Robin watched as the Lincoln swerved back into traffic. A BMW honked.

She could have used another ten minutes (or hours, or days), but Seth was probably beginning to worry. She opened the driver's door and got back in. "Sorry, sweetie. Mommy just… got a little sad."

He was silent for a beat. "Cuz Daddy?"

"Yes, Sweet Pea. Because Daddy died."

Tavis had been in Afghanistan for the entirety of Seth's second year of life, and while saying good-bye again hadn't been easy, for Seth it had been like the end of a long holiday. Tav's presence was more treat than expectation. So explaining his death had been absurdly simple—the first time.

What she hadn't counted on was the difficulty of conveying the absolute permanence of death to someone who barely even had a concept of time. The day after Andrews had delivered the news, Seth had jumped out of bed and asked if Daddy was back yet. To a three-year-old, there was no difference between gone today and gone forever.

"To Jesus?"

She glanced in the rearview mirror. "What, sweetie?"

"Daddy… died to Jesus?" He said it slowly, as if he'd been rolling the thought over in his brain for some time.

"Yeah. Remember, we put his body in the ground? His heart and his mind are in heaven with Jesus now." Robin wasn't strictly sure of this, theologically. If she remembered right, everyone was basically just dead until the end of the world and the resurrection, and then they'd all be brought back at once, together. Or maybe the dead were in some sort of limbo, the whole Old Testament Sheol thing. But her abbreviated explanation felt right for a three-year-old, who still seemed to wonder when this mysterious 'Jesus' guy was going to finally show up. "Jesus will take care of Daddy until we die, too, and then we'll all be together again. But... right now it's sad because he's gone."

Seth considered this. "I like Daddy stories."

"Yes." Robin bit her lip. "I know you love Daddy's videos, but it's really hard for me to hear them right now. It makes me sad, because I want Daddy back." She twisted around and gave him a smile. "And it's a little dangerous to cry while I'm driving, right?"

He looked very serious. "Oh. Sooorry." He said it in his little singsong-voice.

"You don't have to be sorry, Sweetie. Just... save it for later, okay?" She fumbled around down on the floorboard behind her seat and came up, finally, with a foam sword. "Why don't you play with this instead?"

"Kay."

Robin took another moment to compose herself before putting the blinker on and merging, painfully conscious that if a driver behind her was too busy singing along with the radio, or sneaking a look at a text—bam, someone was dead. Odds were it would be the smallest, most fragile person involved. She couldn't lose him.

"Momma?" Seth asked abruptly. "Are we gonna die?"

"Uh... not for a long time, I hope. I hope you get to live a long, long time and have a happy life. I'll probably die before you, since I'm older, but we'll live together for a long time." Said the woman who'd spent the last three days wandering the cemetery with a bottle of pills. "Okay? So don't worry. Mommy's not going anywhere."

Seth was silent for a long while. And then: "Momma?"

"Yes, sweetie."

"I want you to die and me to die and we will die to Jesus and hold hands."

She swallowed, hard, and nodded. "Okay," she managed. "Okay."

Her phone dinged. Had she forgotten something at her mom's? They definitely had Pengie. Everything else was easily replaced. Oh well; if it had been critical, her mom would have called. She concentrated on driving.

By the time they got home, Seth had latched onto the idea of doing bubbles in the back yard and simply could not wait one single solitary instant more, so she dumped his things on the back porch and set him up with soap and a wand before running inside to pee. Before she'd even flushed he was yelling about being *starving*. Sighing, she opened the fridge and was spooning leftover potato salad onto a couple of paper plates when she remembered her mother's text.

Robin licked a bit of salad off her finger, wiped it on the bottom of her shirt, and reached into her purse.

It wasn't a text. It was an email.

From Tav.

3

WAS IT—COULD IT BE POSSIBLE, somehow, that he was not really—

She looked out the window. Seth was still in the back yard, getting into the sandbox now, starvation apparently forgotten. The gate was closed. He wasn't going anywhere.

No. Tavis was dead. He was gone. She had buried what little was left of his body. She had watched the coffin being lowered into the ground. But she hadn't opened it. She hadn't seen his face.

What if, somehow, there had been a terrible mistake—

She tapped the notification. The email winked open.

If you're getting this, it's because... well, it's because the worst has happened.

Robin flung the phone against the wall. She ran to the bathroom, dropped to her knees, and vomited into the toilet bowl.

She couldn't cry. Any moment Seth would notice he was alone and come to find her and she needed to have her shit together when he did. He had already lost too much. He did not also need to lose his mom.

Robin crumpled up a few squares of toilet paper and used the wad to wipe her mouth. She dropped it into the toilet and flushed before getting to her feet.

The phone lay on the tile floor between the kitchen counter and the short back hall. She almost hoped the fall had killed the thing, but after a near-miss with Seth and the toilet she'd bought a case that was nigh indestructible.

She bent to pick up the phone, her legs suddenly rubber.

Maybe she should save it. Tuck it away, like the letter in her purse.

Maybe if she'd never opened it at all. But she'd read the first line. She couldn't just leave it undone. She couldn't even wait until Seth had gone to bed.

If you're getting this, it's because... well, it's because the worst has happened. This was never what I wanted. But it was always a risk. I'm sorry.

God. Where do I start?

Here: Someone died today. I did everything I could and it wasn't enough. I couldn't save him, and I'll spend the rest of my life wondering whether his blood is on my hands. You're probably thinking I'm too hard on myself, that I shouldn't blame myself for not being able to save him when it was someone else who blew him to kingdom come. Honestly, though, it's just a lot more complicated and a whole lot dirtier than I could ever explain. Even if it's not my fault, it's always going to feel that way.

He has a family, Robin. A wife and kid. Technically it's not my duty to write a letter, but I've been sitting here for two hours anyway, with a pen and a blank page and all I can see are your eyes.

He was a good man.

I miss you so much. All I want is to put my nose in your hair and breathe.

Robin let herself sink to the kitchen floor, back against the corner cabinets. She hugged her knees to her chest and breathed.

You looked so sad when I left. Not your face—you've gotten good at hiding behind anger—but I knew. It's the electricity of your touch; in the wary, catlike way you move. The terrible thing is how beautiful you are when you're hurt. You always know what to do in a crisis, and it's not just because you're a quick thinker. It's because you've imagined every awful outcome in advance and prepared for it—so when it happens, you know exactly what to do.

I hate that I've given you the kind of life that makes this necessary.

I worry that there's such a thing as being too strong. That someday there will be something you cannot face alone.

Let me be honest. I fear that the one thing you might not be able to handle is losing me.

Isn't that the most egotistical bullshit you've ever heard?

But when I come face to face with death, all I can think about is you, alone, and how I can't leave you that way. I think of how beautiful you are and how much I love you. Writing down the things I might say, if I knew this was the end, makes me feel a little better.

And I got this idea—a way to leave something, for you. Cyril wrote a script, a sort of program, so I can stockpile these emails. All he needs to do is turn it on. I'm not sure how many there will be, in the end. It's randomized within a few parameters, set up so you'll get something from me once every week or so until they're all gone.

See? He's not entirely bad.

"Mommy?" Seth's voice called from outside. "Moooooommy!"

Robin lifted her head. "Co—" The word stuck, and she had to clear her throat and try again. "Coming! One second!" There was only a little left. She read quickly.

I hope you're not crying. You know I don't want you to spend one minute more than you must in mourning. But if you need to, it's okay. Let your heart out now and then. Keep it bottled up too long and it'll suffocate. Be weak and human. You're allowed. Seth won't be scarred forever if he sees you cry.

Most of all, Robin, please... Be happy. Love Seth. Hug him for me; watch him grow. See his children and his grandchildren if you can. He needs you more than you ever needed me.

And in the meantime, I'll be right here. Waiting on the other side.

"Moooooooommy!"

Robin grabbed the edge of the counter and pulled herself to her feet. Through the window, she could see Seth standing in the sandbox, yodeling at the top of his lungs. Nothing life-threatening was going on. She allowed herself one more look at Tav's words, and then, very gently, pressed her lips to the screen.

"Mommy!"

"Okay!" She shoved the phone into her back pocket and jogged outside. "I'm here, buddy."

Seth looked up at her, his face a mix of confusion and consternation. His arms and legs were caked with sand. Robin was willing to bet his hair was full of it, too. Definitely a bath night. "Mommy?"

"What's up?"

"There's something going on in my butt."

Robin opened her mouth. Nothing came out. She shut it again, but, finally, could not hold back a snort. "Do you—" She bit the inside of her cheek. "Do you think it could be sand?"

He seemed to consider this for a moment before, finally, nodding.

Robin dropped to her knees and threw her arms around him, hugging him tight to her chest as she cried.

4

MOMMY!" THERE WAS HALF A SECOND of lag time between the opening of the bathroom door and Seth swiping back the shower curtain.

Robin didn't even try to cover up. It seemed like only yesterday he'd been gnawing on her nipples, anyway. "Buddy, close the door! You're letting in the cold air!"

He blinked up at her with his frank, open stare. "I'm sirsty." He made a mess with the sprayer every time he used the tap in the kitchen, so she kept a plastic cup for him in each bathroom.

"Okay, well, go ahead! Just shut the door!" The draft up the stairwell was terrible. "Buddy? Shut the door." Her imperative finally registered, and he turned to push the bathroom door shut before jumping up on the toilet seat. Robin whisked the shower curtain back into place, fully aware that this was her reward for taking Daddy Stories away. "You couldn't have gotten water from the downstairs bathroom?"

She hadn't expected an answer, but he said something that sounded like, "A box."

"A box?" She shrank back from the burst of scalding water as he cranked on the tap, full blast. "Oh. Right." Tav's most recent care package, still sitting open and half-assembled on the toilet seat. Snacks and batteries and a toy truck Seth had picked out for Shafik, an Afghan kid who followed Tavis around the base doing errands for candy. A picture of him hung with the family portraits in the stairwell—maybe ten, bright-eyed and impish. He'd reminded Tav of Seth, made him feel a little less homesick. And he hadn't even crossed Robin's mind until this moment.

Where was he? Should she still try to send the package, maybe through one of Tav's friends? A note? What could she possibly say that would make any sort of difference? Nothing she did would change the fact that he was gone.

Seth shut off the tap, jumped to the floor, and thudded out of the bathroom.

"Hey! Close the door!" No response. "Buddy?" Robin sighed and reached for a towel.

Downstairs, she put a hand out as she passed the piano, brushing a spot on the side that was shiny and well worn. If only—

"Mommy! I'm hungry!" Seth's declaration, from the next room, was followed by a soft thump and a sound like sudden rain.

Robin jogged into the kitchen, where the floor was now a mosaic of Cheerios. He looked up at her from his hands and knees, one little O stuck to his cheek. She plucked it off and popped it into her mouth. "Nice job, buddy."

After pouring him a bowl from what remained, she got out the broom and dustpan and began to sweep up, only to come to an oddly startling realization: she was hungry. It was the first time she'd felt a genuine desire to eat since Andrews had knocked on the door.

Sitting across the table from Seth, watching his giant poof of hair bobbing with some music audible only to him—and the thought of suicide seemed suddenly distant. And, honestly, a bit melodramatic.

Her purse still sat on the counter where she'd left it the day before, the large canvas mouth sagging open. Robin put a hand in, rummaged a little, and pulled out the bottle of pills.

Seth's head whipped around. "What's that?"

"The good stuff." That's what her OB called it, after the high of birth was over and it had become excruciatingly clear that she'd torn. She'd powered through the pain anyway, because—well, now she didn't know why. There was too much pain in the world already. Why not erase it if you could?

She toed the lever on the trash can lid and dropped the bottle in.

And then she finished breakfast, got Seth dressed, and walked him to preschool. Five days after his father's funeral was probably too soon, by some arbitrary measure of grief, but if Robin started making excuses now, she wasn't sure she could stop. And she refused to burden him with the responsibility for her emotional wellbeing, even if he was the only reason she was still alive. She existed for him, now. Not the other way around.

It helped that Seth had no reservations whatsoever about rocketing toward Marta, the woman who ran the little home-based preschool. Her eyes widened in surprise and she laughed as she struggled to hoist his wriggly bulk into a manageable side-straddle—but her eyes swept instantly to Robin.

Nope.

Robin offered a quick wave and darted out the door.

Straight into another emotional death trap. "Robin." Tom Buelna put a hand on her shoulder, his fingertips prodding in a way that always felt a little too familiar. "I wanted to come to the funeral, but I couldn't get away from the job. What a terrible, terrible thing."

"Yeah." She stepped back, adjusting her purse. "It's okay."

"Can I—I know this is weird, but—" And before she could object, he had manhandled her into an awkward embrace. "I'm so, so sorry."

Tav had always insisted Buelna was just a friendly guy, maybe a little too lonely since his wife had left, and Robin could certainly sympathize with the intense longing for physical contact. But she didn't see him trying to get all touchy-feely with any of his male clients at the lumber yard. It was exactly the kind of borderline bullshit she'd have called out immediately, three years past. Before she had a kid who didn't need to see her chew out his best buddy's dad. Buelna's kid dashed past them, shrieking joyfully when Seth ran out to meet him on the porch. Still. She ducked and twisted free. "Thanks."

"Look, we should, uh, have coffee sometime." He raked his dark hair backward and ducked his head, seeking eye contact at her level. "I know what you're going through."

"Oh?" Even if Buelna was a creep, the idea of someone else having weathered a similar storm and coming out normal on the other side—or at least not completely deranged—was comforting, in its own strange way.

His eyes, rimmed with thick black lashes, shone with sympathy.

"It's... not easy, being on your own with kids. But you learn to cope. You really do."

It took a moment for that to sink in. "Did you—are you... comparing my husband's death to your *divorce?*"

He straightened. "Well. Obviously it's not the same, but—"

"Not the same? Not the *same?* Not even in the same—the same—" She thumped her chest. "He *understood* me. Like nobody—like nobody ever has, or ever will. Inside out." Robin was aware that her voice was rising in volume, and that at least one other parent who had arrived to drop off her child was now loitering at a cautious distance, but the explosion would not be bottled. "Do you know what that's like? And now he's—he's not just weekends and holidays. He's *gone.*" She leveled a finger at Buelna. "Don't pretend you have any idea what that means. Don't you dare."

She wanted to plant a fist in his face, but she used the last ounce of her self-control to turn and run.

Home. The front door was all but unusable at this point, blocked by a growing pile of bags filled with old clothing and broken toys. Obviously the prospect of sorting through Tav's belongings just wasn't enough—she had become a repository for everyone else's emotional refuse, too.

Robin detoured around the side of the house, jogging down the long drive to her truck, parked in front of the garage. She was panting as she thumbed through her keys to find the one that opened the back of the red camper shell.

Her father had always said that using power tools when you were all worked up was a good way to lose a finger. But work was what he had turned to in hard times, and after she'd lost him it was the only thing that helped. And fingers seemed like relatively small potatoes right now.

Earlier that month, before Tav's departure, she'd started on a window seat that would go between the bookshelves in the master bedroom, and gotten as far as ripping the pieces and gluing the base when the world had fallen apart. If she didn't dally, she could probably get it assembled before Seth got out of school. She yanked the window up and let the tailgate fall.

Tavis hadn't left her things in any kind of order. Why had she expected anything different? He never did. The cord of her circular saw snaked around the compressor and down through a bunch of odds and ends scattered over the bed of the pickup. Pencils, her tape measure, screw driver, the long level... It was a mess. The larger items had ended up near the cab on the right, because Tavis took every corner like Mario Andretti.

Robin slid butt-first into the pickup bed and rolled onto her hands and knees. A prick on her palm alerted her to the fact that she'd just missed impaling herself on a loose screw. They were scattered everywhere.

To be fair, he'd put her tools back exactly as she'd asked the first five times he'd used them that August. But then his deployment had rolled in, sneaky as a sleeper wave, and they'd spent the final week scrambling, like always, and he'd squeezed in one last Counter-Strike binge at Cyril's place and now here she was picking up twelve dozen individual drywall screws.

Why was it so hard to put things back the way they had been?

Robin located the battered Folger's coffee can she'd inherited from her father and dumped a handful of screws inside. The rest she'd flush out later with the shop brush. She tucked the can next to her toolbox, rooted around a bit more, and finally identified the butt of her nail gun. She'd hooked a finger around the magazine and was backing out of the pickup bed when her phone buzzed.

Im really sorry to bother you. LCDR Andrews said he couldnt give me your contact information, but I went on Tavs Facebook page and asked for your #. I know thats creepy but I need to talk to you in person. My name is Deena Walker and I am stationed in—

Robin clicked the screen off and shoved the phone back into her pocket. Whatever this woman wanted to discuss, it wouldn't bring Tavis back.

She was hauling the compressor out of the truck when her phone buzzed again.

I understand you dont want—

"Enough!" She tapped in her code and opened text messaging. It took her a few minutes of frantic poking around, but she found the "block" option and used it on Walker.

That wasn't the end of it, though, was it? This woman was already poking around on Facebook.

Robin dropped the handle of the compressor and watched it slide back toward the cab.

The first room she'd tackled after they moved into the house was the add-on bedroom in the back, behind the kitchen and the laundry room. She'd replaced the ratty carpet with a large-pattern Versailles parquet floor, painted the walls moss green, and finished it off with a nice wide baseboard. Technically the fold-out couch made it their guest room, but in the absence of any guests she'd screwed three planks across a couple of sawhorses, plunked a monitor and keyboard on top, and called it an office.

She didn't go straight to Tav's profile. She started on her own page first, careful not to scroll down more than a couple of days. Her mother was everywhere, engaging in her usual habit of commenting on everything, completely devoid of context. A cousin had posted a photo of his bandmates making lewd gestures; Glennis had replied "Yr dad said U had a kidney stone! Did it pass??? Give him my love! XXOO"

Robin's hand swept the cursor up to open the inbox tab, stopping only just short of clicking. Her mom's faux pas was the sort of everyday amusement she'd shoot a note off to Tavis about: "OMG you'll never believe what Mom did today!"

How many little habits like that would she have to break?

Tavis had written, in the email she'd now read about a hundred times on the tiny screen of her phone, that his letters would arrive once a week or so. Somewhat randomized. So most likely she wouldn't be getting another for a few days. But there was also a chance she *would*. This morning. Maybe if she waited just a little longer.

The notifications on the right side of the page refreshed.

Wish Baback a happy birthday, it prompted. And, beneath that, *Reconnect with Tavis.*

She stared at the postage-stamp sized profile photo, Tav's freckled face and fiery hair partially eclipsed by Seth's exuberant locks. They were grinning like fools.

Tavis had taken a couple of days' leave to get things squared away before his deployment, and on a whim the three of them had piled into the truck and driven to the Santa Barbara zoo. The guys had spent the entire ride making up goofy animal-based lyrics to Twinkle Twinkle, but when they'd arrived, Seth had been more concerned with chasing blackbirds than looking at the flamingos. Robin, no photographer, had taken the shot just as Tavis swept the boy off his feet, shrieking in delight. Somehow, it had come out perfectly.

She clicked on his image. At the top of his personal page was Walker's request: *Anyone have contact info for his wife? Need to talk. Thx.*

Below that was tribute after tribute from his million-and-one friends.

Best corpsman in the service, read the top comment. "Liked" by ninety-odd servicemen.

Tav, you will be missed by all. Thank you for having my back last year, I will never forget it.

'Like' if you're still here because Doc Matheson saved your ass.

Anyone have contact information for his wife? Need to get in touch.

Fuck death. Fuck IEDs. Fuck war. God bless our soldiers.

You may have been a pill-pushing pecker checker of a squid, but you were one of us. Semper fi.

Robin closed her eyes. She took a deep breath and opened them again. Then she highlighted the entire page, scrolling down until she was sure she'd gotten them all. There was no "final comment" from Tav; he used Facebook sparingly, friending everyone but maintaining radio silence for the most part. If he'd made any posts in recent months, they had dropped off the page, too insignificant according to whatever rubric the gods of Facebook used to organize people's digital histories.

She hit Control-C to copy, opened a word document, and pasted. Then she titled it "Goodbyes" and closed the file.

Later.

Right now, she had to get Tav's account shut down.

She filled out a form to let Facebook know that he had passed away, but if her Google search results were correct, all that meant was that, eventually, the word "remembering" would be added above his name. There was a "legacy contact" feature, but Tav hadn't set it up—so unless she could get a password, his page was essentially immortal.

Unfortunately, he'd had an almost inhuman knack for memorization, and his passwords were all randomized mixes of numbers, letters, and symbols. There was a chance he'd saved his Facebook password on his laptop, but that was somewhere between here and Afghanistan. It might eventually find its way back to her, assuming it hadn't been destroyed in the blast, but not before the Navy had stripped it of anything worth saving.

Finally, Robin allowed herself to click the email tab. For a moment her heart stuck in her throat, as she willed the universe to deliver her something new.

Nothing. Not from Tavis, anyway. Walker had gotten her email address, too. Robin deleted the message unopened. She spent a few minutes archiving condolences she would never read, and tapped out a few polite refusals to job offers. One came from the wife of the assistant pastor, but she only needed someone to look at a leaky sink. There were a few more notes requesting similarly trifling repairs, also from church members. Someone must have suggested offering work to help her out.

It hurt to think she might need to start accepting grunt-level piecework. The regular financial support she'd be getting would cover some bills and grow Seth's college fund, but sometime in the next year or two she was going to have to get serious about selling the house, and then... a job.

Fortunately, she did have one thing lined up—was it this week or next? Robin clicked her calendar open and, yes, there it was: Wednesday morning. Some guy in Thousand Oaks who wanted an estimate for a bit of remodel on his condo, out of town until now. Tavis had passed the recommendation along—from Cyril.

Ugh. Did she really want to deal with anyone Cyril knew? Now, of course, she understood his weird reluctance to let her go, at the cemetery. He'd been trying to work up the guts to tell her about Tav's emails. Coward. If there were even the tiniest silver lining to Tav's death, it was that she would never, ever have to deal with Cyril again.

Robin chewed her lip, pulled up the original email exchange with the guy, and reached again for her coffee. He'd been brief and to-the-point. His signature indicated he worked for some architectural software firm, so he had a legitimate career, at least—not some glorified hobby like the snarky tech-review podcasts Cyril recorded at home. Wednesday was her mom's weekly day to come down and take care of Seth, so there was no schedule conflict. And odds were, if Cyril hadn't mentioned anything— which, knowing Cyril, he hadn't—this guy had no idea she was now one of the walking wounded. It would just be her, doing what she did best.

Robin hit *reply* and sent a quick reminder: *See you Weds. at 10.* Then she turned the monitor off, tugged her boots on, and went back to the garage.

She started by taking inventory, exactly as she'd watched her father do throughout her childhood. Making sure everything was in place, clean, and in working order. Then she flipped on the compressor, grabbed her nail gun, and went to work on the window seat.

And, quite suddenly, it was ten minutes to five. She'd meant to go early, to get Seth before any other parents arrived. So much for that plan. She used the air hose to blow the dust off her jeans, darted into the house to take a leak, and hurried out the door.

There were a couple of cars parked in front of Marta's. Robin hung back, watching from around the corner as the parents filed inside, exchanging pleasantries, and came back out again with children in tow. Walking into the middle of that would be like setting off a bomb: the laughter and smiles would die, and everyone would flee.

Finally, the cars drove off and Robin marched up to the house, hands clenched into fists.

A handful of remaining children were gathered in the art corner, outfitted in paint-smeared smocks. She had just enough time to squint, eyes adjusting to the indoor light, before Seth squealed "*Mommy!*" and barreled into her legs. He grinned upward, his face mottled with blue.

Marta was close on his heels. Her eyes said she had seen—or at least heard—everything, this morning. Robin knew she ought to be embarrassed, but the space that had once contained her self-consciousness was hollow.

"Oh, Mama," Marta said, "Seth was having *so* much fun doing our art today!" She called all the mothers Mama, which Robin suspected was mostly because nobody who spent eight hours a day with two dozen three-year-olds could possibly retain enough mental capacity for the names of fifty-odd parents. "And he is *such* a good boy."

"Oh. That's good." Robin stood and bent over the sign-out sheet, and made a show of getting out her phone to check the time, documenting her lateness to the minute. She always felt ridiculously muted in the face of Marta's boundless energy. How did a fifty-year-old woman do this every single day? Robin could barely handle the one.

"Okay, Sethie, you can put on your shoes for Mama, yes? All by yourself?" Marta had shepherded Seth over to the shoe rack. Then, while he was occupied with the Velcro straps, she bustled back to Robin. "And you, Mama?" Her voice softened. "How are you doing?"

How was she supposed to answer that? At the funeral reception, a woman from church had asked how she was holding up. Robin had tried honesty: *My life is broken. Everything's been pushed hopelessly out of plumb, and nothing I can do will ever set it right. The thought of having to live without him for another sixty years is exhausting.* Flustered, the woman had offered her condolences and beat a hasty retreat. If Robin changed the subject, she was clearly deep in denial. If she made a joke, inappropriate. Eight hours ago, she'd screamed and fled, like an angry child. Or a crazy person.

Robin forced a smile and said, with what she hoped was appropriately moderate gravity, "Oh, all right. Keeping busy."

Before she could grab Seth and flee, Marta had her in a hug. "I'm so sorry, Mama," she whispered. "So sorry."

And then Marta was weeping, and all Robin could think to do was pat her on the back and say, "It's okay."

The preschool teacher pulled back, finally, wiping her eyes with the knuckle of her index finger. "You are so brave, Mama. I know it's so hard. Yeah?"

Robin shrugged. "Yeah, I... Yeah."

Marta pressed her trembling lips together. "I'll bring you some food this weekend, okay?"

"Thank you, but we really don't—"

"Some of my chicken and dumplings, eh? Sethie's *favorite*." She bent and pinched Seth's cheeks as he approached, shoes mostly on. "You want my chicken, right?"

"*Yeah!*"

Well, now Robin couldn't refuse. She would find a little more room in the freezer. "That would be wonderful, Marta. Thanks." Quickly, she double-checked Seth's shoes and bundled him out the door.

Rather than taking the most direct route home, Robin turned onto a side street that meandered through a tree-lined neighborhood, hoping to avoid any parents who might feel the urge to pull over and have a good cry on her shoulder.

They'd gone about halfway when she realized Seth was trotting as fast as his little legs could carry him. She slowed and relaxed her grip on his arm. God, what did she tell him? There was no way he hadn't heard her outburst. "Hey, bud," she said, feeling suddenly foolish. "Mommy's sorry for losing it this morning. I just... I got angry. And I yelled, but I shouldn't have. I'm sorry." She wasn't. It had felt good. Powerful.

"Oh," he said.

"So, um. Did you have a good day?"

He nodded.

"Do anything fun?"

"Just art. And play."

Which was the same answer he gave every single time she picked him up from school. Somehow, at three-and-three-quarters years old her son was already a stereotypical male. Maybe tonight, at dinner, he'd blurt out some spontaneous information about his day. Noah likes to wear princess dresses. Abby drew on her arm. We don't say *hey*. Why not? I don't know.

"Cereal!"

Robin blinked and looked down. "What?"

"Cereal!"

"Buddy, it's almost dinner time. We had cereal for breakfast." Although, come to think of it, having cereal for dinner would eliminate the need to figure out which of the fifty-odd funeral leftovers Seth would find palatable today. Maybe this once.

"No—*Cereal!*" Seth pointed.

Robin followed his outstretched arm to the house across the street.

Cyril lived in a granny unit behind what had once been his mother's home, about one step above "parents' basement" in Robin's book. When his mother died, he'd stayed where he was and rented out the house. One of the residents, a guy in a white tank top and green-tinted Virgin Mary tattoos, was out front tinkering with a mower. The grass, or, more correctly, the green weeds, were about two feet high.

"See-ree-uhl!" Seth chanted, stretching as far as he could on the end of her arm. "See-ree-uhl!"

"You *like* Cyril?" Seth often tagged along when Tavis went to Cyril's, but Robin hadn't realized he viewed the visits as any sort of treat. On the contrary, she'd imagined Seth occupying himself with Tav's phone while the guys played Counter-Strike or whatever game Cyril was currently chewing over for review. Hopefully not absorbing too much blood and gore.

"Yeah! Yeah! Yeah!" Seth bounced on his toes.

Lawnmower guy looked up. "He's home."

Cyril was always home. For Robin, being self-employed meant she could set her own schedule and be home with her kid. For Cyril, it meant sleeping in until noon and wearing PJ's twenty-four-seven. "Thanks."

"*Yay!*"

She hated it when Seth misinterpreted a noncommittal reply as tacit approval. But life was sad enough without having to watch his cheery little face crumple into tears.

So she exaggerated looking both ways, a mostly redundant habit now that it was ingrained in Seth's subconscious, and walked him across the deserted suburban street. She gave the renter another nod and released Seth's hand, trailing after him down the long driveway.

Five minutes. In and out. She could handle that. Might even take a certain pleasure in looking Cyril in the eye, now that she knew the truth.

"Seth," she called, "wait for Mommy—"

He hopped up the front steps and rang the bell.

The door swung in just as she caught up. Cyril blinked blearily into the late afternoon light, as if they'd just woken him from a deep slumber. His faded flannel pajama pants and rumpled t-shirt—red, with the word 'Expendable' stamped across the front—appeared to confirm this hypothesis. "Sorry," Robin said, instantly regretting the word. She didn't owe Cyril anything, least of all apologies. "We were walking by, and Seth—"

"Hey little man!" He held out a palm and Seth smacked it as if he'd done it a hundred times. "I got a new game you're gonna love."

Cyril blocked the entire doorway; Seth dropped to his hands and knees and scooted between his feet. Cyril chuckled. "Good kid."

"Thanks for the heads up," she said.

It took him a moment to register her sarcasm. "What, that your dead husband was gonna be sending you love notes?" He shrugged. "Yeah, wasn't quite sure how to phrase that one." He turned and followed Seth inside.

5

THE INSTANT ROBIN STEPPED OVER the threshold, she was assailed by the sour, distinctly male odor of cold pizza and sheets that hadn't been washed in far too long. The place was tiny, with a combination living area and kitchen, and the only thing that had changed since she'd been here last was a turnover in electronic gadgets. Remnants of pre-packaged food were piled precariously on side tables and arm rests, while cardboard boxes overflowing with packing peanuts formed a leaning tower by the trashcan in the kitchen. He must occasionally make a sweep to clean everything out—otherwise he'd be drowning in his own refuse. The place made her skin crawl.

Cyril dropped onto the cream-colored leather couch with a massive *whump*, causing Seth to pop up into the air. He giggled and clapped. Cyril leaned to one side, shifting his bulk over the end of the sofa to pull an iPad off the edge of his desk. He pushed it over his stomach to his other hand before passing it off to Seth.

No way Robin was going to join them on the couch, which left only the massive computer chair—obviously ordered to spec to accommodate Cyril's girth. Or not; there were probably enough morbidly obese computer geeks out there to make it worth marketing an entire line of plus-size office equipment. She pulled it back from the desk, only to find the seat occupied by one of those creepy Guy Fawkes masks used by Anonymous hackers. "Seriously?" She held it up.

"What?" Cyril shrugged. "Thought you had a thing for guys in uniform."

"Wow." Nothing that came to mind was fit for Seth's hearing. The desk was already piled high with papers and empty soda cans, so she tossed the mask on top and sat. How Tavis could manage to be around this guy for more than five minutes, she'd never understood. A draft of warm air brushed her leg, and she looked down to find a computer tower. Cyril hadn't been asleep; he'd been here. Working. Or playing. Which, for him, was roughly the same thing.

She spun the chair to face the room and watched Cyril and Seth tapping at the iPad. They were playing some game with catchy, repetitive music she'd doubtless be hearing in her brain when she tried to sleep tonight.

"See all these parts? You drag them up here," Cyril pointed to the upper left of the screen. "You can put a red one with a green one and—"

"But what about *this?*" Seth could never just do as he was told. Show him how to take a photo and he'd push every button *except* the shutter. Just like his mom, Tavis always said.

Cyril tilted his head to one side, frowning as he watched Seth poke at the screen. "No, see, it doesn't—oh, *in*teresting. Can I—oh." He let out a nasal *heh-heh-heh.* "Cool."

They went on like that for a good ten minutes, except the longer they played, the less they spoke, mostly just making hand-motions and the occasional grunt. Wonderful. Robin pulled out her phone and started to check Facebook before remembering Tavis—and probably Walker— were still there.

She shoved the phone back into her pocket and stared at the pockmarked plaster wall behind the television. The walls were beige and the ceiling was white, which would have been fine except that whoever had repainted the walls hadn't bothered to tape the ceiling, and there were splotches of beige wherever the roller had bumped. The floor was just as bad: it was visibly listing to the west, and there wasn't a single square angle in the room. The window frame was—ugh, she couldn't look without wanting to take a sledgehammer to the entire place.

Finally, she swung the chair around, pushed a microphone on a tripod out of the way, and planted her elbows on Cyril's desk. Her left arm hit something half-concealed by papers, and when she flipped them back she found a brick-sized block with a couple of toggle switches and a big red button in the center. The toggles and the button were housed under a clear plastic casing that opened on a hinge. Some stupid toy. She flipped the cover up.

"*Don't.*"

Cyril had the iPad on his stomach; Seth stood on the couch, shoes still on, leaning against his side. They were both looking at her. For a second she considered jamming her thumb down, but then she let the cover snap shut. "Why? What is it?"

"What does it *look* like?"

"I dunno, some kind of nuclear launch button?"

"Maybe that should tell you something."

Robin rolled her eyes and flopped back into the chair, wishing she'd brought a magazine. The clock on the wall—hung about two degrees off level—was some geek thing that gave the time in blocks of color, so she couldn't tell what it said, but one blinking light conveyed the monotony of a ticking second hand. How many blinks since this carpet had been vacuumed? Every time she steeled herself to stand and leave, Seth giggled and she decided to wait just a few blinks more.

Cyril, though—God. His shirt had ridden up, and every time he lifted an arm to poke at the iPad, his belly shuddered like Jell-O fresh from the mold. It was honestly difficult to tell where he ended and the couch began.

Robin couldn't look at him anymore. Or the room. Not without punching something. She got up and went into the kitchen. And the only thing to be done there—*anywhere* in Cyril's place—was clean. Poking around in a few lower cabinets produced a pair of yellow dish gloves still in the unopened plastic packaging. Way too big for even her callused hands, but they'd suffice. She ran the water, squirted soap over the entire disgusting pile of crusty food and dishes, and went to work.

"Hey." Cyril snapped his fingers twice. "Root beer. Fridge door."

A decent person would have stopped her when she started on the dishes. Any other loser would have interrupted her halfway through, as Cyril had just done, to shamefacedly beg her to stop and let him do it later. Or at the very least admit cleaning anything in this dump was a pointless waste of time.

Root beer? He hadn't even asked. He'd ordered. Blood thundered in her ears.

"What? You're standing next to the fridge." Cyril looked at her son. "You want something, bud? Jell-O? Crackers?"

"Jell-O!" Seth hopped up and down on the couch. "Jell-oh, jell-oh, jell-oh!"

Robin was going to murder Cyril if she didn't get out of here *immediately*. "Sweetie, I think it might be time to—"

"One more minute!" Seth opined. Which, in Seth-speak, meant *as long as I want*. "Please? Oh please oh please oh please?"

Robin should never have taught him the "magic word." He'd taken it at face value and now thoroughly believed that all he had to do to get what he wanted was repeat *please* until she "magically" agreed. She could stand her ground, but Seth was tired and hungry enough right now that a flat refusal would to catapult him into a nuclear-grade meltdown. Better to get some food into him and then try to pry him out of the house. "Ten minutes. Okay?"

"Jell-O's on your right," Cyril said. "Up above."

She opened the cabinet, wholly unsurprised to find a pack of lime Jell-O cups shoved in alongside a stack of canned fruit in syrup. At least there were little bits of pineapple inside. Probably candied. She plucked a spoon from the dish drainer, took it to the coffee table in front of the couch, and swept aside a collection of xBox controllers and monster figurines. "Come down here and eat, okay?" Even as filthy as the place was, letting Seth dump Jell-O onto the couch cushions set a bad precedent. "No hands, okay? Use your spoon."

Cyril cleared his throat. "How about that root beer?"

If Seth hadn't been there, Robin would have told Cyril to go fuck himself. She might, in fact, come back on Thursday when Seth was in preschool and do just that. For now, she looked up and said, very calmly, "What's the magic word?"

Cyril gave her a snide grin. "Root beer... *per favore?*"

Her hand shook as she pulled the fridge door open. Was this setting a good example for her son? Shouldn't she tell Cyril to get his own damn beverage?

All Seth would see was that Mommy didn't like Daddy's friend. The request itself wasn't unreasonable, and she was quite sure Tavis would have amiably gotten up and fetched Cyril a soda without objection, because why not?

She pulled out one can—and then a second, for herself. It was petty, but at least it made the gesture into something incidental; might as well get him a drink as long as she was having one. She went back to the computer chair, sat, and tossed the can at his face.

Cyril caught it easily, set it on top of his stomach, and casually tapped the aluminum tab a few times before easing it open. The can let out a hiss of relief.

Seth went to work on his Jell-O. The spoon was bigger than the kid-size utensils he usually used, and he was determined to dig out each bit of fruit separately, as if mining the cup for treasure.

"Looks like I'll be seeing your friend on Wednesday." Robin hadn't intended to ask about the job—hadn't intended to speak to Cyril ever again, really—but it might be handy to know what she was getting herself into.

"Who?"

"Uh..." She rubbed her forehead. "Cooke, I think his name is? In Thousand Oaks."

"Oh. Yeah." He tipped the soda can toward her. "You're welcome."

"If he's anything like you, I doubt I'm going to appreciate the gesture."

Cyril snorted. "Guy's about ninety pounds soaking wet, so, no."

Robin rolled her eyes. "Personality, not mass."

"He's the most insanely anal person I've ever worked with. You'll love him."

"Oh. Great."

"Probably needs some grab bars in the bathroom or something." Cyril shrugged. "I do contracting work for his company pretty regularly. Figured I owe him."

So he was doing his boss a favor, not her. Good. She tossed a thumb toward the microphone. "I thought reviewing was your job."

"The podcasts? Ha." He waved a hand. "It gets me all this free crap. It doesn't pay the bills."

"So what do you...?"

"I'm a security researcher. A white hat." He hesitated. "Well. Gray."

"What on earth is a—"

Seth shot to his feet. "I gotta pee! Gotta go pee!"

Why did that always occur to him while he was eating? Robin looked at Cyril. "Can we use your—"

"You know where it is, dude."

Seth dropped his spoon and jetted into Cyril's bedroom.

Robin started to follow, but Cyril waved her back into the office chair. "He's got it."

She knew that, of course, but standing guard while Seth did his business seemed preferable to sitting here thinking about all the ways he could, at this moment, be accidentally strangling or drowning himself on the other side of the wall. Not that hanging out with Cyril was much of a treat, either. Robin took a long gulp of root beer and then fiddled with the can, pushing the tab back and forth until it came off.

"So," he said. "Enjoying your letters?"

Had... had he asked what she thought he'd asked? Robin looked at him, and no—she hadn't misunderstood at all.

She opened her mouth. Closed it again. And then: "Fuck you, you piece of fucking trash." Robin had never said anything like that to anyone in her life. Even if she swore, which was rarely, she always thought of the best comebacks far too late.

Cyril never had that problem. Once, in college, she'd shown up at his apartment—which was where Tavis crashed whenever he'd scraped together enough leave—in her workout clothes, ready for an early evening jog. Tavis had ducked into the bedroom to change, leaving her in the living area with Cyril—who hadn't once looked up from the faux-military slaughterfest he'd been playing since her arrival.

It was the first time Robin had seen him since their encounter at the library, and she'd sat at the kitchen table, staring bullets at his back. "Is this what you do all day?" she'd snapped at last. "Just sit here on your butt?"

"Least mine doesn't have JUICY stamped on it."

He hadn't missed a beat.

Today, though, he was just silent.

Then he tilted his head back and emptied the can of root beer with a couple of practiced gulps. He crushed it in one hand and tossed it toward the garbage, where it clattered against the lid and fell to the floor. "You're the one who came over, Chica."

He had a point. "Won't happen again."

"Good."

It had been more than two minutes since Seth had run off. She got up and went into the bedroom, where the stale-sheet smell was even worse. The unmade bed was piled high with pillows, and she had to pick her way through drifts of dirty clothes to get to the bathroom door. "Sethie, are you—"

"I'm *pooping!*"

"Oh." He'd recently acquired a sense of modesty in regards to "number two." Which was ironic, since Robin couldn't even count the number of times he'd come into the bathroom and climbed up on her lap while she was doing her business. She decided to humor him, in the hopes that his desire for privacy would eventually expand to include peeing and after-bath-time cavorting. "Let me know when you're done and I'll help you wipe, okay?"

Seth was silent. He didn't like the wiping. Probably why he didn't want her knowing when he pooped.

Robin sighed and returned to the chair in the living room. Cyril was still on the couch, tinkering with the iPad. Given the effort required for him to get up and down, she wouldn't be surprised if he camped out in one spot most of the day. What about when he had to pee? She looked around, suddenly suspicious of empty beverage containers.

Her hand went to her phone again, just to have something to look at that wasn't Cyril's doughy white stomach sagging between his knees. Speaking of peeing, how did he even...?

Nope. Did not want to know.

Her thumb hit the Facebook icon. "Crap." She closed the app, but not before she'd seen the friendship request pop up from Deena Walker. Programmers programmed these programs, and then the programs programmed you. And then when you were broken, or just gone, the machines kept running, oblivious to your demise. "Facebook," she explained, even though Cyril's glance said he couldn't possibly care less. He was a tech guy, and part of her felt like he was guilty merely by association. "He's still..." She didn't want to admit this. Too late. "I can't get him off."

"Oh." Cyril extended a hand. "Laptop."

She hated how one commanding word made her turn to look for the item before she was even conscious of doing so. This was how Cyril got what he wanted: he exploited the codes of politeness and common decency that most people had trained themselves to observe. He issued orders, and if someone failed to comply, he just moved on to the next unsuspecting schmuck. "Get it yourself."

He shrugged and went back to poking at the iPad.

Unlikely he could do anything, anyway. Sure, he had double-majored in computer science and electrical engineering, but he lived in a one-bedroom apartment and spent his time verbally eviscerating other people's creative work. What could he possibly do about Facebook?

Still. Robin swung the chair around and poked around the junk on his desk until she located the laptop. The grinning Guy Fawkes mask slid off and landed on a haphazard stack of what appeared to be legal documents; Tavis had said Cyril was always getting threatened with lawsuits over his reviews.

Cyril settled the laptop onto his stomach. "*Told* him not to sign up," he muttered, tapping at the keys. "Just one giant repository of social whores sacrificing personal information for the collective delusion of social intimacy."

"Is that a personal quote?"

"Yeah, wrote a piece last month." He looked up. "Do you have any idea how much corporations pay for that kind of detailed consumer data? This is the fucking information age. Knowledge is power. And people just give it away." He opened his fingers. "Poof. Might as well post your social security number, your measurements, and a couple of titty pics for good measure."

Robin's face grew warm. The only reason Tav had a Facebook account was because she'd insisted. Cyril could criticize social media all he wanted, but Facebook was the only reason Robin had any friends—such as they were—at all. Most people could just bump into someone they knew and ask them about last week's game, or how their kid's dentist visit had gone. Robin didn't function that way. She had to work her way back through her own timeline, event by event, until she reached the last time they'd interacted, and then the time before that. Usually by the time she remembered to ask so and so about her ailing mother-in-law, the chance meeting had ended and life moved on.

Facebook had granted her a miraculous visual window into people's lives, where she could study up on names and dates and events at her leisure. Maybe she hadn't made any deep connections, but that was on her. At least she had found people who cared.

Expecting Cyril to sympathize with anything even remotely human, however, was a lost cause.

"He did it for me," she said, knowing it sounded silly. "It's a good way to keep in touch with family and friends."

"Right." Cyril snorted. "Let me ask you this. Have you ever unfollowed someone because all they did was post stupid, offensive shit?"

She shrugged. "Sure."

"Has anyone unfollowed you?"

"How would I know?" That was the point of unfollowing rather than un-friending. The person being ignored couldn't tell.

He pointed a finger at her. "*Exactly.*"

"What, you think I'm talking to a vacuum? I get plenty of likes."

"No. The point is, you don't know who *is* listening. Some people hit that 'like' button on every single fucking thing that shows up on their timeline. Others look, but don't interact. Getting 'likes' is not a measure of whether they are engaged with you personally—it's only an indication of how the technology is used. The illusion of intimacy. Crowdsourcing friendship. Facebook diffuses relationships, dilutes them until they're meaningless." The words came out in a kind of stilted rush, as if he were simply reading words off a page. Abruptly, he broke off, glancing up from the laptop screen. "Anywhere else Tav is still playing ghost in the machine? Twitter? Pinterest? Myspace?"

Was he trying to be funny or just make her mad? "Not that I know of." There was some bank stuff she was going to have to figure out, but that was different.

And then it was as if he simply clicked back to his recitation: "People post offensive shit they'd never say to somebody's face—since it's not directed at anyone specific, it feels like it's okay. But the same is true for the good stuff, too. Like when you invite everyone you know to a party, and everyone else assumes everyone else is going and they won't be missed, and then nobody shows up. It's not personal, it's never going to be personal. But if you get enough likes, you feel like you're all right, that you've got friends. When the reality is, you're alone."

"Right," she shot back, "because you're the expert on friendship."

"I know it's not about quantity." He shrugged. "Sometimes all you need is one."

His sentence hung in the air between them, heavy. Was he being flippant? Baiting her? Or was his apparent indifference only a cover for genuine feeling? She could never tell when he was serious.

Before she could formulate a response, he shut his lap top with a solid click. "There."

Robin frowned. "Meaning what?"

"It's done. He's off. *La fine*."

"Are you serious?" She'd spent over an hour trying to figure out how to get Tavis offline, and Cyril had apparently accomplished the task in all of two minutes. "You're not—you're not screwing with me?"

"In this instance? No."

Robin burst into loud, ugly tears.

This was how grief was: it crept up and pounced when you least expected. She felt Cyril watching as she groped for her purse—with a kind of dispassionate curiosity, as if he found it a little puzzling that any mere human vessel could contain so much raw emotion.

She wanted to explain that it wasn't Facebook—not exactly. It was Marta's hug and Buelna's cluelessness and Cyril's jerking her around and—"This woman—this woman Tav served with? She keeps trying to contact me. Email, text, Facebook." Sometimes all she wanted was to just stop remembering for five goddamn minutes, and now there was no part of her life that was safe from the unvarnished reality of loss.

"And," Cyril said, "you don't want to talk to her because...?"

Robin used a tissue to mop the hot tears tumbling down her face. Hopefully Seth hadn't heard her sobs. "What is she going to tell me? He's dead. Nothing's going to change that. And it's not like I'm afraid—I mean—" She tugged a second tissue out of the little package and folded it over and over, just to have something to do with her hands. "My father always said you don't ask a soldier about things he's done in the field. You can't understand it unless you've been in those boots. If he wants you to know something, he'll tell you."

Cyril scratched the three-day stubble on his cheek. "A wise man."

She looked up, startled by the lack of sarcasm. "He was." If only he were here now, to tell her what she ought to do. Or just wrap her in a huge soft bear hug. As she tucked the pack of tissues back into the zippered pocket in her purse, her fingers brushed Tav's letter. She blinked at it, blearily, and then held it up. "I haven't opened it."

He traded his laptop for the iPad without looking up. "None of my business."

"You asked." Sort of. And he was going to get an answer, whether he cared or not, because she needed someone to know it wasn't just cowardice. "Tav... Tav's writing is so amazing—"

"Yeah, I know." Cyril rolled his eyes.

Of course he did. Tavis told Cyril everything. *He's more than just a friend,* he'd always said. *We're practically brothers.* God, why had he been so loyal? That was what had gotten him killed, in the end. That compulsion to be there, on the front line, with "his" Marines.

"His letters are what kept me going, when he was gone. They're *still* keeping me going."

Cyril cocked an eyebrow. "Thanks to me."

"Yeah, you're definitely the hero of this story." She hoped he choked on a Dorito and died. "Anyway. This one" —she slid it carefully back into place—"is the last. I mean, I don't know when he wrote it, but—it's what he wanted me to read, at the very end. So I'm saving it." Because as long as that envelope remained tucked safely in her purse, Tavis still had something more to say.

"Mom! Moooommy!"

Robin wiped her face one last time, tossed the crumpled tissues on the floor just because she could, and lurched toward the bathroom, grateful for the excuse to get Cyril out of sight. Over Seth's protests, she wiped between his tight little butt cheeks and made him wash his hands, although what she wanted to do was douse him with disinfectant from head to toe.

She was looking down at him in the mirror, making sure he rinsed all the soap off, when she realized the sink cabinet was new, unfinished oak. The nail holes in the trim had been puttied, but not sanded or painted. She placed her finger over one, feeling the slight roughness left behind by the whorls on Tavis's thumb.

She raised her eyes to take in the rest of the bathroom. The fresh baseboard, the brand new tile floor, still un-grouted, and the large commercial toilet like you found in public restrooms. She swept the shower curtain back; the bathtub had been transformed into an oversized shower stall with a handheld sprayer and a crude built-in bench. Robin had taught her husband everything he knew about building, and he was no expert—but this was an obvious rush job, even for him. Tiles were misaligned around the fixtures, pieced together awkwardly in the corners. He'd probably been anxious to get things back into working order before he deployed. Still, every inch of it was unmistakably *his*.

When Tavis had dumped a bunch of her tools in the pickup, he'd told her he planned on helping Cyril with some home repair in between gaming sessions. The truth was probably the reverse: he'd been doing a bit of gaming in between remodel sessions. It made sense, thinking back. He'd come home tired and sweaty, more so than the weather warranted.

"I don't know, Robbie," he'd sighed one evening, stretched out across the bed.

Robin looked at him in the closet mirror, where she was attempting to moisturize her Senegalese twists without destroying them. "Don't know what?"

She saw him clearly in her mind's eye, turning to fold his arms behind his head. "Whether I'm helping... or enabling him."

"Cyril," she'd said, "will self-destruct just fine without you."

When he was around, on weekends or in the evenings after work at the Hueneme base, Tavis had helped her with the house. They had spent an entire weekend crawling around the attic to update the wiring. Tavis had cut all the pieces for the shelves in their bedroom. He'd been the one to help Seth write their names in the concrete they'd poured out front.

And yet the final work of her husband's hands was this: Cyril's bathroom.

Robin splashed her face with water, realized too late that even the towels were not something she wanted to touch, and used a couple of squares of toilet paper to pat her face dry. She dropped them into the toilet and went back into the living room.

Seth was already nestled into place at Cyril's side, looking at the iPad over his arm.

Cyril glanced up, their eyes met, and he knew that she knew. Robin didn't know what that meant—whether it held any significance for him at all.

She cleared her throat to make her voice firm. "Okay, bud. Time to say goodbye."

"But I wanna—"

"Look." She pointed out the window, drawing his attention to the incontrovertible celestial evidence. "It's getting dark. We need to get home and have some dinner. So let's say goodbye and let Cyril get back to work, okay?"

Seth lowered his head and treated her to the frowniest frownie-face he possibly could.

"Wow," she said, feeling her lips curl into a smile. "That's pretty impressive. You gonna say goodbye or not?"

"Bye," Seth said, dropping to his butt and sliding off the couch. Clearly even that one word was a serious imposition.

"Good to see you, kid." Cyril glanced at Robin. If some human emotion beyond cynicism and sarcasm could be attributed to him, there was something in his face she almost would have said was regret. Then he flipped the cover shut on the iPad and held it out. "Here. Keep this warm for me."

Seth's eyes got as round as saucers. He looked at Robin.

What on earth did Cyril think he was he doing? "I can't let you—"

"Yes you can. Anyone who wants me to review an iOS game sends me one. I usually offload them on eBay."

"For quite a bit of money, I'm sure—"

"Just take the fu—" He cut himself off. Rolled his eyes. Rephrased. "It's not for you. It's for him." He looked at Seth. "How old are you? Got a birthday coming up?"

"Free!" Seth declared. "Gonna be four!"

"There. It's a birthday present. Okay? Bye." He rocked forward, shifting his bulk to the edge of the couch, and heaved himself to his feet with a heavy grunt. There wasn't much floor space around the furniture, so walking forward amounted to shepherding them out the door.

"We're not in any financial trouble," Robin said, her voice tight. "If that's what you're thinking."

Cyril leaned against the doorframe and watched, breathing noisily through his mouth, as Seth investigated a plastic water bottle that had been crushed flat in the middle of the driveway. "I don't give a shit about your finances." He shoved the iPad at her chest. "Take the fucking pad."

6

ROBIN HAD MAJOR RESERVATIONS about anyone who would consent to work with Cyril—let alone hire him—so when she hit the buzzer she was fully prepared to cut and run.

Nobody answered.

She shaded her eyes and scanned the condo complex—an upscale community designed around a play structure and swimming pool. All deserted. If everything was as new as it looked, the place might still be sparsely populated. Or perhaps just full of senior citizens. She glanced down at her sneakers and realized, belatedly, that the brown stain on the cement step was probably dried blood.

She hit the buzzer again, twice this time.

"Coming, damn it!"

Great. Now she'd pissed him off. She was patting her back pockets to ensure her notebook, pencil, and tape measure were in place when the door swung in, revealing a guy in neat khaki slacks and a blue checkered shirt.

"Oh," they both said, simultaneously.

"I'm black," she said, just to get it out of the way. Ventura County was absurdly white.

"You're a *woman.*"

"Is that a deal breaker?" Wouldn't be the first time. Or even the fifth. It was why she used the intentionally gender-neutral "R. Matheson" for her email signature. Let him say it to her face.

He grinned. "On the contrary; it's a pleasant surprise." He nodded downward, indicating his crutches. "And yes, crippled."

"Actually, I was expecting—" Someone much older. And a lot less friendly. His artfully mussed hair was shot through with gray, but the faint laugh lines around his eyes said he was forty at the outside. He was probably the only person in America still wearing a wristwatch, strapped next to a medical alert bracelet on one bony wrist. "I'm… not sure what I was expecting, actually."

"But not this?" He laughed and motioned her over the threshold with a crutch, revealing an arm taped with gauze from palm to elbow. "Come on in."

Robin followed him into a slate-tiled living room without a single scrap of furniture. A short hallway on the right led past a spacious pocket kitchen—also bare—and into a bedroom suite with crown molding and a lovely herringbone-pattern floor of reclaimed wood. The furnishings, however, looked like they'd been lifted from a college dorm room: a cheap twin bed frame topped with cotton sheets and a rumpled duvet sat next to a particle board nightstand. Well; at least he had the decency to dress like a human being and put his garbage where it belonged.

The opposite corner of the bedroom had been assembled with greater attention to detail: a desk of brushed steel and frosted glass held three flat-screen monitors and a laptop. The ergonomic office chair, backed with black mesh, was nearly identical to the one Cyril owned, minus the plus-sizing. Cooke probably could have used a "petite" version—Cyril hadn't been exaggerating about his size.

"Do you… live here?" Robin wasn't quite sure how to phrase that in a non-offensive way.

"Oh—no. I work remotely about ninety percent of the time. We're expanding, though, and I've been needed down here more than usual. I sort of… overstayed my welcome with my partner's wife, so…" He shrugged and indicated the bathroom door with one open hand. "After you."

It was about as grungy as she expected of a man on his own.

"Sorry," he said, coming in behind her. "The cleaners just come through to deal with the damage after I leave." He nodded toward the bathtub. "That's priority one. I want some kind of built-in seat. Wood or metal or something. Those padded plastic benches make me feel like I'm trapped in a convalescent home."

Robin pulled her notepad out, sketched a quick floor plan, and jotted "teak slats" with a little arrow toward the tub. Cooke waited for her to finish before describing a few more minor revisions. She nodded and made notes. "Is that it?"

"Pretty much," he said. "Unless you have any suggestions?"

She glanced around the bathroom. Normally she only did this with repeat clients, but... "Look, I don't want you to think I'm trying to upsell you—"

"I'm perfectly capable of saying no."

Fair enough. She stepped back toward the tub. "We could take the liner out entirely. Continue the tile at a slight downward slope, and put in a sliding glass door," she mimed opening it, "right here. I'd extend your bench out of the shower, make both halves independently folding, so you could slide from one end of the seat to the other when you're done." She put a hand on the edge of the sink. "Over here I'd lower the counter and install a hinged stool, for when you want to brush your teeth or shave or whatever. Large hook right here for your crutches. You'd still have some storage over here on the left, maybe add in some shelves on this side, and move your outlet from the blacksplash to the side of the cabinet, so it's right under the sink."

"You," said Cooke, "are *so* hired."

They spent another thirty minutes going through the rest of the condo, batting ideas back and forth about the kitchen counters, the entryway, and the front step. Robin could have redone the whole place, but he wanted to keep it comfortable for his wife, in case she ever came down. Robin offered a ballpark estimate, which he dismissed with a casual wave.

Well. It was always nice to work with an unlimited budget.

She ducked into the bathroom to take a few more measurements, and by the time she emerged Cooke had seated himself in the office chair. "Thanks for coming, Ms. Matheson."

The bony, angular hand he offered was so light she felt like she might break it if she squeezed. "Just Robin is fine. I can get started whenever works for you—although I have to say that I have to work around my son's preschool schedule, so I'm going to be slower than anyone else you could hire."

"No worries; I'm barely here anyway." He put a hand to his breast pocket and produced a newly cut key. "In fact, I'm heading back north in the morning, so feel free to come and go whenever you want. I'll drop you an email next time I'm planning on heading down. How did you do this with Cyril? Some kind of boilerplate contract?"

"Cyril?" she echoed, not sure what he had to do with contracts.

"I assumed you did some work for him."

"Oh—no. He's my husband's friend." She realized the error in tenses a split second after the word came out of her mouth, but couldn't bring herself to make a correction. "Not, uh, mine."

Cooke let out a flat *ha*. "Yeah, he's kind of notorious. Funny as hell, though. Did you hear his takedown of that VP at Sony Entertainment? The Exec's End?"

"Uh, no?" She'd glanced at Cyril's website a time or two, but she was subject to more than enough of his delightful sarcasm in person. Streaming his diatribes in her spare time? Pass.

Cooke held up an index finger, quoting. "Are you so modest that you shrink from a naked sword? Or is it, good sir, the fear of a single honest word?" He shook his head. "Oh my God, I laughed so hard my wife thought I was choking. The entire thing's in rhyming couplets."

Were they even talking about the same person? "I didn't think he could go five minutes without mortally offending someone."

"Oh, he can't. I've fired him twice."

"But not permanently?"

He chuckled. "My own moral failing. Are you familiar with marblecake?"

"Cake?" she echoed.

Cooke waved the word away. "Suffice to say I'm sympathetic to his, uh, extracurricular activities. Most guys who've been dicking around on the darknet as long as he has settle down—find some patron corporation to fund their online hijinks. Cyril would call that selling out. He's loyal to his own unique code of ethics, and it hasn't earned him any friends in high places. So I give him work when I can. When he lets me, I guess I should say." He shrugged. "And honestly, he's reliable. Which is saying a lot for a hacker."

"He's a *hacker?* Isn't that illegal?"

"Depends on context." Cooke fiddled with the cuff of one crutch, as if trying to figure out how to translate his thoughts into layman's terms. "My company deals mostly with architecture, but we do handle sensitive client information, so we need a white hat now and then. A security researcher to identify the weaknesses in our system before someone else exploits them."

"So, like, a good guy hacker." Except Cyril had corrected himself. Gray hat, he'd said.

"As much as that title could be applied to Cyril, yes."

"Huh. Okay. That explains a lot."

He raised an eyebrow.

"My..." *My husband died:* those were the words she should have said. Her first slip had been an accident, and now was the time to correct it. But as much as she felt like she had a duty to Tavis—to his memory—Cooke was the first person in a month who hadn't looked at her like she was missing a limb. "A family member passed away, and I couldn't deactivate his Facebook account. I had Cyril look at it, and he made it disappear instantly." Not exactly the truth, but not exactly a lie.

Cooke frowned. "Facebook?"

"What? Is that bad?"

"Not so much that as—well." He let out a short *hm.* "I've heard of CSP bruteforcing to get user data, but that's basically just accessing publicly available information. Actually getting into someone's account?" He shook his head. "I don't want to... make any accusations here. I'm an engineer, not a hacker. But I know enough to tell you that ninety percent of hacking—more, probably—has nothing to do with code. It's all about finding and exploiting weaknesses. And any system's biggest weakness is, of course, the people who run it. Which makes Facebook, like, ground zero for social hacking. Was Cyril a friend of your... uh, late... whoever?"

She refrained from supplying the word *husband.* "Yes. But he wouldn't have given his password to Cyril. He always used randomized letters and numbers, no birthdates or anything."

"Maybe he didn't know he was giving it. Did he—uh, the dead guy—ever use Cyril's computer?"

"It's possible." In fact, she knew he had—to make the DVDs for Seth.

"Keystroke logger," Cooke said immediately. "Incredibly easy to install. You don't even have to be a hacker for that. If your dead guy logged in to Facebook, say, on Cyril's system, all he'd have to do is pull up this program and see which keys he pushed."

Well that was scary. And totally something Cyril would do. But *why?*

Maybe just because he could.

GLENNIS WAS IN THE KITCHEN, wavy white hair wound into a bun to keep it out of the way while she made peanut butter sandwiches. Robin grabbed the bread from the cupboard and tossed two more slices onto the cutting board. "So that went pretty well. It's some minor remodel work down in T.O. Strange little guy, but nice."

Her mother managed to look ever-so-slightly incredulous. "Well, if you're sure you're ready."

"I am, Mom." As if work was the problem.

"Seth's been to Cyril's, I gather."

Robin pressed her hands to her forehead and dragged her fingers down her face. "The iPad. I know. We were walking by, and Seth just..." She let out a low moan. "He thinks they're best buddies."

"The only thing he's wanted to do all morning is hunt ghosts. With swords. He hit me a couple of times."

"Sorry. I'll have a talk with him later." Yes, he was already reenacting one of the games Cyril had loaded onto the iPad. But he was three; he parroted everything. His swords were foam. No actual damage had been done.

"Well. I hope you know what you're doing."

"I absolutely don't." Parenthood in a nutshell. "Seth's lost enough already. I'm not gonna take away the toy he got from his dad's best friend."

Glennis expelled a heavy I-think-you-know-my-opinion sigh. "Have you at least thought about his birthday? It's coming up fast."

No, really? "Haven't decided."

"You need to start planning if you want any kids to—"

"I know, Mom. We'll figure it out."

Glennis' handmade earrings wobbled as she shook her head. "I just… I wish you'd let me do *something* for you."

Robin gestured toward the laundry room. "You already did the clothes and swept."

"It just doesn't seem like much. Can't I handle any of the paperwork? The bank stuff?"

"No, not really." Robin knew what her mom was looking for. She wanted Robin to open up, to vomit out her heart and soul. Because if she wasn't talking about her pain with her mother, then clearly she wasn't "dealing." As if her mother knew the first thing about handling grief constructively.

"And you've been seeing… who was it? The pastor's wife?"

"Joanie." Robin had completely blown off her first counseling session. Joanie was still leaving messages on her voice mail every other day. "I'm doing okay, Mom. Really." She took the sandwiches her mom had finished, quartered them, and piled them on a plate before taking them into the dining room. "Seth! Lunch!"

There was a half-second of silence, and then footsteps thundered down the hall. "Mommy!"

"Hey, buddy." She got half a hug before he saw the sandwiches and clambered into his seat.

"Oh," said Glennis, coming in from the kitchen. "Sweetheart, let's wash your hands, hmm?"

Seth's head snapped back and forth firmly, his halo of red-brown hair following on a half-second lag. "Don't want to!"

Robin sighed. "You don't have to." Living with a three-year-old was a perpetual germ factory no matter what you did. Might as well throw her support behind the hygiene hypothesis.

Glennis gave them both a disapproving frown and went to wash her own hands on principle.

"Jesus haves dirty hands," Seth informed her when she came back.

Glennis sat down at her place, adjusted her napkin, and gave Robin a *look*.

Robin waved a hand. "We just read that bit where the Pharisees confront Jesus about not washing." And who was she to argue with the Son of God?

"Well," her mother said. "At least you're still reading your Bible."

What exactly was that supposed to mean?

Seth reached for a square of sandwich and carefully jammed the entire quadrant into his mouth. Robin bit her lip, carefully avoiding eye contact to keep from laughing. If he giggled, the sticky bolus would end up on the table or stuck in his throat. Glennis watched with an expression of faint horror, but took a cue from her daughter and didn't comment.

When he finally choked the thing down, he reached for his sippy cup and chugged half the milk.

"Seth," Glennis said, "did you know you have a birthday coming up?"

"Yeah! Cereal gave me the pad!"

"Mom," Robin said. "Don't."

Glennis ignored her. "What do you want to do for your party, sweetie? Grandma can make you a cake if you want."

"Ice cream!" He crammed another quarter into his mouth.

"Mom, I'll take care of it." Robin stared bullets at her mother, but Glennis kept her focus trained squarely on Seth.

"Ice cream? You want Grandma to make you an ice cream cake? And have your friends over?"

"No!" He sprayed crumbs. "Ish keem *shtore!*"

"Oh, you want to have your party at the ice cream parlor? That sounds fun. Who should we invite?"

"Mom," Robin said. "Seriously. I will handle this. Later."

"Sweetheart, we need to get this figured out! Otherwise none of his friends will be able to come. Right?" She turned her smile back to Seth, reaching out to put a veined hand on his. "So tell me, Sethie, who do you want to invite to your party?"

Seth grinned. "You and Mommy and Cereal!"

Robin almost laughed out loud.

Glennis *hmmm*ed. "What about your friends, sweetie? From preschool? Or Sunday school?"

Seth shook his head. "Just you. Mommy. And Cereal."

Glennis looked to Robin for assistance. Robin spread her palms and shrugged. Glennis had brought it up; she could be the one to explain why Cyril wouldn't be coming.

"Well, you think about it some more, okay? Maybe you have some friends your own age you'd like to bring. And we'll talk about it again next week when I come."

Seth crammed a third quarter into his mouth without comment. He chewed thoroughly, swallowed, and took another swig from his sippy cup before plunking it down on the table. "Done!"

"*Now* you gotta wash your hands, bud," Robin told him. "I don't want that jelly on my furniture."

He frog-hopped from the chair to the floor and bounded off.

"And don't touch the walls!" Robin leaned her chair back and watched until he rounded the corner. Then she let the front legs fall to the floor. "Don't ever do that again, Mom."

Glennis collected the napkins and took the empty plate back into the kitchen. Robin grabbed her water glass and beat her mother to the pile of dishes that had accumulated in the sink. The water was running hot and she had the dish gloves on by the time Glennis had put the peanut butter and jelly back in the fridge.

Robin assumed her mother would apologize, however grudgingly, and then go back to playing with Seth. Instead she just stood there, leaning against the counter.

Robin refused to take her bait. She soaped the sponge and started in on plates.

"Sweetheart. You can't do this alone. Please... let me help."

"Oh, like you helped when dad died?" She regretted the words the instant they were out—and yet they were, somehow, a kind of cathartic thrill.

Glennis stood, stiff, looking at the floor. "That's not fair," she murmured. "And you know it."

"Isn't it?"

"Mommy?" Seth appeared in the doorway. How was it that the only time he could sneak was when she needed him gone? His eyes were large.

Robin took a deep, careful breath. "It's okay, sweetie."

He looked between Robin and Glennis, as if evaluating the emotional temperature of the room. "Can I play the pad?"

The little punk. "Yes." She sighed. "Go ahead."

He grabbed it off the counter, chortling with glee, and thudded upstairs to his bedroom. No doubt hoping they'd forget him altogether.

"Look, Mom, can you just give me some space to—"

Glennis stepped forward. Robin tried to duck out of her mother's embrace, but she wasn't fast enough. As if everything would be made right if Glennis could just hug her tightly enough. "Robin, I would never do anything to hurt you. You know if I could have died in his place, I—"

"No." Robin couldn't even look at her. "Just—*don't.*"

"Sweetie—"

"That is *not* how life works." No do-overs. No substitutions.

"I know, sweetie, but if I could have—"

"No." Robin extracted herself from her mother's arms. "You *don't* get to say that." It was the sort of smarmy romantic nonsense people said when they imagined they knew exactly what you were going through. Her mother believed her words were true, but they weren't. "You wanna know the truth, Mom?" Seth was too little. He needed his mother to make play dough dinosaurs and teach him how to put his undies on right-side-out. Maybe later he would need a father, and she would cross that bridge when she got to it—but right now, more than anything else, she had to be there for him. That was the kind of terrible, brutal truth you only faced when something like this happened. "*I* wouldn't have died for Tavis. Even if I could."

Robin watched her mother's face as she wrestled with shock, and then the urge to protest. "You're hurting," she managed at last, tightly. "And I don't think I'm making anything better."

"No. You're not."

"I'm sorry." Glennis went into the living room and lifted her purse off the coat rack. She stepped over the threshold, hesitated, and shut the door.

7

SETH'S SINGING USUALLY WOKE ROBIN a heartbeat before he jumped onto her stomach. So when she woke naturally, gradually, it took her a moment to fit the pieces of her consciousness into place.

Tavis. Gone. Still. Like a hollow in the center of a tree.

And more immediate: silence.

Robin sat up. Had she locked the front and back doors before going to bed, or was the memory just an echo of all the other times she had done exactly the same thing? The two beers she'd had after Seth went to bed hadn't impaired her that much, had they? What if Seth had let himself out—as, yes, he had once done before she'd installed the chain lock—and gone wandering off through the neighborhood? He was surely old enough to know better by now. Surely.

She padded barefoot into the hall. Two years ago, she'd been browsing the internet and come across an article about a mother who'd lost a child when the little girl pulled a dresser over on top of herself. It had been eleven o'clock at night, and Robin had gone into Seth's room with her Makita and screwed every item of furniture to the wall. But there was no point panicking until she had cause.

His door was open. Bed empty.

If something had happened to him—

If he was gone—

She shouldn't have thrown away the pills.

The bathroom was vacant, but there was pee in his potty. She jogged down the stairs; living room empty. Front door shut, but the chain lock hung loose. The bolt had not been turned. Now she ran. Kitchen—empty, including the three beer bottles lined up on the counter. Office—empty. Finally, the back patio she'd glassed in and converted into a play room.

Seth glanced up from the rug, the cheap Ikea one decorated with roads and gas stations and hotels. "Hi," he said, and continued arranging his fifty-plus Hot Wheels cars.

Robin went into the kitchen and made coffee. She drank the first cup black.

The second cup she mixed with milk and chocolate as usual. She stirred it with a spoon and wandered back into the play room, grabbing her phone from the charger on the counter as she passed. The screen informed her that her inbox now contained her mother's obligatory Long-Ass Email of Justification. Because Glennis could never just say *sorry, I didn't mean to hurt your feelings* and let it go.

There was also a text from Trinity, one of the core members of the young couples' group at church, and—unbelievably—yet another message from Walker. From a different number, this time. *I know your grieving, but please can we talk. None of this is what you think.*

Leave me alone, Robin replied. Then she blocked the number. Whatever had happened in Afghanistan could stay there. Tavis had loved her, and she had loved him, and now he was gone.

Two cars collided at her feet, explosive sound effects provided by Seth. He needed to get dressed and eat something before school, but just looking at his little upturned nose was enough to bring a lump to Robin's throat. School could wait. She leaned against the doorjamb, took another sip of coffee, and imagined swiping away the fears of minutes past along with the notifications on her phone.

Now that Facebook wasn't an emotional minefield—assuming she ignored her private messages—she could flip through status updates and shared links without danger. Four weeks, and everyone else had moved on. She read an article about early menopause and checked out photos of a distant cousin's new baby girl.

It was silly, but being able to do this—zone out on social media—was a gift. By whatever means he had accomplished it, Cyril had given her back a little bit of normalcy. Or if not that, at least the power to look at her son without bursting into tears. She smiled at his cars, lined up in neat ranks of eight and sixteen. "Whatcha doin', bud?"

"Dragons."

"Your cars are dragons?" Odd, but not an uncommon substitution.

He pointed to one set. "These guys are little. They need castles to trans."

That was new. "Trans?"

"Yeah." He held up his hands, curling his fingers into claws. "To trans to biiig draaagons!" He moved a car from another group. "But you need money to build castles! See? He needs more! This is his garden. He can sell carrots to make golds! And then he can buy bricks from these dragons to make a castle, like this!" He turned a car from one group onto its back. "But then other biiiig dragons attack the castle! It's not big enough!" He made some explosive sound effects. "So we gotta grow some carrots again!"

Robin set her mug on the windowsill and knelt down. "Hold on. You went too fast for your poor mom. Show me again?"

He pressed a car into her hand. "You be this one."

Robin took the car-which-was-a-dragon and flew it around according to Seth's instructions. It went through the entire cycle, from baby dragon to big dragon, producing carrots and converting them to money and then bricks until finally it built its own castle, where it could store eggs that would hatch into baby dragons that would begin the cycle all over again.

It wasn't perfect, but her three-year-old was using his cars to reproduce a basic economic model of a supply chain.

"Is this… are you playing a game? I mean, a video game?"

He beamed. "Dragontown! From the pad!"

Okay, so maybe Cyril's video games were doing slightly more than rotting her child's brain.

ROBIN SPENT THE REMAINDER of the morning demolishing Cooke's bathroom tile with a hammer and chisel. Not her favorite part of the job, usually, but certainly satisfying. When she finally got the tub liner out, she left it on a drop cloth in the middle of the living room and drove home, ignoring the two calls she'd missed from her mother.

She'd showered and had started on some dinner prep when the doorbell rang. Instantly her pulse rate doubled, and she stood for a moment at the cutting board, breathing carefully.

When the Pavlovian response had faded, she snuck across the floor on tiptoe, avoiding the patches where her weight would produce a squeak or a groan, and squinted through the peep hole.

"I can see you," Trinity sang out.

Robin straightened, patted her hair—as if that could even begin to fix the giant rat's nest it had become—and snapped the bolt open. "Sorry. Just wanted to make sure it wasn't a solicitor." Or Andrews. Or a cop coming to inform her that Seth, too, was gone.

Trinity's lopsided frown said she didn't believe the excuse, but she'd take it anyway. "Can I come in?" She stepped over the threshold and headed straight to the kitchen, a paper bag of foodstuffs cradled against her chest. "You haven't been answering my texts," she called over one shoulder.

Robin plodded after her. "Sorry." She wanted to offer an excuse, but there was none.

Trinity was one of those tiny women who would still be a size zero even if she gave birth a dozen times, with straight blonde hair cut in a severe, businesslike line around her jaw. Tavis had gone through school with her, but only in the most technical sense; she'd been three years behind him, and he said he honestly hadn't known she existed until she married his buddy Benson. Robin chatted with her at church, but she knew she didn't rate more than a casual acquaintance; Trinity was aggressively friendly with everyone, and judging by her Facebook photos she spent most of her "girl time" with Erin.

"You haven't answered any of us," Trinity said, unloading a casserole into the fridge with precise, careful movements. "Teresa and Brianne and Erin and me."

Robin gave her a steady look. "It's barely been a month."

Trinity refused to wilt. "We just want to make sure you're all right. We're your friends."

Were they? The word felt meaningless. Robin watched the other woman finger her necklace, a topaz stone framed by a pair of tiny angel wings, and all she could think about was four years ago, when Tavis and

Benson had volunteered to man the first aid booth at Ventura's annual marathon. They'd borrowed her construction floodlights to light the way for late finishers. Sometime after midnight, she'd come downstairs to find Tavis in the kitchen, bare-chested and covered in sweat as he constructed a late-night BLT. He'd ended up having to resuscitate a runner in cardiac arrest. Even at eight months pregnant, it was the best sex they'd ever had.

"Joanie told me you never came to your counseling session. We're worried about you, honey."

It rankled, having a childless woman five years her junior address her like a wayward teen. Robin had a choice: she could go for real, brutal honesty, in which case Trinity would leave with the conviction that Robin was truly *lost* and in desperate need of help. That would be followed by more friendly interventions, until she snapped and blew up her entire life. Or she could put on a smile and say, "Can I get you some coffee?"

Trinity frowned. "Maybe just some water, thanks."

The kitchen was a mess of half-chopped ingredients, but Robin managed to find a clean glass.

"Smart," Trinity said. "Making two at a time. I always think I'm gonna do that, but I can never get my act together. Plus finding room in the freezer. Lasagna?"

"Yeah." Robin opened the freezer just far enough to inch the ice tray out, hoping Trinity wouldn't notice it was still stuffed with funeral leftovers. The fridge, at least, was clear. She plunked a couple of cubes in the glass and filled it with filtered water.

"Thanks. So did you actually read any of my texts?"

"Um. I don't think so. Sorry." She picked up the cleaver she used for just about everything and continued chopping carrots.

"Okay." Trinity fingered her necklace again. Had the others put her up to this? She was always taking on volunteer assignments—hosting baby showers, making snacks for church, doing childcare for the mom's group meetings... Visiting Robin was probably one more good-deed notch on Trinity's belt. "Have you thought about coming back to church?"

Robin dropped the cleaver. She pushed a hunk of hair out of her face with the back of her hand and leveled her gaze at Trinity. "Look," she said. "I'm not some prodigal who needs saving. I'm still on God's side. I just—I don't feel much like talking to Him right now. And I think He's probably going to have to be okay with that." She felt like it was more than enough, at this point, that she wasn't standing out on a street corner cursing His goddamn name.

"Okay," Trinity said, quietly. "That's, um… understandable."

"Good." Robin went back to chopping.

"Well." Trinity placed the half-empty water glass in the bottom of the sink. "I won't keep you. But—you know," she added, as if whatever she was about to say had just occurred to her, "we're having a ladies' night out next Monday. Just five or six of us. If you're up for it, we'd love to have you along."

Trinity wasn't going to leave the house until she got something.

"Fine," Robin said. "I'll come."

She picked seth up from preschool in the truck. He clambered into the extended cab and insisted on buckling himself into the five-point harness, although it took a good five minutes to complete the task. "Mommy, what's that smell?"

Always flattering. "Just some food, Sweetpea."

"For me?"

"Um… no." She cranked the wheel and pulled onto the street. "Well, sort of. It's lasagna. We're having the same thing tonight." And tomorrow night and the night after.

Her answer stumped Seth long enough to get them around the corner and down the block. He'd just started trying to get his mouth around the word 'lasagna' when she pulled into a familiar driveway.

"*Cereal!*" he shrieked.

"We're not going inside," she said, firmly. "In fact, you're stay here, okay? I'm just gonna drop this off." She grabbed the single-use aluminum pan from the passenger seat and slid out of the cab, ignoring Seth's whiny protests. "Be right back, buddy!"

Odds were, Cyril was home, because he was always home. Odds

were he'd already seen her truck through the window in the front of the granny unit. But odds were he'd do them both a favor and not bother answering if she didn't ring the bell.

She was bending to set the dish on the doormat when the door swung in.

"Great." He reached out and took the lasagna without the slightest hesitation. "Now you can go home and tell yourself you don't owe me anything."

"Owe you? For what?" She kept hold of the pan. "Getting my husband off Facebook? Or stealing his passwords?"

"Oh." He licked his lips. "You talked to Cooke."

She shoved the pan into his stomach, hard. The aluminum buckled slightly, leaking marinara sauce onto his shirt. "You should have told me. About the letters, too."

He lifted one shoulder in a half-shrug. "No matter what I said, you were gonna be upset."

"You know what's worse than saying the wrong thing? Saying nothing at all."

"Well that's definitely not true." He looked elsewhere. "Think what you want. If I hadn't, he'd still be on Facebook."

"That's why I brought the lasagna, asshole. Plus I'd already done the shopping." She turned on one heel—just as Seth leapt out of the truck. He landed on the gravel, his shoes skidding across the loose pebbles before he came to rest, more or less intact, on his rear end.

"*Cereal!*"

"Seth!" Robin tried to sound angry, but mostly she was just astonished that he'd managed to get out of the car seat. Buckling himself in was one thing, but the release button at the crotch was tough even for her.

"Cereal, I got—I got—" Breathlessly, Seth worked his little fingers around until only the middle three stuck up. He held his hand up triumphantly. "I got free stars onna blaster level!"

"Awesome. Did you do the bonus area?"

"Yeah! It's all gold!"

"Seth," Robin said, deciding she couldn't reasonably let this slide, "I told you to stay. In. The. Car."

"But Mommy, I got free—"

As Seth continued to babble about the game, Cyril leveled his gaze at Robin and cocked one eyebrow.

He was right. This was her fault for bringing Seth. If she'd been smart, she'd have dropped the food off before picking him up. And if she were honest, she'd brought Seth along because she'd been afraid of facing Cyril alone. Of what she might do if her kid wasn't there.

She gave Cyril a firm nod. This was not going to continue. This was definitely The End.

Cyril waited until Seth ran out of breath. "That's great, kiddo. But you know what? I can't play. Have fun with your iPad, huh?"

Seth blinked. "Not today?" He seemed to sense the gravity in Cyril's delivery. "But why?"

"Not today. Not any other day. Okay? Go home. Do what your mom says."

"But—"

Robin put a hand on his head. "Come on, Seth. Dinner time."

"Adios." Cyril shut the door.

Seth's fingers cinched around her wrist. "But Mommy? Mommy? Why Cyril don't want to play with me?"

"Because he's busy, sweetie. And he's a grownup. You have other friends to play with, okay? Kids your own age."

Robin could see him trying to be brave. But his lip quivered. A tear slid down his cheek. And then he couldn't keep it inside any more, and his little face crumpled and he buried his face in her legs and sobbed in shame.

Seth didn't understand that Cyril was—well, himself, and Robin didn't like him and didn't want him frying Seth's brains with video games. He didn't get that Cyril had no reason to spend his time with some random kid, even if that kid happened to be the child of his deceased best friend. All he knew was that his friend didn't want to play, and since Cyril was completely awesome there was only one possible reason for the rejection: something was wrong with *him*.

Robin dropped to her knees and wrapped her arms around him and hugged him tight as she could. "Oh, sweetie. I'm sorry. Mommy's sorry. You can play. Okay? This was my fault and I'm sorry."

Was she being too lenient? Was she spoiling Seth when she should be firm?

She didn't care. She couldn't make herself care. And if anyone wanted to judge her she would direct them to the fresh tombstone at Ivy Lawn.

Robin got back to her feet and hobbled to Cyril's door, Seth still wrapped around her legs. She knocked firmly, three times.

It took him a good long while to open the door again. Was he waiting, making sure she meant it? Giving her a chance to change her mind?

"I'm sorry," she said as soon as the latch clicked open. She couldn't quite look him in the eye. "I was wrong."

If there was any hint of emotion in Cyril's face, it was buried in the swell of his double chin and the shadowy hollows of his eyes. "Be sure about this."

"I am. I'm sorry. I am." She would deal with the fallout, whatever it was. Seth's interest in Cyril would doubtless fade with time, anyway.

He was silent another moment. "Okay. This is how it's gonna be. You drop him off. We'll play. You pick him up. That way..."

That way they didn't have to see each other more than necessary. Robin nodded. "Okay." Seth did a little happy wiggle against her legs. "That sounds fine."

"What days does he have school?"

"Uh... Monday and Thursday. Til five."

"I'll pick him up, then. You can come get him at bedtime. That's like seven, right?"

Robin blinked. He was offering to make this into a formal arrangement. Regular visitations. That was weird, but—well, it meant he wasn't planning to drop Seth whenever he got bored. Her kid probably wouldn't die from eating microwave corn dogs and Jello-O twice a week, either. "Okay. I guess—I guess that could work."

Cyril smirked, as if he'd won some sort of battle, and let the door swing in. "Hey, dude. Let's play some games."

Seth tilted his head way back to look up at her, a hopeful light in his eyes. Robin used a finger to brush the tears off his cheeks. "Go for it, sweetie."

"Yoohoo!"

Robin glanced at Cyril. "Yahoo," she interpreted.

"Obviously."

If Robin felt at all as if she had just made some sort of Faustian bargain—and she very much did—her anxieties were mitigated when Seth threw himself at Cyril, wrapping his arms around one massive thigh, and turned to give her a brilliant smile.

She smiled back. "Have fun, sweet—"

Cyril slammed the door.

8

TRINITY WAS WAITING ON THE sidewalk outside Nom, an upscale bistro-bar just down the street from the church in old town Camarillo. She gave a neat little wave and tottered from the curb to the tarmac in her black pumps, arms open for a hug. Robin endured the embrace, feeling absurdly under-dressed in her usual jeans and t-shirt. She hadn't realized this was the sort of thing you dressed up for. She never did.

"So glad you came," Trinity said. "I know you're getting plenty of support from the other Navy wives, but we wanted to make sure you knew we were here for you, too."

"Thanks." Everyone always assumed Robin had closer friends elsewhere. She wasn't sure why. She and Tavis had intentionally moved off-base to avoid all the drama—but how did you tell people that actually, no—after four years in town, they were it? Tavis had been enough for her, but he was gone, and now Trinity was probably the closest friend she had.

"And where's the little man tonight?" Trinity hooked her arm through Robin's elbow. "Benson was sorry he didn't get to babysit."

"Oh—he's hanging out with Cyril." She held the door open and followed Trinity into the bar.

Trinity glanced back over her shoulder. "Cyril?"

"An old friend of Tav's."

"Yeah, I know, I—guess I just didn't realize he was still around." She craned her neck. "Oh! There they are in the back."

Robin had barely scooted into the booth next to Trinity before it started.

"Hey, girl." Brianne, who had taught middle school in Watts before coming home to marry the children's pastor, always pulled out her faux inner-city drawl whenever Robin was around. "How you holdin' up?"

"All right." There was a basket in the center of the table with packets of sugar and a couple books of matches, long obsolete thanks to California's smoking laws. She picked one out and turned it over, tracing the white quill logo with a nail.

Erin, second wife of a guy from Tav's high school football team, put a soft hand on her shoulder. "I can't even imagine. I mean, I don't know how you do it. I didn't know how you did it before, with Tavis deployed, and now..."

"It's not like I have a choice," Robin said. "What am I supposed to do? Pack up and move across the country?" Come to think of it, that might not be a horrible idea. She dredged her brain for a subject change, something to talk about other than Tav. Nothing came to mind. Her future had just gone up in flames, and here they all were with their perfect Norman Rockwell lives.

"I couldn't even *deal* if I lost Derrik." Brianne stuck herself in the arm with a lancet she'd pulled out of her purse. Her fingers were tipped with false nails painted garish hot pink; with quick, practiced manipulations of a thumb and forefinger, she checked her blood sugar and tucked the meter back in her purse. "I think I'd just curl up and die, you know? You're so strong."

Why did everyone say that? "No you wouldn't. You'd pull yourself together for the kids."

Trinity dug into her purse for a pack of tissues and tore it open with a little plastic stutter. "When I heard, I went home and hugged Benson the whole night." She tugged one out and handed it to Robin.

Erin held out a hand for a tissue and used it, carefully, to dab around her mascara. "Yeah. I was having this huge fight with Chris, and we just... dropped the whole thing. It seemed so stupid. Makes you thankful for what you have."

Everyone nodded, murmuring inarticulate mmhmms.

So this was what Robin was, now: an object lesson in gratitude.

There was silence, again, as they all felt the weight of Tav's absence. Robin looked around the table, but nobody met her gaze. She felt like screaming. Instead she said, "Where's Linda? And Yolanda?"

Trinity fingered her necklace. "They couldn't make it." Her eyes stayed on the table.

They'd heard about her outburst at Marta's, of course. "I see." Robin was the epicenter of an emotional earthquake, and these were the women willing to risk the aftershocks.

That ought to have meant something, but it didn't. If it weren't for Seth, she'd have packed a bag of necessities, left her house keys with the local property management company, and simply driven away from it all.

"Remember—" Brianne smiled, tentatively. "Remember when Tavis first brought you to church? You broke about fifteen hearts that day."

Robin forced a smile. At first she'd imagined they were all shocked that he'd brought home a black girl, because she'd been there and done that before. Then she'd realized the looks she was getting came exclusively from young women, and it had nothing to do with the color of *her* skin. They'd been green with envy.

Trinity flagged the waitress with an index finger. "Time to get drunk, girls."

"You're so full of it." Erin giggled. "You and your Shirley Temples." She looked up at the waitress. "I'll have a Sex on the Beach. Do we want some snacks, too?"

After they'd decided on potato skins and nachos, the waitress left and the conversation returned immediately to Tavis.

Remember when he'd shipped off to boot camp? Right after graduation. Everyone had known he'd excel at whatever he put his hands to, and nobody had been surprised when he'd decided to serve his country instead of taking that football scholarship.

Remember when he'd scored the lead in the school play? Everyone had assumed he was just a dumb jock, but he got up there on that stage and damn if he couldn't dance and sing!

Remember when he'd made Eagle Scout and organized that bone marrow drive? He was always such an amazing guy. Incredible that he'd turned out so well, coming from the family he did. Had any of them even come to the funeral? Brianne thought she had seen one of his sisters, maybe. None of them had contacted Robin.

Remember back in middle school, that summer Gretchen had been the lifeguard, and Tavis and his friends had rolled up their towels and sunk them in the deep end, making her think someone had drowned?

Remember when Tavis had teamed up with Cyril in grade school to make that little RC robot? They'd rigged it to make the most awful noise and used it to scare the crap out of the teacher.

Everyone laughed, and Erin let out a long sigh. "You know, we went to prom together."

"Oh gosh," Trinity whispered. "That's right. I'd totally forgotten."

Erin nodded. "I still have the corsage, somewhere. We only dated for, what, two or three weeks, but he was such a—such a—" She put a hand over her face. "Oh my God, I can't believe he's gone."

Brianne wrapped her arms around Erin and Trinity dug out a fresh pack of tissues. Robin used a thumb to flip the matchbook open and closed.

This was why they were here tonight. Not to comfort Robin, but to grieve for a friend.

She liked people, generally, but she'd never had the knack for making them feel instantly loved and valued. Not the way Tavis had. Her father had been like that, too. Neither of them had ever minded her borrowing a friend or two; they'd had plenty to go around. Still, there it was: these were not her friends first. They were Tav's.

But they hadn't known him—the *real* him—the way she had. To them, he was a gentle giant; a sweet, good-natured soldier; more brawn than brains. You didn't get far as an intellectual, in a town like this, and until Robin, Tav's writing had only ever been for himself. What little he'd written down, he'd quickly burned. None of the women around the table tonight knew that his thick skull had housed the most beautiful, perfect part of him: a strong, passionate intellect. In a way, that was a comfort— but it was also a burden, to know she was the sole keeper of his true memory.

Eventually, Erin pulled herself together. Robin could see her searching back over their conversation, mentally, for a change of subject.

"Hey," she said, "whatever happened to Cyril, anyway? Surely he's not still living behind his mom's place."

"He comes by the library once or twice a month," Brianne volunteered. She worked as a part-time assistant, shelving books and reading to kids. "Never checks anything out, just uses the computers."

"Probably looking at porn." Erin wiggled her eyebrows suggestively.

Brianne gave her shoulder a friendly smack. "They're right out in front of everyone."

"Uh," Trinity said, looking embarrassed. She darted a glance at Robin. "I think—"

"He's *huge*, though, have you seen him?" Brianne held her arms out an inflated her cheeks. "Seriously, he has to turn sideways to get through the door. I'm not even kidding."

Erin shook her head and made a little tut-tut-tut noise with her tongue. "Everyone thought he'd move to Silicon Valley and make a million. What a waste."

Trinity opened her mouth to object again—although Robin could have told her she preferred gossip about Cyril to reminiscences of Tav—when the drinks arrived. Robyn stuck the matchbook in her purse and sat back to make room as the waitress placed a cardboard coaster in front of each of them. It was going to be a long evening.

As soon as the server had left, Erin seized her Sex on the Beach and held it high. "Now, let's not forget the original reason for our get-together," she said. "I am done being pregnant, done breastfeeding. Done, done, done!"

Robin looked down at her Bloody Mary and realized it had been eight weeks since her period.

BY THE TIME SHE GOT THROUGH the line at the drug store, it was already twenty minutes past eight—the very latest she'd promised to pick up Seth. She had every intention of waiting until she got home and Seth was safely in bed, but by the time she made it to Cyril's door her eyeballs were swimming. She rapped and let herself in without waiting for an invitation. "I need to use your bathroom."

Seth looked up from where he sat cross-legged on the floor, in front of the TV. "Aw, man!"

Cyril, in his usual spot on the couch, held a hand out toward his bedroom. "I don't see a no trespassing sign."

Robin couldn't even see the bathroom floor for all the dirty clothes. She used the side of her foot to sweep everything out onto the bedroom carpet before dragging the door shut. Tavis had, fortunately, installed a knob with a lock. Not backwards, either, like he'd done the first time at home.

He was here, with her, even if just a very little bit.

The package contained two sticks. She ripped one open and counted to five as she peed over Cyril's double-wide bowl, wondering briefly if half a bloody Mary was enough alcohol to affect the result, if alcohol affected the result at all. Tavis would have known. Then she shook the stick a bit, capped it, and set it in the middle of the newly tiled floor.

Three minutes, you were supposed to wait. She turned and, with a trembling hand, flushed the toilet. Then she washed her hands and splashed her face. "Okay," she whispered. "You got this." She sucked in a breath and looked.

She didn't even have to bend over. That second red line would have been visible from half a mile away.

"You got this," she said again. "You got this."

No, she absolutely didn't. She bent double and puked into the toilet bowl. It was red.

What now? What the ever-loving *fuck* was she supposed to do now?

Robin yanked her purse off the door handle and rooted for her phone. She needed Tavis. If not his arms, then his words. Now.

But no matter how she willed it otherwise, her inbox was barren.

Her hand went deeper into her purse. Her fingers brushed the zippered pocket, hanging open. She pulled the envelope out and held it with both hands, tracing the pen strokes of her name with her eyes.

Not now. Not like this.

She folded it in half and tucked it back into the pocket with her pads. Which she wouldn't be needing for at least another nine months, now would she?

Oh, God.

She couldn't cry. Not with Cyril on the other side of the wall. Even if he didn't hear her, he'd see her blotchy face and know. But if she stepped out now, she was going to fall apart.

She had to *do* something.

Kaiser had an app she'd downloaded a while ago. She pulled it up and signed in. A bit of hunt-and-peck pulled up the appointments tab for her OB/GYN, and she watched as the loading symbol blinked, searching.

Her doctor was booked two weeks out—except for one slot first thing tomorrow morning, probably a recent cancellation. Robin accepted the appointment with a tap. Half a second later, her phone dinged with an automatically generated email reminder.

Next she pulled up her contact list, tapped on Marta's name, and sent her a quick text. *Can you take Seth tomorrow?*

Finally, she picked the test stick up off the floor and stuffed it into her purse, along with the cellophane packaging and her phone.

There. She'd done all she possibly could. For the moment.

She splashed her face again, patted it dry with a few squares of toilet paper, and flushed.

When she returned to the living room, Seth was on his feet, controller in hand, jumping up and down. "Get the guy! Get the guy!"

On the television, a cute little piñata bunny hopped through some grass. Nearby, a diminutive figure wearing a tiki mask had started ripping up flowers.

"I got it." Cyril pushed a button on the controller and a shovel appeared, floating in midair. The view zoomed out and then back in again, square onto the masked figure. The shovel swung forward and connected with a tinny metallic *whack*.

Well. Having her presence completely ignored was, at least in this instance, probably for the best. Robin went to take a seat at Cyril's desk, but the chair, when she turned it around, was piled high with legal paperwork. Cyril spared her a split-second glance. "Don't touch."

Robin's phone beeped and she pulled it out to find a reply from

Marta. *Sorry no! Valerie asked yesterday to put in Freddie. Cannot take any more children that day, its state law.*

Great. Just fantastic. Robin let herself drop onto the couch next to Cyril and massaged her forehead with both hands, trying not to breathe too deeply of his BO.

"Too many Bloody Marys?"

She looked at him, sharply. "How did you know?"

"Hm?" He had exchanged the shovel for a lantern and was using it to chase the tiki guy out of the garden. When the critter stepped over a glowing read boundary line, the music went back to a cheery tinkle and everything sparkled with sunshine. Seth cheered, and Cyril spared Robin enough mental space to look at her again. His eyes narrowed. "Are you drunk?"

"No," she said. "I'm not. How did you know I drink Bloody Marys?"

He shrugged. "I dunno, I picked the first girly drink that came to mind." He waved the controller at Seth. "Here, bud, get the bunny back to his burrow, okay? We'll quit there." When Seth had taken the proffered device and turned his attention back to the screen, Cyril looked at her. "What, you think I left Seth here alone and snuck down to the bar to spy on you?"

"I don't know. No. Never mind. Can you take Seth tomorrow at nine?"

"In the *morning?* Jesus. What about your mom?"

Robin looked at her hands. "She's busy."

"Well, so am I."

"Sleeping is not—"

"I'm not your goddamn babysitter. Ask one of your friends or something."

"They're not—I—look, I have to go to the doctor. This was the only time my OB was available."

"Your hot flashes are not my problem."

"I'm pregnant, okay?" She said it to shock him, to shut him up for once, but he didn't even flinch.

"With Tav's?"

"Yes, with—" She glanced at Seth, who was engrossed in navigating his bunny through a maze that had popped up when he reached the burrow. "Yes, with Tav's kid. Who else?"

"I dunno, he was gone a lot. Plenty of other sailors on the base."

"Asshole." And with that, she knew she'd lost.

Cyril smirked.

"What's ash-hole, Mommy?"

"Nothing, sweetie." She stood, plucked the controller from his hand, and tossed it onto the coffee table. "Come on, let's get you home. No whining, okay? It's late."

"Bye, Cereal!"

"See you in the morning, kid."

9

CYRIL ANSWERED THE DOOR in his flannel pajama pants and a raggedy green bathrobe too small to conceal his sagging belly and sumo-grade man boobs. He squinted in the sunlight, muttered something unintelligible, and shuffled back to his desk.

Seth darted across the floor to his side. "What's going on?"

"Hold on a sec, kid." Cyril's fingers tap-danced over the keyboard. He had about ten windows open on the screen, layered on top of each other, half of them black with tiny white text. He attended to these for a moment before pulling up a chat window and pounding out a couple of sentences at about a hundred words per minute.

As much as she didn't want to admit it, Robin was curious, too. "What *are* you doing?"

"Hm? Uh." He went silent again, and she had just about given up on getting an answer when he said, "Coordinating a DDoS attack. Playstation controller's on the couch. Knock yourself out, kid."

Robin pointed. "Right there, sweetie." She waited until Seth had hopped onto the couch and logged into the piñata animal game. "Um—whatever that is, it sounds illegal."

"Technically." He flipped between windows of scrolling code. "But the U.S. isn't gonna comply with an extradition request from Syria."

"From *where?*"

"Syria?" He glanced at her. "Do you even follow the news?"

"Not since Seth."

Cyril looked vaguely disgusted, but he was quickly sucked back into his attack, or whatever he was doing.

Robin understood his look well; if she had been granted a glimpse into her own future, she would have given it to herself. She'd cared about Big Things, once. Politics, religion, current events. She'd argued vehemently;

made phone calls to her representatives; collected signatures and handed out flyers, even. All of it had seemed so important, especially with Tavis overseas. So black and white.

Now everyone, even the so-called bad guys, just looked like someone else's precious child.

Cyril blew out a triumphant breath of air and pushed himself away from the keyboard. "That's right, fuckers." He grabbed an open can of root beer and took a long pull. "All right. I'm good to go."

Robin frowned. "How long have you been up?"

He leaned back, swiping the backs of his hands across his eyes. "You're assuming—" He paused to let out a long, loud belch. "You're assuming I went to bed."

Wonderful. "Is this gonna be… okay?"

He followed her glance toward Seth. "Kid practically babysits himself. Go. It's fine."

When robin returned, she opened the door expecting to find Cyril at least showered and dressed. Clearly she'd set her expectations too high. He'd installed himself on the couch, as usual, with a bag of pretzels and another can of soda. The robe was gone.

"Mommy!" Seth bounded across the floor, throwing his arms around her legs.

Robin grinned. "Well hello, handsome." Sometimes Seth was completely indifferent to her presence. And sometimes she was the Queen of the Universe.

"Mommy Mommy Mommy! Cereal's coming!"

"*Probably* is what I said." Cyril's voice was still low and throaty, like he'd just woken from a deep slumber. He scratched at the wiry black hair that carpeted his chest. "Pipsqueak couldn't tell me what day."

"Day?" Robin focused on the wall above his head as he yawned and ran a hand over his belly. "For what?"

Seth let go of her legs and slung himself over her purse. "My *birf-*day!"

"Oh. Right." She'd hoped he would forget the whole thing. And he had—yesterday. Not, apparently, today. "Uh... not this weekend, but the Saturday after." Seth went limp, causing the purse strap to bite into her shoulder. "Sweetie, can you just—get off—" She managed to untangle him without strangling him or herself. "That ice cream place by Trader Joe's? Say about eleven in the morning."

Cyril nodded. "Sure. I can do that."

Because his schedule was so packed. "Okay, well, good. Sethie, why don't we go and let Cyril get back to, uh, whatever he needs to do?" Napping, no doubt.

Seth snapped to attention. "No! Wait!" He pointed to the television. "I gotta show you my robots! Cereal said I could!"

"All right, let's see your robots first."

Seth looked at the floor directly in front of his feet. "Where's my troller?"

Cyril shook the last drops of soda into his mouth, crumpled the can in one hand, and tossed it toward the garbage can in the corner, which was the focal point of a more general garbage heap. "I dunno, kid, where'd you leave it?"

Seth dropped to his knees and peered under the coffee table.

Cyril grabbed the arm of the couch and rocked himself to his feet. "Siddown," he said, huffing his way into the kitchen. He didn't so much walk as shove his belly forward with his knees. "This is gonna take a while."

The computer chair was still occupied with files. Robin sighed and took a seat on the side of the couch that wasn't caved into a permanent depression. Seth located the controller and then spent a few long, painful moments attempting to navigate the game system's menu. "Sweetie," Robin said, when he accidentally clicked past his target for the third time, "why don't you let Cyril—"

"No! I can do it!"

She rolled her eyes and slouched back into the soft leather, stuffing her hands in her jean pockets.

Cyril had a can of root beer in each hand when he returned from the kitchen. Robin's first impulse was to get up and move away, but that seemed a shade too rude even for Cyril. She scooted all the way to the arm of the couch as he backed up to the other end, leaned forward, and lowered himself until his center of gravity shifted too far to hold. He dropped the rest of the way, causing the couch to jump beneath her. He passed her one of the cans, beaded with icy sweat.

"So," he grunted. "You take care of it?"

She wrinkled her nose at the smell of BO and way too much antiperspirant. "Take care of what?" If he wasn't going to shower, was putting on a shirt really too much to ask?

"You know." He gestured toward her torso before popping the tab on his beverage. "It."

Robin couldn't even say she was surprised he'd guessed. She used the tip of her finger to draw a squiggly line in the condensation. "No."

"Mommy! Look!" The TV displayed a mirror reflection of him and the room—with the addition of a crowd of little white robots on the floor. Seth flapped his arms, sending them scurrying away from his virtual counterpart. One of them wasn't quite fast enough, and Seth's windmilling hand sent it hurtling into the "surface" of the screen. He shrieked with delight.

"Very cool, bud."

"Now watch!" He swiped at a little pad on the top of the controller and, on the screen, it showed vacuum rays shooting out to suck the robots back into the controller. He chortled and did a happy dance. A couple of remaining robots mimicked his movements.

Cyril took a swig of soda and rested the can on his stomach. "So you made up your mind."

Robin tapped the top of her can and eased the tab open. "Not... yet."

"Well, you can't have very long to decide."

She blinked. He was right, but—"How do you even know how this works?"

"Google is your friend."

Robin wedged a hand into the front pocket of her jeans, feeling the business card the doctor had given her. Two days. And then she couldn't just do it with pills. She'd have to make an appointment at the place on the card.

She looked at Seth, now cavorting with a robot that looked like a floating white helmet.

"Don't," said Cyril. "It's not his brother. Or sister. It's nothing. Not yet."

Maybe not. But it was a little blinking heartbeat on a screen. That wasn't nothing. Three months ago, even contemplating this option would have been out of the question. Life was sacred. She believed that. Still did, always would. Thing was, life was hard. And she was afraid.

"Just take the damn pill." He nodded to the soda in her hand.

She followed his gaze. "This...?" Robin set the can down on the coffee table. Like everything with Cyril, it had come with ulterior motives. She used a finger to push it away. "I don't—they make you do the first one there. At the office."

"So let's go. Right now. Five minutes and it's done."

She put a hand over her eyes. "God. I can't tell if you're being decent or a complete asshole."

"The world doesn't need any more fatherless children. Or children, come to think of it." He took another swig of his root beer, emptying the can. "And it doesn't seem like something you should do alone."

"So... both."

He shrugged. "One swallow. It's over."

Over.

"I don't... I don't think I want it to be." Tavis was gone. But the genetic blueprints which had built him were still there, inside of her. Constructing something new, and yet also *him*.

Cyril tossed the second empty can after the first. "Then you made up your mind."

"You think I'm making the wrong choice?"

"What do you care?" He seemed almost angry. "It's your life."

Robin flopped back into the couch again. She had to admit it was comfortable. She propped a foot up on the coffee table, using her toe to push the aluminum can into the center. Being around Cyril was like revisiting her sullen, rebellious teen years. All attitude, no responsibility. "You really planning to come, next Saturday?"

"You want me to tell him I changed my mind?"

Robin gave him a slow eye-roll.

"Then yes. Not for your sake."

"I got that, thanks." She looped the purse strap back over her head. "All right, Sethie. Let's go. We gotta hit the grocery store."

"Aw maaaan."

It was her general policy not to offer bribes, but she'd had just about as much of Cyril as she could take. "If you jump in the truck right now, no dilly-dallying, we can get you a squeezie."

Seth dropped the controller and bolted for the door.

"Whoa, hold your horses!" Robin jumped up and tried to shuffle around Cyril's legs without bashing her shins on the coffee table. "Wait for Mommy!"

Cyril put up a hand as she tripped, catching her neatly at the hip before she tumbled into his stomach. "Jesus, what's a squeezie? Crack?"

"Sorry." She grabbed his arm for balance and managed, finally, to get around his legs. "They're these little pouches of fruit and vegetable purees. The packaging makes him think they're treats, and I'm not telling."

"Nice."

Cyril's approval made her think she should probably drop the tactic immediately. Had Seth left anything behind? No. He was already up on the running board, attempting to leverage his body weight to yank the cab door open. Clothes and shoes on, check.

She got him into the cab and strapped him in the back before sliding the driver's seat back into place. "Um... One second, buddy."

"Squeezie?"

"Yes, you'll get a squeezie. One second. Stay here. Okay?"

Robin jogged back to Cyril's front door, rapping briefly before opening again. Cyril was bent over the computer chair, one hand on the armrest to support his weight as he used the other to move documents to the desk. He straightened and blew out a breath.

"Um. Look, next Saturday? My mom's gonna be there. Obviously I haven't told her yet, and... I'm not sure when I'm going to. Exactly. So if you could not say anything—"

"You mean you don't want to have a heart-to-heart about this touching moment at a later date?"

"Sorry, I forgot you're only capable of being a human being for thirty seconds or so."

He quirked an eyebrow. "Progress?"

Robin did something she hadn't done since she was fourteen: she flipped him the bird.

10

Robin was drowsing next to Seth's sleeping form when her phone pinged. It was probably her mother. Or Cooke, answering the email she'd sent that morning. It wasn't Tavis. No need to get excited.

She eased her tingling arm out from under Seth's head and stretched before sneaking out. The sneaking was probably unnecessary; once Seth passed out, he'd have slept through a marching band. In the hall, she slipped the phone out of her back pocket and clicked it on with a thumb.

And it was *him*.

Her finger poised to tap the notification, to bring the email up, to suck down every last drop of whatever he had to offer.

But wait.

She'd done all right at the doctor's. She hadn't broken down. She could live without the email for now. She could survive. Wait, and save it for when she was drowning.

Robin plugged the phone into the cord she'd threaded into her nightstand drawer, then forced herself to go into the bathroom and perform her evening routine. When she returned, she slipped into pajamas and slid under the sheets on her side of the bed. Or what had been her side of the bed. She liked to sleep on the edge, a hand or a foot hanging over, so she scarcely took up even a fourth of the mattress.

She closed her eyes and flopped over, facing the nightstand. But she could still feel the emptiness at her back. The bed was just so *big*.

Would it be weird, to sneak back in with Seth?

She reached for the phone.

Robin.

I feel like a hypocrite saying this, especially as a guy, but I will: sex is overrated.

When I go months without seeing you, it's not sex I long for. You're not an object to satisfy my desires. Well, not mostly, anyway. I am human.

You know what I crave? Your smell. You always smell clean and fresh and a little earthy. Like cold water straight from the hose on a sweltering summer afternoon.

I imagine your profile. The precise angle of your forehead and your nose and your chin, and the sweet little dip above your upper lip. That's my appetizer.

The touch of your hand on mine. The warmth of your skin. A feast! God, a single touch from you – I could subsist on it forever.

I sometimes do.

When you're in front of me sometimes it's all I can do to keep from running my hands up and down your body, memorizing every last curve and hollow. Part of me wants to make a complete scale model of you that I can take with me anywhere. Which sounds totally creepy, I know.

And it wouldn't matter, because even the most exact copy would never glow with life and energy the way you do. Your eyes would not overflow with love the way they do when you watch Seth play. You can't bottle that.

I content myself with remembering your hand on mine.

Most of the time, it's enough.

Robin did not cry, because words like that did not deserve tears. She breathed. She laid the phone against her face. And she remembered.

Tav, sleeping next to her. In his underwear, which always made her laugh, because he was perpetually hot. Legs and arms splayed, well over onto her side of the bed. So nice to have some *room*, he always said. In boot camp, his habit of rolling out of his bunk in a dead sleep had earned him the nickname "Thumper." Fortunately, his Marines just called him Doc.

His perfect pectorals and washboard abs—not the reason she loved him, but damn, it sure didn't hurt. The crappy caduceus tattoo on his right shoulder, the one he'd gotten from some hack in Afghanistan; the professional one on his left with her name stitched on a blue ribbon beneath her namesake animal. A little redundant, she'd pointed out. He'd grinned and said, "I love you times two."

The face she'd come to adore: angular, chiseled, but decidedly asymmetrical. His nostril curved up on the left, along with his smile. And those eyes. Ice blue, piercing, rimmed with lashes a shade lighter than his flame-red hair.

Robin reached, eyes still closed, and felt for the nightstand drawer. She pulled out the little bullet vibrator and laid it against her thigh.

She'd felt guilty, the first time, about doing this during his deployment, but when she'd made a hot-faced confession he'd only laughed. "You too? Oh my God, that's hot."

Now, she felt a pang of guilt because he was gone, and lusting after your dead husband was probably the very definition of crazy in the coconut. But she had a feeling that, had he known, Tavis would have said exactly the same thing.

He was—had been—so masculine, outwardly, and yet so privately tender. He had been her first, and he'd been so patient when neither of them could figure out how to bring her to climax. Finally, she'd pulled out the box of letters he'd sent from Afghanistan and asked him to read one aloud. He'd gone deathly pale—and then blushed a deep crimson red.

But she'd insisted, and it had done the trick.

With a flick of her finger, she turned the vibrator on and slid the buzzing bullet between her legs.

He wrote her apologies, from time to time, for not being able to replicate his eloquence in person. "When I look at you, words don't even exist."

She didn't mind. Every moment in Tav's presence was made more vivid in the knowledge that she would experience it again—in his words, reflected through his eyes. She never knew herself more intimately than at the tip of his pen.

Robin pressed the vibrator against herself. Usually, after imagining Tav, it only took a minute or two before she slid over the gulf into orgasm. Tonight, however, she lost the rhythm almost immediately. She forced herself to refocus, not just on Tav's imagined form, but on her body's response to the buzz in her groin.

She tried twice more before deciding it was pointless, but when she turned the vibrator off she was left with a feeling of vague, unsatisfied need.

Finally, she sat up on one elbow, propping a pillow under her arm, and picked up the phone. When she swiped the screen on, the email was still there.

"The touch of your hand," she read, her voice no more than a breath. "The warmth of your skin. A feast. God, a single touch from you—I could subsist on it forever." She clutched the pillow. "I sometimes do."

That was all it took.

She was vaguely proud of herself for not crying, afterward. Mostly, she just felt tired. Spent.

When the screen went black, Robin rolled out of bed, dumping the vibrator back into the drawer. She padded to the toilet and emptied her bladder.

On the way back to bed, she stopped outside of Seth's room. Carefully, she turned the knob, pressing downward to keep the hinges from creaking even as she made a mental note to grab some WD-40 next time she was in the garage. He hadn't moved.

Tavis was gone. But parts of him were still here. Her memories. His letters. And, reflected in Seth, his smile.

What pieces of Tav would she see in this new child?

11

"I'M GONNA HAVE MY FIVE BIRFDAY at our house," Seth announced from the back seat. "With kids."

"Uh... this is your fourth birthday, buddy. And we're en route to get ice cream right now."

"I *know*," he said, as if she'd insulted his intelligence. "I'm having ice cream for my four birfday."

"Right." Seth seemed to be under the impression that his fifth birthday was right around the corner. Who knew; maybe to a being with no concept of time, it really was. "Just so we're clear." Robin traded an amused glance with her mom, in the passenger seat. Things were still a little strained, but with Glennis the best course of action was usually to ignore the drama and move on. "Let's see... Here we are." She braked behind a car vacating a spot three rows away from the ice cream place, which was a miracle in this shopping center. As the car pulled out she realized the spot was labeled 'compact,' but she made it work, putting a hand between the truck door and the chassis of the neighboring vehicle as Seth squeezed out of the back.

When he ran around to join Glennis at the tailgate, Robin straightened and shaded her eyes with a hand. As thrilling as spending the next hour or two with Cyril was going to be, she was going to kill him if he flaked.

She spotted his Datsun just as he nabbed a spot directly in front of the parlor. The door popped open, and he tossed her a wave. She breathed a sigh of relief, or something like it. "This way, Mom."

Glennis fell into step beside her, Seth hopping along on the end of her arm. "Oh dear," she murmured, watching Cyril rock himself out of the car and onto his feet. "I didn't realize he'd gotten so... *big*."

"Mom," Robin warned. But what could she say, really? An elderly woman on the sidewalk performed a disgusted double-take as she passed

Cyril. What else did he expect, assuming he even cared? He spent his days sitting in front of a computer screen eating pizza. There was no metabolic issue or tragic disease. He was just a miserable slob. "Remember this is for Seth, okay?" She said it as much for herself as for Glennis.

"I'm the one who taught *you* how to behave, my dear."

Cyril was impossible to miss in his bright red Star Trek shirt, but Seth was so short he didn't see him until they'd circled his car. "Cereal!" His ear-to-ear grin made it all worthwhile.

"Hey, bud." He held out a box wrapped in green cellophane. "Happy Birthday."

"Cyril..." Robin gave him a disapproving frown. "You already gave him the iPad."

He rolled his eyes. "Relax. It's just some candy."

"Yay yay yay yay *yay!*"

Robin put a hand on Seth's shoulder, squeezing firmly as he started to rip into the box. "Seth, why don't we get our food first?" For whatever value of "food" ice cream could be considered. Hopefully he would still be coherent enough after the sugar rush to be sufficiently thankful for the gift; Robin had picked eleven o'clock in the morning with the aim of avoiding a sucrose-induced meltdown.

"Hello, Cyril," Glennis said, enunciating crisply. Robin had been on the receiving end of that tone often enough to know exactly what it meant: even though you weren't polite enough to acknowledge my presence, I'm still civilized enough to hold up my end of the social contract. "How long has it been? Since the wedding, I think."

Had it been that long? No wonder her mom was shocked. Cyril had been plus-sized then, too, as Tavis's yearbooks showed that he pretty much always had been. But nowhere near what he was now.

Cyril looked at Seth, as if reminding himself to be on good behavior. "Sounds about right."

"Okay," Robin prompted again. While they'd been standing there, a gaggle of middle school boys had beaten them into the shop. If the line got any longer, Seth was going to be bouncing off the walls. She took her mother's arm and started for the door. "Let's get some ice cream."

Being in the middle of a commercial block, the place had no windows except the glass double doors, and the space was awkwardly deep and narrow. Instead of plastering a wall or two with mirrors to create "space," the booths along the left wall had been custom built into a crescent, arcing outward at the center and tapering off to the smallest booths at the door and the far end. Combined with a palette of rich natural colors, the shop felt cozy rather than sterile or institutional. Still, there wasn't a cleaning agent known to man that could deal with the layers of grime that accumulated from thousands of sticky little hands. It was like eating from Seth's car seat.

Cyril stepped up to the counter. "All right, buddy, what'll it be?"

Seth stood on tiptoe. That proving ineffective, he darted around to Cyril's other side, squeezing himself in behind the last kid in line. The boy, about thirteen or fourteen, started slightly at the unsolicited butt-touch, and rolled his eyes when he saw Seth. He hoisted a sporty messenger bag higher onto his shoulder and checked to make sure his headphones were still settled fashionably around the neck of his puffy gray jacket. The illusion of maturity was broken by his nails, ragged and bitten to the quick.

Seth hopped up and down, still unable to see. "I want rainbow!"

"Dude, rainbow is not a flavor. Look." Cyril pointed up at the pictorial menu on the wall. "You ever had a banana split?"

Seth cackled, as he did whenever a new phrase struck his three-year-old brain as being particularly hilarious. "Banana split?" He made a karate chop motion and cackled again. "Banana... *split!*"

"I'll take that as a no."

"Robin." Glennis tugged at her arm and nodded toward the booths. It was an unseasonably warm day for late October, so even at this early hour the place was about half full. There were a couple of senior citizens, some parents with a group of grade-school-aged children, and three sweaty women in spandex from the 24-hour fitness place next door. All of them were darting furtive glances at Cyril. A little girl giggled and raised a finger to point, but her mother grabbed her arm and wrenched it down with a cautionary hiss.

Robin wasn't sure what she was supposed to be looking at. "Yeah?"

Glennis raised her eyebrows meaningfully. "He's not going to *fit.*"

Robin eyeballed Cyril's back side. Glennis was right. The booths were the only seating available, and barring some sort of miracle of physics there was no way he was going to squeeze in.

"What are we going to do?" her mother whispered.

"I don't know. Let's just… um. Let's get our ice cream." They would figure something out. Eat outside? Was there a park nearby?

"But—"

"We'll figure it out." She stepped up to the counter, away from her mother. She couldn't think with Glennis whispering in her ear. "Sethie, did you pick something?"

He stuck his hands in the air and hopped. "I can't *see!*"

Robin shifted her purse to pick him up, but Cyril was one step ahead.

"Hey," he said, tossing the word at the gray-haired man behind the counter. "You got a chair around here? The birthday boy needs something to stand on."

The server went a bit wide-eyed behind a pair of thick-rimmed glasses. His hand shook as he scraped together a scoop of espresso for the kid in front of them. "Um. I, um, don't think—"

"Oh look," Cyril said, with no pretense of subtlety. He nodded toward the swinging door that led to a back room. It had a circular window which he was presumably tall enough to see through. "There's a chair right back there."

Much as Robin hated it when Cyril pulled that kind of bullshit on her, she had to admit it was effective. The server mumbled something apologetic, dropped the ice cream scoop, and darted into the back room. Her back would thank him, in any case.

"Seriously?" said the kid with the headphones. He offered Cyril a disgusted sneer. "Wait your fuckin' turn."

"Hey," Robin snapped. "You watch your mouth."

The kid looked her right in the eye, no shame whatsoever. Robin was about to suggest he consult his mother about that attitude when the server came around the end of the bar with the chair. One of the kid's buddies socked him in the shoulder. "Hurry up, Brett, I'm hungry."

Even after all the kids had made their choices, it took Seth a good ten minutes to make up his mind. But with Cyril coaching him on how best to exploit his birthday-boy status, he finally settled on a banana split with scoops of vanilla, chocolate, and, unfortunately, bubblegum. Chocolate syrup yes, nuts absolutely not.

"Get your camera ready," Cyril said. "I'll have a scoop of strawberry cheesecake in a cup." He used the back of his hand to give Seth a little tap, and when he hopped off the chair Cyril picked it up and followed Seth to the booth nearest the door. Seth jumped onto the red vinyl seat; Cyril set the chair down at the end and settled himself carefully on top. He looked like a boulder teetering on the edge of a chasm.

Robin looked at her mother, who shrugged. Apparently Cyril could take care of himself.

She and Glennis placed their orders, argued briefly about who got to pay—something Cyril had taken for granted, naturally—and took their ice cream to the table. Glennis booted Seth out momentarily so she could slide in next to him and he could sit by his "ah… friend."

Robin went back to the counter for the banana split. As she passed the table of middle-schoolers, two booths down, one of them followed her with something that sounded like "Mmm, dat ass." When she turned to look, the kid with the headphones slid his tongue across his upper lip. They all snickered.

God, did it start that young? Nine, ten years, and Seth would be in the middle of it all. And without a man in the house to set the example. Unless—

Robin couldn't think about that right now. Maybe not ever. She slid in across from Seth, plopped the banana split in front of him, and laughed when he pantomimed cartoonish slavering. "Now hold on. We have to sing the birthday song." A brief expedition into her purse produced a pack of rainbow candles and the book of matches she'd picked up at Nom. She popped four candles into the ice cream, adjusting one as it sagged downward, and lit them all with a single match.

Before Seth, Robin had sung only when she was assured of being truly by herself: in the shower, when Tavis was on deployment, and occasionally in the car. In church she just mouthed the words. But Seth had been a nightmare as a newborn, and the only thing that would calm him down—at least momentarily—was *Rock-a-bye Baby*.

Then, of course, there wasn't a point at which you could just *stop* singing to your child. The first time he'd demanded *Row, Row, Row Your Boat* in the park, in full view of eight or ten other adults, she'd found herself groping for an excuse. But two-year-old Seth hadn't known that singing in public was embarrassing—and Robin didn't *want* him to know. The world would be a darker place without his husky little voice.

She had sung then, and she sang now, belting out the opening lines of the birthday song. Glennis chimed in and Cyril added a low harmony. For all his snark, he had a wonderful singing voice, deep and sonorous.

Seth folded his hands in his lap, squinted his eyes into happy little crescents, and beamed. He looked like a flower soaking up the morning sun.

When the song ended, they clapped, and Seth didn't so much blow as spit the candles out. Robin handed him a spoon. "Dig in, Mr. Four-Year-Old."

They all watched as he shoveled the first enormous bite—chocolate with chocolate sauce—into his mouth. "Cold!" he shrieked, and spat it back out.

Cyril laughed—not his usual snicker, but a hearty belly laugh that shook him all the way through. "Pace yourself, kid."

"It's icy! Ice cream is made of *ice!*" As if this were a revolutionary discovery.

Glennis sampled her vanilla. "You have a beautiful singing voice, Cyril."

Cyril snorted. "At least I've got that going for me, huh?" He gouged out a chunk of strawberry cheesecake the size of a golf ball and shoved it into his mouth.

Robin closed her eyes. Not now. She couldn't take this right now.

"I *love* you guys," Seth said. There wasn't a hint of sarcasm in his tone. He hadn't yet learned that it was possible to be anything other than one hundred percent genuine.

She let out a breath. "We love you too, buddy. Happy Birthday."

Cyril and Glennis let it drop, thank God, and Seth filled the silence with running commentary on his birthday treat.

It had been a while since they'd had ice cream—since that day at the zoo with Tavis, actually—and Robin lingered over her rocky road. She took a couple of pictures of Seth, and then Seth with Glennis, and then Seth with Cyril. Knowing from experience that she was no expert photographer, and there was no guarantee that Seth would be still at any given moment, she immediately tapped her phone into viewing mode to make sure she'd gotten at least a couple of decent shots.

Every last one had been photo-bombed by one of the teens. The angle of the booths had made it easy for them to work around the three ladies in spandex at the table in between, and they'd successfully managed to fill Robin's camera with middle fingers, tongues, and crossed eyes. About half the photos showed one or more of the kids puffing up his cheeks and holding his arms wide in mockery of Cyril. One shot had even captured one of the spandex women casting a disapproving glare that said, "Ice cream? No wonder you're five hundred pounds."

Robin narrowed her eyes and glared. Mr. Headphones held up his ice cream cone, tilted his head sideways, and gave it a long, suggestive lick. "Mmm," he said, slurping loudly. "*Soooo* good."

"Oh my God," another gushed. "I could eat this all day. I could eat this every. Single. Meal."

Robin thumped the phone down on the table and slid to the edge of the bench.

Cyril put his hand on top of hers. She glared at his fingers, and then at him. He shook his head minutely.

Robyn let a breath out through her nose and slid back into the booth. He was right; it wasn't worth it.

Cyril lifted his hand, declining yet another offer of ice cream from Seth. "I've got plenty, kid." Seth, bless his generous little heart, was an enthusiastic sharer. Especially of food.

The world would be a much better place if everyone were more like Seth—who, in his childish wisdom, observed differences without attaching meaning. Once, after explaining the concept of homelessness, she'd purchased a stack of prepaid grocery cards and told him they could hand them out to people who looked like they needed food. He'd proceeded to grab one and gift it to the woman behind them in line, standing there in heels and a business dress. Robin's attempts to broach the topic of race had, so far, gone completely over his head. Similarly, he had no idea how food and nutrition correlated with weight, or that excess weight was even a bad thing. When discussing his extracurricular activities with preschool friends, she'd overheard him refer to Cyril— proudly—as "my big friend!"

Robin had forgotten to have Seth wish on his candles, but she made one for him: that he would stay, in spirit, forever exactly as he was today.

"Gramma? You share?"

Glennis held up a hand, mirroring Cyril. "No thank you, sweetie." And, as Seth attempted to forcibly spoon some into her mouth, "No, sweetie, really. Thank you, but no. *No.*"

"Sethie," Robin warned, "Grandma said no. Thank you for sharing, okay bud? But that ice cream is just for you. We all have our own."

"Awwww, man."

She sighed. "Here. Gimme some chocolate." She leaned forward and got a mouthful of half-melted bubblegum. "Wow. Um. Thanks."

"More!"

She pulled out a pack of wet wipes and wiped sticky bubblegum residue off her chin, noting peripherally that the middle school boys had started to pick up. Finally. She'd try and get some better photos after they left. "Nope. No more. I'm good." She showed him her empty ice cream cup. "All full."

"But I'm full too!"

She used her spoon to do a little excavating in his dish. "Did you even eat any banana?" So much for the nominal nutritional content.

She glanced up just as the middle schoolers—five of them—passed behind Cyril. His chair blocked the right side of the double doors, so they had to go around him to exit through the left. As they did, a kid with straw-yellow hair mimed falling against Cyril's back and bouncing off.

"Hey," Robin snapped. Her mother *tsked* and muttered something about manners. "Take it somewhere else."

The one with headphones stopped and met her with that same unwavering stare. Then he held his fists up and mimed dry-humping Cyril from behind. His buddies whooped, high on the thrill of his chutzpah. He let his hands drop and shook his head. "You are way too much of a MILF to be hanging out with this fat ass."

"*Excuse* me? You need to—"

Cyril shoved himself back. The legs of the chair grated over the tile floor with a shriek of protest that set Robin's teeth on edge. He planted his palms on the end of the table, leaned forward, and pushed himself to his feet. At six-plus feet he dwarfed the middle schoolers, and with one step to the side he blocked both doors.

"Sorry," he said, in a low, clear voice. "Didn't quite catch that."

Mr. Headphones squared his shoulders. "I said she's a MILF. You know." His buddies snickered. "Mother I'd like to—"

"No. After that."

The kid's eyes got very wide. Then he screwed his courage to the sticking post and blurted out, "Fat."

A woman waiting in line at the counter cleared her throat and said, loudly, "So anyway. Can I sample the raspberry cappuccino?"

"Fat." Cyril didn't raise his voice, but every single person in the shop heard that single crisp, clear syllable. "That's all you've got? Fat?"

He shrugged. "Everyone's thinkin' it." His glance around the parlor suggested the increasingly awkward silence spoke for itself.

Cyril seemed to give the kid's words serious consideration. Then he shook his head. "That seems like such a waste, though, doesn't it? The entire English lexicon at your disposal, and you pick *fat?*" He said the last word with a sudden sharpness that made the boy flinch. "I mean, accurate, granted. But it lacks a certain... panache. And no points for creativity whatsoever." He lifted his head and looked around the shop. "Am I right?" He shrugged. "Something to work on, kid."

"Whatever, asshole."

"*Stop.*" Robin rose half out of her seat. Glennis had clapped her hands over Seth's ears, but he was already wiggling free. "Cyril, just let him go. And you—don't use that language in front of my kid."

Cyril inclined his head toward her as if to say, bear with me just one moment. But he didn't take his eyes off the boy. "She's right. Brett, was it? Your vocabulary is pretty tired. Not much of a reader, I take it?"

Now the kid was turning red. He seemed to struggle for a clever response and, finding none, motioned to his buddies. "Come on, guys." He made a feint to the right.

Cyril didn't move. And he was solid: nobody was going to move him unless he wanted to be moved. "Now, hold on. I feel a little responsible. I mean, it's society's duty to educate our youth, isn't it? If your vocab is limited to the ten tired expletives you learned from the janitor, how far are you going to get in life? Sure, maybe your mom will pay for an arts degree at some half-priced junior college, but how are you gonna earn your iTunes money? McDonald's burger flipper? Starbucks barista?" He let out a heavy sigh. "We've failed you. Truly."

Brett pointed a finger at Cyril, just short of actual physical contact. "Go fuck yourself, dick—"

Cyril stepped forward into the finger, forcing the boy to back up before he was knocked out of the way. His faux-friendly tone descended abruptly into a sharp growl. "Was the lady not clear enough for your diminutive little dinosaur brain? You want to deal with me, let's deal. But no obscenities in front of the kid. Unless you'd care to escalate this conflict to an entirely different level."

"You can't threaten me, you—"

Cyril held up a finger. "One more four-letter word comes out of your mouth and I'll..." He raised his eyebrows at Seth. "I'll *sit* on you."

Seth giggled.

"*That's* supposed to be funny?" This from the yellow-haired kid. The other three were hanging back now, looking like they might be having second thoughts about their choice of companions. "Maybe for a two-year-old."

"I'm *four!*"

Glennis grabbed Seth and hugged him to her chest. She shot a pointed look at Robin.

I know, she mouthed. This was absurd.

"Sometimes art isn't *for* you." Cyril held a hand out toward Seth. "It was for him. And he laughed. Which is more than I can say about anything you and your friends have said in the last half hour. I could rattle off insults all day and still come up with better material than you. I mean, really, at the very least you could've pulled out a good fat joke."

"Okay," said Brett. "Like what?"

"Yeah," yellow hair chimed in, suddenly gleeful. "Go ahead, neckbeard. Tell us a fat joke."

"Aw, someone discovered Reddit. That's adorable." He shook his head. "Man, Eternal September gets younger every year."

"We're still waiting."

Cyril looked up at the ceiling. He let out a short, heavy sigh. "Fine. Challenge accepted." Then he cleared his throat, dramatically. "But I don't want to waste anyone's valuable time, so let's do this fair and square." He leaned to one side, groping around in the folds of his baggy black pants until he located a pocket, and pulled out his Android phone. "We'll use my D-20 app."

The kids looked at him stupidly, unwilling to admit ignorance.

"D-20?" He flicked his thumb across the surface of the screen, then held it up to display the digital die. "A twenty sided die. Is that too old-school for you? Jesus." He glanced at Robin, the smirk still fresh on his face, but seemed to realize she was unwilling to be drawn into this ridiculous confrontation. He held the phone out to Seth instead. "Give it a tap, buddy." He glanced at Brett. "Whatever number comes up, I'll give you that many insults better than *fat.*"

Seth lurched forward to oblige, one knee on the tabletop as he watched the digital die totter around the screen and then, finally, come to a stop. "Twenty!" he crowed. Other than one hundred, it was the largest number he could identify by sight. "Twenty!"

"Twenty," Cyril echoed. He cleared his throat again, with slightly less confidence.

Now it was Brett's turn to smirk. "Well?"

Cyril nodded. "Who's counting?"

"Me!" Seth got to his feet and hopped up and down on the vinyl seat, one arm held high. "I can count! A four-year-old can do it!"

"You got it, buddy. Tell us what comes first."

"Number *zero!*"

Robin looked at him. "What?"

"Whoops," said Cyril. "That's what I get for teaching him integers. Okay." He hiked his pants up. "Number zero. We'll start with something classic. Yo' Momma so fat—well, I *thought* your Momma was fat, but then I saw *you*."

Seth jumped up and down, snorting with laughter. Robin was pretty sure he didn't actually get the joke, but knowing something was supposed to be funny was usually enough to tickle his funny bone. He held up one little finger. "Number one!"

Cyril rolled his eyes upward, pensively. "Hmm. Okay, let's go with childish." He pointed over Brett's shoulder and exclaimed in falsetto: "Look, Mommy! It's the red balloon!"

Seth did get that one. Comprehension was as thrilling as the joke itself, and he shrieked with delight.

Brett shook his head. "Stupid."

"Hey, I'm warming up." Cyril spread his palms. "I mean, think about how much you could do with a simple change of tone. For instance, helpful." He held his fingers up like a telephone. "Hello, Macy's? We've located your missing blimp! Or... complimentary: Your shirt is just lovely. I had no idea they made tents in such a subtle shade of rose. Practical: Hey, if you ever get stuck on a deserted island, at least you'll last a while. Naïve: Excuse me, what are the visiting hours at this monument?" He looked at Seth. "How many was that?"

Seth frowned over his fingers before holding up one hand. "Five!"

At this point, nobody was even attempting to pretend they weren't watching. Another group of 24-hour fitness escapees had come in just before the altercation had begun, and they all turned around, leaning hips against the ice cream case as they watched. "Keep going," one said.

Cyril gave her an ironic little nod. "Confused: I've heard of watching your figure, but honestly I'm having a hard time seeing anything else. Envious: I get wrong-number calls constantly. Must be so nice to have your own area code." That one drew a few reluctant titters.

"Seven!" Seth announced. He was echoed by a couple of kids from another booth.

The bell on the door tinkled and Cyril started forward slightly as the door hit his back. He stepped aside to admit two more women in spandex. The pair looked around, bewildered by the stares aimed in their general direction. "You might wanna take a rain check on the ice cream," Cyril suggested.

One of the women at the counter beckoned the ladies over. When they came, still looking confused, she pulled them into a huddle and filled them in, presumably, with a furious whisper.

"Robin," Glennis started.

She waved her mother to silence. Cyril had stepped away from the door, but at this point there was nothing to be gained by leaving. Seth had already been drawn into this thing, whatever it was, and attempting to leave would cause more of a stir than simply sitting tight and waiting for it to end. And Cyril, at least, seemed cognizant of the fact that half his audience hadn't even hit puberty.

"Well?" prompted Brett.

Cyril nodded somberly. "Yes. I think it's time we addressed the elephant in the room." He turned, pantomiming speaking to himself. "Cyril?" He paused, and after a short beat there was a chorus of laughter from the kids. "Mmm... Cautionary: Don't get on his bad side. You'll have to take a train and two busses to get back. Religious: The preacher said Jesus lives, but nobody told me Buddha was just down the street! Philosophical: If there's any justice in this world, you must be incredibly beautiful on the inside. Zoological: I had no idea whales beached themselves this far inland." For that one, Cyril was rewarded with an eruption of laughter, adults included. He raised an eyebrow at Brett and his companions. "Seth?"

"Twelve!"

"Automotive: You must have to get your tires rotated every month." Silence. "Think about it, folks." At the belated round of chuckles, he looked at the ceiling. "Okay... Aha. Geological: Oh, so you're in town! I was wondering about that earthquake last night. Puzzled: I'd ask you what your favorite restaurant was, but I wouldn't know whether to eat there or burn the place down." He stopped to suck in a couple of deep breaths.

One of the women from the fitness center passed a bottle of water to the woman in front of her. It went from one hand to another until it came to Brett, who looked at it stupidly. "Not you, jerk," the woman said. He flushed and handed it to Cyril.

"Much obliged." He mimed tipping a hat, then cranked open the cap and chugged half the bottle. "Seth?"

"Fifteen!"

"Five more. No problem." He squinted.

"Come on!" someone said.

"Okay, okay. Idiomatic: You certainly take 'making a mountain out of a molehill' to a whole new level."

"Sixteen!" This came as a chorus from all of the children.

"Sincere: Please be careful when you go to the beach. I don't think Japan can take another tsunami."

Everyone joined the chant: "Seventeen!"

"Literary: If I were you, I'd watch out for guys named Ahab."

"Eighteen!"

"Astronomical: Is this child with you, or did he just fall into your orbit?"

"Nineteen!"

"One more," Robin heard herself say.

"We'll go with a classic." He turned to her and, with a sly grin, nodded at the dish of melted ice cream and banana that was Seth's sundae. "So." He wiggled his eyebrows. "You gonna eat that?"

Robin laughed.

12

GLENNIS DROPPED HER purse onto the kitchen counter. "Well, that was lovely. What a fantastic role model for your son."

Robin leaned around the doorway, making sure Seth was fully absorbed in his favorite Magic Schoolbus episode. "I know, Mom, but... at least he was standing up for himself."

Glennis rolled her eyes heavenward. "Against a thirteen-year-old."

"An incredibly *obnoxious* thirteen-year-old. You didn't hear what he said to me." How did Robin always end up defending Cyril to her mother? Insanity. "Anyway, Cyril didn't get physical. He settled it with words. And I'm pretty sure most of it went right over Seth's head. How is that setting a bad example?"

"That kid could have been carrying a knife, Robin. Or who knows, a gun."

"Oh, come on. This is Camarillo. And" –she didn't want to, but— "admit it. He was *funny.*"

"It's just..." In the space of about two seconds, her mother switched from disgust to misty-eyed almost-tears. "I'm sorry. He's not Tavis, Robin. Not in the least."

Robin flinched at Tav's name, but she'd be damned if her mother was going to rattle her. "Well, neither am I." She snorted. "So what? Being someone else doesn't make him evil." Being an asshole and a hacker, maybe.

"I guess I just don't understand why your opinion of him changed all of the sudden."

"Mom, it's not all of *the*—" Robin bit her tongue.

"What, sweetie?"

"Nothing. Look, Mom..." She sighed. "Cyril is not my friend. He's Seth's. I'm... I'm trying to look on the bright side, okay? He may not be an angel, but he's not the devil incarnate, either."

Glennis shook her head. "Well. I better use the bathroom before I head home."

Discussion over, apparently. "Use mine upstairs, Mom. I'm in the middle of cleaning the other one." At least, she had been. The can of powdered bleach was still sitting on the office toilet where she'd abandoned it two days ago. Pregnancy was easy on her, as those things went, but anything with a strong scent made her nauseous.

"Thanks, honey."

The moment her mother left the room, Robin clenched both fists in the air, mouth open in a silent scream. Glennis always had to have an opinion about everything in Robin's life. And nothing was ever quite the way *she'd* have done it.

Whatever. What. Ever. Robin opened the fridge and rifled through the veggie drawer for the bag of baby carrots. They'd gotten Seth home before his sugar crash, and if she could get a bit of real food into him while he was zoned out on TV they might be able to skate through the rest of the day without a mega-meltdown. The bottle of ranch was so empty she couldn't get anything out of it even after a few vigorous thumps, so she tossed it and went hunting in the pantry for another.

"Robin."

Glennis stood in the middle of the kitchen, something clutched in one hand.

"Mom? What's wrong?" The bottom dropped out of her stomach. Was Seth—

"How many weeks?" Her voice was quiet. Gentle.

"What?"

"Tell me how far along you are, Robin." She set a bottle on the kitchen counter with a careful *plunk*.

In the half-second before her mother's words registered, Robin thought Glennis had, somehow, found the pills. The other pills—the ones she'd thrown away. But it was just her prenatal vitamins. Just. Oh, God. Could she get away with saying they were left over from Seth? No; they were prescribed, because her stomach couldn't handle iron, and the date was stamped right on the side. "Mom, I—"

Glennis closed her eyes and shook her head. "Is it his, Robin?"

"What? Whose?"

"Tavis. Is this Tav's child?"

"Mom! Who else's would it be?"

"You're the one who had to ask what I was talking about. You tell me."

"I don't even know what to say." She had expected Glennis to be angry when she found out, yes, but—what on earth *was* this? "Are you accusing me of sleeping around?"

"I don't know, Robin. I don't know anything. You don't talk to me anymore. You don't go to church. And if you're pregnant, you're at least... three months along now?"

"Mom, I'm sorry. I didn't know what to do. I wasn't even sure—" She stopped herself, but her mom knew her well enough that she might as well have spoken the words out loud.

"Robin." Glennis looked at Robin's stomach, concealed beneath the baggy shirt. "That is my *grandchild*."

"I know, Mom. I know." And that was exactly why Robin hadn't been able to talk to her. Because there was no gray area for Glennis. No extenuating circumstances, no room for human weakness or error. Robin knew that, because it was what she had been like, too. And then Tavis was gone, and suddenly the world was nothing but gray.

Had Glennis attempted to enfold Robin in a hug, she would have pulled away. But Robin felt lost, somehow, when her mother didn't even try.

Glennis shouldered her purse and got out her car keys. When she lifted her eyes, they were sad and old. "I'm your mother, Robin. So I'll always be here for you. And Seth. You know that. But I'm not going to force myself into your life if you don't want me."

Robin heard her stop to give Seth a kiss and a hug on her way out.

"Wait," Robin whispered. Too late. Much too late.

She wanted to be angry with her mother, for playing the martyr. The wounded one. She was always so *hurt*.

But this time, Robin couldn't say she was wrong.

Outside, her mother's Prius hummed to life. Robin stood in the middle of the kitchen, using her knuckles to knead her brow as the sound faded. Then she reached for her phone.

It was a week since she'd gotten this email. The longest, so far, that she'd managed to save one. What if it were the last? She should wait until she got another, just to make sure.

It wasn't. Surely not. Even if it was, she still had his final letter.

She needed him now.

Robin.

I like that you're a lone wolf. No—don't argue. You always get upset when I talk about it, but we both know that you have acquaintances, not friends. It's okay. It's who you are. I like you that way, because... Well. This is selfish, but I like it because it makes me feel like you—the real you—is just for me. The way this—my writing—is only for you.

But unless you're in your sixties and I've been storing up these emails for thirty-plus years, they aren't going to last forever.

Which means I'm going to be gone, Robin. And you'll be alone. In truth, you already are.

I know you'll try and shoulder this burden yourself. I know you. And yes, my proud beauty, you are strong. But not this strong.

Find someone. You're too much your father's daughter to want to see a shrink, but consider it, at least. Talk to your mom. She loves you, Robin, even if she doesn't always get things right. Think about how much you love Seth. That's how she feels about you. When I see the two of you together, the way she looks at you, it's plain as day.

Or if you can't do that, try one of the older ladies at church, or a support group. Find someone you can trust to handle your feelings, even the bad ones. Especially the bad ones.

Robin—don't do this alone.

She just stared at the screen for a moment, shaking. Then she clicked the phone off, placed it back into her purse, and stepped into the living room, in front of the TV.

"Hey!" Seth said. "I can't see!"

It was the only way to make sure he truly heard her when he was watching television. "Mommy's going to be in the garage for a little bit, okay?"

"Oh-*kay.*"

Robin went back through the kitchen and out the back door. Across the grass and into the side door of the garage. She shut it behind herself, grabbed the edge of the nearest shelf, and screamed.

How could he? How *dare* he?

He had done this. *He* had left her. In spite of all her pleading, he had re-enlisted. After two deployments, he could have easily stayed stateside, either in Port Hueneme or any other goddamn place that wasn't fucking *Afghanistan.* But he hadn't. I have to be with my guys, he'd said. They need me. This is what I do. And she'd agreed, because he had a calling and she wanted him to be happy and fulfilled.

Three folded beach chairs were propped up against the base of the garage shelves. She drew a foot back and kicked. The stack fell over. She picked one up and slammed it against the storage bin that held Tav's clothes.

"*You!*" she screamed. "*You* left me!"

When she was done crying, she pulled down her box of maternity clothes.

13

ROBIN SAT ON THE CURB around the corner from Marta's house, a reusable grocery bag dangling between her knees as she watched the parade of parents through a gap in the bushes. If someone spotted her she was going to feel like a freak, but it was marginally better than having to explain the slight curve of her belly, now artfully accentuated by one of the umpteen maternity blouses her mother had purchased during her first pregnancy.

Cyril was on time; five minutes early, actually, lumbering around the corner on the other side of the street. There was a step up where the sidewalk met the path that split Marta's lawn in half, and when he reached it he paused to tug his shirt down over his belly. He planted one foot on the step, sucked in a breath, and sort of heaved himself forward and up.

Robin didn't generally waste her time worrying about Cyril's wellbeing, but Jesus—he was about ten pounds shy of a Wal-Mart scooter. In the time it took him to get from the sidewalk to the front porch, another parent passed him, went inside, and returned with her daughter. She ducked a quick acknowledgement as she led the girl around him, in a wide circle through the grass.

Marta appeared on the front porch with Seth, his shoes and backpack already on. "Be a good boy, Seth!" She gave him a pat on the back.

"Cereal!" Seth launched himself down the steps without so much as a backward glance. "Do you know a game of Airlanders?" His shrill little voice carried all the way to the end of the block.

Cyril said something affirmative.

Seth grabbed his hand and pulled him toward the street. "Philip has *ten* Airlander guys! Blastshock and Endzone and Dualbite and—"

Cyril stopped to tug his shirt down again before tackling the step down to the sidewalk.

Robin stood, brushing off the back of her pants, and shouldered the reusable grocery bag. She glanced down the street to make sure the coast was clear before stepping into view. "Hey guys."

"Momma!"

Robin crossed the street and bent to give Seth a hug. "I brought dinner."

He squinted up at her, clearly suspecting some kind of bait and switch. "For Cereal too?"

"For all of us. Go on." She waved him forward, and he trotted on down to the end of the block.

Cyril lifted an eyebrow. "What, did Saturday's little performance magically win your respect?"

He said it with a snide, sarcastic twist, but Robin shrugged. "Well... yeah? Kinda?" Everyone in the shop had been looking down their noses at him, and in the space of about ten minutes he'd had them laughing and cheering for his success. That took some kind of talent, or charisma, or *something*. He really could be charming, when he wanted to.

"Oh." The confused frown lasted for about half a second before giving way to a sardonic half-smile. "If you think that was—"

Robin held up a finger. "Don't." He was going to infuriate her at some point, but it didn't have to be right now. "Just... don't. For like five minutes. Okay?"

He lifted an eyebrow and snorted. "Um... yeah. Fine."

Seth might have managed to share the sidewalk with Cyril, but Robin couldn't do it without colliding, so they fell into an awkwardly staggered formation—Seth darting up ahead, Cyril bringing up the rear, and Robin in between.

"So," he said. "You told your mom."

Robin cast a questioning glance over one shoulder, and he gestured to her attire. "Oh. Well, not *told*, exactly. She found my prenatal vitamins."

"Jesus." The word came out a breathy huff; walking and talking at the same time was an effort.

She stopped and turned. "What, now you're on her side?"

"No." He cleared his throat. "You're usually just more straightforward. Especially with your mother."

"Really." She cocked an eyebrow. "And exactly how do you know what I'm like?"

"You think a guy who spends all his free time writing love notes doesn't talk about you *incessantly?*"

"Oh." Robin had never thought about that, actually. But now that she did, she felt... naked. Exactly how much *did* Cyril know about her personal life?

"Like being the third wheel in a goddamn threesome."

"Ew."

"Thanks."

"I didn't mean—" Okay, she had meant that. If she'd been even the least bit interested in such a prospect—and she was most emphatically not—she could scarcely wrap her brain around the idea of him having sex at all. The physical logistics alone were... sizable. "I—"

"Yep. Got it."

Robin bit her lip. "Sorry." For what, she wasn't sure.

Seth, having exhausted his patience during the thirty seconds he had waited at the corner, turned around and zoomed back. Robin put her hand out, but he ducked under her arm and stuck his hot little paw into Cyril's palm instead. "I wanna go to the park." He looked between them and added, "With Cereal."

"Sweetie, it's dinner time." An absolute lie by omission: she'd stuck paper plates and plastic forks in the bag in case Cyril didn't have any clean dishes. Which meant they could totally eat at the park. "Anyway, the sun's going down."

"Why?" Seth whined.

"Why is the sun going down? Because this is when the sun goes down."

"On the other days, you came when the sun was up. Before." This was clearly an accusation: she had left him at school too long.

"I still pick you up the same time every day, bud." Although, yes, she had occasionally let him burn off some steam at the park before going home. "The sun isn't up for as long in the fall, but there are still the same number of hours in each day. Which means we still eat and go to bed at the same time." A white lie, this time. She put Seth to bed a full hour earlier in the winter, because she could get away with it and he needed the sleep.

Seth blinked up at her with an expression that said clearly she was the crazy one.

"He's got a point," Cyril said. "We're the ones who choose to conform to arbitrary demarcations of time. In an agrarian culture, we'd already be asleep. Look." He freed himself from Seth's grip and held up both hands, curled into fists. He wiggled one. "Here's the sun. And here's the earth. During summer, our part of the earth is tilted toward the sun, so we see the sun longer each day." He tilted the earth-hand back. "But during winter, the earth is tilted away from the sun, which means the time we see the sun each day is shorter. Right now it's fall, and we're heading into winter, so the days are getting shorter."

"Yeah," Seth echoed, aiming the word at Robin. He seemed to think Cyril's little educational demonstration had been an argument in his favor. "Shorter."

Cyril snorted. "Kid, I think you missed—"

Robin waved him to silence. "Whatever. Ten minutes."

They rounded the corner instead of crossing the street, and as soon as they came into view of the park Seth darted off. Robin followed Cyril through the gate and set her bag on the first picnic table with a view of the play structure. Now that she'd caved, did she get the food out and let him see she'd had the means to make it a picnic all along, or save it and hope he didn't see it later? If she got the silverware out, he might think she'd been trying to avoid being seen with him in public. If she left the bag alone and he saw the silverware later, he might think—well, he'd probably think roughly the same thing.

"Ten minutes?" Cyril lowered himself onto the bench, back shoved against the table, and nodded toward the streetlamps overhead. "There's lighting. And it's not like we're gonna get mugged in the middle of suburban Camarillo."

"Ten minutes in Seth-adjusted time. Works out to more like half an hour."

He plucked at the sleeves of his T-shirt, ventilating sweat-ringed armpits. "No wonder he has no concept of time."

Robin seated herself on the table, planting her feet next to him on the bench, and reached into the bag for napkins. Who cared what Cyril thought? She was starving. "If he did, he'd figure out that his bedtime is rarely ever *actually* eight o'clock."

Cyril shook his head. "Funny, what turns out to be hereditary."

"Meaning what?"

He gestured to Seth, who had zeroed in on a couple of older boys and was somewhat unsuccessfully inserting himself into their game, which involved removing their shoes and chucking them down a slide. "Tav was exactly the same. Ten minutes, two hours—it made no difference to him, if he was doing something interesting."

"Oh." She'd been prepared to be defensive, and the oddly pedestrian conversation caught her off guard. "You're right. It drove me so crazy when he—" She cut herself off.

"When he'd drop by my place and stay for five hours?"

She shrugged and continued unpacking the bag. "It's hard to believe other people don't have internal clocks when you've got one yourself."

Cyril put a hand on his own wrist, as if covering a watch. "Prove it."

"Mm, I can't do it to the minute." The casserole dish was still hot. She pulled the lid off and used a plastic fork to coax some baked macaroni and broccoli onto a plate. "But it's five fifteen, give or take ten. Maybe a little more. Say five seventeen."

He leaned to one side and fished around in his pants pocket, finally pulling out his phone. He showed her the screen, which glowed 5:17. "Nice."

"It's a gift." She grinned and stuck the fork in the macaroni before tossing it onto the table next to him.

Cyril turned sideways on the bench, inching one knee up as far as he could get it and draping the sagging flesh of his left arm over the table. He slid his right hand under his belly and grunted, shifting the mass until it was, presumably, positioned comfortably on his thighs. Only then, as he reached for the fork, did he frown. "Silverware?"

"Easier than doing your dirty dishes."

"Ah." He took a bite. "Not bad."

"Gee, thanks." She tilted the dish and forked out some macaroni for herself.

They ate, watching Seth as he jumped on the rope bridge and the sun went down.

Robin glanced at Cyril. She shifted.

"Uh oh," he said, without looking at her. "Shit's about to get real."

She rolled her eyes. "I just... Can I ask you something?"

"You can try."

Robin sucked in a breath. This shouldn't be hard, except that it determined what came next. "Why didn't you come to the funeral?"

"I told you. I don't need to—"

"No," she said. "Not the piss-me-off reason. The real reason."

She expected him to shoot back something flip about how he was an atheist and dead was dead, so who cared about ceremonies for people who no longer existed? Instead he cranked his head around and gave her a look of incredulity, as if he were astounded that anyone with a pulse could be so stupid. "You saw what happened at the ice cream shop, and you ask me that?"

As if he'd been some sort of victim, there. "You picked that fight and you know it. None of Tav's friends are anything like those boys."

He snorted. "Fuck the boys."

"What, then?" Everyone looking at him? If he'd ever cared before, she hadn't noticed.

He studied her face for a long moment. Then he shook his head, turned his attention pointedly back to Seth, and shoveled macaroni into his mouth. "Forget it."

"No. Explain it to me." She hesitated, attempting to tone down the sarcasm. "Please." She was not entirely successful.

He didn't look at her. "You ever seen a fat guy cry?"

"I..." She couldn't think of a specific instance, no, but it was more of a rhetorical question. "You have as much of a right to tears as anyone else." Tavis was his best friend, after all. Most of the time she was so busy being pissed at him that she forgot, but... "Maybe more than most."

"Tavis..." He looked down at the empty paper plate, half-crumpled in his hand. "Tavis was my only real friend. If I were even half the man he was, I'd have sucked it up and kept my shit together for his—for the service." He turned back to her, suddenly, and forcing himself to raise his eyes to meet hers was obviously so difficult that he shook with something between grief and rage. "But I'm not, am I? And yeah," he whispered fiercely, "My corpulent carcass may be nothing better than a quarter-ton of wasted space, but so long as I'm breathing nobody—*nobody*—will laugh at any tear shed in your husband's name." He swallowed. "Least of all mine."

Robin stood there for a moment with, she was sure, her jaw on the ground. In the space of three sentences Cyril had dropped every bit of his solid steel armor, leaving himself all but naked before her. It took all her willpower not to avert her eyes.

"Omy*gawd*," he said, mimicking a valley girl drawl. "The monster has *feelings*." He tossed his plate onto the table and leaned forward. "Adios."

"No, wait—" Robin reached out. "Hold on. Just—wait." He sat back with a heavy grunt. She wasn't sure he'd have been able to get up on the first try anyway. "All... All those jokes you made. On Saturday—" He was quick on the draw, but not *that* quick.

He looked at her hand, resting lightly on his shoulder. "What, is that my internal monologue? Please. I know how the game is played. Better to say it yourself than hear it from someone else." He shrugged away from her touch. "So you can put your goddamn doe eyes away."

Robin told enough half-truths to recognize one. Still, she nodded.

"Momma!" Seth barreled toward the picnic table, bashing himself against her shins, and then stood there with his mouth open, making little "unh unh unh" noises like a baby bird.

"Nice. Couple more minutes, okay?" She shoveled some macaroni in. Seth chomped down on the plastic fork and she had to yank it out. "Look, kiddo—"

He dashed off, yodeling at the top of his lungs.

She sighed.

Cyril brushed a few crumbs off the front of his shirt. "You're a good mom."

"Sometimes I think I might just be completely insane."

"Well, I wasn't gonna say it, but… you have been looking a little nuts."

Robin popped him on the arm. "What's that supposed to mean?"

"Ow! Jesus." He rubbed his shoulder. "Just—I dunno. It's been three months, and you still look like you just walked out of the jungle or something."

"Are you—I—did you actually just—" Robin couldn't even find the words. Finally, she threw her hands up in the air. "Jesus H. *Christ,* Cyril! The second I start to think you might be an actual human being, you go and open your goddamn mouth."

"Better ugly and honest than pretty and false."

"Is that what you tell yourself? God." Robin had nothing to say that wasn't an expletive. She got up and flung her plate into the garbage can.

"Look," Cyril said. "I just meant—I meant, are you okay."

Robin stuck her hands in her armpits, covering her dry, ashy knuckles. "So you're not racist. You just think you're my mother."

"No, but apparently you do." Cyril grabbed his waistband and rocked back, freeing the leg he had propped up on the bench before pushing himself to his feet. "I mean, you keep coming to me with the shit you should be telling *her.*"

"Shut up." Robin shoved the casserole dish into the bag and shouldered it. "Just—shut up."

He put a hand down on the end of the table and sucked in a sharp breath. "Fuck, my leg's asleep."

Seth approached the table, cheeks flushed. "Done," he announced, in a robotic monotone.

Robin blinked. "Uh… what?"

"Ready. To. Go." He turned and walked stiffly toward the street, knees locked.

She looked at Cyril. "I think that's the first time he's ever voluntarily left the park. Ever."

Cyril waved at the play structure. "He had an argument with the other kid."

"Oh." Robin felt weirdly negligent. While she'd been fuming over Cyril, he'd been keeping watch over her son.

"Don't be too thrilled." Cyril nodded toward Seth, who reached the sidewalk and made a sharp left. "He thinks he's going to my house."

Robin looked heavenward. "Ugh. Do you mind? Five minutes and he'll be happy as a clam."

"Sure. I'll be up all night anyway."

"More, uh... Anonymous stuff?"

"Nah. Dungeon raid."

They fell into formation: Seth at the front, Robin in the middle, Cyril picking up the rear. His glacial pace, his huffing, his throat clearing—everything about him made her want to scream. "Hey," she said finally, over one shoulder, just to drown him out, "Why do you do that stuff, anyway? With Anonymous, I mean. You don't strike me as a hipster."

"Hipster?" He snorted. "You mean the Occupy Wall Street crowd. They sorta co-opted our image for a while, but it was probably a good thing. Now everybody thinks the movement's old news. Real Anons don't advertise."

"So why do you do it? Those raids and stuff?"

He shrugged. "Somebody's gotta keep the authorities in check."

"What, or else America's gonna turn into a police state?" She shook her head. "I understand the paranoia, especially these days, but I don't know how you could have been friends with Tav and still think the military is full of thugs."

"I don't know how you could have been married to the guy and still think every asshole in a uniform is a saint."

"I didn't say—Sethie, stop!" She darted ahead and caught his arm, then waited for Cyril to catch up so they could all cross together. The next block was Cyril's, so when they were safely on the sidewalk again she let Seth go and he skipped ahead. "I didn't say that," she started again. "And you know it. But the guys who sign up? They're not doing it for the money. They do it because they think it's right. My dad, Tavis, all the people they worked with—"

"Oh, so he never told you about the uneducated rednecks with no real-world skills who join because their only alternative is poverty, and thought of shooting people gives them a hard-on? No complaints whatsoever?"

She turned and walked backwards, because she wanted him to have to look her in the eye. "No, but being a moron doesn't mean you're out there, I dunno, killing for sport—"

"How many bad apples does it take?" He stopped, because apparently walking and talking at the same time was just too much effort. "One? Afghanistan, March of 2012: soldiers line the locals up and threaten to execute them after a roadside bomb injures a few of their comrades. Three days later, Army sergeant Robert Bales murders sixteen civilians, including women and children." He held up two fingers. "Two? July of 2011, four Marines from the 3rd battalion are videotaped as they laugh and urinate on dead bodies. That's a Geneva convention violation, by the way. The video goes viral. Three? January of 2010, Staff Sergeant Calvin Gibbs directs two of his men to kill an unarmed fifteen-year-old boy doing farm work for his father. They strip his body and pose for photos—"

She put up her hands. "Okay, I get it."

He held up an index finger. "One psychopath and fifty guys who don't want to say anything. Because they're afraid of looking disloyal, or breaking the code, or whatever. Semper fucking fidelis. That's how these things work. Or didn't you ever learn about Nazis?"

"I'm not stupid." Although he was certainly an expert at making her feel that way. She glanced over her shoulder to check on Seth. "Look, I don't know everything. I focus on what I can do, which, right now, is raising my kid. But what I do know is that Tavis loved his work. He believed in what he was doing—helping, healing. And I know, without a shadow of doubt, that he was the kind of guy who'd speak up."

Cyril grunted an affirmative. "On that much, we agree."

He was right, of course. Whatever else stood between them, there was still Tavis. And now, it seemed, Seth. And... it was nice to know Cyril believed in something, at least. Even if she didn't agree.

Robin stepped down into the gutter. Cyril lifted an eyebrow as she fell in beside him, but made no comment.

She shoved her hands deep into her pockets. "Did Tavis ever mention I didn't start college until I was nineteen?"

"Sounds vaguely familiar."

"My dad died a month after my high school graduation. Mom... fell apart. For..." She pulled a hand out and counted on her fingers. "About nine months. I deferred my enrollment and spent pretty much the whole year cooking and cleaning and paying the bills while she hid in bed."

"I just assumed you got held back."

Robin ignored the obvious bait. "Anyway. I can't help resenting her for that. For forcing me to be strong when I was just a lost kid, you know?" She shrugged. "So now, what—she wants to be 'there' for me? To, like, trade places or something? No. Sorry. It doesn't work like that. It can't—I have Seth. But she thinks if I'm not a complete mess, I'm in denial. She can't accept that I'm not falling apart. That she's just... I don't know."

"Weak."

"No, I mean..." Maybe that was exactly what she meant. "Just because I'm not going to lie down and fall apart doesn't mean I didn't love him. Because I did. I do. I'm just..."

"A survivor."

"I guess so." She didn't feel like one. But he was gone, and here she was.

"Again—you're telling me this why?"

Robin swallowed. "I need someone. Not my mom."

He stopped walking. Turned. And gave her a long, hard look. "You," he said finally, without a trace of humor. "Are out of your fucking mind."

She felt suddenly, remarkably calm. "I'm having a baby, Cyril. I can't do this alone."

His voice dipped down into a gravelly rasp. "I am *not* the one you want."

She shrugged. "You basically already are."

"That's not my fault. Go find someone else."

"No."

"Jesus Christ. Why?"

She nodded to Seth, who had reached the end of Cyril's driveway and started to perform a little dance of impatience. Or maybe he had to pee. "Because he loves you. And so did Tav."

"Those are pretty shit reasons, Chica."

She spread her hands. "Okay, fine. You're the only one who even comes close to understanding how much I've lost."

"Come *o-on*," Seth called. "You guys are so *bor*ing to me!"

Cyril looked at Seth, and then back at Robin. He shook his head and headed for his house.

Robin stepped out of the gutter and followed. Even at her slowest shuffle, she caught up with him halfway down the driveway, where he'd paused to wheeze.

"Just so we're clear," he growled. "I'm not doing any fucking Lamaze."

Part Two
Winter

14

ROBIN HEARD CYRIL BELLOWING at his computer from the doorstep. It was almost routine at this point—in the past three months, she'd walked in on him ranting into his microphone for a podcast, muttering to himself while carrying out some less-than-legal computer raid (which he later referred to as "SQL injection" and then declined to discuss), and cussing out Cooke on the phone.

She brushed the dusting of light rain off her shoulders and rapped, loudly. His chair creaked as he shifted, but he didn't respond. She turned the knob and leaned in over the threshold. "Hello? Can I come in?"

"Protector? I have no protector but my sword!" He had his headphones on, the computer screen bright with explosions in a simulated fantasy world she now recognized as World of Warcraft.

"Hellooo?"

"Oh, you dare challenge me?" He threw his head back and let out a throaty laugh of triumph. "I am at your humble service, gentlemen. Please, raise your hand if you'd like to die today!"

She crossed the room and tapped him on the shoulder.

He lurched backward. "Oh—fuck! Fuck, you scared the—hold on. No, not—Jesus Christ. AFK, assholes." He ripped the headphones off and punched a button on the keyboard. "What the hell?"

"Sorry," she said, and couldn't quite contain a snicker. "What were you *doing?*"

He held a hand out toward the screen. "It's a role-playing game. I was playing my role." He walked his chair around to face her. "It's nine in the morning. You're here. Did I agree to babysit and forget?"

"Um, no." She smoothed her shirt over her belly. "Seth's playing pad in the truck. I... today is my twenty-week ultrasound. That's the anatomy scan? You see the baby, they usually tell you what sex it is."

"And you couldn't give me a day's warning? I do work, you know." He rolled his eyes. "Whatever. Bring him in. Raid's a wash now anyway."

Robin looked at the floor. "It's Monday." Seth's school day. Which meant that if she'd wanted him out of her hair, she'd have dropped him off with Marta as usual.

When Cyril didn't answer, she glanced up and found him staring at her blankly. Then his eyebrow slid up. "You want *me* to come? Seriously?"

"Look, I know it's weird, okay? I was gonna take Seth by myself. But it turns out—it turns out I can't." Not without losing it completely. Somehow, she'd managed to make it through the holidays without having to explain to Seth why the smell of gingerbread made Mommy sick, or why her tummy had gotten so firm and round. But this was it. Today, *fetus* would become *girl* or *boy*, and Robin could no longer justify leaving him in the dark. "I'd leave him at school, but he deserves to be a part of this. Without having his mom fall apart. I'm sorry if it's a major imposition, but if you could just—"

Cyril held his hands up. "Yes. Okay. Jesus, I'll come." He gestured to his plaid pajama pants and the rumpled black shirt that said, in large white letters, *There's no place like 127.0.0.1.* "Now? Like this?"

"You've got half an hour to shower."

"So generous."

"Honestly, I expected to find you sleeping."

ROBIN WAS SEATED IN THE CAB, door hanging open, when Cyril came back out. His hair was wet, combed back over his scalp, and he'd replaced the PJs with pants that looked pretty much like PJs, only black. He toed blindly into a pair of flip flops and then started toward the Datsun.

Robin leaned out. "Seriously? It's like two miles. Just get in."

Cyril leveled another long gaze at her, as if she were quite possibly the stupidest person on planet earth. He unlocked the car door, braced his forearm against the frame, and leaned in. When he straightened, he held up a seatbelt extension.

"Oh."

The entire starboard side of her truck sank when he stepped onto the running board, then bounced back a couple of times as he shifted himself fully into the seat. He rocked his bulk toward Robin once and then a second time to get the door shut.

Seth giggled. "Again!"

Robin cranked the ignition. It was only two miles.

WHETHER IT WAS THANKS to Robyn's gargantuan companion or the small child bouncing off the walls, the nurse roomed her fast. Nobody in the overcrowded waiting room objected to their line jump.

"All right," the nurse exhaled, once they had squeezed into the cubicle-sized exam room. "Sorry if we seem a little rushed; it's been a crazy morning." She consulted a manila folder with Robin's name on the label and flashed a quick smile. "I see we're doing your twenty-week anatomy scan?"

"Nineteen weeks and four days, I think," Robin said. She didn't know whether that was important.

"I see, yes. Close enough. If you could just take a seat...?"

Robin slid up onto the exam table, paper sheet crinkling beneath her thighs. "Sethie, no touching please." His grubby hands were already reaching for the dials on the ultrasound machine, a large model docked permanently next to the table. "We don't want to break anything."

"I won't!" he whined. "I'm careful."

"I know you are, sweetie, but sometimes accidents happen."

"But it won't!"

"C'mere, kid." Cyril kicked the doctor's rolling stool out from under the sink.

Seth needed no instruction: he plopped onto the stool stomach-first and held on for dear life as Cyril gave him a good firm spin.

The nurse looked for a moment as if she would object, then shrugged and forced another smile. "Let's get your vitals."

Robin held out her arm for the blood pressure cuff and the nurse started to pump, manually.

"How old is the little one?"

"Four!" Seth shouted, before Robin could answer. "Not little!"

The nurse smiled. "And we're all hoping to find out if baby's a girl or a boy?"

Robin nodded, although that wasn't entirely the whole answer. Seth was too busy shrieking with laughter to catch the nurse's question. Perhaps she'd have time to prep him while they were waiting for the doctor. Or maybe he'd just figure it out when the baby popped up on the screen.

The nurse listened to Robin's pulse before jotting down her numbers. After that, she stuck a thermometer into a plastic casing and instructed Robin to bite down. Seth got off the stool, staggering a bit, and began to spin it himself, sans rider.

The nurse cast her exhausted-fake smile toward Cyril. "Is Daddy hoping for another boy?"

Robin froze, thermometer clenched between her teeth.

Cyril's gaze swept over the nurse, almost lazily. "How charming," he said, voice dripping with condescension, "that you even pretend to entertain the notion. But no." He gave her an equally fake smile. "I'm just the nanny."

"Oh my goodness, I'm sorry. Um." The thermometer beeped. "There we go. Perfect. I, um. I'll just let the doctor know you're ready. As I said, we're a bit busy, so it might be a few minutes, but I promise she'll be in." She edged the door open and scooted out.

Robin pressed her fingertips into her eyelids, trying to stifle her laughter before it turned into tears. Finally she shook her head again and pulled one foot up to unlace her tennis shoe. Whenever she had to lie on an exam table for more than five minutes, her feet went to sleep. Taking her shoes off helped a little.

"Again!" Seth demanded, plopping himself back on top of the stool.

Cyril did the honors. He glanced up as Robin removed her second shoe. "You're not getting naked, are you?"

"Just my stomach. Is that gonna be too titillating?" Tavis had mentioned Cyril's extensive digital porn collection on more than one occasion.

"I'll live." He shifted from one foot to another and glanced at the chair by the door. It was broad, but it had arms, making sitting a risky proposition.

There was another knock and Cyril squeezed to one side to admit a petite woman with dark hair pulled into a bun. She smiled at each of them in turn, then offered a tiny little hand to Robin. "Ms. Matheson? I'm Fatimah. I'll be doing your ultrasound today."

"Oh. Are you, uh, Doctor Gracie?"

She flashed her little white smile again, a polite apology. "I am a trained ultrasound technician. Dr. Gracie will review the results after I have completed the scan."

"Oh," Robin said again. Did she not even get to see the doctor?

Fatimah looked at Cyril and held out a hand toward the chair positioned just inside the doorway. "Please, have a seat."

They did a little shuffle-dance around one another until Cyril stood in front of the chair. He hitched his pants up, sucked in a breath, and sat. Robin winced, sure he was going to break the arms off the thing, but he managed to squeeze in somehow.

"Sethie, let the doctor have the stool," Robin said. Nurse? Technician? Whatever.

He hopped off immediately, giving the little woman a winning smile as she took the seat. Always so well-behaved for others. What Robin needed was a rotating string of strangers visiting the house each day. Maybe she should clear out the extra bedrooms and start a B&B.

She lay back on the exam table and pulled her blouse to her ribs, lifting her arms out of the way as the other woman folded a papery cloth over the elastic band of her maternity jeans to protect them from the gooey ultrasound gel. Fatimah fiddled with the machine for a minute, flicking on a few switches and entering some numbers in the keyboard.

Seth appeared at the woman's elbow. "What's goin' on?"

Robin pointed at the ultrasound screen. "Keep your eyes up there and tell me what you see."

Fatimah squirted a bit of gel below Robin's belly button and pressed the club-headed wand against her stomach.

"I don't see anything," Seth noted loudly. Static filled the screen.

"Give it a minute." Robin was painfully conscious of her pulse, thudding loud and quick over the speaker.

And there it was, in perfect profile. Big alien head, spine curving down to a little rump with twiggy appendages. It squirmed and was gone.

"Ah, there you are." Fatimah pressed the wand more firmly against Robin's belly. "We've got a jumper."

Seth's little forehead wrinkled as he watched the baby reappear on the screen.

"Well, buddy?" Robin asked. "Did you see it? What's in Mommy's tummy?"

His eyes followed the cord from the wand to the ultrasound machine. Then he looked at her. "I don't *know*," he said. "Something *weird*."

"Best guess. What's it look like?"

"I don't know."

Robin saw the realization dawning in Seth's eyes, but he didn't like making guesses. He wanted to know an answer was correct before he spoke. "Cyril," she said, "what do you think?"

"Hang on." He threw his weight forward with more force than usual, and managed, mostly, to clear the chair. It came up a few inches before clattering down behind him. Robin tried to ignore his wet, heavy breathing as he came around to see the screen. He cleared his throat. "Looks like some kind of parasite to me."

Seth threw his arms around Cyril's leg, laughing loudly. "Nooooo!"

"Do you even know what a parasite is, kid?"

"It's not a parasite," Robin said. "What is it, Sethie?"

He was confident now. "A *baby!*"

The ultrasound tech finished scanning the brain and appendages, which were all there, and began to move down through the organs. "Well," she said finally, "shall we see if baby's being cooperative?"

Robin nodded.

Fatimah fiddled with the wand a bit more, trying to get a good angle on the legs.

"Oh, look, Sethie. Look." Robin pointed. "See the little foot?"

Fatimah pushed a button and the machine chattered as it printed a copy of the image. She moved the wand again, and the V of the baby's twin femurs appeared. And between them—

Robin didn't have to ask. It had been just as clear for Seth. "Buddy, look! His little wee-wee!" She laughed, and then, suddenly, clapped her hand over her mouth. She was not going to cry, not again, not in front of Seth.

Cyril tousled Seth's hair. "Looks like you're having a little brother, kid."

Seth's eyes got big. "Right now?"

He laughed. "No, not now. In… uh…"

Robin looked away. Her heart was too full for words.

"Twenty weeks," Fatimah supplied. She made a little white arrow on the screen and typed "it's a boy!" before hitting the print button again. "About four months." She cleaned the wand with a sanitary wipe before replacing it in the machine, then handed a few wipes to Robin. "Thank you, Ms. Matheson. Dr. Gracie will review my measurements and meet with you in her office before you go." She peeled off her gloves and bent at the waist—not very far—to meet Seth eye-to-eye. "You have been a very good boy. Would you like to follow me and pick out some stickers while Mommy cleans up?"

"Yeah!"

"More excited about the stickers than another kid." Cyril shook his head. "I'll be in the hall."

Robin's stomach was a bit of a mess, so she wiped carefully before sitting up and pulling her pants back into place. Fatimah had forgotten to give her the ultrasound printouts, so after Robin slipped her shoes on she took the liberty of tearing them off the machine.

Strips of sunlight filtered through the blinds in the still-dark exam room, illuminating his little profile, a footprint, and the relevant anatomy…

His.

The vast and nebulous potentiality condensed, suddenly, into reality. No longer *baby* or *it* but *him.*

Robin reached for the rush of affection she'd felt when she'd learned her firstborn was, in fact, little-boy-Seth. Tavis was the one who had stumped for the name, while she—positive the baby was a girl—had wanted Sonora. Finding out her instincts were wrong had been a shock, but a good one. She was well suited to being the mother of a rough-and-tumble boy.

Mostly what she remembered was Tav's hand, closing tight around hers. Even when he was away, she'd been able to turn to him for insight, to try to figure out what was going in Seth's little caveman brain. It wasn't as if Robin were a completely different species—she had always been a Daddy's girl and a tomboy—but there was no denying that there were major differences between the sexes. Or perhaps it was simply that Seth took after Tavis so much more than her.

Now he was gone, and she was about to be the mother of boys. Plural.

The door opened a crack. "You taking a nap or what?"

"Lemme get my purse." Abruptly, the floor around the exam table was a watery blur. Even the light from the hall didn't help. "Hold on." She fumbled around her feet. "I just…" She stood, wiping her dripping nose with the back of her hand. "I can't do this, Cyril." Not without him.

"Little too late for that."

She made another swipe at her eyes. "Thanks, Captain Obvious."

There was no fixing this. Option one had been taking the pill, and she hadn't had the courage to follow through. Option two was giving him up—which was no option at all, because this was Tav's child, Seth's brother. She would never forgive herself. No; she needed to have this baby. It would be hers.

But not like this. Not alone.

She could teach her boys to pee standing up and how to shave and whatever else, but nothing she could do would ever change the fact that this precious baby boy would grow up without ever even having held his father's hand.

Was that so much to ask of the universe? That a father see his son before he died?

"Do you ever think," she whispered, "that life is just too sad?"

Cyril squeezed through the door and shut it behind himself, making the room suddenly very small. He cleared his throat. "You're wrong. You can do this. And you will."

Robin looked up. "You don't know that."

"I know Tavis never would have married a woman who couldn't handle a couple kids on her own."

"I know I can *handle* it." She held out the flimsy photo paper, crumpled slightly in her grip. "But what about him?" He deserved so much more.

Cyril moved slightly, and whether it was toward her or away she couldn't have said. But suddenly she didn't care that it was Cyril, or what Cyril thought, or anything. She threw her arms around him.

"Uh," he said.

"Shut up," she choked. "Just shut up. Just…" She just needed someone warm.

He didn't say anything. For a moment he didn't move. And then, finally, he put an arm around her shoulder.

Something about the weight or the warmth of the gesture took her instantly back to her father's all-enveloping embrace. She hadn't even realized it was something she missed, desperately, until that moment. She pressed her face into the soft crook of Cyril's elbow and sobbed.

How could she possibly go on? How did anyone just go *on?*

Seth would be back with the nurse, or the doctor would come in with the results, and there was no time. That was how. She put her hands on Cyril's belly and pushed herself away.

"So," he said. "You're human too."

"Shut the fuck up." She found her purse and stuffed the ultrasound photos inside.

"No, I…" He frowned. "Well. Whatever. You okay?"

"I'm about to raise two boys by myself," she said. "And the only man they have to look up to is you."

15

AFTER LETTING CYRIL OUT at the end of his driveway and dropping Seth off at school, Robin headed home to change into her work clothes and pick up a drop cloth or two. Cooke had texted the night before to say he'd be on the first flight down in the morning, and naturally she'd just laid into his kitchen with a sledgehammer. It was short notice, but the least she could do was try and get the place into a habitable state before he arrived.

There was a woman on her front porch.

She wasn't in uniform, but she didn't have to be. Everything about her screamed military, from her severely cropped white-blonde hair to the way she unconsciously snapped to attention when Robin pulled into the driveway.

Robin cranked the window down to chin-level, shedding rain droplets like tears. "Leave," she snapped, glad she'd already dropped her passengers off.

The woman jogged down the front steps and approached the truck with a quick, firm stride. "My name is Corporal Deena Walker—"

"I know who you are. And I've asked you to leave me alone. Repeatedly."

"I know. And I'm incredibly sorry for—"

"Clearly you're not." Walker's last attempt at communication had come nearly three months ago. Robin had felt safe in assuming the woman had given up. So why now?

"I'm sorry," Walker insisted, "because I can't in good conscience respect your wishes." She pressed her hand to the window. "Please, Ms. Matheson. This was the first leave I could get. I've been driving all night."

"Not my problem." Robin backed into the street.

SHE DIDN'T KNOW what else to do. So she went to work.

Her maternity blouse was hardly appropriate, but she found one of Tav's ratty old workout shirts stashed with all the other crap in the extended cab. It smelled like him. It also did a pretty good job of hiding her belly. Cooke didn't strike her as the kind of guy who'd axe her for being pregnant, but it wasn't a topic she wanted to discuss, regardless of his stance.

She'd gotten the water running back through the sink and was sweeping tile fragments into a dustpan when a key rattled in the lock.

"What on earth—" It was a high-pitched woman's voice.

"I know, I know." That was Cooke's slightly nasal kvetching. "Furniture is on order, okay?"

Robin smiled. He was totally lying.

There was a low thump of an umbrella being closed, and then heels clacked across the bare living room floor. "Well, it's nice, anyway. Where's the bathroom? Do you need help? It's been almost three hours since—"

"Oh. My. God. Would you *please* stop treating me like a fucking kindergartener?"

"No need to be nasty." She said it in a weary, offhand way that suggested a lengthy acquaintance with Cooke's attitude. "Where should I put the bag?"

"Bedroom. End of the hall. And yes, I know it's a mess, thanks."

Robin tugged Tav's shirt down over her belly as the heels clacked into the hall and stopped, abruptly, in the doorway.

Cooke's wife was a slender woman in a pencil skirt and four-inch heels. She had black hair that hung straight to her rear and a delicate gold ring in one nostril. "Oh." Her dark eyes swept down over Robin. "I didn't realize—"

Cooke came up behind his wife. "Hey."

Robin rubbed her palms on her jeans. "Nice to meet you, Mrs. Cooke." She was a little surprised—but then, it was always the nerdy rich guys who bagged trophy wives, right?

The woman blinked at Robin's out-held hand. "Oh my goodness, no." She looked at Cooke and let out a sharp, silvery laugh. "I honestly think

I'd kill myself!"

He quirked an eyebrow at Robin. "This is my partner's wife, Sheena. Sheena, Robin."

Sheena set his rolling suitcase upright and took Robin's hand. Her velvet-soft fingers started to pull away—and then tightened, suddenly, as her eyes locked on Robin's stomach.

Robin froze. Not now. Please not now.

There was a split second of silence—and then Sheena dropped her hand. She glanced at Cooke, a sudden spark of humor in her expression. "Does Greta know? About her?"

Cooke rolled his eyes. "Greta knows she doesn't have to worry about competition. Look, can you just put the damn—"

"Yes, yes." Sheena turned on one heel and jerked his suitcase down the hall.

"Sorry," Cooke said to Robin. "Please tell me I have a car."

"Hm? Oh." He'd asked her, a few weeks ago, to take delivery for his new purchase: a little powder blue Fiat with orange trim. Robin opened the drawer to the left of the stove and pulled out a set of keys. "In the garage, all ready to go." The hand controls had arrived via UPS, and she'd installed them with no trouble. "It's adorable."

"Well, shit." He pocketed the keys. "I was kind of going for cool."

She laughed. "It is cool. Also, adorable."

Sheena reappeared, sans suitcase. "So I'm done shuttling you?"

"Abso-fucking-lutely."

She gave Cooke a sour look. "Do you kiss your wife with that mouth?"

He grinned. "Oh, I do a whole lot more than that."

Robin choked back a laugh and busied herself sweeping.

"You're terrible." Sheena ran her fingers through her hair. "I'd better get going. Unless you need some groceries or something? Priya won't mind if I'm late."

"I'm good."

"If you say so." She lifted a hand in a little wave toward Robin. "Take care of yourself. And don't worry, he's all bark."

"*Bye,*" said Cooke. He stood watching Robin sweep until the door thunked shut. "Sorry," he apologized again. "We have, uh… history."

"I understand." It felt strangely familiar, in fact—like watching herself and Cyril. Was that how he saw her? The uptight goody-two-shoes who had stolen his best friend? "I'll show you the bathroom if you want—it's done."

"Oh. Uh, yeah, sure. I should use the facilities anyway."

Cooke got himself turned around and headed down the hall, his knock-kneed shuffle looking shakier than she remembered. Assuming he wasn't going anywhere, he probably didn't want her banging around with power tools in the kitchen. But if she finished cleaning up and went home, would Walker still be standing on her porch? "Would it bother you if I—"

His right arm buckled. He had been in the process of turning to look at her, and all she had to do was put her hands out and catch him under the armpits. He was as light as a doll. "*Shit*," he spat.

"Are you okay?"

"Yeah." He shook his arm out and let her boost him back up onto his crutches. "Just—ridiculously tired."

And he hadn't wanted Sheena to know. Figured. Robyn ushered him to the bathroom, where she flipped down the bench she'd installed outside the shower.

Cooke collapsed onto it with a sigh. He slid his arms out of his crutches and pulled a silk handkerchief from his shirt pocket, unfolding it to wipe his brow. "Had to get up at four to make my flight, and the airline took—oh my God." He lifted his hand up off the bench, as if he'd touched something filthy.

"Is something wrong?" The sealer had dried weeks ago; even with the damp weather, it couldn't still be green.

He blinked at the shower, and then the toilet and the counter. "This is amazing."

Robin's face grew warm. "Glad you like it." Quickly, she showed him the seat that swung out from under the sink, and the pull-down shelves she'd installed in the upper cabinets. "I know you said not to bother with anything above shoulder-height, but I found these and I thought they'd work perfectly. If you don't want them I can—"

"No, no, it's fantastic. All of it." He tucked the handkerchief back into his pocket. "Seriously. If you ever want to come up north and do some work, I'd be happy to put you up. Your husband too. And kid. My wife loves kids."

"Um—thanks, but I don't think I could make that work right now." She started to back out, before he could ask why and she had to buckle down and tell him about Tavis and the baby and she ended up crying or something stupid like that. She gestured to the toilet. "I'll let you—"

"Damn it. Is this going to be awkward? I'm sorry."

He thought she was embarrassed about having to help him to the bathroom. Or maybe that he'd been too aggressive about the work invitation. "No," she said quickly. "Not at all. I mean—I've got a four-year-old. Nothing's awkward." It was hard to top having someone watch you poop.

"Good." He grabbed the side of the bench and leaned forward, catching his crutches neatly on the hook she'd built in. "I know you said you weren't close, but you never know what that means for people."

She stopped in the doorway, hand on the knob. "Wait, what are we talking about?"

He spread his palms. "Cyril?" And then dropped his hands. "You didn't know."

She was almost afraid to ask. "Know... what?"

He unbuttoned his collar, and then his cuffs. For a moment, he looked like he was about to say it wasn't something he could disclose. Then he shrugged. "I had to fire him. Like, permanently. It was kind of spectacular, to tell you the truth."

"What? Why?" And why did this even surprise her? It was Cyril.

"Well, um... Hm." He glanced at the toilet. "You know what, let me, uh, take care of this, and then—"

"Oh. God. Of course." Standing in the middle of a client's bathroom was not the most ideal place for conversation. Robin backed out, shut the door, and had started for the kitchen when she hesitated. What if he fell or something? He was still shaky. Other than the crutches, she had no idea what was wrong with him. Quietly, she sat down in his office chair to wait.

At rest, it was harder to ignore the gurgle in her stomach. With Seth, she hadn't understood the sensation as anything more than gas, but this time the slow shift-and-stretch was clear. She put a hand to the curve of her belly, and as if to proclaim his autonomy, her son responded with his first definite *kick*.

Was Walker still waiting on her doorstep? What if she refused to go away? Or came back when Seth was there? Or just started shouting at anyone who'd listen?

She pulled out her phone and thumbed to the contacts list, finger hovering over Andrews' name. If the woman wouldn't respect Robin's wishes, surely she'd have to listen to Andrews. He could report her or something, right?

Maybe she'd drive by the house first.

"Hey." Cooke's voice came through the door. "If you're just gonna sit around, how about getting us some sandwiches?"

WHEN SHE RETURNED from the deli down the road, Cooke was seated on the edge of the twin bed, legs dangling, talking into a phone the size of a hand mirror. "Yeah, I know what they want, but they're not gonna get shit unless—" He paused, listening. "It happened. The Feds have been notified. If they think we're going to—Well, fuck if I know." He glanced up. "Look, lunch is here, we'll discuss this when I get in tomorrow." Pause. "Yeah. Sorry. The flight kinda fucked me up. No, it's fine. Don't—no, seriously, don't. I'm hanging up. Bye."

Robin dropped the bag next to him on the bed. "Sorry," she said. "About... whatever. I can see how that might get annoying."

"God." Cooke tossed the phone onto the bed, next to his crutches. "My wife is the only person on the fucking planet who treats me like an adult. Not that she wouldn't have done exactly what you just did, so fuck me anyway. Oh, Coke. Thanks." She had gotten two bottles and two sandwiches; he took one of each. "You're putting this on my bill, right? Yours too."

"Sure." She took a seat at his office chair again, unfolding the white butcher paper to cover the surface of the desk, and used the soda bottle to anchor one corner. "You know, I can get you some furniture if you want." Interior decorating wasn't her wheelhouse, but she liked being given leeway to do her own thing, and Cooke was that kind of client.

"Oh?" He nodded. "Good idea. Yes. Do that."

"Any preferences?"

Cooke tipped his coke bottle toward the bathroom before twisting off the cap. "You obviously have good taste. I'm not picky. As long as it's—oh my *God*." He smacked himself on the forehead. "When I said awkward, you thought I meant—" He waved toward the bathroom again. She nodded. "I'm a little slow today. Yes. That too. *Any*way. You wanted to know about... right. Mr. Blanchard."

"Not sure I do, but yeah." Robyn picked up half of her sandwich and sat back, propping her heels up on the foot of his IKEA bed. Probably the first piece of furniture she'd replace.

He shoved his hands under one knee and yanked up, pulling his leg onto the bed. "Hard to explain in layman's terms, but let's just say he seriously abused his access to a database that deals with some extremely sensitive information." He unwrapped the sandwich and nestled it in the triangle formed between his foot and thigh. "Like military contract stuff. And then he basically blew it up."

Cyril was an asshole, but he wasn't an idiot. "Why would he do that?"

Cooke shrugged. "No idea. But the mess he left behind? Christ. It's why I'm down here. And I don't usually even deal with this stuff. After what he pulled, nobody in InfoSec's gonna touch him with a ten-foot pole."

Did she care? So far as it concerned Cyril's continued ability to live and work, yes—and Cooke seemed to be implying that he'd just committed career suicide. But Cyril hadn't brought it up, so maybe it wasn't any of her business. She sighed. "Pissing people off is like an Olympic sport for him."

"Oh, he's definitely a gold medalist in fuck-you. Guy like that can't shut it off even if he tries. Pride's his armor." Cooke took a huge bite of his turkey on rye and chewed, thoughtfully. "I dunno, though. I envy him, in a way."

"You envy a five-hundred-pound guy living behind his mother's house?"

"Does he?" Cooke seemed to find that amusing. "No, I mean part of me misses... living at odds with the world. No compromises, no concessions. Everything's so much sharper when you work under the eyes of those who hate you, you know?"

It was impossible to be a woman working in a male-dominated profession and *not* feel the constant pressure to prove your excellence. Mediocrity was a forbidden luxury. "So what changed?"

He wiped his fingers on the bedsheets, picked up his phone, and poked at it a moment before handing it over.

Robin found herself looking at a photo of a girls' basketball team—high school, maybe. "Your... daughter?" She didn't see an obvious resemblance in any of the faces.

"My—oh! No. Here." He reached over the edge of the screen and used a thumb and forefinger to zoom in on the coach. "My wife. She hates being photographed, so I have to take what I can get."

The real Mrs. Cooke was large and blocky, standing with hands folded over her chest. Her rough, unsmiling face suggested a sense of humor was not her strong point. Not a trophy wife by any stretch of the imagination. "She seems..."

"Formidable?" Cooke laughed, obviously amused by her reaction.

Robin handed back the phone. The expression on her face when she read Tav's letters was probably not, she guessed, too different from the look Cooke gave his wife's photo now, as he clicked off the screen. Her heart hurt.

"Marriage is the ultimate compromise," he said. "You can't burn all your bridges when someone else is standing on them."

"That's how I felt about having kids," Robin said. "It was sort of the opposite, with—" She cleared her throat. And found, suddenly, that she wanted to talk. To this man who knew nothing of her or Tavis or any of it. "With my husband."

Cooke lifted an eyebrow, inviting her to continue.

"I was a business major when we met. I thought I'd manage a restaurant or... something, I don't know. Something practical. Successful." She'd had her hair relaxed and spent an hour every morning doing her makeup and wore tailored business suits to all her presentations. "I was treasurer of the women's business society. I networked with women pursuing the same goals. Then I met Tavis, and..." She shrugged. "We didn't have much time together before he deployed, but he wrote, and—you know how sometimes someone you don't even know can see you better than you can see yourself? He made me realize I had spent so much time being the person everyone expected that I genuinely believed I was the person I was trying to become. Except it wasn't. Reading his letters, it was... It was like seeing myself in the mirror for the first time. Through his words, I found *me*."

"So now you're a badass carpenter," Cooke said.

Robin had to laugh. "Yeah." She got a little angsty, now and then, about being that girl who didn't wear makeup or dress up or style her hair or go out for cocktails. Or have girlfriends. But not uncomfortable enough to want to keep pretending. She hadn't realized how exhausting it had all been until she stopped.

"What's he do? Your husband?" Cooke had finished half of his sandwich; he put the remainder down and rolled it back up in the butcher paper.

"He's a Navy corpsman." And with that, the lie was not just one of omission. No going back now. "Kind of like a medic."

Cooke used a knuckle to knead the inside of the elbow that had failed, earlier. "Over at Port Hueneme, right?"

"Sometimes. Mostly Afghanistan. He deploys with the Marines."

His smile fell. "Oh. So... you know what it's like to be apart. And here I thought a couple of weeks was bad."

"No, it's hard. No matter how long." She nodded to his phone. "It must be hard for her, when you're down here."

"Oh, God no. This is the only reason she hasn't killed me yet."

He was oddly cheery about the fact. "I'm... sorry?"

"No need." With a few deft movements, he rolled up his shirtsleeve. Underneath, a neoprene sleeve covered his elbow. "If it's not obvious at this point, I come with a lot of crap." He peeled the brace off and dropped it next to his crutches. "And as Sheena would be happy to tell you, I'm not the easiest person to live with. Greta gets fed up with me, I take a hike, and my business gets a boost. Really, this is how we *stay* married." He shrugged. "The Christian woman's substitute for swinging, I guess."

Robin clapped a hand over her mouth, too late to stifle the explosion of laughter.

"Oh God," Cooke said. His pale face turned a splotchy red. "That was totally inappropriate, wasn't it. God. Dammit. This is why I don't teach. Sorry. Really sorry."

Robin could only shake her head. She bent, hands on knees, and tried not to choke on her own spit. Finally, she straightened, forcing herself to breathe. "I haven't laughed that hard since—" She wiped tears from the corners of her eyes. "In a long time. Oh my goodness."

"Sorry," Cooke said again, obviously embarrassed.

"No. Don't be." Robin wanted what he had. The kind of relationship that saw truth and loved anyway, warts and all. That was how Tavis had loved her.

Dead or not, she owed him that much in return.

WALKER HAD LEFT A NOTE, wedged between the front door and the frame. *Motel 6, rm 24. I'll be hear for 2 days. Please. It's importent.* The last word was underlined seven times.

All the motel's rooms were exterior. Robin's legs felt like rubber as she walked up the rain-slick cast iron steps, sucked in a breath, and knocked on number twenty-four. A rustle inside was followed by the clack of a chain lock. Walker blinked, and then stepped back. "Oh." Her gaze traveled downward, to Robin's stomach. "I didn't know—"

"Does it matter?" Robin brushed past her. Inside, the furnishings were unsurprisingly cheap, and Walker had kept the spread of her own belongings to a tidy minimum. Robin pulled a chair out from the desk in the corner, sat, and set her purse in her lap. "Well? Go ahead. Unburden your conscience."

Walker took a moment to close the door and re-fasten the lock. When she turned, she hesitated, eyes darting over the room. She looked nervous. "My... conscience?"

"Was it a one-time thing, or are we talking long term?"

The woman's milk-white skin flushed a rosy pink. Suddenly she looked very young. "Oh my God. No." She waved her hands in the air, as if to scrub the slate clean. "No, no, no. That is *not* what this is about. Honestly. I would never—*Everyone* knew he worshipped you."

Robin studied her for a long moment. Walker was telling the truth. The knot in her chest loosened, ever so slightly. "Then..." What *was* this?

Walker put her hands over her face. "I'm so sorry you thought—"

"It's okay." Robin put her purse on the floor. "It is now, anyway."

Walker crossed the room and flattened the bed sheets with a sweep of one hand. She sat, facing Robin, and propped her hands on her knees. "Okay," she said, blowing out a slow breath. "Honestly, I'm not sure if this is better or worse."

Robin wished she'd brought a bottle of water. "Let's just get it over with."

Walker nodded, once. "I think Doc Matheson's death might not have been accidental."

"What?" Robin's body tensed. The life in her stomach—her son—responded with a sharp jab. "Are you... telling me they lied? That—that it wasn't an IED?"

Walker shook her head. "No. It happened like they said. I talked to the guys who saw the, um... the aftermath. It's just..." She closed her eyes. "I don't think it was a coincidence that he was there. That he was the one who died."

And suddenly there were a thousand questions.

Had someone set him up? Why? Why would anyone want to hurt Tav, let alone kill him? Everyone liked him, didn't they? Was Walker sure? What if she was just some nut? How did she know—

Robin shook her head. "I think I'm gonna need a drink."

OFFERING HOSPITALITY to a representative of the vocation which had consumed her husband felt... wrong. It was impolite—bordering on superstitious, really—but Robin left her in the back yard while she ducked in to the kitchen for a couple of Coronas. The rain had stopped, anyway.

She popped the caps off and handed one bottle to Walker as she leaned against the porch railing. The Adirondacks by the fire pit looked inviting, but the wood was damp.

Walker cast a skeptical glance at the bottle in Robin's hand. "Is that okay?"

Robin tipped the bottle back and took a swig, just to make the other woman squirm. "As long as I'm not doing it every day, yeah. It's not like beer has any alcohol content to begin with."

Walker laughed and took a sip. "My girlfriend calls it ant piss."

They stood in silence for a few minutes, watching wan rays of sunlight scatter yellow-tinted rainbows through the beer.

"So." Walker cleared her throat. "I feel like I need to say this first. I love the Marines. My dad was a Marine. His dad was a Marine. This was all I've ever wanted to do. So this is not... I'm not, you know, some sort of, uh, activist."

Which meant she was about to say something that wasn't going to reflect well on the service. "I understand," Robin said. "Nothing's perfect. Not even the Marines."

Walker nodded. "I'm a translator. My last deployment was on a FET in Afghanistan. That's Female Engagement Team." She shook her head. "A lot of guys didn't like us being there, at first, or didn't understand what we were there to do. Doc Matheson got it." She took another long pull of beer and wiped a hand across her upper lip. "Anyway, none of us were real happy with our command structure. I don't know how much you know about how things work, but..."

Robin nodded. "I know he wasn't thrilled with the way they were handling relations with the local police." Tav's second deployment had been a rocky one, with a new command and some superiors he'd butted heads with. It was also the first time he'd had nightmares, when he came home. But as usual, he'd glossed over his complaints with a smile. He hadn't wanted to burden her more than necessary—but more than that, it was just his nature to look on the bright side. Still, she'd known he wasn't happy, and she'd been furious—and confused—when he'd not only re-upped, but actually *volunteered* for immediate deployment. Again.

"Yeah. So much depends on who's in charge. Most commanders run a tight ship—they don't tolerate having soldiers get drunk or harassing the locals or, you know, shit like that. But some overlook things, and that allows certain soldiers to start pushing boundaries. For me that meant getting groped and harassed on a regular basis."

"I'm sorry."

Walker shrugged. "My partner got raped, so I guess I got off lucky."

Robin had no idea what to say to that. "I—I'm sorry," she repeated.

Walker looked like she was about to say something, angrily, but then she shook her head. "That's another issue. Sort of. Anyway. There was an incident with some local contacts. Couple of farmers and a kid."

Robin's stomach turned. She almost didn't want to say the name. "Shafik?"

"Oh. Yeah. So you know." Walker looked relieved.

"Know... what?"

Walker sighed. "Story was that a couple of Marines on patrol got a tip, followed up, and stumbled onto Shafik's father and uncle meeting with a known insurgent—insurgent fled, and the brothers turned on the Marines. Guess who ended up dead."

Robin swallowed. "Shafik, too?"

Walker nodded. "I was only two weeks into my deployment. I didn't know the Marines or the locals. But Doc did. Said no way these guys were aiding the enemy. I told him to let it go, but—"

"He was the kind of guy who'd speak up," Robin whispered. That's what she'd said to Cyril, and it was true. The first time Tavis had heard a couple of redneck ag majors yell "nigger" from a passing truck, he'd taken down the license plate number and stormed halfway to the campus police station before she stopped him.

"Yeah." Walker shook her head. "Command told him to go fuck

himself, pardon my French. Assigned him to some seriously crap details just to make it clear. There's a lot of stuff that goes on over there that doesn't sit well with anybody, but it's... it's just something you deal with. This, though—it sorta put Doc over the edge. He made it clear that once his time was up, he wasn't coming back. Ever."

"But he changed his mind," Robin said. His reasoning—that he needed to be there for his team—had never made sense to her, even as loyal as he was. He hadn't told her. About any of this.

Walker nodded. "Two days before he shipped home, one of the locals came to tell him that he'd seen Shafik—alive."

"Alive? How—"

"I don't know. He was apparently dancing bacha bazi for one of the local head honchos. Had about twenty seconds of shaky footage on his phone to prove it."

Robin frowned. "What's bacha bazi?"

"It's... Oh, God." Walker cleared her throat. "They say it's a cultural thing. Basically boys—ten, twelve—used as dancers, and then..." She shrugged. "They buy them from poor families, mostly. Or just take them off the streets. Keeping a boy is a—it's a sign of power, for a lot of these guys."

"Oh my God."

"It's beyond fucked up, I know. But there's no good solution, you know what I mean? We work with the local authorities, we give them guns, we train them to police their own communities. But the guys we support turn around and do shit like this. And we can't do anything about it, because supposedly it's up to local law enforcement, but these guys *are* the local law. If we kicked them out and backed someone else, they'd go out and get their own boys. It's just all..." She shook her head. "Fucked. I think it was easier for Doc, in a way, because he knew he was there to help. Our guys, the Afghans, anyone he could. Except, with this kid... it really ate him up."

"So he went back," Robin whispered. He'd told her he'd be in less danger, when he re-upped, now that he was E6. "Mostly desk duty," he'd promised. Which, while it might have been technically accurate, was not the truth at all. That was why he hadn't told her any of this. Because if she'd known, she'd have killed him herself before she let him go. Or at least handcuffed him to a load-bearing beam.

"Yeah." Walker sucked her upper lip between her teeth and let it go with a soft *smack*. "They moved my partner and I up north, so I don't know exactly what happened, after that. But after he—after his death, I heard from one of the other corpsmen. He said it was weird that Doc had been assigned to this one detail. I don't know if that's true. He might have gotten it wrong. Maybe someone arranged for this to happen. Or maybe someone just strategically 'overlooked' some intelligence. Or, you know, maybe this is all a coincidence." She scraped the heel of her boot on the edge of the porch, then kicked at the clod of mud. "It's Afghanistan. People get fucking killed."

"I want the names of those two Marines," Robin whispered. She would track them down. Demand answers. Follow the trail, just as Tavis had—

"Okay, hold on. Look." Walker set the beer bottle on the railing and folded her arms, squaring herself to Robin. "I'm gonna tell you the same thing I told Doc. You can't rush into this. You gotta cover your ass. Don't be stupid. Okay?"

Robin wanted to grab Walker by the neck and shake until the woman gave up everything she had. Instead, she slipped past her and stepped off the deck. "Okay," she said. Because of Seth. She set the empty Corona on the edge of the cinderblock fire pit and took a slow lap around the edge of the patio. When she got back to the deck, she put her hands on her hips and looked up at Walker. "I'm glad to know this," she said. Because it was marginally better than harboring the secret, niggling suspicion that the man she loved had cheated on her. "But why are you here? If this is all conjecture, I mean. Why did you feel like you needed to get this off your chest, even if I didn't want to hear?"

"Because..." Walker scratched the side of her nose. "The other corpsman told me that Doc—two days before he died—said he had everything he needed."

"For what?"

"I don't know. To find Shafik? To go up the chain of command with whatever happened? I mean, something dirty was going on. We weren't supposed to know this kid was alive, right? Why not?" Walker shrugged. "No clue."

Robin folded her arms over the top of her belly. She took a deep breath, held it until the baby kicked, and then slowly let it out. "So where is it now? The evidence? Or whatever?" And then she answered her own question: "You think *I* have it."

Walker nodded. "Files? A laptop, USB drive? Anything he kept here, or sent back?"

Robin shook her head. "All I got was a package with his uniforms, some pictures, a few—" It all seemed so clear, suddenly. So obvious. She pointed to the gate. "Let's take a walk."

"Uh, okay. Can I ask why?"

"Let's just say I'm not the person you should be talking to."

ROBIN USUALLY LET HERSELF in when she picked Seth up from Cyril's, but with Walker at her side it seemed more appropriate to knock. There was an audible creak as he got up from the couch and plodded across the floor. Walker glanced at her, lifting an eyebrow, just as the door opened.

Robin held out a hand toward Walker. "This is Corporal Deena—"

"*Shit.*" Cyril threw the door open wide, grabbed Robin's shoulder, and dragged her over the threshold. "Get the fuck inside. Both of you. Get in. Now. *Shit.*"

Seth looked up from where he sat, cross-legged, in front of the television. "Mommy? What's going on?"

Cyril snapped the blinds shut. "Nothing. Everything is fine, kid. Your mom and I just need to have a grown-up conversation, okay?" He held a hand out, indicating his open bedroom door.

Seth's eyes jumped from Robin to Walker and back again.

"It's okay, sweetie," Robin told him, although suddenly she had no idea if that were true. She bent and gave him a quick hug. "You didn't do anything wrong. We just need to talk."

"Okaaaay," he said, eyeing Walker skeptically. She gave him a little wave and a smile. He shrugged and went back to his game.

"Kids," Walker said, as they followed Cyril into his bedroom.

"Video games," Robin corrected.

Cyril kicked through drifts of dirty clothing and bent to shove what looked like clean-ish laundry to the far side of his bed. Then he turned and sat down in the space he'd cleared.

Walker glanced at Robin. Robin shrugged. "Cyril, Deena is—"

"I know who she fucking *is*," he hissed. "What the *fuck* are you doing here?"

"I'm sorry," Walker said. "But I have no idea who you are."

"*Good.*"

"You knew," Robin said. "You knew what Tavis was doing."

"Of course I did. Jesus. He had no idea how to keep his shit secure. You know what they do to people who go digging into military fuck-ups? Chelsea fucking Manning, that's what." He turned on Walker. "Tavis gets himself killed, and you go find his *wife?* Jesus fucking *Christ.*"

"Look," Walker said, "I'm not—this is not my battle. I just wanted to make sure she knew the truth, and had whatever evidence—"

"So she could do what? Get herself thrown in prison?" He ran a hand over his face and scratched at the stubble on his second chin. "Okay. Here's what's going to happen." He leveled a finger at Robin. "You and Sergeant Stupid here are going to leave this room and go home. Take Seth. If someone says they saw you with Walker, you're going to say she showed up to offer her condolences, and you brought her along to pick up the kid. The both of you are going to go home, wait at least ten minutes, and then go out on the front porch and say a nice fond farewell." His finger arced toward Walker's chest. "You. Are going to leave and never fucking contact either of us, ever again. And if you do that, maybe—*maybe*—none of us ends up in jail."

"Hold on," Robin said. "What—"

"I'll see you on Thursday. As usual." Cyril pointed to the door. "Now get the fuck out."

16

CYRIL HAD BROKEN A KEYBOARD in half once, playing Counterstrike. Robin knew because Tavis had brought the evidence home. "He's a class-A rage-quitter," he'd said, laughing.

So it was hard to know, two days later, whether his paranoid freak-out had been justified. Walker had seemed shaken when she left, and hadn't called or texted since—which seemed to indicate she'd taken Cyril's admonitions seriously. But did she really know any better than Robin?

She decided to follow Cyril's directive, as silly as it seemed: to pretend, at least outwardly, that nothing out of the ordinary had happened. She would wait until Thursday evening, when, as usual, Cyril would pick Seth up from preschool. And then she would make him answer every single one of her questions.

In the meantime, she shopped for Cooke's new furniture, placed a few orders, made a few inquiries, and finally checked herself into a local day spa.

Taking care of herself, physically, was something her mother had been nagging her to do since the funeral—although not recently, now that they were on speak-only-as-necessary-for-Seth terms. And maybe she was right. Off-season prices were a steal, and Robin had her nails trimmed and polished, her face steamed, and every inch of her body oiled with something that smelled faintly of peppermint. They even had a stylist confident enough to take a pick to Robin's matted locks, and now her curls hung to her shoulders in neat, well-oiled order. She'd spent most of her down-time plotting the next stage of renovations on the house, but work was the best kind of escape, anyway.

Shedding her ashy skin and untamed hair felt like coming out of mourning, in a way. Although the world as she knew it had come to an end, she still lived on. Robin smoothed the plush white robe over her belly, spreading her toes to soak up the warmth of the patio heater. "Like it or not," as her father had said, "a body's gotta eat and breathe and pray."

Someone had killed Tavis. An insurgent or someone in Tav's command or a collaboration of both. If the evidence existed to prove who that person or people were, she would make them pay. But for the moment—for *this* moment—she was content to know that the man she loved was all that she had imagined. The Tavis in her letters was and would forever be hers. Nobody could take that away.

She dipped a hand into her purse and felt for her phone. Tav's emails had continued to appear in her inbox at a more or less steady rate, and though they couldn't last forever she'd managed to save up seven, still unread. She tried to save them for emergencies, for when she needed them most. But maybe now, today, she would read one—not because she was on the edge of collapse, but simply because she loved him.

Everyone loves a hero. The guys who make big, bold sacrifices for truth or justice or whatever noble ideal you want to plug into that spot. Even if it means leaving family and country behind, it's worth it in the end. It's worth missing a kid's birthday or a graduation—they won't understand now, but when they get older they'll realize the importance of doing the right thing.

Bullshit. All of it, Robin. It's something we tell ourselves so we can sleep at night. Which sounds absurd because some of the things people do in the name of heroism will haunt them for the rest of their lives. PTSD and all that.

And yet I think, as humans, action always feels better than inaction, doesn't it? When there's a problem, we need to do something, because the alternative is acknowledging our helplessness. And the thought that we might be powerless is the most terrifying thing of all.

Which is to say: I did something stupid, Robin.

I'm not going to lie. What I did—or what might happen because of what I did—isn't best for you or me or Seth. Honestly, I don't even think it's best for our country. Maybe in the long run. I don't know. If I wanted to do what was best for all of us, I'd muddy my conscience and live with it for Seth's sake. It takes a certain kind of strength to be able to live with injustice so your kid has someone to tuck him in at night. That's the real sacrifice.

I know you'd do it in a heartbeat, Robin. I know you already have. I thought I could. But I can't. I've tried, and... and I just can't.

So let's be honest: I'm doing this for me. I hope you can forgive my selfishness.

What kind of man goes to war and tells himself it's love?

Robin clicked the screen off and pressed it against her cheek. There had been a couple of other emails like this, or at least in the same vein, but without the same... finality. Until now, she hadn't even recognized that he was referring to anything specific. He'd often questioned his work—whether he ought to be involved at all, whether he was hurting more than helping—but always came back to the fact that doing something was better than doing nothing.

She couldn't hate him. Not for this. Not any more than she hated him for going off to Afghanistan in the first place. She'd accepted that when she married him, along with all the rest: good and bad, better or worse.

Mostly what it meant to her, right now, was that the letters couldn't last for very much longer. He'd written this one after deciding to go ahead with—well, whatever he'd done. Collecting evidence, or perhaps confronting his command. She'd picked this letter at random—the sixth of the seven. The seventh might very well be his last.

An employee strolled by, bearing a steaming teapot cradled in a thick white towel. He paused, and Robin held out her mug for a refill of cinnamon-apple tea. She had switched her phone to silent when she checked herself into the spa, so it was only because she was still holding it that she felt it buzz. She looked at the screen; it was Marta.

"Hello?"

"Hi Mommy. You at home?"

Robin sat up. "Uh... no, but I'm not far. What's wrong?" She looked at the clock on the wall. It was fifteen minutes past five.

"Your friend, he was supposed to pick up Sethie today?"

"He didn't show?"

"He forgot, maybe."

Robin reached under the lounge chair for her purse. "Sorry. Give me fifteen minutes."

They'd been doing this going on four months now, and he'd just forgotten? Right. Was he trying to avoid discussing this with her? He had to know that wasn't going to work. *Deal with me however you want,* she already heard herself telling him, *but don't you dare take it out on Seth.*

Marta met her with a sad, knowing smile.

Robin couldn't take it anymore. "Yes, I'm pregnant." It had been completely obvious for a while now, anyway. "Seth's probably told you, but it's a boy."

Marta reached for her hand and squeezed. "Anything I can do, Mommy. You just ask."

"I will." Robin wasn't usually comfortable accepting charity, but if there was one circumstance which justified assistance, it was being pregnant with your dead husband's baby. She still hadn't been back to church, but the news of her pregnancy had gotten around and the front-porch-dumping had started up again, this time with diapers and onesies. And she took it all. Why the hell not? No guilt, no reciprocation. Whatever anyone offered, she would accept. "Let's go, Seth."

She had him mostly buckled in before she realized he was trying to communicate. Sometimes when he was unsure of himself, his speaking volume fell below her audible hearing range. She made herself stop and look him in the eye. "What's up, bud?"

"What happen to Cereal?"

She frowned. "I don't know, buddy. He might have forgotten what day it was." She smiled. "Maybe he thinks it's Saturday!"

Seth's expression remained grim. "It's *not* Saturday. It's Cereal day."

"You know what, bud? You're right. Let's go tell him." Let him look her kid in the eye and try to lie. She climbed into the cab and started the engine.

Her foot hit the break the moment she turned onto his street. She shifted into reverse, but it was already too late. "Mommy!" Seth shrieked. Two police cruisers and a big, official-looking van were parked at the end of Cyril's driveway.

He was dead. His heart had finally had enough. Or he'd suffocated while he slept. Or he'd done it intentionally, a bag over the head. Whatever had happened, he was dead.

But how would anyone know? Maybe he'd had time to call the paramedics, or maybe his tenant had come to deliver rent and found him and now what the hell did she tell Seth? How could she tell him he'd lost not only his Daddy but his best friend?

"Mommy!"

You couldn't have pried her fingers off the steering wheel with a crowbar. "Sethie—"

There was no ambulance. No fire truck. Maybe they'd already declared him dead and couldn't fit him into a regular ambulance so they'd found a truck...

A balding, red-haired cop ambled down the driveway and leaned against what was presumably his cruiser, writing something on a pocket-sized notepad. He glanced up as a second man, dressed in black and carrying a big file box, followed his path from the house to the drive. At the sidewalk, the second man turned toward the van, revealing the letters printed across the back of his shirt: FBI.

Oh *shit.* He hadn't been paranoid. And now—oh God. What the hell was this?

Robin cranked the steering wheel to the left and parked a good forty feet behind the cop car—far enough not to be a threat. If she got out and approached them, was she going to end up in handcuffs? She flipped down the visor and checked herself in the mirror. Her face glowed, her hair was fantastic, and she was wearing a fashionable but modest maternity blouse. Surely a visibly pregnant woman in upscale clothing was not someone small-town cops would tackle first and question later. Thank God she hadn't just come from work. "Sethie, Mommy's gonna talk to that police man, okay?"

Seth looked at her with big eyes.

"Can you play a game on my phone, maybe?" She held it out.

Normally this offer would have been completely irresistible. Her phone was forbidden territory. Now, he just looked at it as if she were holding a small brick in her hand. He shook his head, mute. Terrified.

Robin sighed. "Okay, kiddo." She got out and popped the seat forward. "We'll do this together." When she unbuckled him, he stretched his arms out toward her neck. She grabbed him and situated him, as best she could, on one hip. Pregnant woman with small child was even less of a threat—at least, she hoped so.

The cop looked up as they approached, noted Seth, and gave him a friendly salute. "Hey, boss. Nice hair."

Robin relaxed. She let Seth slide to the ground, though she kept a firm hold on his hand. Down at the end of the long driveway, Cyril's front door was open, and a second cop emerged, this one carrying two stacked boxes. "We're friends... of Cyril Blanchard?" She cast a meaningful glance at Seth, hoping the guy had kids of his own.

The cop straightened. He gave a curt nod and then trained his smile on Seth. "Have you ever seen where we put the bad guys?" He reached into the front of his vehicle to hit a catch. The back door popped open. "Climb on in."

Robyn started to object, but Seth was faster: "I'm *not* a bad guy," he said.

The cop laughed. "All right, you can sit in front. Here." He leaned into the cab and fiddled with the equipment for a moment. "Okay, go for it. Don't drive off without me, okay?" He waited until Seth jumped in, then let the door swing shut just far enough to touch the frame without latching. He stepped away from the vehicle, keeping Seth in view, and crossed his arms.

Robin turned her back on the car. "What on earth is going on?"

The cop's smile disappeared. "We're executing a search warrant."

"Oh my God." Her heartbeat ratcheted up another couple of beats per second. "What happened? Is Cyril—he's—"

The cop shook his head. "Wasn't real happy about the whole thing. Ended up taking him into custody."

"You mean—arrested? You arrested him?"

The cop shrugged, almost apologetically. "He was trying to destroy evidence. It's unlikely he'll be charged. For now, anyway."

She covered her mouth with her hand. "I don't even know what to say." The obvious conclusion was that this had something to do with Tavis. But wouldn't the military have been involved? Or did they turn it over to the FBI because Cyril was a civilian? Had Walker's arrival somehow tipped them off? Oh God, it was *actually* the FBI. Did that mean they'd already been watching Cyril?

And... what if it wasn't about Tavis at all? Cyril had said nobody would care if he hacked Syria or wherever. What if he'd been wrong? Or—wait, did this have something to do with losing his job? Cooke had said it involved sensitive information—*government* information—and she'd overheard him mention the Feds on the phone.

The whole thing was crazy. Cyril wasn't a criminal—not a real one. He was just a jerk. He was just—he was just *Cyril*.

"What can you tell me about his activities?" The cop's hand twitched, and Robin realized he had just aborted a gesture to pull out his notepad.

The first week after her father's retirement had moved them back stateside, he'd been pulled over for "dim headlights." Robin remembered sitting in the passenger seat as he politely accepted the fix-it ticket. He'd even told the officer to have a nice day. But she could see by the way he gripped the wheel that he was sweating like a sinner in church. When the patrol car pulled away, he'd rubbed his palms on his Sunday pants, gaze fixed on the windshield as he told her to stay clear of cops, if she could. Don't dress like a hooker, keep your car in good shape, and drive like your baby was in the back seat. "Not all of them are gonna see you as the enemy, honey," he'd said. "Not even most. But enough. And if you meet that one, his brothers are gonna have his back, you can bet on that. Just stay outta his way and hope he stays outta yours."

And—God forbid she were ever arrested—admit nothing. Don't volunteer information. Just because you were innocent didn't mean something couldn't be used against you. Or someone you love.

Robin didn't love Cyril, God no, but he was certainly... well, *someone*.

"I don't know," she said. Would that half-truth get her in trouble, if they discovered otherwise?

The cop's eyes narrowed. "Well. What I can tell you is this: We're working with the FBI to execute a federal search warrant. A grand jury doesn't issue one of those unless they're pretty sure of finding something."

"Like what?"

"That's for the FBI to determine. They'll examine the evidence and file charges, if they decide a crime has been committed." Which, he seemed to imply, they almost certainly would. He pulled out his notepad, flipped to a blank page, and scribbled some digits. "Assuming he doesn't get riled up again, your friend will probably be released tomorrow morning on his own recognizance. If you want to pick him up, he'll be at the Ventura facility. Call this number and they'll let you know what his status is."

Robin took the page. "Jesus," she said.

17

SETH WAS SILENT all the way home, and when Robin started dinner she didn't even have to ask him to go play by himself. She'd have to tell him something. But what? Sorry, kid; your best friend—that guy you worship? He's sitting in jail tonight. Because the FBI thinks he's a criminal.

How dare he? How *dare* Cyril befriend her son—do nothing but encourage the kid to fall completely head over heels in love with him—while at the same time knowingly engaging in dangerous—potentially criminal—behavior? All without telling her. What if the cops showed up at her house? What if they assumed she was involved?

For all she knew, she was. If this was about Tavis—well. She was never going to forgive Cyril for hiding it from her. Her husband. More importantly, her kid. She had a right to know.

But the more pressing question was whether Cyril was going to prison. Like, permanently. It was almost worse than having to tell Seth he was dead.

When they sat down to spaghetti and steamed broccoli she looked at Seth across the table and took a deep breath. "Sweetie? About Cyril. He's... he's in a little bit of trouble."

Seth looked at her, eyes wide.

"I'm not sure why, okay? But the police had to take some things out of his house."

"Oh." Seth ate.

The cogs were turning in his head. He was thinking about this, and hard.

After dinner, she ran him a bath, got him into his PJs, and—after five too many stories—finally into bed. Robin folded her hands around his and closed her eyes, knowing he was watching her, and prayed. "Dear

God, thank you for this day. Thank you that Seth got to have fun at school today and thank you that we have food and a house. Tonight we pray for our friend Cyril. We don't know what's going on, exactly, but we pray that you will watch over him tonight. Amen."

She gave his hands a little squeeze and kissed him on the forehead. "Good night, my sweet. Sleep good, okay?"

He nodded. And then: "Momma?"

Here it came. "Yes, sweetie."

"Is Cereal... a bad guy?"

Everything in his little world was all so black and white. "Well," she said, slowly, wanting—needing—to get this right. "I think... everyone has good and bad inside. I mean... sometimes you do bad things, right?"

Seth nodded, albeit a little reluctantly.

"But even though you do bad things sometimes, you're still a good guy, right?"

"Yeah."

"Well... most people aren't all bad or all good. Most people are a mix of good and bad. And I think most people are mostly good. Or they try to be."

Seth digested this for a while. Then, in a very small voice, he said, "Sometimes... sometimes when I'm outside and I have a wrapper, I just toss it behind."

Robin frowned. "What?"

He looked at his fingers. "Sometimes when I have a wrapper, I just toss it behind." He made a throwaway motion.

"Are you telling me you litter? You throw your garbage on the ground?"

He nodded, unable to meet her eyes.

He was confessing. To the most terrible crime he could imagine, apparently. "Oh, sweetie." She wrapped her arms around him, laughing, and blew raspberries under his chin. "Sethie, you are the best little boy in the whole world." If only she could roll him in bubble wrap and keep him forever.

She tucked Seth in and kissed him once more before turning off the bedside lamp.

"Mommy?"

"Yes, sweetie."

"Is Cereal gonna be all right?"

She brushed Seth's hair back from his forehead. "Yes, sweetie. He'll be fine."

But as Robin closed his door, she wasn't sure she had told him the truth. She'd never seen the inside of a jail, but if what she'd seen on TV was anything like reality, Cyril would be spending the night in a cold cell with a very narrow bunk. He was barely comfortable in his own skin, let alone any seating arrangement outside of his own house. He wouldn't be sleeping.

And honestly, imagining his discomfort granted her a petty sense of satisfaction.

What had he *done?*

With Seth in bed she had the whole house to herself, but somehow she ended up in the laundry room, in the dark, with the phone pressed against her ear. "Mom?"

"Robin! You, calling me? Is it April Fool's?"

"Mom... not now. Okay?"

Glennis sobered instantly. "What is it, sweetie? What do you need?"

"Cyril just..." She didn't even know what to say. "I'm not sure what's going on. Cyril's in jail."

"*Jail?* What on earth—?"

"I know. He hacked someone or something. I don't know. Can you just... come? Here? They're gonna let him go in the morning and I don't want Seth—"

"Robin. Honey. Please tell me you're not planning on picking him up."

"Mom, I..." Robin needed to know what he'd done, but Glennis was right. Cyril was nothing to her. Or she'd thought he wasn't. But he'd been there when she needed someone, and if you just ignored the stupid shit that came out of his mouth he was actually capable of being an okay guy. "Mom, he's Seth's friend. He was Tav's friend. I have to do something. I can't just—"

"You absolutely can."

She bit her lip. Again, her mother was right. And you didn't go pick a guy up from jail just to prove your mom wrong. Robin didn't, anyway. Cyril probably deserved whatever he got, but... "Mom," she whispered. "It's what Tavis would do."

Glennis was silent. Then she sighed. "I'll be there first thing."

18

ROBIN DUG INTO THE BACK of her closet for a sedate black maternity dress with ruched sides, and then added a lavender cardigan, heels, and a pair of modest gold studs. It had been so long since she'd worn earrings she could barely work the posts through the holes. She even touched her face up with a bit of lip gloss and mascara.

And still, when they patted her down, she felt like a criminal. Worse: a statistic. Just one more black girl roped into the system. It barely even mattered that she wasn't on the inside. She was involved.

The waiting area, when they let her in, was a single small room with a bunch of plastic chairs and a uniformed corrections officer standing at moderate attention in the corner. A family of about ten people, in ages ranging from a toddler to an ancient grandmother, had pulled some of the chairs into a circle, where they sat chatting lowly in Spanish. On the other side of the room a middle-aged man with stringy yellow hair and skin like leather nodded along to music delivered via earbuds plugged into his iPhone.

Robin cast a glance at the guard in the corner, hoping for guidance, but he gave no indication of having seen her. There were no signs, except for a few warnings by the door about no guns, no knives, no… Robin squinted. Bras with underwires? Her hand went to her chest, heart suddenly pounding, when she realized the list was restrictions for visitors. She was here to pick up, not go in.

She'd gone thirty years without seeing the inside of a jail, and here she was. Thanks to Cyril.

Quickly, she stepped across the floor to the desk on the far end of the room, where a woman with a ponytail as severe as her frown sat behind a wall of bullet proof glass. Robin leaned forward and spoke into the cluster of drilled holes. "Hi. I'm here to pick up Cyril—" For a moment she blanked on his last name, and a wall of panic hit her. "Cyril, um—" What if her behavior seemed suspicious? Was this like the airport, where they could take you into a little side room and interrogate you and violate all your civil liberties at the whim of some minimum wage employee with a badge?

She had no idea what her rights were. She should have listened more closely, all those times her father had talked about knowing what to do at the airport, or at the border, or whenever you were confronted by authority. Her mother had always laughed it off as libertarian paranoia, but at this moment her comfortable Berkeley liberalism seemed small and far away.

"Blanchard!" There it was. "Cyril Blanchard. I'm here to pick him up?"

The woman behind the counter gave no indication that she was even aware of Robin's presence. Her hand rested on the mouse, clicking a few times as she continued to stare at the screen on her desk.

Robin was about to raise her voice and try again when the woman's lips moved. No sound came out. "Sorry, what?"

She didn't look up. "He's in *processing*. Have. A. Seat."

"Oh. Okay. Um. Thanks."

An hour later, Robin was still waiting. So was everyone else, including the folks who had trickled in after her. Nobody else seemed surprised or agitated, so… maybe this was just the way it went.

At the two-hour mark, she approached the window again. A man in uniform had come into the room behind the glass and was talking to the woman at the desk, who had turned her back to the counter. The man looked directly at Robin, but he didn't alert the woman or even have the decency to nod at Robin and let her know she would be taken care of in due time.

Eventually, he left and the woman swiveled back into place.

"I'm sorry," Robin said loudly, "but do you have any idea how long it's going to be?"

"Ma'am, I don't have any control over the process. All I can say is that it'll happen as soon as it can. Some things are just out of our control."

Robin sat down near the exit this time. Out of their control? What did that mean? Prison riots? Stabbings? Did that sort of thing go on here? The facility was big enough that it had to house people serving out actual sentences in addition to overnighters and those who couldn't make bail.

The whole thing felt like a trip to the ER. If you weren't bleeding out on the table, you were sitting with a bunch of junkies and impoverished seniors until some doctor had a moment to put a couple of stitches in your busted thumb. Which could be hours. Then, once you were roomed and patched up, you went to the absolute bottom of everyone's priority list. Whether you got out in one hour or five depended solely on your chronically overworked nurse remembering to grab a FAQ sheet and the discharge forms.

So maybe that's how this was. Cyril had, presumably, been fingerprinted and catalogued and whatever else, and now he was idling at the bottom of everyone else's list, waiting for some minor piece of paper to sign before they could let him go home. He was probably sitting in a room that looked very much like this one, sandwiched between a Mexican kid and a middle-aged biker.

Glennis texted at the three-hour mark. *Everything OK?*

Still waiting, Robin wrote back.

Typical. The text came along with a picture of Seth in the back yard, clutching a water gun in one hand and a bouquet of wilting sourgrass flowers in the other. He had his sweet smile turned on full blast, but Robin knew from long experience that this would be one in a long series of photos which were necessary to capture Seth while not spinning or hopping or otherwise cavorting. Each half-blurred photo presented a different expression: fierce, adoring, goofy, faux-sad. When Robin looked at the adorable little boy smile in the photo, she saw all the other faces, too.

After three hours and forty-five minutes, there was a buzz from somewhere deep within the building, just like on TV. Funny, what turned out to be real and what was completely made up.

The corrections officer turned to the door at his right, peered through the little window laced with chicken wire, and then stooped to press his badge against a sensor on the wall.

For some reason she couldn't explain, Robin's heart lurched into her throat. She gulped it down.

A second, more diminutive buzz sounded, and the metal workings of the door clacked as he hauled it open. It was a grungy-looking kid who couldn't have been more than twenty, looking really, really hung over. When he saw his entire family in the corner he put his hands over his face, but didn't shy away as his mother lit into him with the tongue-lashing of his life.

Cyril was going to get a tongue-lashing of his own when he finally showed up.

It was another hour before the buzzer sounded again. Half her day gone, and it probably wasn't even him, yet—

The angry speech she'd spent the morning composing died on her lips the moment he shuffled through the door. He was in flip-flops, pajama pants, and the ratty bathrobe that didn't close around his middle. The purple circles under his eyes made it obvious that, despite his attire, he hadn't slept a wink.

"Jesus," she breathed. "Are you okay?"

It took his eyes a moment to find her face and bring her into focus. Then he just shook his head in disgust. "Get the fuck out of here."

"You're welcome. Come on." Robin reached for his arm, but he jerked away with a sudden violence that made her flinch.

"I am *not* your friend." His voice was a low, ragged growl.

Robin couldn't deny that it hurt, a little, to hear him say that. But he wasn't wrong. "You owe me an explanation."

"I don't owe you shit."

"You owe Tavis."

"That particular social contract expired the moment an IED turned him into pink mist."

"Pink—" She couldn't even say it. "Is that what your Counterstrike buddies call it? When you all play pretend soldiers?"

He flashed an artificial smile. "That's what your husband called it, honey." The smile vanished, and his voice dropped back to a growl. "Now get the fuck out of my face."

IT WASN'T PERSONAL, she knew that: he was powerless and on the defensive and so everyone was his foe. Still, she was so blinded by rage it took two passes through the lot to find her truck. Mostly she was angry at herself, for expecting Cyril to be any kind of reasonable. When she swung around the traffic circle, she saw him shuffling down the sidewalk, his raggedy bathrobe flapping in the icy February wind.

It was tempting to stomp on the accelerator and plow through the muddy water pooled by the curb, but she needed answers. Instead she hit the brake, slowing to a crawl, and cranked the window open. "Planning on walking all the way back to town?"

He gave her an emphatic middle finger.

She waited. He made it another ten or twelve yards before he stopped. He didn't turn around.

The curb was red and there were certainly plenty of patrol vehicles in the vicinity, but there was enough room for other cars to get by. Robin cranked the wheel to the left and pulled up beside him. "Get in the damn car."

He reeked of sweat, cigarettes, and stale beer. Robin left her window down and turned on the heater full blast. When she merged onto the freeway, the wind in her face was worse than the stench, so she reached down and cranked the glass back up. Then, because she was tired of not looking to her right, she glanced at him.

"Oh my God." The left elbow of his robe had been torn open, revealing a mess of dirt and dried blood. "What happened?"

"I fell."

"What, like, when they arrested you?"

His silence was affirmation and... something else. As if it weren't quite as simple as all that. Had the cops been rough with him? Had he *forced* them to be rough, by resisting?

"They said you were trying to destroy evidence."

"*Me?*" He snorted, as if it wasn't even worth his time to refute such a blatant falsehood. "Oh, the irony."

Now Robin was completely lost. Not that she'd ever had a clue. "What's going on, Cyril? What did you *do?*"

"I pushed the red button."

She was so done with his cryptic bullshit. "What does that even mean?"

"I literally" –he lifted a thumb and jammed it into his palm—"pushed the button."

"You mean that stupid nuclear launch thing? That actually *did* something?" Or did the cops just freak out because that's what it looked like?

"You don't want to know."

"Yes, actually, I do."

"Legally." He cleared his sinuses noisily, rolled down his window, and spat. "It's better if you don't know."

"Oh. Great." Absolutely wonderful. "Look, can you just give me a general category here? Is this connected to what Tavis was doing? Or is this your Anonymous hacking crap? Or is this about Cooke?"

His head swiveled to look at her. "Cooke?"

"He said he had to fire you."

"Oh." Cyril turned back to the windshield. "Yeah. That. Plus the Anonymous stuff."

She wanted to pull over and strangle him with her bare hands. "So... this doesn't have anything to do with Tavis?"

"Nah."

"I don't even know whether to believe you."

He shrugged again. "Believe whatever you want."

She didn't even have the energy to be angry. "I should have known better than to let Seth get close to you. No—I did know better. But I kept telling myself, Seth's lost Tavis, and for some reason he idolizes you, and you're at least a little part of his dad, or maybe I just needed to see him happy, but... You're not Tavis. You can't bring him back. You're just..." She shook her head. "For some crazy reason I didn't think even you would befriend my child while you were—I dunno, hacking the Pentagon or something?" She glanced at him. "Are they gonna put you in prison?"

"I hope not." He was silent for a moment, and when he spoke again his voice was low. "But yeah. Maybe."

"So it's not enough that my child loses his father, now he's gonna lose his best friend, too." She slapped the steering wheel. "God. Fuck you."

Cyril didn't apologize. He was probably thinking about going to jail. Good. Robin hoped they stuffed him in some windowless cell and threw away the key.

When she pulled into his driveway she put the truck in park and sat there with the engine idling, staring out the windshield. She felt him look at her, and then away.

Finally, he cleared his throat. "What are you going to tell him?"

She snorted. "I'm not telling him anything. Whatever the hell this is, you're going to explain it to him yourself."

"I thought—"

Robin stomped on the parking brake. "What? You thought I'd never let you see him again? No. It's too late for that. You don't get off that easy, you worthless fuck."

He sat there for another moment, staring at the center of the dash. Then he gave a short nod and fumbled for the handle. The door popped open against the press of his bulk, and he rocked to the edge of the seat before grabbing the frame and heaving himself out. He stumbled forward, catching himself just short of falling into the muddy gravel.

"Whoa." Robin jumped down from the cab and circled to his side. "Here." She gestured for him to put an arm around her shoulders.

He shrugged her off. "I'll break you like a twig."

"I'm stronger than I look."

"Not that strong."

He was right. "Keys."

Cyril fished around in the pocket of his bathrobe. His keys came out, along with a sheaf of paper that dropped to the ground.

Paperwork from jail. Robin picked it up and stuffed it back into the pocket. She took the keys from his hand.

"The copper one."

She crossed the fifteen feet of gravel, inserted the key, and pushed the door in. "Do you think—oh."

They had taken everything.

The furniture was there, and the television. Everything else—Playstation, iPad, computer tower, controllers, even his garbage—was gone. The place looked like a cheap pre-furnished rental. With bonus grime.

Robin turned and watched as Cyril pushed off the side of her truck and staggered toward the door, thighs shuddering with each weighty step.

"I'm sorry," she said, but he shoved past her without even pausing to survey the damage. He put a hand against the wall and hobbled into the kitchen, where he began flinging open cabinet doors. With a grunt of satisfaction, he pulled out a double-sized package of Oreos and a bag of salt and vinegar chips. He pinned them under one arm and wall-walked over to the dining table.

Once he was seated, he pried the bag of Oreos open and tossed three into his mouth. As he was chomping those, without, it seemed, even stopping to savor the taste, he opened the chips and grabbed a handful. Robin watched with a kind of detached horror as he sat there alternating between sugar and salt. When he stopped, she felt a kind of secondhand relief, but he only hesitated long enough to belch and say, "Grab me a soda, if you're just gonna stand there."

"What are you *doing?*"

He looked at her as if she had asked a completely nonsensical question. "You know what they give you in jail? Stale peanut butter and jelly. One, at midnight. The bread was moldy."

Robin could have sworn it was her mother who blurted, "Oreos and chips are *not* breakfast."

He held his arms out wide, indicating his girth, as if no further explanation were necessary.

She went to the fridge, grabbed a Sprite, and slammed it down on the table. "I want it. Whatever you were helping Tavis hide."

"What, so you can go all *Wrath of Khan?*" Cyril twisted his arm around, but couldn't get it far enough to get a good view of the gash on the back of his elbow. "Fuck no."

Robin had never sat through a single Star Trek episode in her life, but she got the gist of the sentiment. "What I do with it is my decision, not yours. Tavis was my husband. I have a right to—"

"Oh, get off your high horse. You have Seth." He waggled a finger at her belly. "And now that one."

"No," Robin said, and then she stopped, because the only thing standing between her and perhaps the most important thing her husband had ever done was Cyril. It would have been one thing if he'd been adamantly against giving her the information—but he wasn't. He just didn't care all that much, and he thought it was amusing that she did.

Pig-headedness could be dealt with. It could be cajoled, persuaded, bribed. Indifference was infinitely more terrifying. She imagined grabbing a knife from the kitchen and threatening to stab him, but she knew he would laugh. He wasn't afraid of pain. He didn't care about his life, or what she could do to him. He just didn't *care*.

Cyril raised an eyebrow. "No?"

Robin clenched her hands into fists. She had to find exactly the right words to make him give this to her. And she didn't know what those words were.

"No," she whispered again, finally. "You don't get to take this choice away from me because you think I might make the wrong one. You *don't*."

He shrugged. "I already did."

Her pulse was so loud in her ears she couldn't hear. "No."

He repeated the same motion he'd made in the car—pushing a thumb into his palm. "Kaboom."

Robin snapped her arm back and buried her fist in his face. She hadn't expected to hit anything other than soft flesh—hadn't thought about the action at all, really—but her knuckles connected with a sharp *crack.*

He sucked in a breath and rocked forward, covering his jaw with a hand. "What the *fuck!*"

Her hand wasn't too happy, either. She pinned it under her armpit. "Tavis risked his life—he might have *died* trying to help that kid, and you destroyed whatever information he had? How can you even live with yourself?" There were tears on her face. Damn it. "He was your best friend!"

Cyril rubbed his face. "Trust me, he got the better end of that arrangement."

"Oh my *God*, you're an asshole."

Cyril leaned one arm on the table and got to his feet. He shuffled past her into the kitchen, brushing a fly out of his face. "Christ. You think that wasn't what he asked me to do?"

"I—" Robin turned to watch as he opened the freezer and pulled out a bag of tater tots. "Why would he do that?"

"He didn't want you involved in any of this. In case that wasn't clear from him, you know, telling you jack shit. So if you need a punching bag, look elsewhere. God." He pressed the bag against his cheek. "Want one?" He reached back into the freezer and pulled out a bag of peas.

She took the package and looked at it, dumbly. "Peas?"

"I think they were here when I moved in." He opened the fridge and pulled out another Sprite.

"Can you—can you at least tell me what it was?" The freezer-burned peas gritted against her knuckles. "What he had?"

"How much did Walker tell you?"

"That a couple of Marines shot Shafik's father and uncle and supposedly Shafik. Except that Tavis found out he was alive. Being used as a dancer or... something."

Cyril gathered the Oreos and chips from the table and took a moment to adjust his clothing before installing himself on the couch. "That's about the size of it. Dumb bastard couldn't let it go. Insisted on re-upping, so he could go poking around. Trying to save the kid, if he could, which he fucking couldn't. Digging up paperwork, interviewing people with this stupid little camera—God. I shouldn't have—" He rubbed his forehead with one hand. "He didn't know how to keep that shit secure. I helped him encrypt it and hide it on a third-party server. Sort of. I mean—" He shook his head and waved the details off like a pesky fly. "Technical bullshit. You don't care."

She sat on the edge of the dining table. "Did he... figure out what happened?"

"More or less. The Marines, the ones that did the killing—just following orders, of course. The head honcho in the region—Afghan, not U.S.—had a hard-on for the kid, but the kid's dad wouldn't sell him. Poor bastard thought his relationship with the Marines would protect him. Let's see, how did Command phrase it in the paperwork? A 'tactical necessity.' To 'maintain regional stability.' Because if they didn't work with the guy in power, the situation was going to deteriorate, and nobody wants more instability, you know? More fighting, more death, more Americans going home in caskets. Bad for everyone." He lifted a shoulder. "Meanwhile this kid is getting gang raped at parties for the greater fucking good."

Robin covered her face. "You shouldn't have," she whispered, when she could speak. "You shouldn't have destroyed the evidence. I don't care what he told you to do."

"Yeah, well." He twisted his arm in another vain attempt at examining his elbow. "Superheroing's not really my bag."

"Clearly not." She went to the fridge and flung the peas back in the freezer. "I'm not sorry I punched you."

"I'm not sorry I deleted the damn evidence. What exactly did you think you were gonna do with it, anyway?"

She slammed the freezer shut and turned on one heel. "Seriously? You think there wouldn't be complete outrage about something like this going on? About the U.S. military condoning the abuse of children, covering up murder? If this made it to network news—"

"Oh," Cyril said, with a snort. "Oh, that's rich. Little Miss I-Don't-Watch-the-News."

"Just because I don't watch it doesn't mean other people—"

"Oh, you mean everyone in your little Facebook bubble? Because clearly the people you associate represent an accurate cross-section of America." He swatted the air with a hand. "Nobody cares."

"You don't know that."

He snorted again. "I absolutely do. I'll prove it. Give me your phone."

"Um, no."

"Fine. Pull up your browser and type in 'bacha bazi.' You know what you'll get? I'll tell you: a Frontline documentary about the whole thing. An article from the New York Times about how soldiers coming home can't sleep because they had to listen to these men raping little boys *on the base*. You'll find actual fucking YouTube videos of boys dancing, in case you like that sort of thing." He fluttered a hand in the air. "Everyone knows. Afghanistan is stale. The media cycle's moved on to Syria and Russia and whatever the fuck else. If there's outrage, it lasts until that next God-bless-our-soldiers Facebook post. Nobody cares. Nobody."

"Fuck you." Robin walked out the door. She opened the camper and ripped her first aid kit off the Velcro holding it to the wheel well. Cyril said nothing when she walked back in and plopped down on the couch next to him, but jerked away when she grabbed his elbow.

"Keep your goddamn hands off me."

"Touch your elbow." She tossed the kit onto the coffee table and nodded to his arm. "Go ahead."

He grabbed another handful of Oreos. "Go fuck yourself."

"You can't, can you. You can't even touch your own elbow, and from the looks of it, that's not going to change any time soon." She hooked a leg of the coffee table with one foot and dragged it close. "So shut the fuck up."

He didn't pull away when she swabbed his elbow with alcohol.

"There's still gravel in here." She fumbled for the tweezers and spent a few minutes digging around in his flesh. "What did they do, push you down and then stomp on it?"

"Sorta what happens when six hundred pounds of force comes down on one joint."

"Six—Jesus Christ, Cyril. Are you serious?"

He shrugged. "My scale tops out at four-fifty. That was like, I dunno, two years—*Ow!* God dammit!"

"Sorry." Robin glanced up. Beads of sweat were rolling down his temples. "Well, for—" She grabbed the topical anesthetic and sprayed. "A few more minutes, okay?" It had already been festering a good twenty-four hours. Cyril was putting up a tough front, but for a guy of his size, a neglected wound could get out of control pretty easily. That's what she remembered Tavis saying, anyway.

As she picked at the gravel, Cyril sat and consumed every last Oreo in the package. He ate with the same kind of single-minded focus Seth got when he was trying to perform some new physical feat, as if the entire world had narrowed into this one concerted action.

It was impressive, in a kind of sick, sad way.

She shook her head. "I don't know how you can live like this."

"What, fat?"

"I think you're a little beyond fat, Cyril." She sat back, wiping her eyes with the back of one hand. "Seriously, why do you do this to yourself?"

He lifted his free hand to indicate the room. "Because all my shit is gone. Because my best friend is dead. Because I got reckless, and now I'm probably going to prison. I dunno, pick your excuse." He crumpled the Oreo package and sent it arcing toward the garbage can. It hit the wall and bounced a few feet.

"Have you ever thought about... you know, getting help?"

"Wow, you know, you are the first person who's *ever* suggested that." He finished off the second can of Sprite and tossed it after the Oreo bag. "How about you? Ever thought about getting help? Or you just gonna keep showing up at my door?"

"I'm not killing myself."

"Aren't you?"

"Uh... no?"

"Funny. I used to know this woman who never swore. I mean, I didn't *really* know her, because she was too smart to bother hanging out with an asshole like me. But I know she went to church on Sundays. Had half a dozen friends or so, a career she loved, and a great relationship with her mom." He dragged the back of his hand across his mouth, loosening a few crumbs that had caught in his two-day grizzle. "Whatever happened to that chick?"

Robin grabbed another antiseptic wipe and cleaned the wound a second time. It was too big to cover with the largest band-aid in her kit, so she pulled out some gauze and tape. "I don't know," she said, quietly. "I'm not sure she ever really existed."

"Well. Girl or ghost, whatever you are, how about sticking a frozen pizza in the oven?"

"No."

"Then leave. Because I'm going to eat until I want to puke, and then I'm going to take a handful of Ambien and pass out for twenty hours."

Robin looked at him. He looked back, unblinking. "You're scared," she realized. A night in the county lockup had treated him to a glimpse of his own possible future, and it terrified him.

"No shit."

She finished taping off the wound. "Walker said... she said she thought maybe they killed him. Tavis. Or... got him killed."

"Who? The Marines? Or someone in command? Maybe. Maybe not. Even if I gave you everything Tavis had, you'd never know. Nothing you could do."

Except take it all to the media and let the public be the judge. But Cyril had destroyed even that small chance at justice.

"They'd put you in jail, you know," he said. As if she'd spoken the accusation aloud. "The information he collected, it was... it'd put you in jail. No matter what happened to the other guys. A breach like that, from a civilian—they couldn't let you off."

Or him. "So you destroyed it. To save your own neck."

"If it makes you feel better, the Feds are still doing their absolute best to put me away."

"So instead of going to jail for something worthwhile, you're getting put away for—"

"The lulz?"

"What?"

He snorted. "Forget it."

Robin packed the remains of the kit, then collected the wrappers from the antiseptic wipes and crumpled them in one hand. "You gonna be okay to pick up Seth on Monday?"

He lifted an eyebrow. "Does it matter?" He lifted a hand to encompass his abode. "Assholes took my fucking *Xbox*."

"Oh. Right." Seth would probably be happy staging imaginary battles with silverware or whatever else happened to be on hand, but... "Come to our place. He'll be over the moon to show you all his toys."

On her way out, she chucked the pizza in the oven.

19

LUNCH WAS WAITING on the table. Robin could tell her mother was trying—and completely failing—to project an air of disinterest. The reality was that Glennis wanted all the dirt. Most of all, Robin guessed, she wanted to hear her daughter admit she'd been right about Cyril. As if Robin's refusal to cut him out of her son's life were equivalent to making him her best friend.

She didn't care about satisfying her mother's curiosity. She cared about Seth. "So," she said carefully. "I picked Cyril up from jail."

Seth picked up his fork and danced it along the edge of the table.

"Sethie, your mother is talking—"

"Mom, it's fine." Seth's response to social discomfort was to act like he wasn't listening. Of course, he heard every word. "Apparently he made a mistake at, uh, his work. I don't know if he did it on purpose or on accident, exactly. Maybe some of both. The police are going to investigate him and decide if he broke the law. They had to take him to jail for one night because he..." How did she put this? "He got a little upset when the police came. He was scared and angry, and the police needed to have him out of the house for a while." She hesitated. "Okay?"

Seth's fork got to the corner of the table and did a pirouette. "Kay."

"Are you done eating? You can go play."

He slid off his chair and was gone in a flash. Robin sighed. Doubtless there would be more questions later.

"So what *happened?*"

Or now, apparently. "Basically what I said, Mom. He's in some trouble at work." No way was she getting into the whole thing with Walker, although it did make Cyril look slightly better. Except for the part where he'd deleted everything. So Robin didn't feel like doing him any favors in her mother's eyes; not that he cared. "He did something illegal, I have no idea why, and now the FBI's involved. He could go to prison."

Glennis' eyebrows shot up. "And what on earth are you going to tell Seth?"

"I don't know. All I can do at this point is play it by ear."

"Would you like me to start coming on Wednesdays again?"

Robin swallowed. "Mom, I—I never wanted you to stop."

Glennis waited—presumably for Robin to apologize. When it didn't come, she took a long, careful sip of water. "If you need me to, I can fill in on Mondays and Thursdays."

Which was to say, Cyril's days with Seth. So subtle. Why was she trying to set this up as an either-or situation? "I'm not cutting him out, Mom." She felt the urge to offer some sort of explanation—but aside from not having anything rational to articulate, Robin didn't have to justify her decisions to anyone. Not even her mom. She shrugged.

"Well." Glennis sighed. "Did you finally go to a salon? Your hair looks lovely."

"HEY, BUD." Robin slid up onto the twin bed next to Seth and brushed his hair back from his face. He gave her a sleepy smile—and then jackknifed his entire body, kneeing her in the groin. "Ow! Buddy, be careful!" She put one hand on his chest, pinning him down as he giggled and squirmed, and the other on her belly. "Remember? Your brother's in here. He's small and you gotta watch out for him."

"Oh *yeah.*" Seth let his body relax. "Sorry."

She grabbed a couple of his larger stuffed animals and piled them next to his pillow to recline on. "So," she said, willing her voice not to break, "you know Daddy died."

"To Jesus."

"Uh, yeah." She still wasn't entirely sure what that meant to him, but it seemed to confer some sort of comfort. "So, he's gone. But he left me some letters." She twisted and pulled her phone out of her back pocket and tapped her email settings to pull up the archive file she'd entitled *Emergencies.* She scrolled past the unread messages she'd managed to stockpile, to one of the most recent ones she'd opened. The subject line read *You and Seth.* "I want to read you this one, okay?"

Seth said nothing for a moment. Then, slowly, he nodded.

"Okay." She cleared her throat.

The day we met was the best day of my life. I know I've said that a thousand times, and you always smile and nod, because you don't want to make me feel bad by not agreeing. It's fine. I know that for you, nothing in the whole of history could ever top the day Seth was born.

I feel like a jerk even admitting this, but I was jealous. I spent hours composing the perfect letter about, I don't know, motherhood and heredity and all sorts of nice esoteric concepts—and you set it aside, unread, because you couldn't take your eyes off him. For you, the day Seth was born became the reason you are alive. For me, it was the day I became second in your heart.

Maybe it was that rush of oxytocin or just you becoming wholly and wonderfully you, but Seth became your entire world. And me? Don't get me wrong; I was happy that you and he were both healthy and whole. But I looked at that wrinkly old-man-baby face, and I didn't know what it meant. I don't know if that's what all guys feel like, or if it was just me. But suddenly I knew I was just... extraneous.

I'm not sure when that feeling changed. You came home, and Seth started eating and crawling and walking and talking and... somewhere along the way, I fell in love. Deeply, permanently in love.

You and me, Robin, we've made our choices. We decided which books to read and which classes to take and what careers to pursue. The choices we've made will determine, in large part, where we go from here.

But Seth? All of that is still before him. He's his own person, Robin, and yet when I look at him—he's everything we could have been, but chose not to be. He is every single one of those missed possibilities, and a thousand we never even dreamed.

It kills me to even contemplate not being there to see what he'll become. To teach him, to help him grow and make all those thousand-and-one choices that come before us each and every day. I want to be there, Robin. I want to hold him and play with him and love him with all my heart. Sometimes I get jaded, but then he leaps into my arms and I realize this, right here—this is what it's all about. I never imagined myself saying that about a child. A woman, yes. You, absolutely. But God, Robin, I love him.

If I'm not there... hug him for me. Don't tether yourself to the past, but... remind him, now and then, that I loved him too.

Seth had nestled up against her, slipping his hands around her arm as she read. She looked down, expecting to find a sleepy smile. His eyes were closed, and his breath came in soft pants from between slightly parted lips. Content.

She buried her face in his hair, pressing her lips against the top of his head. "We'll get through this, bud," she whispered. "Whatever happens. You and me."

20

SETH HAD THE FRONT DOOR OPEN before the door chime finished playing. "*Cereal!*"

Robin dried her hands on a kitchen towel and followed him into the entryway. Cyril stood outside on the porch, Seth clinging to one leg like a carrot-topped anchor.

"Oh my God," Robin said.

He touched the left side of his jaw, gingerly. It was purple. "Looks worse than it is."

"I'm so—" No, she wasn't sorry. She stepped back. "Come on in."

He looked down. "Lemme go, kid." He grabbed the door frame to help himself over the threshold.

Seth took his hand the instant it was free. "Come to my play room!" He cast a glance at Robin. "You go wash dishes."

She rolled her eyes. "Yes, your highness." Seth was trying to get rid of her so he could have Cyril to himself. He did the same thing when her mom came.

"Well," said Cyril. "I see who wears the pants in this house."

"*Bossy*pants," Seth corrected. "That's what Mommy says."

"You and I are going to have a chat about that attitude, Mister." Robin leveled a finger at Seth, and then moved it to Cyril, who wasn't even trying to hide his smirk. "I pick my battles. If you think I'm a pushover, let's see how well you're doing in two hours."

THE CASEROLE needed to cook for a good fifty minutes, and with nothing better to do Robin looped a scarf around her hair, grabbed a can of spackle, and got down on her knees to do the baseboard she'd been avoiding for months. She'd gotten through Seth's room and was working on the window seat in the master suite when she heard the floor creaking downstairs—Cyril coming out of the playroom. Did he need something? She rose to her knees, cracking her neck to relieve the tension, and heard Seth's voice, high and excited. Cyril rumbled something indistinct when he paused. Well, if they needed anything, Seth could find her easily enough. She bent her neck the other way and then knelt back down.

The can of spackle ran out about the time she needed to check on dinner, so Robin rinsed the chalky residue off her hands and headed downstairs.

"I didn't find it." Seth's little voice, clear as a bell, made her pause on the landing. He and Cyril had come into the living room.

"Did you look under the couch?"

"Oh. I forgot." Seth's footsteps pattered around the room. Robin decided to go back upstairs; if she interrupted now he'd probably start whining for dinner. "Here it is!" There was a crack as he slammed whatever it was against the coffee table. He cackled. "He's in jail! Like you, right?"

Robin stopped.

"Uh." Whatever Cyril was sitting on—the couch?—groaned as he shifted. "Yeah. I, uh, I had to go to jail for one night."

Should she intervene? No; she trusted Cyril to keep it kid-friendly. She didn't trust him enough not to eavesdrop, though. Robin sat down on the step above the landing, just around the bend in the stairs. Seth was her child.

"Was is scary?"

"Yes."

"You shouldn't go if it's scary."

He chuckled, almost sadly. "Well, I didn't really have a choice. The police took me. Because... some people think maybe I did something illegal. Um. Against the law. Something I wasn't supposed to do."

"Are you a bad guy?" Seth's voice was small.

"I don't think so. I mean. Well." He cleared his throat. "Some people think I did something bad. I don't. I think what I did was right. I did it to help people."

Right—the FBI had gutted his house because he was out there

performing random acts of cyber altruism. Was he lying so Seth wouldn't think his best friend was a criminal, or did he believe his own bullshit?

"Like Daddy," Seth said.

Robin would have put an end to the conversation right there if Cyril hadn't immediately replied, "*No*. Not like your Daddy at all. He was much, much braver. And he did much better things. I just did something small."

He was that honest, at least.

"Oh." Abruptly, Seth's *Frozen* wand started tinkling the notes to "Let It Go." Conversation over.

Now what? Sneak back upstairs and pretend she hadn't overheard any of it? Or casually walk down and offer Cyril a knowing shrug?

"Will the police take you there again?"

Okay, not over. Carefully, Robin leaned against the wall.

"Jail? Yeah, maybe. I hope not. I'd rather stay here and play with you. And these chomping guys." There was a clink of plastic.

Seth giggled. "*Chomper* guys!"

"Right, right. Sorry." Whatever he was sitting on groaned again. Not the couch; that was more high pitched, at least when Seth used it as a trampoline. Not the rocking chair—

She realized where he was half a second before the fallboard thunked up.

No, she wanted to scream, but Cyril's fingers were already tripping aimlessly over the keys. And what had she expected, anyway? For the piano to sit collecting dust for the next twenty years? Seth would have gotten around to poking at the keys eventually, and what then? Was she going to lock it shut? No.

Still.

"Do *Frozen!*" Seth ordered.

Cyril cleared his throat and then, slowly, tapped out "Twinkle Twinkle." And suddenly, the second time around, the tap turned into a full two-handed, jazzy rendition of the classic tune.

That she had not expected.

"No, *Frozen!*"

"Hold your horses, kid. It's been a few years. Uh... play it again."

Robin heard Seth fumble with the snowglobe-topped wand. The tinny little melody played a second time.

Cyril grunted an affirmative. "Okay. Lemme know if I get this wrong."

And then he played. Only the snippet from the wand, but in a complete arrangement of chords. The second time through he changed it up a bit, adding some twists and flourishes. Tavis could play the piano—from sheet music. Not like this.

"Let it go!" Seth shrieked, at approximately the appropriate time.

"All right, gimme something else. 'Itsy Bitsy Spider' or something."

"Falling down!"

Cyril dropped the jazzy tone and performed a lilting, lullabye-esque "London Bridges." Next came "Row, Row, Row Your Boat." Seth sang along, shouting his usual, "Merrily, merrily, merrily, like a spot a dream."

"'Life is but a dream,' kiddo."

"Huh?"

Cyril played a quick set of scales and then started again, this time singing along with the traditional lyrics. His voice was as rich and smooth as it had been at the ice cream parlor, and with the perfectly pitched piano accompaniment, the simple melody sent a shiver up Robin's spine. "See? It's 'life is but a dream.'"

"No," Seth insisted. "Like a *spot* a *dream*."

"Well, fine, if you wanna go and make up your own lyrics—" Cyril began once again, adding a jaunty tinkle. "Stomp, stomp, stomp your feet, all around the room—if you stomp them hard enough, you'll bounce up to the moon."

It was silly and ridiculous and by the time he hit the last note Robin was curled up on the landing, hands pressed over her mouth to stifle the sobs.

Seth shrieked with laughter. "Again! Again!"

Cyril sang it through again, then switched it up with some verses about robots and mummies. "Okay," he said, after what seemed like an eternity. "That's all for now." And before Seth could whine, he added, "Here. Go build me a blue one of these, okay? And a red one."

"You come too!"

"I told you, kid, if I sit in that rocking chair again you'll never get me out. Go on. I'll wait here."

Seth let out a small huff of frustration, then bounded off without further protest.

Robin swallowed and wiped her face with the bottom of her shirt.

"Sorry," Cyril said.

She froze.

The piano bench protested as he got up. "I'll go."

"No—" She wiped her face again and then rolled to her feet, stumbling down the stairs. "How—how did you know?"

He glanced over his shoulder and then turned, slowly, to face her. "Know what?"

She punched his shoulder, harder than she probably should have. "Don't play games with me. That—" She almost couldn't say it. "That was their thing. Tavis—Tavis would always make up silly rhymes to sing—"

"Oh. The filking." He looked at the floor. "We did it too. As kids. Making up new words to songs. It was just a stupid game. Sorry, I... didn't realize."

Robin stared at him, hard. Wanting to be furious. Because the songs belonged to Tavis. Tavis and Seth. It was theirs, not Cyril's. But apparently it had been, long before Seth. Tavis had never said. Was that Cyril's fault or Tav's?

"I won't do it again."

"Good," she snapped. "No. I mean—" She stuck her fingers in her hair and yanked. "God."

He turned and shuffled toward the kitchen. "Christ, but you're wound tight. I need a drink."

Robin followed. Cyril grabbed a glass out of the dish drainer and filled it from the tap. "There's filtered water in the—"

He grunted a negative, leaned against the counter, and chugged.

His pose felt familiar. "Did he make you read Magic Schoolbus?" Those always left her parched.

Cyril held up two fingers.

She winced. "Sorry. I usually limit him to one."

He dropped the empty glass on the cutting board. "Those things should be off limits until kids can read for themselves. I tried to skip the side bars, but—"

"He knows you're skipping." She opened the fridge and pulled out the carafe of purified water.

"Sharp kid." Cyril picked the glass back up and held it out for a refill.

Robin topped him off and got a second glass for herself. "Sometimes I wonder how he's interpreting all of this information. After my last doctor's appointment? He kept asking me—I forget how he phrased it, but I finally figured out that he wanted to know whether I was giving birth to another *him*. Like a clone."

Cyril chuckled. "A respawn."

"Oh, so it's your fault."

He shrugged.

Seth's small voice came, faintly, from the other side of the wall. He had gotten lost in his own little world, singing something fairly close to Cyril's robot song.

Robing closed her eyes. "Don't stop," she whispered.

Cyril raised his eyebrows.

"It hurts, but—" It was exactly what Seth needed. *He's like my brother,* Tavis had said of Cyril, and Robin had never understood how or why. But she had thought Tav's songs were gone, and that her son's memories of his father would gradually slide into the fog of early childhood. Now, maybe he would forget, over time, that the songs had been Tav's. Maybe it would become something between him and Cyril. But when he got older, she would tell him, and he would know. Even if Cyril sang the words, these would be his father's songs.

"But hey, I'm better than nothing?" Cyril snorted. "I just hope I don't screw him up in the long run."

Because he didn't expect to be around forever. "You're not dying," she said. He didn't even know he was going away, for sure.

"Yeah, well, I don't think they do play dates in prison."

"Who cares?"

"I dunno, it seemed like you might."

She shook her head. "You don't get it."

He lifted an eyebrow. "Enlighten me."

"There is no long run, Cyril. Yesterday I was going to spend the rest of my life with the only man who has ever known me, the real me, and today I'm alone." She pointed at the tile above the sink. "The only thing in the entire universe I give a shit about is sitting on the other side of that wall, singing your song. I'd die for him, Cyril. I would *kill* for him. No question. You may be an asshole and a criminal and tomorrow I may end up having to explain to my son exactly what federal prison is, but—today? Today you make him smile. And as far as I'm concerned, that's the only thing that matters."

THEY SANG AGAIN, after dinner. Seth begged and Cyril started to tell him no, but Robin put up a hand and said, "It's okay."

And somehow, it was.

Cyril occupied the entire piano bench, so Seth dragged a chair in from the dining room and stood on it. Robin sat on the couch, next to the end table with the Kleenex in the drawer, just as a precaution. Though he only seemed to use the notes as general guidelines, Cyril flipped through the sheet music on the rack for inspiration. Robin could hear him getting a little hoarse after a couple rounds of "Camptown Races" and "Swing Low," so she slipped into the kitchen and came back with his glass of water.

"Thanks," he said, downing half of it as soon as she handed it to him. "Uh, where..." He looked for a place to set it.

Robin grabbed a coaster from the end table and set it on top of the piano. "*Oh,*" she said.

Seth and Cyril looked at her.

"Shhh." She pressed Seth's hand to her stomach. "Feel that? That's your brother."

Seth's eyes got big. "What's his name?"

Not Tavis. She couldn't. "I don't know."

The baby kicked again, hard. Seth squealed. "Cereal! Feel!" He grabbed his hand off the keyboard.

"I don't think your mom wants me groping her belly, kid."

Normally Robin would have agreed, but he looked so ridiculously uncomfortable that she laughed and reached for his hand. "Go ahead. Cop a feel."

"Uh, right." His fingers brushed the soft black polyester of her shirt and immediately drew back.

She snorted. "Come on, don't be chicken." She took his hand and pressed it firmly against the lower left side of her abdomen, where little whatsisname did most of his kicking. "Now just wait."

Then, of course, the little guy really *did* make them wait—until Robin was starting to think maybe she should let Cyril off the hook. Then she felt the familiar turn and pull, and—"*There* he goes."

Cyril stiffened, his eyes locked on a point somewhere on the floor behind her. The baby kicked again, a sharp one-two-three, and then shifted away. Cyril didn't move.

"Hello?"

He snatched his hand back. "Yeah. Okay." His fingers danced out a couple of staccato chords. "Let's do one more song."

Robin joined them in a couple verses of "Low Bridge" before breaking the news that it was time for Seth to go to bed. She expected the usual moans and groans, but he grinned and said, "Cereal do stories!"

"Buddy, I think we better let him go. He's been here a while, and—"

"And I got nothing to do at home," he rumbled.

"*Yessss!*"

"Well, if you're sure." She waved them up the stairs. "By all means, go."

Cyril shut the lid over the fingerboard, slid to one end of the bench, and heaved himself to his feet. Seth shot straight up the stairs and Cyril followed, pausing to wheeze like a walrus after every single step.

"No more Magic Schoolbus!" Robin called.

STORY TIME STILL LASTED a good forty-five minutes. Robin had cleared the table and cleaned up the kitchen and was on the couch flipping through the channels when Cyril made his way laboriously back downstairs. By the time he reached the living room, he was huffing like he'd run a marathon.

"Hey," Robin said, muting the television. "Have a seat." She'd refilled her own glass, but now she leaned across the cushions and set it on the other end table. The last thing she wanted was him having a heart attack on the walk back home.

Her mom's old floral-pattern couch was too low; he had to spread his legs, lean forward, and fall back with a heavy *whump*. Quickly, he tugged his shirt back down over the top of his exposed belly. He tried to pull his pants up as well, but he couldn't reach the band. He tried shifting himself to one side, but the angle of the couch was too steep.

"Jesus." Robin leaned forward, located his waistband, and yanked it up over his gut. "There. Now we both got to cop a feel."

He gave the side of his stomach a firm slap, making his flesh shiver. "Yeah, I bet that's real titillating."

"You may find this hard to believe, Cyril, but it's not your size I find offensive. It's *everything else*." She flipped the volume back on. "Drink your damn water."

Diplomatic relations with China were on edge. The situation with North Korea had deteriorated even further. A cop in New Jersey had shot an unarmed black man. Edward Snowden was still in Russia, still talking about the NSA's privacy violations, but the thing that really had everyone riled up was an insult the president had tweeted at an aging actress. Come back for more outrage after this commercial.

Cyril shook his head. "Can't believe anyone still pays for this shit," he muttered.

"For what?"

"*Cable.* This is not journalism. It's a pseudo-intellectual strip tease. They'll do whatever it takes to keep you watching long enough to flash *that* in your face." He waggled a finger at the screen, where a slender, blonde-haired woman was blissfully wiping down her kitchen counters with a branded cleaner as laughing, modestly-dressed preteens ate an after-school snack at a white-tiled island. "And you *pay* them for it."

Robin rolled her eyes. It wasn't that she thought he was completely off the mark—she just didn't have the emotional energy to expend on this right now. "My priorities are kind of—" She sucked in a sharp breath as fire shot down the inside of her right thigh.

"You okay?"

Like he cared. "Baby just jammed his feet into my crotch. Probably be up half the goddamn night." She shifted and pressed two fingers into the side of her belly, trying to coax him off the nerve.

Cyril looked at her. "It's fucking weird to hear you swear."

"Makes me feel better."

"You're not gonna have to say a bunch of hail Marys or something?"

"I'm not Catholic, moron. And if God's okay with letting my husband die, I think He can handle a couple dozen fucks."

The news came back on. Robin flipped channels until she landed on a documentary. Something about ancient cryptography. Cyril snorted when the 'expert' came on. She flipped some more.

Peripherally, she was aware of Cyril drinking the glass of water. She felt him look at her again, and glanced up just as his eyes flickered away from her belly. He looked genuinely embarrassed. "Really?" She laughed. "Why the hell not." She took his hand and put it on her stomach. He tried to pull back, but she tightened her grip and, finally, he relaxed. His fingers were warm and slightly damp.

"I just—I never—"

"Yeah. I get it." Even Cyril was human. Occasionally.

Robin ended up back on the news. They sat in silence, only the baby moving, watching something about an event at the White House. It was followed by a segment on world news, which contained a two-sentence soundbite on Afghanistan, and then the hosts launched into a discussion about celebrity divorce. Robin hit the power button and tossed the remote aside. "You know what gets me? Seth thinks littering is bad. Like, that's literally the worst thing he can think of doing."

Cyril pulled his hand back. He made a fist, briefly, before letting his palm rest on his belly. "He's a good kid." He tugged his shirt down.

She shook her head. "Someday? I'm gonna have to tell him about slavery. The Holocaust. The killing fields. Stuff like that."

"Didn't you just tell me that today is the only thing that matters? That seems like a few years off."

"Yeah? No. I dunno. Everything is shit right now." She let her head fall back against the couch cushion. "That's not even the worst, right? I mean, Hitler's bad. But it's not..." She flung an arm toward the TV. "It's not personal. How do I tell a kid who feels guilty about *litter* that someone killed his dad with a bomb made out of nails and rusty scrap metal? *Intentionally?* That's fucked up, Cyril." For lack of a better way to express the complete absurdity of the universe, she grabbed the remote and turned the TV back on. A few more flips brought her to a DIY channel airing a remodel show. The hosts were adding on a covered porch. "They're framing it wrong."

"They're still walking around."

"Of course they are." She held a palm out toward the screen. "It'll be fine until the first hard rain, and then—"

"The people who did this. They killed those farmers, and maybe Tavis, and sold that kid into slavery. And they're still walking around. Scott free." Cyril's face was... dark, somehow.

She sucked in a breath. "You—you know who they are." And he'd destroyed the evidence. "*You're* not thinking of going all *Wrath of Khan*, are you?"

He avoided her eyes. "What if I could?"

"Don't." Maybe a month ago. Maybe a few months ago. "Not now."

"Why not?"

"Because Seth loves you. And I—"

Cyril looked at her.

She shrugged. "I'm... sorry about your jaw."

He snorted, and then they just sat there, watching the stupid remodel show.

Something jolted her. A moment of disorientation, and then the realization that she was still sitting on the couch.

"Damnit." Cyril had gotten himself to the edge of the cushion. "I was trying not to wake you." He was red-faced and panting.

Robin swiped at her eyes with the backs of her hands. "What time is it?" They were watching a different show. Out the window, the sky was dark. She got up, quickly, and for a second her vision went black. "You've just been sitting here this whole time?"

He held up his iPhone, screen dark. "Played some games."

She held out a hand. He looked at it, seemed to consider offering a snide remark, then shrugged and accepted the offer. With his other hand, he gripped the arm of the couch and rocked himself forward. Robin pulled. She wasn't much against his mass, but it was enough to get him to his feet on the first try.

Cyril did his usual shirt-pulling and pants-hiking before turning to locate the phone on the arm of the couch. He tucked it into a pocket.

"Wait—is that new? They took your phone too?"

"And froze my bank accounts. Lawyer's working on it. Fortunately I hid some cash in the peas." He cleared his sinuses. "Thanks for dinner."

She followed him to the foyer. "Come back on Monday, if you want. I'll have something better than baked macaroni. And I promise I'll get you out of here before—" She glanced at the clock in the living room. "Ten thirty. Geez. I'm sorry."

"No worries. It's basically my lunchtime." He braced himself on the railing and stepped off the porch.

"Hey, um—are you gonna be okay?" Much as she disapproved of his lifestyle, she hated to think of him sitting alone in that little house, with nothing but his phone and the food in his fridge.

"I'm sure the thought of the pie waiting in my freezer will sustain me on my long journey home."

"No, I just—" She was so tired of this shit. "You know what, forget it." Robin stepped back and started to close the door.

"Wait." He said it quietly, but she heard. And she did. "I'm... fine." He leaned to one side to fish in a pocket. His hand came out with his ring of keys and a piece of crumpled paper.

"Okay?"

He fingered the paper, smoothing the edges. "New laptop and mic arrived yesterday, and I got my site back up, so... I'm okay."

"Oh. Good. Well. Good night."

"Wait," he said again. He put his hand on the porch railing. "Will you be home Saturday?"

"Saturday? Seth's off to my mom's for the weekend."

Cyril licked his lips. "No, I mean—you."

"Uh... yeah, I'll be here. Why?"

Cyril looked down at the piece of paper in his hand. He stuck his keys back in his pocket and used both hands to unfold it, squinting in the dim porch light. "Yes," he said, letting the word out with a heavy breath of air. "I am reading this from a piece of stupid fucking paper, because I am attempting to be a decent human being and I don't want to fuck it up by going off script. So. Here's the thing." He shook the paper as if to jostle the words into place. "I know Saturday is your birthday."

Robin swallowed. How...? He didn't give her a chance to ask.

"I know Tavis treated it like a national holiday. I know he always made sure it was special, even when he was deployed." He glanced up from the sheet. "A couple times I helped, um, arrange stuff."

Her ears burned.

He looked back at the paper, crumpled again because he was clutching it so tightly. "Okay. Um." He was looking for his spot. "I know it's going to be hard this year. He's gone, and there's nothing I can do about that. But I was hoping maybe—uh—I could do something. To. Make it a little bit better." He looked up at her, questioning.

Maybe it wasn't the smartest thing to do, but she nodded.

He cleared his throat and looked back at the paper, his focus trained so intensely on the page that it looked like he was trying to burn holes through it with his eyes. "I don't... I don't want you to be alone. So. If. If you are okay with it, I—" He cleared his throat again. "I would like to take you out to dinner." He shook his head and spat out an emphatic "*Fuck.*"

Robin felt her mouth twitch into a very small smile. "Was that in the script?"

"Damn it. No. Forget it." He crumpled the paper and flung it into the bushes. "Stupid idea. Okay? Never mind." He turned and walked away, one heavy step at a time.

"Cyril." He kept going. "Cyril, stop."

He stopped. He didn't look at her.

She'd thought he'd opened up before, that night in the park, but this was exposing his soft underbelly. Her instincts were right: he was a decent guy. Way, way, *way* down underneath. Which, in retrospect, she ought to have expected of anyone who Tavis called friend.

"Sure," she said. "Why not."

"Well," he said, "I could think of a few reasons."

21

CYRIL DRESSED... WELL, not exactly nicely, but nice for him. Black slacks, not just sweatpants, a black button up shirt with subtle damask stripes, and, perhaps most shockingly, a pair of black leather loafers. He was clean shaven, pink-cheeked, his hair still damp. The bruise on his jaw had faded to a pale blue.

"You didn't buy all that for tonight, did you?"

He looked down at himself. "I... bought it for the funeral."

"Oh." So backing out had been a last-minute decision. Robin grabbed her purse from the hook inside the door and stepped out onto the porch. "I've already cried three times today. So, you know, no promises."

"Uh... okay?" Cyril looked back at his car, idling in the driveway. "We don't have to, um—"

"Just try to be nice, is all I'm saying."

He stepped down off the porch and, to her shock, opened the passenger side door. For a moment she just stood there, blinking, and then she shrugged and got in.

He shut the door and went around to the drivers' side. When he'd finally wedged himself in behind the wheel, he glanced at her and said, "Wouldn't it be better if I were an asshole?"

He had a point.

Cyril avoided the freeway, and a few minutes later they pulled into the parking lot at Wood Ranch, a steak house on the north end of town. Robin wasn't big on steak, but his restaurant choice was a wise one for reasons which had little to do with her preferences. Couples and families milled about on the lawn in front of the entrance, waiting for coaster-shaped pagers to buzz. It was obvious, from this small cross-section of clientele, that this was a place where big people came to order big meals. They weren't all large, or even anywhere near Cyril's size—but this was one place he could dine without anyone blinking twice.

Robin volunteered to duck inside to give her name and pick up a pager, and discovered that most of the seating was booth-style, with some regular tables around the edges of the floor. "Excuse me." She pointed at the tables. "We're going to need to sit over there."

The hostess gave her an absent nod and put an X next to Robin's name. Apparently this wasn't an unheard of request.

During her brief absence, Cyril had scored them seating on one of the wooden benches along the outer wall. He'd claimed the entire thing by sitting smack in the middle; when she approached, he inched himself over.

"Fifteen minutes." She handed him the pager. "That's what they said, anyway."

"It's always crowded."

"Do you come here often?" She was surprised by the thought of him dining out. Alone?

He shrugged. "They have a pick-up counter around the back."

Robin watched as a family of five filed in to be seated. There were maybe another two or three groups before their number came up, assuming they didn't have to wait longer because of the table choice.

She glanced at Cyril. He just sat there, staring straight ahead, breathing. Like he was trying not to move. "Is this gonna be super weird?" she asked. "It is, isn't it."

He let out a breath he had apparently been holding. "Sorry. I'm trying not to, uh…"

She filled in the words he was trying to edit out: "Fuck up?"

"Yeah."

"It's okay. It's mostly about the effort, I think."

He didn't say anything.

He was really, really uncomfortable, she realized. To be with her? Or was it just that she was human? And female? In all the years she'd known him, he'd never had anything even close to a girlfriend. Or even a friend. "Hey," she said. "How come you never hooked up with anyone?"

He treated her to an *are-you-fucking-serious* look.

She spread her palms. "What? Everyone does online dating now, and you're a minor internet celebrity, right? There must be at least one woman out there who'd put up with you."

He rolled his eyes. "Yeah, well. I'm not into fat girls."

Robin opened her mouth, but nothing came out. "Wow," she managed, finally. "That's, um… quite the double standard."

"Look." He blew a breath out of his cheeks. "Let's just say I'd rather be alone than put up with the person who'd put up with me."

Robin shook her head. She'd worried that agreeing to dinner with Cyril would feel like some sort of betrayal. But how could it? He couldn't even begin to compare.

A year ago today, she'd woken to find Tavis gone, his imprint still fresh in the sheets on his side of the bed. The house smelled of pancakes and coffee, and when she'd helped herself to some breakfast she found a heart-shaped note in the middle of the kitchen table. It had been the first in a string of clever riddles that led her in a scavenger hunt across town, revisiting the memories they'd made in each place. It had ended at the beach in Ventura, where he'd used a rake to draw two giant interlocking hearts in the damp sand. When she ran down to the shore and hugged him, she discovered two super soakers wedged into the back of his belt. The rest of the afternoon had consisted of the most epic water gun fight in history.

Cyril… Cyril was an asshole, even when he was trying his best to be nice. But it seemed appropriate to spend the day she would miss her husband most with the one person who understood the magnitude of her loss. And if anyone did, it was the guy who had quite literally lost his only friend.

She patted his knee, or roughly where it seemed his knee ought to be. "Thank you, Cyril. For doing this. I really do appreciate it."

"Even though—"

"Yeah." She laughed. "Even though." The pager buzzed and she stood, resettling her purse on her shoulder. "Although I might need some wine to make it through the rest of this meal."

She'd been half joking, but when the waitress gave them the

rundown on the specials Cyril invited her to order a glass. Robin chose an Alexander Valley merlot and asked whether he didn't want one too? A single glass wouldn't even come close to incapacitating a man of his size.

He shook his head and waved the waitress away.

"You don't drink?"

"I'd probably have binged myself to death by now if I did." He slid the silverware out of the napkin and shook the cloth open with a snap. "I'm not good with moderation. In case that wasn't obvious."

Robin wasn't sure how to respond to that, so she unrolled her own silverware and draped the napkin across her lap before picking up the menu.

Even with his stomach pressed firmly against the table, Cyril's mouth was still several feet distant from where his plate would be. He held his napkin up like a flag of surrender. "Would you prefer I wear this like a bib or walk out of here with my shirt covered in barbeque sauce?"

Robin let the menu drop. Was he seriously going to turn this into a repeat of the ice cream shop? Maybe she'd been an optimist for hoping this evening could turn out to be anything other than a disaster. "Look." She leaned over the table, lowering her voice to ensure that he'd be the only recipient of the piece of mind she was about to dish out. "You are huge, Cyril. And it's kind of disgusting. But it's your life, not mine, and unless you've been cloned or body-snatched there's still a human being in there somewhere. It might be an issue if I were considering *dating* you, but as a friend? I don't care. I really don't."

"So… you don't care, unless you actually *did* care."

She rolled her eyes. "Yep. That's exactly what I meant."

"Sorry," he said. "Just trying to be funny."

"And that's all you've got? If you're not cutting me down to size, you're cracking jokes at your own expense? You're a smart guy, Cyril. I think you can do better than that."

He thumbed his shirt collar open and tucked the napkin inside. "You're funny or you're irrelevant. At least in my world."

"Which would be what, the internet?" A million voices all vying for a piece of mental real estate. And what rose to the top? Anything shocking—shockingly funny, shockingly offensive, shockingly true. Also cute. Cyril didn't have much in the way of that commodity. "Maybe you should get a cat."

He snorted. "I'm allergic."

"So could we possibly just have a normal conversation?"

"About what? The only thing we have in common is a dead guy, and we've already established that I'm attempting *not* to make you cry."

She held up the menu. "Well, I was thinking about the Carolina pulled pork; is that any good?"

"Oh." He looked down at the description. "Uh... yes, it's excellent. But get the sauce on the side."

The waitress returned with Robin's wine and two mason jars filled with ice water. She was surprised when Cyril proceeded to order for both of them. Not exactly in line with her feminist side, but it showed he had some manners, anyway.

"So," she said, after the waitress had gone. "How's it going with the, uh, legal stuff?"

His nose wrinkled. "Well, I'm not getting my crap back any time soon. But I've upgraded from legal paper-pusher to serious-fucking-lawyer, and the judge agreed with my guy's motion to release my bank account, seeing as I don't have another income source at the moment."

"Cooke said nobody was going to want to hire you after what you did."

Cyril shrugged.

"So what next? Is there going to be... a trial or something?"

"Probably. They're still investigating, so basically everything's in limbo until they decide to file charges on... whatever they manage to dig up." He shrugged. "I cover my tracks pretty well. Usually."

She had to ask. "What exactly *did* you do?"

He snorted. "What *didn't* I do? It's not a question of what I did. It's what they can *prove* I did."

"So... it was some Anonymous thing?"

His eyes narrowed. "This is where I start to wonder if you're wearing a wire."

Robin laughed. "I'd be sitting here sweating bullets if I was. I'm no good at faking."

"Exactly what I'd expect you to say if you wanted to throw me off."

She twisted, lifting her shirt far enough to show him the small of her back. "See? I'm clean."

"Your phone's the size of a credit card, and you think a wire still looks like a brick?"

"Oh." She laughed. "I watch too many old cop shows."

"*Now* I believe you."

A busboy appeared, briefly, and dropped a basket of rolls on the table. Cyril used a finger to flip back the starched white cloth. He offered her the basket before taking one himself, tearing the roll in half with one quick, savage bite.

"So. Uh." Robin attempted to saw hers in half with a butter knife, but it was so soft and fresh that the dough collapsed. She tore a piece off with her fingers instead. "Was it worth it? Whatever you did?"

"You mean, is it worth going to prison?" He tossed the other half of the roll into his mouth, chewed twice, and swallowed. "It had better be."

The waitress approached, bearing dinner. "All right, you had the pulled pork... and you had the ribeye. Can I get you two anything else? Butter? Catsup?"

Cyril gestured to his mason jar, which was nearly empty. "I could use a coke."

"Of course; I'll get that right now." She turned to Robin. "Do you need a refill on the wine?"

"No thanks." She tapped the lip of her mason jar. "This'll do."

The waitress bowed herself away from the table.

Cyril's hand went to the napkin on his front, double-checking that it was still tucked into place. "Well." He looked uncomfortable. "Do you want to, uh..."

She quirked an eyebrow at him.

The waitress returned, and Cyril moved his arm so she could swap the empty jar for one filled with carbonated syrup. When she had gone again he said, "You know, pray?"

"Pray?"

He got a little red around the collar. "Jesus. Seth always makes me pray."

Robin burst out laughing. "Oh, God, I'm sorry." She slapped a hand over her mouth. "Seth—oh, I'm sorry. We do. At home. When it's just us. I don't..." She couldn't quite stifle a final giggle. "Oh God, I'm so sorry."

"No. It's okay. It's... good to hear you laugh again." He gave a lopsided smile that might almost have been genuine. "Even at my expense."

She seized her knife and fork. "Good bread, good meat; good God, let's eat." It was one of those little things Tavis always said, acting like it was funny and clever every single time. Mostly, she was pretty sure he just liked to hear her groan. She took a stab at her pork, but the next time she glanced up Cyril's eyes found hers, and she knew he knew. He gave a little nod of understanding.

"It's good," she said, after they'd spent a couple of minutes chewing in silence.

He grunted an affirmative, then turned his attention to sawing off another bloody hunk of steak. "So," he said. "We're friends."

"What?"

He stabbed a chunk of steak and used it to point at her. "You said, 'but as a friend.'"

"Oh." She chewed and swallowed. "Um. Yeah. I guess... I guess I did say that." At this point, she wasn't sure what else to call it. Comrades in grief?

"I'll try not to abuse the privilege."

"You know," she said, "that's something I've always wondered, about you and Tav."

"Hm?"

"You don't have to talk about it if you don't want, but... How did you become friends? In the first place?"

Cyril seemed surprised. "He never told you?"

She waved a hand. "You know how he is. Was. He's always been friends with everyone, forever and ever amen. I know you guys grew up here, and he stayed with you and your mom when things got rough with his dad. But he never really said how you guys met."

"It's a small town. We were both born here. We both went to school. So he's right—we've always known each other. But what you're really asking is why a popular jock would want to hang out with the geeky fat kid. Right?"

"Well… yeah."

"Third grade. My dad. His mom." He made a circle in the air with his fork.

"Oh," she said.

He stuffed half a roll into his mouth, chewed once or twice, and swallowed. "A bunch of O's, apparently. They weren't real, uh, discreet. Eventually they took off, made a kid, or maybe two or three, who knows; that was the last we heard. Anyway, we have a half-sister in common. So he's right when he says we're siblings, at least by the transitive property."

"That's terrible." She'd known Tav's mom had left him and his two older sisters, but he'd never mentioned that she'd done the leaving with Cyril's father.

He shrugged. "Mom decided to eat everything she could fit in her mouth. Tav's dad picked up a belt. His sisters picked up guys, and he started crashing on our couch every weekend. Until he got big enough to hit back, anyway."

That explained why Tavis had avoided the topic. It wasn't that he'd been dishonest or cagey; he was just the kind of guy who found a silver lining in any cloud, refusing to dwell on the negative. So he'd told her about the good times—escapades with friends, sports, school—and she hadn't pressed him about the rest.

It also explained his insistence on seeing something worthwhile in Cyril. Much like the bonds he'd developed with the Marines in his unit, Tavis and Cyril's shared history had forged a loyalty stronger than their differences.

"Hey." Robin put her utensils down and reached for her purse. "There's something… something I wanted to share. Today. I hope this isn't too weird." She also hoped she could do this without bursting into tears. Locating her cell phone, she thumbed through her recently read emails. "I just... I know you don't believe in an afterlife. Which is fine, I'm not saying that's wrong. But Tav wrote something that made me think about how there's more than one way to live on, even after your body dies."

Cyril rested the heel of his hand on the edge of the table, fork pointed up. He was suddenly very still.

"Um. He says he loves me, some other stuff..." Robin cleared her throat. "Been missing you more than usual. No particular reason, I guess, since our last goodbye was only three days ago. Sometimes the distance between us just seems so impossibly far. But I was talking to one of my guys about a project, and something popped out of my mouth and I thought, that wasn't me—that was Robin talking. That was exactly what she'd say. And I realized it *was* part of you, in me, reaching out to help this guy. You've changed me, Robin—I carry little pieces of you around, so deep inside my heart I don't even know until I hear your words come out of my mouth. And maybe it's arrogant, but I like to hope you carry a little bit of me around, too. I can't hold your hand and touch your face, but maybe we can still touch across this distance—not physically, but in other, more important ways. Maybe—"

Cyril slammed his fork down on the table.

The words died on Robin's tongue. "Are you—"

"I don't want to hear this." He ripped the napkin out of his collar and swiped furiously at his hands.

It looked more like he *couldn't* hear it. "I'm sorry," she said, hearing the rasp of tears forming in her own voice.

He tossed the napkin onto the table and grabbed his utensils, attacking his steak with vicious concentration. "Pointless," he growled. "Stupid. Fucking. Words."

"I thought they were beautiful," Robin whispered.

"Then you're just like every other stupid bitch on the planet, aren't you."

Robin had never been slapped, but she was pretty sure this was what it felt like. Cyril had insulted her before—many times before—but never so directly.

This was the first time, however, that she saw the pain behind the violence.

She slipped the phone back into her purse. "You can call me whatever you want, but Tavis was your friend. His words matter."

"Words? Words are nothing. They're less than nothing. Words are for telling lies."

"Not everyone," she said, "is as cynical and jaded as you."

"This isn't about me. It's about Tavis. And I don't give a fuck what he said. I care what he *did*. I care that he had nothing—no family, at least not one that gave a shit, no money, no nothing—and worked his ass off to get through school and then boot camp. Not so he could make a million and retire, but because he wanted to do something to help people. He went to Afghanistan not once, not twice, but *three* times, voluntarily, because he wanted every one of those guys to get home in one piece. His dad—" Cyril's voice broke, finally, and he had to stop to breathe. He massaged his temples with one hand.

"Cyril." Robin reached across the table.

He jerked away from her touch. "No. His dad—you never met the guy, did you? His dad beat the shit out of him, and instead of growing into just another bully or asshole Tavis turned around and became the best—the best father any kid could ask for." Cyril flung a hand toward her. "And I'm sure he fucked pretty well, too."

She blinked. There was no rush of fury from within. "He did, yes."

Cyril looked up—startled, perhaps, by her calm—and then around at the other tables. A few people averted their eyes. "Fuck." He shifted in his seat. "I'm gonna—" He shifted again. The legs of the chair grated on the Spanish tile. "I'm gonna take a piss."

Robin watched, slightly open-mouthed, as he made his way to the doorway in the back. He turned sideways to get past a couple of tables, but everyone saw him coming and gave him plenty of space. The table nearest the restrooms was empty; as he passed it, Cyril reached out and knocked a chair out of the way.

The waitress appeared at her elbow. "Is everything all right?"

"Oh. Um… yes, I think so. I'm sorry, we're… a friend passed away. We were talking about him."

Sympathy flooded into the woman's expression. "Oh, gosh. I'm sorry. Well. Let me know if there's anything I can do."

Robin nodded and the woman moved to the next table, reassuring the other patrons that the remainder of their meal would continue undisturbed.

Robin ate a little more and then checked her cell phone, feeling suddenly conspicuous by herself in the middle of the dining floor. Particularly after Cyril had just drawn everyone's attention to their table.

What was he doing in there? Well, peeing, probably—Robin's eyeballs would have been floating if she'd drunk the two big glasses he'd downed. A second cell phone check told her he'd only been gone a minute or two. It seemed like much longer.

The bigger question was this: What was she still doing here? Why hadn't she stormed out? Maybe she should just get up and leave. It would take an hour or so, but she could walk home.

But she wasn't offended. She wasn't even angry, really. Not anymore.

With other people, Tav's death was always about them. Glennis cried about Tavis because it reminded her of her husband. Trinity and the other girls wept for a lost friend, and the realization that the ones they loved were mortal, too.

But Cyril? His pain was her own.

He came back as she was checking her cell a third time. It looked like he had splashed his face with water, but that didn't necessarily mean he'd been crying. He lowered himself into the chair without looking at her, lifted his stomach a couple of times, and ran a hand under each armpit to pluck out the bunched folds of his shirt.

"Are you okay?"

"Just dandy." He leaned forward as much as the table allowed, picked up his napkin, and tucked it back into his shirt.

They ate. Robin finished well before Cyril, although she continued to pick at the leftovers so he wouldn't feel like she was sitting there staring at him. He kept touching the edge of the plate with his left hand, as if he had to keep overriding the impulse to pick it up, set it on his stomach, and shovel. She could tell he was pacing himself—trying not to go too fast, too carelessly. He was doing okay; there were a few crumbs on his shirt, but that was all.

Finally, Cyril cleared the last few bits of food. The waitress came and loaded their dishes onto one arm, reserving Robin's plate for her free hand when she requested the leftovers to go.

The waitress returned with a compostable container and a dessert menu.

"Oh," Robin said. "I don't think—"

"Oh, come on." Cyril pulled the napkin out of his collar and used it to wipe the grease off his fingers. "You have to get something on your—"

Robin shushed him. The last thing she wanted right now was an off-key serenade from a bunch of wait-staff.

Cyril tossed the napkin onto the table and gave the dessert menu a once-over. "Okay, I'll have the chocolate cheesecake. She'll have a—"

"No, that's fine. We'll share."

Cyril looked confused. "Uh—okay."

"I mean, unless you—" She was about to say *unless you seriously planned on eating the entire thing yourself,* but cut herself off.

He cleared his throat. "Sure. Okay. We'll share." He nodded, handed the menu back, and the waitress went away.

"Sorry." She'd spent so much time growing up in countries where meals were served family-style that she often caught herself being a little more communal about food than most Americans were comfortable with. "Is that too weird for you?"

"No, I—just didn't think you'd want—"

"What, to share your food? I'm not your biggest fan, but I don't think you're contagious." She cocked her head to one side and raised an eyebrow. "I mean, we're friends now, right?"

He cleared his throat loudly. "I, uh, thought maybe that was off after I called you a bitch."

"I'm not saying it's okay, because it's totally not, but... you're right. Sometimes words are just lies."

"Here you are, folks." The waitress set the plate between them and held out two forks. "Enjoy."

"Oh. That does look good." Now that Robin saw it, she wished she'd ordered her own.

Cyril pushed the plate towards her with one finger. "Go ahead."

She used her fork to clip off the tip of the wedge. "Mm. Yeah. Delicious." She pushed it back.

He hesitated before carving off an equally small bite. Quickly, he returned the plate to her side of the table.

"*Now* you're making it weird." Was he worried he was going to inhale the whole thing next time she blinked? He just had no idea how to share. Robin picked up her chair and scooted it around the side of the table, so she sat at ninety degrees to him rather than across. She used the side of her fork to draw a line down the middle of the cheesecake, demarking two smaller wedges. "There. Better?"

"Sorry."

"No worries." Now that she was closer to him, she could smell the tang of his antiperspirant. A glance at his armpits confirmed that he was indeed sweating like a pig. Either his button-up shirt wasn't very breathable, or he was incredibly nervous. Probably both.

His arm brushed hers as they both went for another bite. "Sorry," he said again.

"Look, I'm not—" Her phone rang. "It's my mom. Hello?"

"Hi sweetie. Seth wanted to say good night—aaaand he just ran off to use the potty."

Robin laughed. "Any time he stops for five seconds he realizes he's got to go."

"How are you doing?" And the unspoken prepositional phrase: on your birthday?

"I'm fine."

The waitress, of course, chose that moment to bring the check. Cyril held out a hand for the slim leather folder. "Here you are. Thanks so much for coming."

"Oh," Glennis said, brightening a little. "Sounds like you're out somewhere?"

"Yeah, decided to get some dinner." She looked at Cyril and rolled her eyes, sticking out her tongue.

He pulled a credit card out of his shirt pocket and tucked it into the folder.

"With who? Trinity?"

The waitress tucked the bill under her arm. "Is there anything else I can get? Looks like you two won't be needing a box for that dessert!"

"No." Cyril frowned at the woman. "We're fine."

He kept his voice low, but not low enough.

In the silence that followed, Robin imagined her mother trying to tell herself this was none of her business and, ultimately, failing. "*Robin,*" she finally gasped. "what are you *doing?*"

Robin got up, quickly. "Excuse me."

Cyril picked up her box of leftovers. "I'll meet you outside."

Robin zigzagged her way back to the entrance, breathing deep as fresh, cool night air hit her in the face. "Mom," she said, and abruptly realized she had no excuses. No carefully constructed rationale. She just didn't care. "Don't freak out. He just wanted to take me out. So I wouldn't be alone."

"I would have done that if you'd let me, Robin."

There was no way to explain the difference, not even to herself. "Look, nothing's going on between us, okay?" It felt weird to even be denying that—as if there were even the remotest possibility it could be true. "It's just dinner."

"Oh, sweetie." She sighed. "Does *he* know that?"

"*Yes*, mom." God. Did her husband's death mean she had to live out her teenage years all over again? She felt self-conscious amidst all the loitering diners-to-be, so she headed out across the lot to Cyril's car. "Is Seth out of the bathroom or what?"

"I think so. Hold on." Glennis's breathing changed slightly as she walked through the house. "Sethie? Here's Mommy."

Robin felt her mouth curve into a smile. "Hey, how's my little man?"

"Good." He was always very terse on the phone.

She leaned against the back end of the Datsun, crossing her ankles.

"Did you and grandma have some fun at the park?"

"Mm hm."

"Good. I love you, sweetie. Sleep good, okay? Give Pengie a big hug for me."

"Kay."

There was a rustle and a laugh from Glennis as, most likely, Seth shoved the phone back at her face. "Sorry," she said, "I think that's all you get."

"I'm surprised he wanted to call at all. What time should I get him tomorrow?"

"Oh, I'll bring him home. I need to swing by that print place again. We'll take some lunch to the park after church and head out when he gets tired. I'll give you a call."

"Thanks, Mom."

Glennis was silent for a moment. But she couldn't just leave it at that, could she? No. Of course not. "I hope you know what you're doing, Robin."

Robin held the phone out and watched the little photo of her mother's face wink away. Then she turned and delivered a roundhouse punch to the Datsun's rear window in Seth-inspired slo-mo.

"Epic."

She stuffed the phone back into her purse, feeling like an idiot as Cyril huffed his way across the last twenty feet of asphalt.

He handed her the takeout box. "Before you pound it into a heap of molten slag, remember I don't have collision coverage."

Robin was too embarrassed to think of a witty reply, so she just watched as he unlocked the driver side door and got in. Wedging himself between the seat and the steering wheel was a serious ergonomic accomplishment.

"Coming?"

"Oh." She hurried around to the passenger side.

Cyril pulled out of the lot and turned south. As the Datsun curved around the freeway onramp, his bulk shifted to the left and he propped a hand against her headrest to keep himself from tipping into her space. "Sorry," he muttered.

"It's okay."

Robin had to admit this much: she didn't hate him. Not anymore. Simply not-hating him, though, did not mean she felt anything even resembling love. More like pity mixed with disgust and a certain amount of empathy, at least where their mutual loss was concerned. She didn't understand Cyril at all, but maybe that wasn't as necessary as she'd imagined.

She heard the echo of her mother's voice: *Does he know that?*

Who was she to know what was going on, deep down in the incomprehensible depths of his psyche? Probably best she didn't.

Cyril swerved into the left lane, muttering as he passed a driver doing about forty-five, then whipped back into the right lane just in time to make the exit to their side of town.

Pride was Cyril's most valuable commodity, and he'd sacrificed a great deal of it by asking her to dinner. He'd paid, of course, since the whole thing was kind of a birthday present, and she's split dessert with him as she would have with anyone who wasn't a complete stranger. But what did that casual intimacy mean to someone who hadn't been on a date—*ever?* What if her willingness to spend time with him had signaled, if not desire, then at least possibility?

She waited until he pulled into her driveway and set the emergency brake. "Cereal."

He cocked an eyebrow.

Then she realized what she'd said, and they both burst out laughing.

Robin wiped the corner of her eye. "Clearly I spend way too much time with that kid."

He pulled the takeout box off the dash and held it while she fumbled in her purse for the house keys. "You know, that's what Tav used to call me. When we were kids."

"Oh?" Her grin melted. "Oh, God, I had no idea. Do you want me to get him to stop?"

He shook his head. "It's fine."

"Okay. Just—let me know if it's not." She took the box from his hand. "You were going to say something?"

She sighed. "I feel silly for even thinking this now. I just—I wanted to make sure you knew. That... this isn't the kind of story where the soldier's widow falls for her husband's best friend." She glanced up, not quite meeting his eyes. "You do know that, right?"

Silence for a moment. A long moment.

Then he snorted. "How could I *not?* A forever-alone neckbeard like me and an attractive, intelligent woman? Trust me, I know my place."

She ought to have known better. "Cyril, you know that's not what I—"

"Isn't it? Isn't this where you put on your little sympathetic pout and pretend you're not secretly laughing at the thought of my being with a woman above a three?"

"Three? What does that even mean?"

"One to ten." He drew a line in the air and used his finger to punctuate the lower end. "Three."

She gaped. "Are you serious? You give women *numbers?*"

"At least I'm honest. Which is more than I can say for your kind."

"My kind." Normally that would have been a reference to the color of her skin. But from Cyril? "You're sitting here ranking women like—like bitches at a dog show, and you think *my kind* are, what, dishonest? You put a dog in a cage, he doesn't give you love. He does what he needs to get a bone. Fuck you." Robin shoved the car open and had one foot on the ground when she turned back. "Is that really what you think women are like? What you think *I'm* like? I mean, really?"

"No."

Not exactly the comeback Robin had expected. "What the hell is that supposed to mean?"

He frowned at the seat she had half-vacated. "It's not what you're like. It's how I am."

Like, what, she was supposed to feel sorry for him? She got out of the car. "I'm sorry, Cyril. I'm sorry you're like this and if I could help you I would, but your problems are too big and too deep for me right now. I've got all I can handle at the moment." She tossed the takeout box onto the empty passenger seat. "Keep the leftovers. I'm sure you'll enjoy them more than me."

Robin marched around the front end of the car. She was followed by a methodic squeak as he cranked the window down.

"Nine," he barked. "In case you were wondering."

22

WHEN THE SUN PEEKED over the hills, Robin wrapped her hair in a lavender scarf, pulled on her rattiest pair of maternity jeans, and dumped her grouting supplies into the back of her truck. The tool belt seemed inadvisable at this point, but she added it anyway. Then she got her tile saw out, loaded it into the truck bed along with everything else, and drove down the street.

She pounded on Cyril's door until he answered, wearing nothing but his standard pair of black pajama pants. "Thought you were the fucking FBI," he growled, squinting at the five-gallon bucket dangling from her right arm. "What—"

"I can't fix you. But I can fix your bathroom." She squeezed around him before he could shut the door in her face.

She was using her foot to push his dirty laundry out of the bathroom when his silhouette loomed in the bedroom doorway. "Hey," she said. "Did Tavis leave a bag of grout mix around here? Or did he run out after he did the shower?"

Cyril just looked at her.

She put her hands on her hips. "If I need to run to the hardware store I'd like to know now."

He nodded toward the wall on the other side of his bed.

Robin went around the mattress, kicked a blanket, some candy wrappers, and a few empty soda bottles out of the way, and unearthed a twenty-five-pound bag of sanded grout next to a stack of leftover tile. "This'll do." She went into the bathroom to take stock of the tile, many of which had come unglued, probably from a combination of dampness and the daily weight of Cyril's feet. She squatted and flipped a couple over; Tavis hadn't done the best job gluing, so between redoing that and adding grout, they'd hold up all right. There were a couple of edge pieces she wanted to re-cut, too.

Cyril was still standing in the middle of the bedroom when she emerged.

She grabbed a stack of tiles and gestured toward the door as she headed for it. "Gonna set up my saw on the tailgate so I don't cover your floor with dust."

"Robin."

She stopped. Why did that sound so strange to her ears? She turned to face him. "I think that might be the first time you've ever used my name."

"Why are you doing this?"

"I just told you." She pointed at the bathroom door. "*That's* something I can fix. And yeah, I know I'm pregnant, okay? A little low-impact carpentry isn't gonna hurt."

"Here." He pointed at the floor. "Why are you here? Why do you keep coming back? Do you think I'm going to magically transform into someone you like? Because that's not going to happen. What you see is what you get."

"Tavis kept coming back."

"So? You're not him."

She shrugged.

"God, you're crazy. What if I just say no?"

"Go ahead. Lock me out." She took the tile and went outside.

After she'd grabbed her bucket of adhesive and a spatula, Robin filled her bucket from the outside spigot and tried the front door. It was open. Cyril was on the couch pecking at his new laptop, still looking bleary-eyed. He'd put a shirt on. "I'll be in here a while," she told him. "You want to shower first?"

He considered a moment before shaking his head.

Robin shrugged and went to work with the adhesive. When she came back out, Cyril was gone. Puzzled, she went out into the driveway and saw that his car was also missing, two grooves in the gravel where he'd edged the Datsun around her truck. Well, whatever.

A while later she heard him come back in, his footsteps creaking on the kitchen floorboards. The water went on and then off again.

The tile she'd re-glued would have to wait at least twenty-four hours before grouting, but she'd filled the sections around the toilet and the outer edges of the floor. The water in the bucket was now a cloudy gray, so she tossed the sponge in and hauled it into the living room. "Hey, do you have an electric fan anywhere? It'll cut down on the drying time."

Cyril was unpacking groceries from a few paper bags. "Uh." He scratched the side of his face. "Maybe the back of the bedroom closet somewhere. You want me to, uh." He glanced at the bucket.

She looked down. "Nope." She took it outside, rinsed and refilled it, and hauled it back to the bathroom, where she set it in the shower before checking Cyril's closet. There was a lot of crap—a lot—but no fan that she could see. And she didn't want to go digging.

As she finished the remainder of the grouting project, she could hear Cyril still in the kitchen, doing something that involved rattling an aluminum bowl. His footsteps were easy to track, and he let out a heavy grunt every time he reached up or bent over. Making himself breakfast, probably.

Hanging the mirror and medicine cabinet were up next on her mental list, so she washed up in the sink and checked around for any hardware Tavis might have stashed. His craftsmanship might have been amateur, but she could always count on him to plan ahead.

The brackets for the mirror were in the drawer to the left of the sink, still inside the packaging. Medicine cabinets usually came with their own hardware, so she tipped it forward and ran a hand over the back and then opened it up to check inside.

Two rows of pill bottles and blister packs stared out at her. Not just your average household painkillers, either. Diuril, Miralax, Zoloft, Lipitor, potassium gluconate, naproxen, Prevacid…

Robin shut the cabinet. This was none of her business.

Then she remembered what she was looking for and opened it again. The hardware was taped down in the bottom right corner. As she used a nail to pry out the little plastic bag, her eyes wandered back to the collection of drugs.

She picked up her phone, opened the browser, and tapped in "Diuril." It was for blood pressure. Miralax was for constipation.

Totally, definitely none of her business.

Her phone trilled just as she had finished wrangling the mirror into place, which was convenient since she was going to need a little breather before tackling the medicine cabinet. She sucked in a breath and answered. "Hey, Mom. Heading home?"

"Just packing up at the park. You sound strange, can you hear me?"

She flipped the toilet seat down, stood on it, and opened the window. "I'm in the bathroom. It's kind of echo-y." The clean air was so refreshing she pressed her nose against the screen and breathed.

"Oh, that's it. Well—just so you know, I suspect someone may be a-s-l-e-e-p when we arrive."

"Don't count on it. He can keep himself awake now."

"I've got some nice, calming music."

Robin laughed. "Do your best. See you in forty-five?"

"Mm, probably at least an hour. We're not quite picked up here and I think there's traffic."

"Okay, drive safe." She clicked the phone off, stuck it in her pocket, and packed her things back into the toolbox. The medicine cabinet could wait until she came back to finish the tile.

When she opened the bathroom door, the scent of chocolate rolled in like a warm wave. She followed it into the kitchen. "I didn't know you baked."

Cyril jerked slightly. "Damn it." He was hunched over something on the counter.

Robin set down her toolbox and went around to the other side to see what he was working on.

It was a cake. Round and two-layered and all chocolate. He had a cone of yellow frosting in one hand and had just finished writing *Happy Birthday Robin* on the top. Well—that was what it was supposed to say. Now it read *Happy Birthday Robim.*

"I always did think my name was too common."

Cyril used a butter knife to lift off the second hump. "There." He put the knife down and wiped his hands on his shirt. "Sorry."

"For..."

"Last night. I fucked up." He started to wipe his hands again, then looked down and saw that his shirt was covered with flour and frosting. "I *am* fucked up. I thought I could—I don't know." He reached over one shoulder and pulled the shirt off over his head. He balled it up and flung it toward the bedroom door. "I honestly just wanted you to have a good time. Not—any of that other shit."

"So... you baked a cake."

"Yeah."

Robin looked at the cake. "Probably should've just done that to begin with."

"Yeah."

She opened the cupboard and got out two plates. "Well, let's see if it tastes as good as it smells."

Cyril took the plates and waved her toward the dining table. He rinsed the butter knife off and used it to carve out a single thick slice, added a fork, and set it in front of her.

Robin helped herself to a generous first bite. "This is fantastic."

"Nobody bakes a better cake than a fat guy."

"I wish you wouldn't—"

"What? Say I'm fat? Because guess what?"

"No, I—never mind."

"God damn it. I just—" Cyril cut himself off with a low growl. "I'm gonna go take a shower."

"Um, okay. Wait—" She held up a finger. "Try and keep off the center tiles if you can. Put down a towel or something, too. And keep the water, um, low in the shower, so it doesn't—"

"Got it." He slammed the bedroom door.

Cyril came back out in a clean shirt. Or at least a different shirt. He sat down across from her and watched her scrape the last crumbs off the plate.

"So," she said. "Not that I care what you think of me, but you were wrong about me not valuing Tav's service."

"Look, I said I was—"

"I know, I know." She got up and went back into the kitchen. "I just need to say it, okay?"

He rolled his eyes. "Fine."

She pointed at the cake. "I'm gonna have another slice. You want one?" He shook his head, so she shrugged and helped herself. "My dad was a naval officer, you know? If I was looking for a Navy guy, I'd've had my pick. I've known dozens of guys just like Tavis: dedicated to serving God, country, and family." She opened the fridge. "You got any—ah." She pulled out a quart of milk, which, by the looks of it, he'd bought expressly for baking. There was one plastic cup in the dish drainer, so she filled it and brought it back to the table. "This really is good cake."

"My mom's recipe."

"Mm." She chewed and swallowed. "So that's the thing with guys in the service. Good men, but family comes third. Even if you make it work, it's rough. The time away, moving around, everything. I lived that life with my dad, and it was good, but—it wasn't what I wanted for myself. I wanted someone who'd be there, for me, for our kids. In the flesh."

"So... you ended up with Tavis in *spite* of the fact that he saved lives and served his country."

"Cal Poly doesn't even *have* a Navy ROTC program." She shook her head, smiling. "I mean, what are the chances? It was fate."

"So... you're saying if a slob like me wrote you letters like that, you'd have picked me over Tavis?"

She snorted "I didn't say *that*. I mean, it's not—it's not about the pretty words."

"Isn't it?"

She rolled her eyes and ate another bite of cake. "Cyril, look at me."

His eyes made a quick sweep from head to foot before he cocked an eyebrow.

"I don't *fit*." She held up a hand to head off the obligatory wisecrack. "And yeah, I know *you* don't fit. What I mean is, most of my childhood was spent in places where my defining trait was being 'the American.' But back here in America, I'm the black girl. Unless you're asking my cousins in Louisiana, in which case I'm apparently 'too white.'" She started ticking the list off on her fingers. "I'm an attractive female with the fashion sense of a lumberjack. Not quite a single mom, not quite a housewife, not quite a career woman. I work in an industry dominated by men. I'm a Christian who believes in evolution and a woman's right to choose. I don't know. Sometimes I feel like I've spent my entire life... in between."

He grunted. "Yeah, I can sorta see that."

"But, you know, as a kid? It didn't matter. Because I had my dad. When he looked at me, I knew exactly who I was. His daughter."

"And then he croaked."

His word choices didn't bother her anymore. She heard the underlying sentiment. "I felt so lost. I'd look in the mirror, and all I saw was this random collection of odd parts. But then Tav—" Robin cut herself off. Swallowed hard. "He saw me. The black girl and the American and the foreigner and whatever. He saw all those things. But beyond that, when he wrote? I was always just... me."

Cyril grunted again, a kind of disinterested acknowledgement.

Robin watched him watch her eat another bite. "You on a diet or something?" It was unkind, but she didn't feel like he deserved a whole lot of consideration right now. Even if the cake was good.

He shook his head. "It's for you."

"If you insist."

He shifted, looking uncomfortable. "I have, though. Lost weight."

"Oh. Good for you? I guess?" He didn't look any different to her. Was she supposed to be impressed?

"From..." He waved a hand toward the window. "Picking Seth up."

"From walking three blocks?" Did he literally spend his entire life parked on that couch?

"And... I cook better. When he's here."

Robin put her fork down. "Are you trying to say something? Because if you are, you should just say it. I have no idea where you're going here."

"Just... I'm sorry. Not only for last night. For... everything."

"Everything?"

"Shit. I dunno." He looked over her shoulder. At the sink. At the wall.

"For... getting myself into legal trouble. After Tavis died, I... didn't think it mattered."

"You didn't think what mattered? Your *life?*"

He shrugged.

"That's... really sad."

He used a fingernail to pick at a crack in the oak tabletop. "Just. Thank you. For not..." He frowned. "For... giving me access to Seth. You don't have to. But it... makes a difference."

"Oh."

"God. That's a shitty way of saying it. I fucking—" He let out a low growl. "I suck at being... genuine. Okay? I try, and then I fail and I—I hurt people. You. But here's the thing. I like your kid and he makes me feel like maybe the world isn't completely fucked. And he makes me laugh. So yeah. It's fun to hang out with him. Fun like I used to have with Tav. And— you let me spend time with him, so I—I appreciate it. Also the bathroom." He breathed out a sigh of relief, like he'd just staggered across a finish line.

Robin laughed. "You sure you don't want any cake?"

"I really, really want cake."

She took the remainder home. Cyril had zero saran wrap in the house, so she set the plate on the passenger seat and drove carefully. The grade from the street to her driveway was steep enough to be risky, so she parked at the curb and carried it to the front door.

She was turning the key in the lock when she glanced down and saw a bit of white paper caught down behind the bushes lining the front face of the house. Plenty of stray candy wrappers and pizza delivery advertisements had accumulated back there as well, but this bit of detritus looked familiar. She set the cake on the railing, jogged down the steps, and wedged herself just far enough between the porch and the bush to reach it with the tips of her fingers.

It was the paper Cyril had read his little speech from, a week or so ago. Robyn grinned as she smoothed it over the firm curve of her stomach.

The actual words he'd spoken that night would have taken up perhaps a quarter of a page, but there were so many cross-outs and rewrites that his scrawled handwriting went all the way to the bottom of the page, one final line curving up around the side. Trying to puzzle out his rough draft seemed rude, so she folded the note into quarters and slipped it into the inner pocket of her purse. Next to Tav's envelope.

Cyril's composition didn't hold a candle to even the briefest note from Tavis. And yet—because of who Cyril was—precisely because he was just *not* that kind of person—his awkward little speech was one of the nicest gifts she had ever received.

She picked up the cake. Maybe this was Cyril's way of being a little bit of Tavis, too.

23

FOR THE PAST COUPLE OF WEEKS, while Cooke had been in residence, Robin had made a point of showing up after he'd left for work and leaving before he came home. He was friendly enough, but he struck her as the kind of guy who'd appreciate her staying out of his private space. So when she let herself in on Monday morning, she was surprised to hear the bedroom door kick back against the wall.

She waited in the living room, adding "door stopper" to her mental to-do list.

"Hey," he said, when he appeared in the doorway. "I was hoping to catch you before I went back north."

"Did I miss something else?" He'd already emailed her about the malfunctioning outlet next to the sink.

He cocked his head to one side and grinned. "I wanted to beg you to come work your magic on my house. I'd get down on my knees, but, you know."

Robin looked at the floor. "That's flattering, but I'm sure you could find—"

"Oh come on." He stumped past her into the living area, where she'd arranged a couch and a recliner on top of a short-pile rug, all in rich reds and browns. He positioned himself in front of the couch and flopped backward into the cushions. "Did you think I wouldn't notice?"

She bit her lip, then shrugged and smiled. "Most people wouldn't."

"This is the first couch I have *ever* been able to escape from with my dignity intact." He tapped the recliner with the end of a crutch. "That one, too. Did you measure me on the sly, or are you just that good at eyeballing?"

"Not you—your office chair." She'd taken two inches off the couch legs; the recliner had been perfect just as she'd found it, not too deep or soft.

"Oh, of course. And that little trolley thing? Oh my God, I can't believe I never thought of that. I don't know where you got it, but can you have one shipped to my house?"

"Uh, sure." It was just a little stainless steel dining cart on casters; she'd thought it would make it easier for him to get food from the kitchen to his bedroom or the table. "Glad you like it."

"I will seriously pay you whatever you want to come up and give my house a makeover. I'll put you up in a hotel, a rental house, whatever."

"I'm flattered, but honestly I just... I can't. Not right now."

"Oh—no, no, of course not. Whenever you're ready. Like, what, six months? Is that enough? Sorry, I know absolutely nothing about babies."

For a moment, Robin was speechless.

Cooke grinned. "I may be a basement-dwelling computer nerd, but I'm not blind."

"I—I'm sorry," she stammered. "I didn't want it to—"

"Your body, your business. I figure if you're here—hell, if your husband's okay with you being here—then you're fine." He hesitated. "You are fine, right? I mean, everything's okay with..." He nodded toward her stomach.

"Yes, he's fine. We're both fine."

"Oh good. God." He chuckled. "For a second I thought I'd put my foot in my—"

The doorbell rang.

They each gave the other an inquiring look. Cooke shook his head; it wasn't for him.

"I'll get it." Robin stepped around the end of the couch and opened the door.

Two women in casual professional attire stood on the front stoop. They were both blond-haired and blue-eyed; the shorter one held a clipboard.

"I'm sorry," Robin said. "I don't think we're interested in whatever—"

The woman with the clipboard smiled. "We're not selling anything. My name is Stephanie Hopkins, and this is—"

"What the hell are you two doing here?" Cooke demanded. "This is my private residence."

Robin stepped back, allowing him a clear line of sight from the couch.

The taller woman leaned in slightly. "I apologize, Mr. Cooke. We're actually here to talk to Ms. Matheson." She looked at Robin. "My name is Jennifer McDonald. Steph and I—"

"About *what?*" Cooke interjected. "She's not involved with any of this."

McDonald gave him a slightly pained smile. "Ms. Matheson's connection to both you and Mr. Blanchard makes it necessary to ask a few questions. We thought she might prefer to be approached here, rather than at home where her son might be present."

"My son?" All of Robin's internal alarm bells went off. "Exactly who are you?"

McDonald shot another glance at Cooke. He shrugged and she pulled a laminated ID card out of her purse. "Steph and I are with the FBI office in Los Angeles."

Robin put a hand over her mouth. "Oh. Um." She'd worried this might happen, but when Cyril had gotten out of jail and a week had passed with no knock at her door, her concerns had faded. And now they were here. What had he told her? What was she supposed to do? What if they asked about Tavis?

Hopkins put a hand out, touching Robin's arm. "It's okay," she said. "It's our job to make inquiries. May we come in?"

Robin looked at Cooke. It was his condo, after all.

"Up to you," he said. "You don't have to talk to them."

"And then we'll get a subpoena," McDonald said, as if it weren't any skin off her nose whether or not Robin wanted to do this the hard way. She pulled out a phone and checked the time.

Robin didn't want to get involved in any of this. She certainly didn't want to get into any legal trouble or hire a lawyer. Maybe if she let them ask their questions and answered honestly, they'd realize she had nothing to do with Cyril's activities. "Okay." She looked at Cooke, who was getting to his feet again. "Do you mind if we use the dining table?"

He beckoned her over with an upward nod. "Look," he said, when she approached, "they've been very helpful and unobtrusive, at least where my company is concerned. But this is the FBI. They are not on your team. Okay?"

Robin nodded.

"So if you're going to talk to them, at least record it. Do you know how to do that?"

"Um, can I just start a video on my phone…?"

He shook his head. "It'll burn through your memory in five minutes. Run into the bedroom and grab my phone. I've got an app installed."

Robin did as he directed. It wasn't on the nightstand, or his desk… She started looking under things, then pulled open the nightstand drawer and found it there.

Hopkins and McDonald were in the kitchen, seated at the four-person breakfast table. Cooke had pulled himself up onto the section of the counter that she'd lowered, feet dangling. He held out a hand for the phone and then spent a minute or two tapping at the screen. "You want me to sit in on this?"

Her first instinct was to say no, that she'd be fine on her own. Truthfully, though, she was scared. "Would you mind?"

"Not at all. Here. It's running." He handed her the phone, grabbed his crutches, and slid to the floor.

Robin was gratified to see him pull out the nearest chair and sit without difficulty. The table setup had taken the most work—she'd cut the chair legs down and added casters to the bottom, but then they'd rolled so smoothly over the tile that she knew he'd have a hard time sitting in one without it sliding away. So she'd tried a couple of rugs, settling finally on a short-pile rectangle in geometric browns. When she came around and sat opposite him, he flashed a crooked smile as if to say, *Yes, I noticed that, too.*

Robin set the phone in the middle of the table. "Okay. Let's get this over with."

Hopkins let the pages fall back into place. "Thank you for speaking with us, Ms. Matheson. First, on behalf of both of us, we just wanted to say how thankful we are for your husband's service, and how sorry we are about his death."

Robin's mouth went dry. Her eyes focused on the phone in the center of the table, but she could see Cooke in her peripheral vision, his face frozen in a half-grimace of confusion.

The silence stretched, until McDonald cleared her throat. "I apologize if—"

"I'm sorry," Robin blurted. She was, suddenly, overwhelmed with guilt at having lied—even if only by omission—to this adorable little man. Who had she thought she was fooling, anyway? She covered her face with her hands. "He was killed in Afghanistan, almost six months ago. I didn't say anything because—because—"

"Because was none of my business," Cooke finished.

"I'm sorry." She forced herself to look at him. "I'm so sorry."

He seemed to understand, somehow, that he wasn't the one she was apologizing to. "It's okay," he said quietly. "You do what you need to survive."

She nodded. Drew in a deep breath. And turned to the women at the table. "Okay. Go ahead."

Hopkins flipped the first page of the clipboard up, let it flutter back into place, and let out a sigh. "Essentially, Ms. Matheson, we're here to determine whether your involvement with Cyril Blanchard extends to his online activities, or if it's purely romantic in nature."

"I don't know anything about—" Robin stopped herself with a short *ha*. "Um, I'm sorry, is this some kind of joke?"

McDonald's mouth flattened into a grim line. "This is absolutely not a joke."

Robin looked at Cooke, who looked as confused as she felt. "You're— I'm sorry—you're actually suggesting I have a *romantic* relationship with Cyril?"

McDonald exchanged a glance with her partner. They might have been playing poker for all that look revealed. "You deny that this is the case?"

Robin snorted. "Um, yes."

Hopkins consulted her clipboard again, frowning. "You've spent a lot of time at his house since Mr. Matheson's death."

Robin looked between the two women. "How do you even know that?" This was getting weird. Were they spying on Cyril? Or her, too?

"I'm not at liberty to discuss how we obtain our information. But you acknowledge it's true?"

"Well, yeah." Robin's pulse quickened. The correct thing to do would probably be to end the discussion and get a lawyer. But if she did that, they'd leave thinking she had some weird thing going on with Cyril, and then what? Would they station a cop by her house? Start following her around town? Pull her over for not using her blinker a full 100 feet before a stop? Find some excuse to cuff her and haul her off to jail? "Of course I've spent time at his house. He was Tav's friend. He's also my son's friend. Most of the time I'm just picking Seth up or dropping him off."

"And yet he's visited your house a few times as well."

"Since you took all his stuff, yeah."

The FBI agents looked at her for a long, steady moment. Like they were expecting her to volunteer some sort of incriminating evidence. Robin had no idea what that might be. Whatever they thought they had was ridiculous. She had nothing to hide.

McDonald tucked a stray bit of hair behind her ear. "You and Mr. Blanchard went out for dinner, did you not? Last Saturday. Was your son involved then?" The hint of smugness in her tone said she knew perfectly well that Seth had not been present.

"No, it was my birthday and he didn't want me to spend it alone." This was becoming absurd. "Look, I don't care what you think—my *involvement* with Cyril is based completely on his relationship with my son and my husband. We might at the very least be friends, but we are *not* romantically involved. Have not been, never will be. Period."

McDonald looked at her partner, as if passing the interrogation baton. Hopkins nodded and turned her ice blue gaze on Robin. "I'm sorry," she said, "but we find that very difficult to believe." She flipped through the pages on her clipboard, selected three, and pulled them out. "Do you deny receiving these emails?"

"Emails?" Robin leaned forward and realized, abruptly, that they'd gotten them. Tav's notes. They'd gone into her private email or through Cyril's computer or something, and they had taken them out and *read* them. She snatched the papers from the woman's hand. They were only copies, of course, but she couldn't bear to have this woman touching them. "You have no right to these," she hissed. "They have *nothing* to do with Cyril. These are between my husband and me."

A crease formed between McDonald's eyebrows. Whether her confusion was genuine or feigned, Robin couldn't tell. "Your husband was killed six months ago, Ms. Matheson. Surely you don't think he's writing from beyond the grave…?"

"I'm not an idiot." She folded the pages in half and then in half again, slipping them into the back pocket of her jeans. "He wrote these before he died. Cyril just triggered the program that sends them to me." She looked at Cooke for support. "That's—that's totally possible, right?"

He nodded. "Fairly simple to arrange, actually."

The look the agents shared this time was clear: Robin's response was completely unanticipated, and neither one had any idea how to react. Hopkins mouthed a silent word; McDonald returned a shrug and then shook her head.

When McDonald turned her attention back to Robin, her expression softened. "Is that… Is that what he told you?"

Robin's stomach dropped over the edge of an eighty-foot rollercoaster.

Hopkins licked her lips. "Ms. Matheson, we…"

"Don't fuck with me," Robin said. "Don't you dare."

"What kind of proof do you have?" This came from Cooke.

Hopkins pulled a few more pieces of paper off her clipboard and passed them to Cooke. They were covered in what looked like code. "Obviously we can't discuss our data collection methods. But I can say without any reasonable doubt that Mr. Blanchard typed those emails himself, at home, sitting in front of his own computer. As recently as— well"—she flipped to a paper at the bottom of the stack—"yesterday."

Robin looked at Cooke, who was scrutinizing the papers with a deep frown. Finally, he looked up and shrugged. "This could be faked," he admitted, "but it's an awful lot to go through for... I'm not sure what."

"No," Robin said. "Cyril did not—this is ridiculous. There's no way he could—" She pushed back the chair and stood, reaching into her back pocket for her phone. She held it up. "This is Tavis. This is what he sounds like. I *know* my husband. Cyril—there's no way he could—"

"Ms. Matheson—"

"This is just you trying to get me on your side, isn't it?" She backed up, past Cooke, through the kitchen.

"Robin," he said quietly.

"*No.*" She pointed to the agents. "You want me to give you information or tell you he's a horrible person or I don't know what. But I don't have anything. I don't know anything. Okay? He hangs out with my son. He took me to dinner on my birthday, because Tavis is gone, and I *don't believe you.*"

McDonald rose, holding out a hand. "Ms. Matheson, please calm down. Let's sit down and—"

Robin fled.

SHE DIDN'T KNOCK. She could see Cyril through the blinds on his living room window, sitting on the couch with his laptop on his stomach.

For a moment she just stood there, watching, not knowing what to think or feel. Then he looked up, and she couldn't quite see him well enough to meet his eyes.

Robin stuck her hand into her back pocket and pulled out the printouts of Tav's posthumous letters. She slammed them against the single-pane window. It rattled in the frame.

"Did you do this?" she demanded, raising her voice to carry through the window. "Did you pretend to be him?"

He didn't say "What?" or ask if she had lost her mind. He just sat there, unmoving. Then he lifted a hand and shut his laptop.

Robin wanted to scream "Fuck you" or "I hope you burn in hell." Instead all she could do was burst into tears. "Why? Why would you? Why would you do that? Why would *anyone* do something like that?"

She stood there at the window, crying loudly, until she heard the door open.

"No." She stumbled backward, turned to flee, but he was surprisingly quick and suddenly his hand was locked around her wrist and she flailed and struck his face, but nowhere near as hard as she wanted to, and it was all like some horrible dream where she just couldn't quite find the strength to break free. She let out something between a cry and a scream.

"Would you shut up?" he said. "Jesus. Calm down."

She tried to pull away again, and this time he let her go. She stumbled backward and then stood there, rubbing her wrist, unable to see anything of him except a giant pale blur. "I don't understand," she said. "I don't understand why you would pretend to be him. After he died? How *could* you?"

"I'm sorry," he said.

She didn't care if he was sorry. She wanted it to all make sense. Wanted the pieces to fit together in a neat, rational way. "Just tell me why."

"I've seen plenty of his letters to you over the years. Words are—it's what I do. Copying his style was... it felt like having him back, a little."

"That's why you did it? To feel like he was here?" That was crazy.

"No." He shook his head. "No, I... you..." He paused. "At the cemetery, when I..."

"The pills," she realized. They had rattled, and he'd looked down, and she had known that he'd known. "You knew."

"You just seemed so sad. So... incredibly sad. And... you would never... nothing I could say would make it any better, because I'm... me. I didn't even think I'd ever see you again. But I thought... Tavis. Tavis could always make you smile."

She stood open-mouthed, staring at him. Her vision cleared slightly. He was looking at the ground.

It made sense. A certain sort of sick and twisted sense.

"I thought you were good," she whispered. "Underneath."

He lifted one shoulder, slightly. "It worked, didn't it?"

"Oh, so I should *thank* you?"

He didn't answer. Didn't lift his eyes.

"How long were you planning on doing this?"

"As long as it seemed like you needed... him."

"Forever."

She didn't know what she hated more: the fact that he had done it, or the fact that she hadn't been able to tell. Cyril was right: she hadn't even thought to question the emails because she had so badly needed them. Without the FBI's tactical blunder, she might never have known. She would have continued to save those letters, treasure them, memorize them, and read them to her sons.

Robin bent over and vomited.

"Jesus," Cyril said. "Let me get you some water. Stay—"

"I don't want anything from you." She dragged the back of her arm across her mouth. "Except to stay the hell away from me. And my child." She crumpled the printouts, dropped them in the puddle of half-digested breakfast cereal and ground them into the gravel with her heel. "I hope they lock you away for life. I hope you starve."

Driving home, blinded by tears, she remembered the letter in her purse.

Was that one real? It had her name on the front, in Tav's handwriting. It was sealed. But it certainly wasn't out of the realm of possibility that Cyril had faked that, too.

She almost circled the block, to go back and demand an answer. But how would she know if he was telling the truth? He'd been stringing her along for months and she'd never so much as suspected a thing. If he could do that—he was capable of anything.

Then again, why would he fake a final good-bye letter when he was also planning to do the emails? Unless he was telling the truth about why he'd done it, and hadn't decided to do the emails until after delivering Tav's final letter. In which case, the letter was probably genuine. It seemed like something Tavis would do. Then again, so were the emails.

God.

She couldn't even rip it open and see for herself, because she no longer trusted herself to know the difference. And if it *was* real—she'd never forgive herself for reading his last words like this, in a vain attempt to cleanse herself of Cyril's filth. For now, she left it where it was.

At home, she parked and went inside, past the television, past the piano, and upstairs to her bedroom. She dropped to her knees beside the bed and pulled out the final box of letters. She yanked out the stack of fresh, clean, neatly folded printouts and tore them in half. Then she crumpled them and threw them toward the door.

Her cell phone. She had it in her hand, ready to delete every single email from existence—

But what if she needed them for evidence? She had no idea what scenario would result in her needing to prove that Cyril had sent her a bunch of emails in her dead husband's name, and surely the FBI had everything, but... well, who knew. She didn't trust any of them. Not Cyril, not the agents, nobody.

So she pulled up the folder she'd created for the counterfeit emails, three of them still unread, and changed the title from *Tav* to *Lies*. She hid it from view.

Enough of Cyril. She had wasted too much time, too much emotion, too much caring on him.

Robin reached back into the box of letters, *Tav's* letters, and pulled out one he had written by hand, in his neat little chicken scratch capitals. She would read them all. Here, right now. Or as many as she could get through before she had to pick Seth up. From preschool. He would be devastated. How was she going to explain that?

It didn't matter. She would try. He would be sad, or angry, or both. She would hug him and tell him it was going to be all right. And, eventually, it would.

She unfolded the letter, smoothing it carefully with one hand.

Do you have any idea how weird it feels to be called a hero? Everyone thinks "strength" means living in a desert for months on end and carrying a gun and then stitching people up when they get shot or blown up.

You know what strong is? Strong is carrying another human being inside of you for nine months like it was nothing. It's giving birth to the most beautiful baby boy in the universe. It's staying up to breastfeed all night and all day and all night again. It's being able to do that alone, because your husband is on the opposite side of the world and who knows when—or if—he'll be coming home—

Robin folded the letter—quickly, carefully—and slipped it back into the envelope.

You know how you were complaining the other day about movies? How, unless it's a chick flick, the dude is always the protagonist? I didn't say anything then, but I was thinking it: did you know that you're the protagonist in our story? Half the time I'm just playing backup. You're the real star of the show. You may be quiet, and maybe not many people can tell, but you have the real talent, the brains, the courage. All I know how to do is look cool and play a couple of backup chords, but I'm gonna do that as best and as long as I can, no matter—

Were all his letters about death? Had she just never noticed before, or perhaps simply not wanted to see? Or was she reading too much into them now, after the fact?

She pulled the next one from the middle of the stack.

I'll never forget the first time I made you laugh. I was surprised to see your teeth, because – and don't take this the wrong way – most people with a mouth as crowded as yours get braces. If not as a kid, then as soon as they can afford them as an adult. But your father must have told you how beautiful they are, and you must have believed him. I like to think they're all shoving for room, vying for a place in your big, beautiful smile.

It's addictive, you know – your laugh. Once you threw your head back and let out that completely unselfconscious chortle – once that happened, all I wanted was to make it happen again and again.

I'm not a funny guy. I mean, I can be, but most people don't really see me that way. I don't always get everything right, especially not face-to-face, but when I write to you, I imagine you reading, and I hope more than anything that these ridiculous little words occasionally make you smile.

Robin closed her eyes. She held the note to her nose and breathed. *That* was him. Cyril could write like him, yes. But not like *that*.

She felt tears coming and quickly, carefully folded the letter and filed it back into place. These were going to have to last the rest of her life. She couldn't afford tear stains. Strange, how even in the midst of grief, her brain still had room for these practical thoughts.

Robin reached for another letter, but couldn't even read the address on the envelope. It didn't matter. She had most of the letters half-memorized anyway. She held the paper against her chest, then slipped it into her shirt, against her skin.

It was like losing him all over again for the first time.

She was tucked into a fetal position on the carpet when the doorbell rang. The baby jolted, and she had half-risen before she realized it was either the FBI or Cyril, and she didn't want to talk to either.

She jerked upright at a noise in the hall, heart catapulting into her throat. But it was not an intruder. Not a malicious one, anyway. "Mom?"

Glennis stopped in the doorway, taking in the scene of her bleary-eyed daughter surrounded by piles of Tav's old letters. "What's going on?" she asked, slowly.

Robin didn't think she had any moisture left, but she burst into fresh tears. Glennis put her arms out and Robin lunged up and forward, falling into her mother's embrace. She pressed her eyes into the older woman's bony shoulder.

After a while, the sobs stopped, or at least tapered off. Glennis put her hands on Robin's shoulders and pulled her back just far enough to see her face. "What on earth happened?"

Robin pulled the bottom of her shirt up to wipe her nose. "Why are you even here?"

"Cyril called. He said you needed me."

Part Three
Spring

24

OBIN WEDGED HER PHONE between her thigh and the end of the pew, so nobody could tell she wasn't listening to the sermon. She opened her little collection of wedding photos and tapped on her favorite: Tavis looking at her as if there weren't another human being on the planet, an effect accentuated by the fact that it was a group shot of the wedding party. She used a thumb and forefinger to zoom in, cutting out Cyril's smirk on the left.

On the right was a girl Robin hadn't seen hide nor hair of since about a month after the wedding. When Robin had asked her best friend to be her maid of honor, Suzannah had been genuinely taken aback. "*Me?*" she'd said, and then, trying to backtrack over the awkwardness, "I mean—I guess I just didn't think we were *that* close."

That was when Robin had known it wasn't her itinerant childhood, or her introversion, or the color of her skin. She'd worked damn hard to make friends in college, and ultimately that look of embarrassed shock was all her efforts had earned. Whatever component it was that allowed women to form bonds of sisterhood, Robin was missing it. Not once in her life had she ever been her best friend's best friend.

That realization had stung, but it hadn't been devastating—because she'd had Tavis. Somehow, even through his gregarious extroversion, through his multitude of friends, he'd seen her for exactly what she was. And he'd loved it. Her. Nothing had ever been better than to know and be known.

And now he was gone. Truly, finally gone.

Even now, two months after the fact, she still found herself wishing desperately that Cyril's emails had been real. That Tavis could still speak into her life, even if from beyond the divide of time and space. Perhaps even more desperately, she hated Cyril for making her need this thing which could never be.

Rather than fall down that endless rabbit hole of longing, Robin clicked her phone off and tried to turn her focus back to the sermon. It was something from Matthew—the Beatitudes? Yes. *Blessed are those who have been persecuted for the sake of righteousness, for theirs is the kingdom of heaven.*

But that only brought her back to the fear that had prompted her to pull up the wedding photo to begin with: What if this was the end?

What if there was no heavenly reunion? No sweet hereafter? What if they were all just kidding themselves? What if June twenty-seventh had truly been the last time Tavis would ever wrap her in his arms?

There was a touch on Robin's leg; she looked down to see Trinity's petite white hand. Her eyes followed the hand to the face, and Trinity nodded toward the back of the sanctuary.

She'd been caught.

"Sneaking" was not a feat that could be accomplished by a woman eight months pregnant, but Robin ducked her head to make her profile slightly less obtrusive as she headed for the big double doors. She pushed into the foyer and turned, just to get this over with as quickly as possible. Trinity would give her a hug and ask if she were all right, and Robin would assure her that yes, everything was fine, and Trinity could go on with her life without feeling that nagging sense of guilt or doubt or whatever it was that made her think Robin's happiness was in some way essential to her own.

Trinity didn't stop. She slipped through the second set of double doors and turned to hold one open, beckoning with a finger.

Outside, the early-morning rain had turned into a drizzle broken by brilliant rays of sunshine. Robin raised a hand to shield her eyes.

Trinity pointed to the café on the corner. "Let's get some coffee."

They crossed the street and ordered a couple of sugary-syrupy drinks topped with whipped cream and seated themselves in two big leather chairs in the sun. A few pedestrians walked by on the other side of the window, and a few minutes later an usher came out the big wooden doors of the church and propped them open. Another minute or two and congregants began filing out, squinting and tucking away umbrellas.

Robin felt Trinity glance at her.

"I know everyone says this." She touched Robin's arm, briefly. "But I wanted to tell you again that I'm totally there for you. Whatever you need. You can put me on your speed dial. Meals, babysitting, grocery runs, middle-of-the-night emergencies, anything. Okay?"

"Thanks." Robin sipped her mocha, which had finally cooled to just-below-scalding. "But I think my mom has dibs on pretty much everything." After this next week, anyway. On Wednesday, Glennis would head out of town—and out of cell phone range—on her annual women's retreat. It was cutting it a bit close, but it was always the highlight of her mom's year and chances of the baby making an appearance three weeks early were slim to none. Robin hadn't even had any Braxton Hicks. No reason Glennis's life should come to a grinding halt, too.

"I know." Trinity blew on her coffee and sighed. "But it really does take a village, you know? It's selfish, but—in a way, helping with other people's kids helps me heal. So if you feel like it's an imposition, believe me, it's not."

Robin usually ignored passive-aggressive attempts to get her to ask for more information, but something in Trinity's tone said this was a topic she thought Robin was already privy to. She took the bait. "Heal?"

"You know, my... oh. You don't know?" Trinity fingered her little angel-wing necklace and gave a half-hearted laugh. "I just assume everyone does." She shrugged. "We lost our little girl to retinoblastoma. Just before you and Tavis moved back to town. Well, I guess *you* weren't moving back. Sometimes I forget not everyone's been here forever."

"I had no idea," Robin said.

"I guess it's not the kind of thing you post on Facebook, right?" She forced a smile. "I know I'm that crazy lady who kidnaps any kid she can get her hands on, but I promise I'll give them back!"

Robin should have known. The necklace, her childlessness in spite of her obvious love for kids... "I'm sorry."

"It's okay. Really. And, you know, God's been so good to me. Emmaline's in heaven with Him, and I've been able to use this experience to help so many other women. So—" She choked slightly, but managed to go on. "*So* much good has come from her life, even though it was very short."

Robin nodded, but she knew the words were merely a thin veneer over a wound that ran deep and dark as the sea. Trinity wasn't lying—she was telling herself this truth, repeatedly, in the hopes that if she did it long enough, maybe someday it might feel true.

She shook her head. "Anyway, I'm sorry. It's not the same as losing a husband, so please don't think I'm comparing our experiences at all."

"No," Robin said. "It's fine. I'm—not sure which is worse, actually." A lie. She'd have killed Tavis herself to save Seth. How had she never noticed that Trinity bore those same invisible scars? Tav's death had blinded her to all pain but her own. The worst thing was that, even knowing, she didn't have it in her to care. Trinity's daughter was nothing to her.

"I don't think you can measure grief like that." Trinity looked down into her cup and then, abruptly, set it aside. "Want to take a walk?"

They ambled down the sidewalk, passing the church again on the other side of the street, and were surprised by a momentary shower. They ducked under the awning at Sprouts, a boutique children's clothing store. Trinity pressed her forehead against the darkened window. "Look at that little tiny suit," she said. "And the hat! Do you think your little one will have Seth's hair?"

How did she do this? Robin could barely stand to see a man in uniform. How could Trinity look at these tiny clothes and not drop to her knees? "Does it… get better?"

"Hm?" Trinity looked up, her eyebrows lifted in question. "Oh. Um. Yes… and no." She turned, leaning with her back to the window, and fiddled with her necklace. "There is no *better.* Other people… think you get over it, move on. You don't. It's like…" She frowned. "It's like breaking a vase. At first you're just trying to glue the pieces back together. If you could just do that—but you can't. And you realize even if you could figure out where everything goes, it'll never hold water again. So you carry the pieces around for a while, and eventually you start to see… hey, maybe I could make a bowl, or a cup, or, you know, some sort of modern art sculpture. And it's a good cup or sculpture or whatever. And you learn to love it. It's just... not ever going to be a vase."

"Oh." Robin put a hand out, palm up. The rain had stopped, at least for the moment.

Trinity pushed off from the wall and took Robin's arm, turning them toward the grassy plot on the corner that sometimes passed for a park. "Sorry. That wasn't very encouraging, was it?"

"No, it was, in a way. I guess. It's... hard to let go of the vase." It was exactly why Robin had fallen so easily for Cyril's sham. Why a small, hateful part of her still wished she had never discovered the truth.

There was a chirp from Trinity's purse, and she dropped Robin's arm to pull out her phone. "Oh shoot, I forgot Benson and I were having lunch with the Fasolds. Where did you park?"

"The lot behind the music center—but I need to rescue Seth from Sunday school first."

"Oh! Right. Well, it's on the way." Trinity hooked her arm through Robin's as they retraced their steps, and Robin didn't pull away. "You will be able to feel joy again, you know. Even if it seems like all you're doing is going through the motions. The sadness will never go away, not completely—but you'll figure out how to live with it. And you'll find joy."

Robin bit the inside of her cheek. "Promise?"

Trinity gave her arm a squeeze. "I promise."

It was Robin's turn to be interrupted by a phone; she felt for the buzz in her purse. "Hey, Mom. What's up?"

"Robin, turn on the TV."

"I'm walking down the street in Old Town. I can't—"

"Then go home. Turn on CNN. Or any news station. *Now*, Robin."

Trinity had been politely pretending not to eavesdrop, but her head snapped up at Glennis' last words. "Oh my God," she moaned. "Not another shooting. Or a bomb?"

"Mom, is it—"

"No, no." Glennis had overheard. "Nobody killed. Sweetie, it's Cyril. He, um—oh gosh, I don't know how to explain any of this nonsense."

"Cyril's on *television?*" What on earth had he done now? "Okay, well—we'll figure it out. Thanks, Mom."

Trinity pointed down the block, to the hanging sign with the white feather. "Nom. They have a TV behind the bar."

As pregnant as Robin was, hurrying was more like a slow shuffle. Trinity broke away from her about twenty yards from the restaurant entrance, leaving Robin to huff along behind, one hand under her belly in an attempt to ease round ligament pain. Probably not too different from how Cyril felt all the time. Good.

Trinity was already arguing with the woman behind the bar when Robin caught up. "Two minutes," she was saying. "I can call George if you want, but we just—"

"Oh, go on ahead." A grizzled old man sitting at the end of the bar with a beer and a bowl of chili waved a spoon at the screen, which was tuned to a professional soccer game. "Ain't gonna score anyway."

"Thank you," Trinity said.

The hostess gave the old man a sour look, but she pulled out a remote and started flipping channels. An infomercial, a cooking show—

"There," Robin said.

The screen showed a stock image of papers stamped with CLASSIFIED in big red letters, and the headline above it read, "Whistleblower Arrested; Leaked Documents Point to Marine Misconduct."

"—starting to comb through the documents he's released in a very widespread, public manner." The image faded to a long-lashed woman at the CNN news desk. "Again, I want to make it clear that while this evidence is technically classified, it has been released so publicly that containing it is essentially, well, a lost cause." She looked to her left as the camera panned back to include a man in a Navy blue suit and tie. "Gerald, can you give us a rundown of what this information is, and exactly how a civilian like, ah—" She glanced down at the desk in front of her. "Like Cyril Blanchard might have gotten access to such classified material?"

"Well, Una, we're looking through everything as fast as we can, but the main takeaway here is that it's not *just* documents. I mean, I mean—" He pushed his glasses up. "Yes, the documents are the bulk of the classified material here, and—and honestly, this is almost a—I don't want to say it, but a Snowden-level leak, which is to say that we're going to be combing through this data for months to come. But the real focal point here seems to be a single Afghan boy, identified only as 'Shafik.'" A familiar snapshot of a grinning, gap-toothed boy appeared on the upper right of the screen, followed a moment later by grainy video footage of him keeping a red, white, and blue hacky-sack in the air using only his feet. "The really damning bits are a series of, of informal interviews that appear to have been, ah, conducted by an American soldier on the ground *in* Afghanistan. We're working on some translations for the folks at home as we speak, but the evidence strongly implicates that this boy's father and uncle were both—well, I don't want to say murdered, but—perhaps *eliminated* would be a more appropriate term for the time being—in a move that was not only known about by superiors, but actively covered up. We're not sure who this soldier is, or what kind of connection he has to Blanchard, but we're working as fast as we can to identify—"

"I'm sorry to interrupt, Gerald, but I've just been notified that our correspondent has arrived at Blanchard's residence in Camarillo, California. Let's go to Tyra Ramirez for the latest. Tyra?"

There was a lag as the station switched to their on-the-ground reporter. Finally, the image of the news desk, anchors holding their smiles, blinked out and was replaced with a very familiar shot of Cyril's driveway. There were cop cars everywhere.

"Holy smokes," said the guy at the end of the bar. "Isn't that just over off Lantana Street?"

"Yes, Una, I'm here on the scene and—and I'm afraid we're a little too late to catch the action, but I'm told the FBI has *just* taken Cyril Blanchard into custody. We have not yet been able to obtain the official charges, but this is essentially about distributing highly classified military information. I've been told by the officers here that Blanchard was *already* under investigation for abusing his access to sensitive information through a tech company doing some military contract work, but whether or not that is related we don't—"

"Tyra, thank you—I'm sorry I'm going to have to cut you off for the moment—thank you for that update. We've managed to obtain a photo of Mr. Blanchard, and I'm told our media team is—ah, there it is, up on the screen now."

The screen fragmented for a moment as the digital feed struggled to keep up with the changing image, and then a headshot of Cyril appeared to the right of the news anchor. It was about five years out of date, judging from the fact that his face looked significantly less bloated.

"He certainly doesn't *look* like the next Edward Snowden, does he Gerald?"

Gerald chuckled. "Well, Una, what he looks like to me is a hacker. If you—if you Google his name, you find out pretty quick that he's a podcaster who's, who's got a reputation for ruffling feathers. I think that's really what we're looking at here. This guy is not an insider, he's not a whistleblower. He's a computer geek who likes making trouble, and somehow he stumbled into something juicy. Odds are he realized he'd gotten himself into hot water and thought maybe he could vindicate himself in the public eye. Unfortunately, that doesn't mean much from a legal standpoint. If you think the FBI's going to turn a blind eye to this kind of hacktivism just because the military ends up with egg on its face, you're wrong. If we've learned anything from Brad—I'm sorry, *Chelsea* Manning, it's that—"

Gerald kept talking, but Robin wasn't listening. She got up and walked outside. She was aware, dimly, of Trinity coming out the door behind her.

"Robin?"

"He lied." Every single thing he'd ever said was a lie.

"What?"

Robin looked at Trinity. "He said he destroyed the evidence. Everything. He said there was no solid proof—he said the FBI was investigating Cooke's company, or maybe his hacking—"

It was all connected. Tavis had gotten himself killed for the sake of this boy. Or he'd gotten killed before he'd had a chance to try. Even if they'd known, nobody would have cared. And so... Cyril had decided to make it impossible to ignore.

Robin fumbled in her purse for her phone. She brought up Cooke's number and hit the green button.

He answered immediately. "Are you fucking seeing this?"

"Language," a low female voice cautioned, in the background.

Robin stuck her fingers in her hair. "What on earth is going on?"

"Look, I—I don't know who's listening in on this right now, okay? I kind of have to assume someone is. And officially, I have to say that I don't approve of any of this, because he hacked my goddamn company, but—"

"Language." The voice was a more forceful this time.

"Oh my *God*, Greta, I am having a fucking emergency here."

"So take it in the other room."

"Hold on." There was a familiar aluminum clatter, followed by a rhythmic rustle of cloth and breath. "Sorry," he said, finally. "My wife's babysitting. Not that this kid hasn't heard it all."

"When did you hire Cyril?"

"The last time? Um, Jesus. Let's see. About eighteen months ago, I guess."

Right after Tavis returned from his second deployment.

"And in case you were wondering, yeah, he knew who we were working with. This was not coincidental."

"No," she said. "I didn't think so."

"Honestly, Robin? Your friend has just royally fucked himself. My partner's on the other line and I gotta go to damage control, but, uh… if you see him? Tell him I said good luck."

25

S HE WATCHED IT ALL UNFOLD from her living room couch. Some free speech activists had started a GoFundMe page for Cyril's legal fees, and he got a lawyer from the ACLU who, it was speculated, would get him out on bail almost immediately. The hashtag #findShafik was trending. Translations of some of the videos were aired—an elderly Afghan woman speaking in a near-whisper of her son's death, and her grandson's kidnapping; a middle-aged man who shrugged and stated, with no particular vehemence, that his wife's opinion was irrelevant as she did whatever he told her to do. Only Robin—and Cyril—knew the face behind the camera was Tav's.

It couldn't last forever. The doorbell rang at six o'clock Monday morning, and when Robin peeked out the window, she found four news crews camped on her front lawn.

The bell hadn't woken Seth, so she hurried downstairs, grabbed a chair, and stood on it to disconnect the ringer. Whoever was standing on the porch heard. "Mrs. Matheson? Robin? Could we have a word?"

She double-checked the locks, then retreated to the office and pulled out the baby monitor. She hadn't used it in a good six months, but the broadcasting end was still plugged in upstairs—Seth's room was on the back side of the house, fortunately, but if the noise outside did wake him, she wanted to catch him before he ran downstairs and stuck his face up against the front window.

When she flipped it on, the monitor exploded in a burst of static and voices. She turned it off again.

The first thing that appeared when she opened Google News was a photo of Tavis. His boot camp graduation portrait, to be exact; he looked so fresh and earnest it hurt. They'd identified him not because any servicemen had ratted him out, thank goodness, but by simply asking around town. If you were looking for people who associated with Cyril, there was basically one answer.

Her phone buzzed. She looked at the screen, but it was a number she didn't recognize. Almost simultaneously, someone outside realized that she'd disabled the bell and started knocking. Not a polite little tap, either. She silenced her phone and started reading.

They didn't have much—nothing more than what she already knew. Tavis had been conducting interviews with folks on the ground in Afghanistan, and he'd pulled together a paper trail which made it clear that not only had his superiors known about the incident, but that they'd actively orchestrated the whole exchange. Cyril's part in all of it was more vague; various analysts were speculating that he'd helped Tavis encrypt the videos, or that he'd been the one to build the paper trail by hacking his way into the military's records through the work he was doing with Cooke's company, Architective.

There was already a bit of speculation about Robin, too: they'd gotten her name, and Seth's, but no photographs.

Facebook. "Shit," she whispered. Thanks to a healthy paranoia instilled by her father, she'd kept her privacy settings tight, and the only photo that came up when she performed a Google image search for herself was her profile photo—a picture of an inlaid wood jewelry box a long-time client had commissioned last year. Still, there were twenty-six new friendship requests when she opened the tab. Robin deactivated her account.

"Mommy?" Seth was in the kitchen.

"Yes! In here, sweetie!" Robin hurried to meet him in the hall, bracing a hand on the wall as she squatted to give him a hug. "You want some breakfast?"

He still looked a bit bleary-eyed. "I heared something."

As if on cue, the banging started up again.

Seth's eyes lit up. "Gramma! It's a Gramma day!"

Robin caught his arm as he lunged forward. "Hold on, bud. It's not Grandma." How the hell did she explain this? "It's... well, we can't answer the door, okay?"

"Why not?" She could see the panic in his eyes: if he didn't get to the door soon, the visitor would give up and go away! If only.

She put a hand on her knee, pushed herself to her feet, and paused to let the stars clear from her vision before she patted Seth's head, giving him a gentle push toward the play room. "It's... really hard to explain, buddy. But there are a bunch of TV people outside who want to talk to me, and I don't want to talk to them."

He tilted his head back to look at her. "But why?"

"They want to know things about Daddy. Private things. Things..." Things she was probably going to have to talk about in court, at some point. "Things Daddy wanted to keep a secret." Sort of.

"But why?"

Robin sighed. "Bud, I'm sorry, but I honestly just don't know how to explain this one. Think of it like—like we're in a castle and the bad guys are trying to get in. We don't want to stick our heads out because someone might shoot an arrow and get us."

"*Arrows?*"

"They don't really have arrows. It's just—" She let out a growl of frustration. "I'm sorry, bud. It's stuff you'll understand when you grow up. It's really hard to explain right now." She stopped in the kitchen, briefly, to pull a yogurt from the fridge. "I just really need you to stay away from the windows, okay? Don't let anyone see you. Kind of like hide-and-seek."

Seth, still a bit wide-eyed, allowed her to usher him into the play room and set him up with some yogurt at the art table. It was a bit of a treat, since he normally wasn't allowed to eat in here, and that was enough—she hoped—to keep him out of sight for the time being.

"Gramma still coming?" he asked, as she was backing out.

"Oh—um, yes. Well. Maybe." Robin had forgotten: since Glennis was heading off to her retreat on Wednesday, she'd planned to come down and play with Seth today. If this circus continued for any length of time, it was good she'd be out of town. But even better if she could stay out of it entirely. Robin went back to the office for her phone, which now catalogued twelve missed calls and twice as many texts. She scrolled through them, just to make sure there was nothing from her mom, and then attempted to ring Glennis.

No answer. It was a little after eight, which meant her mother was likely already headed down the coast, and was, for once, heeding Robin's oft-repeated plea not to answer her phone while driving. Robin went to the settings on her phone and assigned a chirpy tinkle to everyone she knew, so when Glennis returned her call half an hour later she didn't automatically silence it.

"I can't get to the driveway! I'm over on Daily."

"I know," Robin said, "I don't know what to do." Seth had finished his yogurt and was bouncing around her knees, trying to get her to look at something he'd made out of Legos. "Sweetie, one second. I'm on the phone." She left the play room, but he followed her into the kitchen. "Can you try honking? I don't think they're supposed to block traffic, right?"

"Even if I can get to the driveway, they'll catch me on the way into the house!"

Glennis had a point. Robin didn't want her mother on the news any more than she wanted them filming Seth. "Maybe we can get to the truck and meet you somewhere." But they'd have to walk through the back yard to get to the garage, and the fence was only four feet high. Could she throw a blanket over Seth? She'd already had to bribe him with chocolate to get him to stay away from the front windows. This was absurd. "Hold on for a minute, Mom. Let me think about this and get back to you, okay?"

"I'll go get my coffee. Honey, I'd think about calling the police."

And give them an excuse to ransack her house like they'd done Cyril's? No. "I'll see. Love you." All Robin wanted to do was scream, but she squatted down awkwardly next to Seth and summoned her patient-mommy voice. "Okay buddy, show me." And please let it be quick.

He thrust his Lego creation at her face. "It's a demlo!"

It looked kind of like a giant mouth with a single foot. "Cool! What's a demlo?"

He gave a dramatic sigh. "I already *told* you! Demlos are super-fast squares that you can't even go faster than!"

Obviously. "Is this from a show? Something you saw at Grandma's?"

He stamped a foot. "No! They're not pretend! I already told you!"

"Oh, okay. Sorry. I guess I forgot." She put a hand on his shoulder. "Hey, buddy? You know how there's a bunch of people—" Her phone chirped. It was Andrews.

"Outside? I can look now?"

Robin caught his wrist. "No, sweetie, not now." Robin didn't want to talk to Andrews, but if there was ever a time she could use some military assistance it was now. "Hi."

"I just turned on the news."

"Yeah. It's kind of crazy." She pinned the phone between her ear and shoulder and used her free hand to give Seth the "sh" signal. Then she started toward the back of the house, dragging him by the arm.

"Tell me what I can do for you."

"I—I don't know. They're all—I'm sorry, one second." She pulled Seth back into the play room and pointed at his upturned tub of Legos. "I need you to play in here for another few minutes, okay? By yourself. If you can do that while Mommy's busy, we'll make some cookies after lunch."

He opened his mouth as wide as it would go and let his tongue hang out, slavering. "Coooookies!"

She gave his head a rub before stepping out and closing the door. She leaned against the doorjamb, sighing. "I don't want anyone to see Seth," she told Andrews. "I don't want him involved in this." If it weren't for him, she'd have been outside screaming bloody murder.

"Are they on your property?"

Robin went into the living room and peeked through the drapes. Cameras flashed. "All over my lawn. There's a news van parked in the driveway."

"Mrs. Matheson!" a voice shouted. "We want to hear your side of the story!"

She squeezed her eyes shut. "Oh my God, what do I do?" What did they even think she could give them?

"Okay, Robin," Andrews said. "I'm gonna hang up and make a few calls. Okay? And I'll let you know. Or—do you—would you want me to come over and be with you until this is resolved?"

"No—I mean, thanks, but no. Actually, wait. My mom—she's hiding out over at the Starbucks by Safeway." Glennis loved Andrews. "I don't want her involved, either. Do you think you could—"

"Absolutely, Ms. Matheson. I'm already on my way." Knowing Andrews, he wasn't exaggerating—he'd probably been calling from his car.

Robin sank down on the couch and put her head in her hands. Even if Andrews could get a few men out to stand guard, what was that going to do? The crews would move back to the sidewalk and they'd still be trapped in the house.

Her phone continued to buzz with an endless stream of texts. She was going to have to change her number. She scrolled through them quickly, hoping for some sort of update from her mom or Andrews, even though it was too soon for him to have gotten to Glennis. It was just a bunch of journalists, begging her to contact them or promising her some sort of exclusive platform for her agenda, whatever that was. And then: *Sprinklers.*

Robin frowned at the screen. Sprinklers? What the—

She jumped to her feet. She ran to the back of the house, past the play room, and into the back yard. Nobody could see her unless she went around the corner of the house or across the grass to the garage—and, fortunately, the control panel for the sprinkler system was right outside the back door. She flipped the cover open and flicked the switch from AUTO to ON. There was a sputter, and then—

A chorus of shrieks.

She grinned as she let herself back inside. This time she jogged upstairs, to the finished window seat in the master bedroom, and peered out over the front lawn. The crowd of reporters and camera crews had become a crowd of wet, angry reporters and camera crews. One of the reporters who was particularly soaked was standing next to her van, screaming at her underling to find a towel or, if none were available, to give her the shirt off his fucking back.

And then, as she watched, a woman inside the van parked in the driveway leaned out and called for the attention of her crew. She held up a cell phone and motioned urgently. In what seemed like seconds, they'd packed up and driven away. The remaining crews had begun speculating about whether they were missing some critical breaking news when a guy in a striped polo shirt held up his phone and shouted, "Oh shit!" In less than ten minutes, only one van remained. A man and two women milled around, looking at their phones, at the end of the drive.

Robin's phone rang. It was Andrews.

"Did you do something?" she asked.

"Um—no, why?"

"They're gone."

"Oh. Good. That's good." He sounded excessively relieved.

"Are you okay?"

"I'm fine. I—well, it's not important now."

It didn't sound unimportant. "If there's something I should know, I'd rather hear it from you."

He sighed, heavily. "I tried to call in some favors. It's... well, people don't know what to make of what's happening. And they don't want to be seen assisting a possible, um—"

"Traitor," Robin filled in.

"I'm sorry. Nobody's saying he was. It's just, with all this going on, it's... risky."

"Oh, I get it." She shook her head. Cyril had been right. One bad egg and fifty guys unwilling to speak up. Or in this case, one good guy and fifty guys unwilling to stick out their necks.

"Please don't think it's everyone. Tavis has friends for life here. Just not... anyone in a position of power."

Which was precisely why Tavis had felt he'd had to do any of this to begin with.

Why hadn't he *told* her?

"Thanks," she said. "Send my mom home, okay?"

He signed off, and Robin shifted so her back was to the window. She tapped the text icon and watched that single word blink back into view: *Sprinklers.*

You lied, she typed.

An ellipsis appeared, indicating that a reply was being composed.

Finally: *I didn't want to risk involving you.*

She stabbed at the screen with her thumbs. *That wasn't your choice to make. It was mine.*

At least I'll be the one in jail.

He genuinely thought he was playing the hero. *I never asked you to sacrifice yourself for me.*

The ellipsis came back, and then winked out. She stared at the screen for a long moment, and was about to get up and go downstairs when the ellipsis came back. She waited.

Tell Seth I love him.

Robin bit her lip. "Fuck you," she whispered, and clicked off the phone.

"Robin?" It was her mom, downstairs.

She shoved the phone deep into her pocket and hopped up. "Coming!"

Seth was already hanging on Glennis, who hadn't even had a chance to put down her purse. "Play demlos with me!"

"Hold on, buddy, give Grandma a chance to take a breath." Robin grabbed an arm and dragged him off. "Sorry, Mom." If she didn't have a conversation about jumping on people with Seth, soon, Glennis was going to end up breaking something, or worse. "You want—oh, you already had your coffee."

"Lieutenant Colonel Andrews paid. He's such a gentleman. You should invite him over for dinner sometime, to say thank-you."

Robin didn't know whether to take that as a passive-aggressive criticism or some weird attempt to hook them up. Either way, she ignored it.

Glennis put her purse down on the floor by the piano. "Your grass has been destroyed. There ought to be *something* you can do."

"I'm just glad they're gone. For now, anyway." Robin peeked out the front window to make sure.

"I wonder where they all went?"

"Good question." Robin located the remote and turned on the TV.

"...word that Cyril Blanchard is about to be released on bail. He's stated, via his lawyer, that he will be granting an exclusive interview to at least one journalist, as yet unnamed. He was apparently scheduled for release this morning, but so far there's been no word—"

Robin flicked the television off with a laugh.

"What?" Glennis asked. "Did I miss something?"

"He texted me. Fifteen, twenty minutes ago."

Glennis looked blank.

"He wasn't texting from prison, Mom. He's already out. He's gone. He's jerking them around." He'd gotten them off her lawn.

"Oh. Well, ah, I suppose that's a good thing?"

Seth grabbed Robin's hand and went limp, jerking her over to one side. "I'm *huuuungry!*"

"Well!" she said. "We'll make lunch, then. And we'll eat in the back yard—enjoy our freedom for as long as it lasts."

They were reclining in the Adirondacks, feet propped up on the fire pit, watching Seth try to bury himself in the sandbox. Glennis reached for her back pocket. She pulled out her phone and frowned. "It's... him. He says he wants to apologize."

Robin only had to glance at her mother's face to know who she meant. "Block his number." She grabbed the phone. "Here, I'll do it for you."

Glennis watched as she pecked through the settings. "I'm sorry, sweetie, but can you explain all this to your poor old mom?"

Robin looked up and realized, suddenly, that her mother was still completely in the dark—except, of course, what she'd been able to gather from the news. She sighed. "I'm sorry, Mom. I..." She took a deep breath. "Okay, so—the news is mostly right, I guess. Tavis got mixed up in something that looked like a couple of Marines murdering some Afghan civilians, one of them a kid."

Glennis glanced at Seth, as if to ask whether they should be discussing such things in front of her grandson.

Robin shrugged. He was going to hear about it one way or another; better he become familiar with the narrative now, even if he couldn't quite comprehend it all, than have it sprung on him somewhere down the road.

"His command wouldn't pursue it, and he found out that the boy was still alive, working as a kind of—of sex slave. That's why he re-enlisted. Cyril was helping him to, like, protect the information or something. Or store it. I don't know. You know that guy I did the condo remodel for? He owns the company Cyril hacked. They have some military contracts and Cyril was… getting into stuff through them, or something. I didn't have a clue any of this was going on until a couple of months ago, and when I tried to get the whole story out of him he told me he'd destroyed the evidence. Except he didn't."

Seth scowled at her from his bucket full of sandy mud. "Are you guys talking about Cereal?" While he'd accepted her explanation that Cyril had hurt Mommy's feelings very badly, he rejected the notion that it couldn't be fixed with a simple "I'm sorry." So now, of course, it was all her fault.

"Yes, sweetie." Honestly, Robin couldn't say he was wrong. It *was* her fault for thinking anything good could come out of letting Cyril spend time with her son. Seth still asked about him every other day. He asked about Cyril more often than he asked about Tav.

Seth glared at them for another minute, then returned to digging.

"So what now?" Glennis asked, lowering her voice.

Robin handed back her mother's phone. "I don't know. What they did was totally illegal. If Tavis was still alive, he'd be facing a court martial. So they'll have a trial or something." She shrugged. "Cyril thinks he's probably going to prison."

Glennis picked up her iced tea and drank, carefully. Robin knew she was thinking, wanting to say something Robin wasn't going to like.

"What?" she prompted, finally.

Glennis sighed. "I know what he did, Robin. With… the letters. It's inexcusable. But with this… I mean… it sounds like he's done the right thing."

"What, you're on *his* side now? I don't care what he did for Tavis. I mean, I'm glad he didn't destroy the evidence. I was furious when he told me he had. But he *owed* Tavis that much. Doing what he should doesn't make him a hero." At the very most, it made him something marginally closer to a decent human being.

"These days, sometimes I think it does."

"Well, my standard was Tavis, so I guess that bar's set a little higher than the general population."

Glennis looked at her, realizing suddenly that Robin was getting genuinely angry. "Sweetie," she said, "you know I'm on your side. No matter what."

Robin sat back. "I know, Mom."

Seth got up, shook a bucket's worth of sand out of his shorts, and sat back down.

Glennis reached out and touched Robin's hand, gently. When Robin didn't pull away she said, "If I hurt you, before, I'm sorry. I didn't mean to."

Robin squeezed her mother's fingers. "I know." The last thing she wanted to do was rehash all the details of their conflict. "I just..." Maybe she had just needed someone to be angry with. "I'm sorry too."

They sat watching Seth for another few minutes. Glennis finished her iced tea and got to her feet, collecting the glass and her phone. "Well. With all this nonsense going on, I'm thinking I should just cancel my trip."

"Your retreat? No. Mom. Please don't. I don't want this to screw up your life too."

"Sweetie, I'll never forgive myself if something happens and I'm not here. What if those crews come back?"

"Then I'll call Andrews again." Robin got up, following her mother to the porch. "Or just go to your house. I have your keys. I can hole up there with Seth, no problem. Cooke probably wouldn't have a problem with me crashing at his condo while he's gone, either. It's gated."

"And what if the baby comes early?"

"He's not going to. Not *that* early, anyway. Remember Seth?" He'd been two weeks overdue, and they'd had to induce, and even then she'd had to labor for over twenty-four hours. "I haven't had any Braxon Hicks yet. Nothing."

"You never know, Robin. With you, I thought—"

"You never know anything in life, Mom. I thought I had it all planned out, and I don't. The last thing I want you to do is give this up just because something *might* happen. Anyway," she added, "Trinity is more than happy to help out. I can sign Seth up for a few more hours at preschool if I need to, but it's not like I'll be working much anyway."

Glennis raised an eyebrow. "*Much?*"

"Oh, mom. Detail work around the house is not going to kill me."

"You take care of my grandsons, Robin. Both of them."

26

SETH DRAGGED HIS LITTLE BLUE CHAIR across the kitchen floor. The back legs grating across the tile made Robin cringe, but she gritted her teeth and smiled as he hopped up next to her at the cutting board. She encouraged autonomy wherever she could these days; in less than a month, she was going to be doing all of this plus a baby, too.

"I wanna dump it!" he reached for the cup of uncooked rice.

"Whoa, buddy, not in the bowl. Rice goes in the rice cooker. One second, I'll get it out." She put a hand between him and the ingredients. "Wait for Mommy, okay?"

"Kay."

She crossed the floor, gripped the counter, and squatted in front of the cabinet, trying to stifle a grunt.

"Are we making two?"

The rice cooker had somehow gotten pushed to the very back of the cabinet, so she had to get down on her knees and crouch. "Yes, sweetie."

"One for Grandma?"

"No, this one's for the sick lady from church. Grandma's at her retreat, remember?" She made one final lunge for the cooker pulled it out.

"With Jesus?"

Robin rested her forehead on the cool tile floor, not sure whether to laugh or cry. She'd tried to explain the spiritual significance of setting aside time to listen to God, and… failed, apparently. "Um. No, Grandma is not in heaven." Thank goodness they were clearing this up before Seth asked Grandma for a rundown of her visit with Daddy. "She's at a camp. Out in the woods. She'll be back in a few days."

"Ohhh-kay." Seth hopped off his chair and picked the rice cooker up by the handles.

Now why hadn't she just thought to have him get it out to begin with?

Her brain was clearly not getting enough blood. She pulled herself up, slowly, and blinked away the black spots in her vision. This was the point at which she started thinking all her problems would be solved when the baby came out—which was a lie, because then she'd have a *baby*. Having a perpetual infant or being continually eight months pregnant were two eternal hells she was glad she'd never have to choose between.

She was helping Seth slide the cooker up onto the counter when the doorbell rang. He dropped it and ran. Robin set it in place and waddled after him. "Hold on, buddy. Let me look first." After the TV crews had realized Cyril had given them the slip, they'd come back to her place in fits and starts. One woman had camped out in her car for over twenty-four hours, until a patrol car came and told her to move along. One of the neighbors had probably called—they couldn't be too pleased with all this activity, either.

It wasn't a news van, but her heart sank anyway—it was Andrews. That was unusual; he almost always called to ask permission before coming over. And she almost always found a reason to beg off. Had something happened? Robin flipped the bolt back and opened the door.

He looked bizarrely casual in jeans and a polo shirt, especially with his high-and-tight buzz cut. Either it was his day off, or he'd finally realized she'd be happy if she never saw another uniform again. He held out a large cardboard box. "This was on your porch."

"Is it a present? Is it for me?" Seth threw himself against her legs, and she had to catch herself against the door frame.

"Buddy, you cannot do that! I am eight months pregnant!" Whatever internal gyroscope her body used to stay upright had finally been compromised by the size of her belly.

"Sorry." He hopped around her. "Is it my train books?"

"I don't know, bud. Just—chill out for a minute, okay?" She took the box and set it inside the door. "Sorry. Come in." She stepped back, giving Andrews just enough time to cross the threshold before she shut the door. In case anyone was watching. "Did something happen?"

"No, no, nothing." He smoothed his moustache with a thumb and forefinger. "Your, ah, mother asked me to check in on you. While she was gone."

"Seriously?"

He winced. "I thought it might be a good opportunity to update you on the situation. Have you been following the news?"

She'd texted with Cooke a couple of times since the whole thing had broken, but beyond that... "I've been trying to ignore it, to be honest." Andrews looked surprised, but Robin couldn't come up with the words that would make him understand what it meant to be carrying someone inside of you. To know that everything you saw and felt and experienced might have an impact on that little person ten, twenty years down the road. Her house could burn down, the city could flood—her husband could die—and her first thought would still be to worry about the impact it would have on her kids. She smoothed her shirt over her stomach. "I suppose I need to keep up with things, though. Better you than CNN." If only by the slimmest possible margin.

She got him some water and sat down across from him at the dining table. Seth performed a stealthy disappearing act, but a moment later they could hear him in the front hall, attacking the box.

Andrews jerked a thumb over one shoulder. "You want me to...?"

Robin shook her head. "It'll keep him occupied for a while." Odds of Seth getting through the packing tape with his safety scissors were low. She took a gulp of water, realizing as she did that she was parched. She took another drink. "Okay. Tell me what's going on."

He nodded, and she could almost see him consulting a mental list. "So—first of all, if you don't know, Cyril was arraigned yesterday. He pled not guilty. So now it's the pretrial, uh, 'discovery' phase. Honestly, with a case of this complexity and, uh, magnitude, that could last five, six months. If you get subpoenaed, it won't be for a while."

"And he's just out, free, until then?"

"I think he's prohibited from leaving the county."

"Not like he'd get far if he ran for it."

"Yeah, his, uh, size makes him a low-flight risk."

Robin had heard that on NPR the other day, before she switched it off. They'd been having an actual, serious discussion about which Federal prisons, if any, could accommodate Cyril.

Andrews cleared his throat. "As for the rest of it, I assume you heard about the Secretary of Defense's press conference."

Robin's eyebrows went up. "As in the head of the DoD?"

Andrews nodded, and she got the sense that this was satisfying for him: to be able to give her something concrete, something positive. "They found him."

"Him?"

"The boy. Shafik."

Robin covered her mouth. "Are you—are you serious?" She cast a glance toward the front of the house, where it sounded like Seth was now kicking the box against the front door. "I didn't even know—" It had never even entered her mind that it was a possibility. "I didn't think anyone *cared*."

Andrews shrugged. "Honestly, it was the best possible PR move they could have made. Well. The *only* possible PR move they could have made."

Cyril had said nobody would care. "I thought—this happens to kids all the time. Over there."

"Yeah," he said, in a low voice. "Well." He cleared his throat. "It's the security breach that makes it headline news. The whole thing reflects badly on the armed forces—and particularly on this administration. But the information that was leaked was—well, for most people it's just a fact. It doesn't *mean* anything to them. Afghanistan is just background noise at this point. But this kid puts a face on the whole thing. Without him, the hack might have been breaking news for a day or two and then blown over. But all those photos, the videos—it's a major headline wrapped in a personal interest story that can't be ignored."

"So he… he's safe?"

"Shafik?" Andrews nodded. "He's been relocated with some relatives in another part of the country and placed in school. He'll be safe and educated."

Robin looked down at her hands. She laced her fingers together and pressed her fingertips into her knuckles. He'd done it. Tavis had saved Shafik. It was small comfort—for Robin, in any case—but… it was something. Better than thinking his death was pointless and in vain. "Are—are they going to investigate Tav's death?"

Andrews shook his head. "I don't know. The Secretary didn't say anything about it. That... may come later."

Or never at all. "They're always going to see him as a traitor." She looked up. "Aren't they."

Andrews opened his mouth to speak, and then closed it again. As if he'd realized she didn't want him to sugar coat the issue. "Many will," he murmured finally. "But some won't."

She nodded. It wasn't okay, not even close to okay, but—"I think he knew that." Saving a child—someone else's child, half a world away—had meant more to him than all the glory and honor in the world. More than his own life. That was Tavis to the end.

They chatted another minute or two more. Andrews asked, as always, if there was anything he could do. Told her he'd be there wherever and whenever she needed. Squeezed her hand, briefly, before taking his leave. Robin breathed a sigh of relief when he was gone.

Immediately, her brain started replaying that moment: the ring of the doorbell, Andrews standing there with his hat in his hand—

"Fuck," Robin whispered, forcefully. She had to do something else, something to distract herself. She wasn't going to spend the rest of the day reliving that horror. "Seth? Where'd you go, bud?"

He'd dragged the box into the play room and had ditched his safety scissors for the sharp corner of a ruler in his attempt to hack through the reinforced packing tape. Robin got down on her knees and wrapped her arms around him from behind, burying her face in his hair. "I love you, buddy. I love you."

Seth twisted around and looked her straight in the eye. "I love you too, Mama." He gave her a peck on the nose.

How did he know? How did he know when she needed that most?

Robin blinked back the water in her eyes and put a hand on the package. "Okay, dude. Let's get this open." Getting back on her feet again was going to be a bit of an ordeal, so she stuck a hand in her pocket and pulled out her keys. She used the house key to rip the tape down the center.

Seth was practically drooling with anticipation, but when she pulled out the contents of the box his face fell. "A *purse?*" He flapped his hands and made a noise of disgust. "Hungry."

It was a diaper bag. Robin pulled the plastic wrapping off, and confirmed her first impression: it was one of those fashionable high-end bags that ran two hundred dollars and up. Not something she'd ever have bought for herself. In fact, she'd been planning on reusing the canvas tote the hospital had provided when Seth was born.

She reached into the box and pulled out the packing slip. The note printed on it said, *No idea if this is early or late. Took my best guess. – S Cooke*

"*Hun*gry!" Seth whined again. "I want Jell-O!"

She shoved the bag back in the box and got to her knees. "Hold *on*, bud! Geez." She knee-walked to the wall, leaned a hand against it, and managed to get to her feet. In the kitchen, she carved out a two-inch square of her grandmother's lime Jell-O salad, and made Seth carry it—carefully—to the table. Then she rinsed her hands and pulled the phone out of her back pocket.

Got the bag, she thumb-tapped. *Thank you so much.*

The reply came half a second later: *My pleasure.* And then another line: *It's returnable.* Cooke always replied in a series of snippets rather than a coherent block of text, so Robin stood there waiting until he was done:

friend's wife is pregnant...
fourth time...
asked her what ideal present would be...
said this bag...
now apparently I owe her one too...
whoops...

Robin grinned. *It's beautiful*, she wrote back. *And it's going to get destroyed. But thank you.*

So you'll come up north?

Robin laughed out loud. *I'll let you know. Bun's still in the oven, so it'll be a while.*

No worries. Will still be crippled when you arrive.

She rolled her eyes and stuck the phone back in her pocket. "You done, Buddy? Ready to start on this casserole?"

Seth slid down from his seat at the dining table and came back into the kitchen. His eyes wandered over all the items on the counter, which she'd carefully measured ahead of time so that he could participate effectively. "I wanna play cars."

Robin sighed.

Three hours later, she loaded the larger of the two casseroles into her truck, buckled Seth in the back, and drove across town to the house of the ailing church member—a sweet elderly woman recovering from pneumonia. Robin never knew how to act in these situations with near-strangers, but Seth was her ace in the hole. He did a little goofing off for the benefit of the octogenarian and then turned sweet and snuggly when she requested a hug. She insisted they share the meal with her, and in the end, Robin had to drag Seth out of the woman's house with the promise of another visit sometime soon.

"All right, bud, time to get you into bed," Robin said when she pulled into their driveway. There was no answer. She set the parking brake, turned off the motor, and bent the rearview mirror down to see into the extended cab. Seth was out cold.

She was two months past being able to lift him, especially as dead weight. But if she woke him, he'd rocket into hyperdrive and be up until two in the morning. So now what? Grab herself a pillow, ratchet the seat back, and sleep in the car? Or maybe plug the baby monitor in out here?

As if to answer her unspoken question, her belly tightened in a long, slow squeeze.

Great. She'd been on her feet too much today, and now she'd gotten Braxton Hicks started. Kind of a relief, actually—to have some sort of timeline, even if it meant the end of sleep. These would keep her up at night for a couple of weeks until she went into labor or they had to induce.

Robin breathed slowly, trying to calm her body, and waited for the false contraction to end. Slowly, her belly relaxed. There. No problem. No sleeping in the car; that was silly. She'd wake Seth up and deal with the consequences. "Hey," she said, unbuckling her belt. "Hey buddy."

Her stomach tensed again. This time it hurt. Just a little. She clenched her teeth as she waited it out.

Okay, well, even assuming this turned into full-blown labor, which was unlikely, she still had plenty of time. They always told you to stay at home for a few hours, labor in the shower, get things going before you packed it up and went to L&D. She'd had three false alarms with Seth, and she remembered well the knowing smiles of the nurses. *You're not in enough pain yet, honey.*

"Sethie?" She couldn't twist around, but she snaked an arm back and patted his leg. "Buddy?"

He was out. Seriously out. She could leave him here, take a nice hot shower, and come and wake him up and try to get him to bed. Or, if the contractions continued, give Trinity a call. Robin double-checked her purse for her phone. There. Nothing could go really, seriously wrong while she had her phone. Thank God for technology.

Her stomach seemed to have calmed down, so she slid out of the cab, leaving the door open and the parking light on, and went into the house. She was upstairs, running the water in the tub, when it hit her. She dropped onto the toilet seat, hard, and grabbed the toilet paper roll, moaning through clenched teeth as her nails tore into the soft paper.

Denial evaporated into a cold, hard *knowing*. Thirty-seven weeks or not, she was having this baby. Tonight. Possibly right now.

The contraction eased, and she reached for her phone, tapping the icon she'd created specifically for Trinity. Robin switched the call into speaker mode and set the phone on the edge of the sink, so she could concentrate on deep-breathing.

The phone rang five times.

"Hello!" Trinity's bright voice said. "This is Trinity Winsor. I'm not available right now, but go ahead and leave a message. I'll get back to you as soon as—"

With a jab of her index finger, Robin ended the call. Trinity called or texted at least once a day—wore a freaking Apple watch—so of course the one time Robin desperately needed her to answer, she didn't.

Robin moaned through another contraction, this one no weaker than the last. When she could breathe again, she texted Trinity. *Pick up, please. Having contractions.*

Robin didn't even have a hospital bag ready. She opened the cabinet under the sink and pulled out her travel kit, which was missing toothpaste and deodorant. She had to stand to reach both, shelved above the toilet, but that simple physical action triggered a third contraction.

There was no time for this. She needed to leave the house, immediately. She zipped up the travel kit, sans toothpaste, and headed for the stairs, propping herself up against the wall with a hand. Contractions stopped her twice before she got to the bottom. Still, it wasn't like she was going to squat down and deliver the baby right here on the floor. Her water hadn't broken. Her cervix still had to dilate. Well, probably *was* in the process of dilating at this very moment. But it all took time. Enough time.

Several more contractions overtook her on the way back to the truck, but she managed to slide in behind the wheel and plop her bathroom kit on the passenger seat. She waited for the last one to subside, then reached into her back pocket for her phone. She'd try Trinity once more, and then Andrews.

Except there was no phone.

It was upstairs, in the bathroom.

Robin heard herself whimper. Even if she could make it up those stairs again, no way she'd be able to get back down. Panic rose like bile in her throat. What did she do? Start honking? Hope someone heard?

A faint snore reminded her of Seth, in the back seat.

"Seth! Sethie!" She reached back and shook his leg. "Wake up, buddy. Mommy needs you. Come on." Finally, even though it probably made her the worst mother ever, she pinched him.

He cried out, a sad little half-asleep sound, but in the rearview mirror she saw his eyes flutter and his head come up.

Her stomach tightened again. She grabbed the steering wheel and moaned.

"Mommy?" Seth mumbled blearily. "Is it brekfess?"

Robin gulped a lungful of air. "No, sweetie. Mommy—"

This was not going to work. How was she even going to get him unbuckled? He'd gotten himself out that once, but he was half asleep and barely coherent. What if she sent him into the house, and he got distracted and never came back out?

Only one possible solution presented itself. It was the very last thing she wanted. But at this point, she was too desperate for pride.

Robin keyed the ignition, turned her emergency blinkers on, and drove.

The streets were empty, thank God, and twice she braked to wait until a contraction passed. They were coming fast and hard, now. She remembered what the crown of Seth's head had felt like, pressing into her pelvis, and fortunately she wasn't feeling that yet.

Cyril's blinds were shut, but there was a light on inside and Robin breathed a heavy sigh of relief when she saw his fingers spreading the slats. She honked. Not because she didn't think he would have come out anyway, but—just because.

He was dressed. Black shirt, plaid pajama pants, but *dressed*.

Robin cranked down the window. "Hurry." The word came out a whisper as every muscle in her body pulled inward.

"Are you—?" His eyes widened, abruptly. "Oh. Oh shit."

"Cereal!" Seth shrieked, from the back seat. "*Cereal!*"

He put a hand up, index finger extended. "Hold on," he said. "Just hold on." He turned and disappeared into the house.

Robin moaned.

"Mommy?" Seth was wide awake, now. "What's happen?"

Robin dragged herself over the gear shaft and into the passenger seat. "Sweetie—honey—Mommy's body is having the baby. We're—oh God." She paused, breathed. Waited. The pain washed over her, head to toe, and then dissipated. But even when the contraction was over, her stomach was still tense. Just prepping for the next one. Quick. "Mommy's going to make some funny noises, okay? It might be a little scary. But it's okay. Mommy is okay. Everything is going to be fine. Having a baby hurts, but it's normal. Okay?"

Seth was silent for a moment. "Kay," he decided, at last.

Cyril appeared in the doorway again. He stepped out, locked the front door, and shuffled across the gravel to the driver's side window.

"Get in," Robin tried to say, but it didn't come out as anything comprehensible. She flapped a hand toward the steering wheel.

Cyril tried the handle, found the door locked, and reached through the window to pop it open from the inside. He levered the seat back as far as it would go, then gripped the wheel and heaved himself in. Robin's left leg was still draped over the gearbox, and she didn't object when he shoved it out of the way.

The contraction let go of her, and she tried to get everything out at once: "My mom's out of town and Trinity isn't answering and I left my phone upstairs and I can't get it and I don't remember her number but her last name is" –deep breath– "oh my God what is it Winsor that's it. I'm only thirty-seven weeks which should be fine but I need you to get me to a hospital *right* now and I need you to take care of Seth because I don't want him to be scared."

"Which hospital?"

This time, it was excruciating. All she wanted to do was scream *fuck* at the top of her lungs, but Seth was in the car and she couldn't curse in front of him so she bit her lip and it came out as one long *ffffffffffffffffuuuuhhhh*. She curled her fingers into a fist and punched the dash. It hurt like hell, but in a good way, in the sense that it distracted her ever so slightly from the greater pain in her abdomen.

When she regained her senses, they were approaching the freeway onramp. Cyril glanced at her. "Which hospital?" he demanded.

"Uh—oh God, um—" She was blanking. How could she be blanking on the *hospital?*

"Pleasant Valley? Kaiser Oxnard? Community Mem—"

"Kaiser!" she blurted. "Kaiser in—"

All she was conscious of, after that, was Cyril's profile, him staring bullets out the window, and Seth shouting "Too loud! *Too loud!*" as she screamed.

Then they were at the hospital, and Cyril pulled up outside the double doors of the ER, the spot designated for ambulances, and bellowed *Help* as he spilled out of the truck. Robin felt as if she was watching it all from afar, somehow, even as she moaned and wailed.

Someone came with a wheelchair and a clipboard because even though she was giving birth right here and now they were still going to make her fill out the goddamn paperwork and someone told Cyril to take his wife up to L&D because there was no head coming out of her vagina and they didn't want her in the ER.

Then they were in the elevator, which was the slowest elevator anyone had ever made in the history of the whole world, why would they make an elevator so slow, and she was sitting on the edge of the wheelchair seat, gripping the handles and screaming and trying not to move a muscle because moving at all somehow made it hurt even impossibly more. Seth, her baby, was clinging to Cyril's leg, deathly silent as Cyril tried to fill out the paperwork from the information he'd found in her purse, which was looped over his arm.

Then there was an innocent little *ding* and another five thousand hours later the elevator door slid open and Cyril stabbed at the intercom and told them to come "Fucking *get* your patient because she is about to give birth in the *fucking* hall! Sorry, kid."

Eventually there was a buzz, just like when she had picked Cyril up from jail, and a nurse opened one of the fire doors. The instant she saw Robin she said, "This way," and cleared a path through the center of labor and delivery. And then they were in a nice, spacious room with several nurses and they were trying to get Robin to move to a bed but she couldn't lie down or even get out of the chair because every time she moved every muscle in her body contracted into an explosion of pain. She couldn't talk or even look at anything, anywhere, because the lights were too bright and it was all just *too much*.

Someone helped her undress, or rather undressed her while she sat, every muscle taut, concentrating on the floor and not moving, and then tied her in a loose gown. At some point she transferred to the bed, though she remained perched on the very edge, balanced with the balls of her feet just *so* on the floor, and with her next full breath she screamed for an epidural and didn't stop until Cyril squeezed her shoulders and spoke into her ear, firm and low: "It's too late. You're at eight centimeters."

It was then she realized the thing she was holding was his arm, and her nails were tearing bloody tracks in his flesh. "Sorry sorry sorry," she exhaled. She tried to let go but she couldn't move. "Sorry sorry."

"It's fine."

Seth. Where was he? Cyril needed to be with him. He must be terrified. She wanted to tell Cyril to leave her and go to him but all that came out was "Seth."

"One of the nurses has him outside with some crayons. He's okay."

"Get in closer, Daddy," one of the nurses said. "Here, try sitting on the bed. Support her."

"I'm not—"

But it didn't matter. He was something to hold onto, and she *held*. Someone tried to coax her into lying down, again, and she only shook her head and mewled. All she could manage was to inch up onto the bed on her knees, arms wrapped around some part of Cyril, and slam her forehead into his soft belly, over and over. Her rear end, which the airy hospital gown completely failed to cover, hung over the end of the bed, and she couldn't possibly have cared any less. "Okay," one of the nurses said. "We'll make it work."

She had no idea how long it went on. Five minutes, eternity. Every moment so swift and slow as molasses at the same time. She had never been so *present*. "It's okay," Cyril said, over and over. "You can do this."

Finally, she managed to lift her head long enough to scream, "*No. I. Can't!*"

He shut up after that.

"Oh, Robin. I'm so sorry I didn't pick up." Trinity's voice broke through the unending agony. "I'm here now. I'm here for you."

Robin wanted to ask how Cyril had contacted her, or had she put the information on the birth plan she'd filed with the hospital, or what? But the thoughts ran, broken ticker-tape through her mind. The rest of her was too busy trying to avoid pain to speak.

Cyril squeezed her shoulders again. "I'm going to take Seth home."

"Okay," she huffed. "Yeah. Okaaa—" The last word disappeared into ragged wail.

"Sweetie," Trinity said, somewhere close to her ear. "You need to let go."

But she couldn't. She just *couldn't*. Cyril was not a person, he was a physical object, and he was holding her together. When he tried to slide off the bed, she whimpered and clamped down. Then she buried her face in his stomach and let out something between a scream and a sob. He smelled terrible and that was fine, because his smell was something other than agony.

"Mommy?" Seth said, from somewhere to the left. What was he doing here? Who had let him in? Robin hoped he wasn't standing there watching her lose control of her bowels.

Confusion. Nurses talking. Someone inserted a hand into her vaginal canal.

"Just take him," Cyril said. "It's fine. No. Go. You have a key—okay. I'll call you when—yeah. Go."

"You're at nine centimeters, honey. Doing real good. Can I break your water?"

Robin screamed.

"I'm going to break your water, and then you need to push. Okay?"

She nodded into Cyril's stomach.

He translated: "Go ahead."

There was a sharp poke which seemed like it ought to have been painful, but it wasn't, and a gush of liquid down her thighs. Suddenly the bed beneath her was slick, and her knees slid apart. And then it was coming.

"Hold on, hold on," a nurse grunted. "Don't push yet. Daddy, you need to hold her up, kind of like a squatting position? It's awkward, I know, but grab her thigh—there you go. Good. Just like that."

Robin tried to ask a question, but all that came out was a high-pitched whine.

"What's that, honey?"

She clawed at Cyril. "Can I?" she mewled. "Push?"

"Is it okay to push?" he relayed.

"Oh—yes, yes! As hard as you can. Whenever you want."

Robin pushed.

"There's the head! Excellent. Breathe, honey, breathe. Okay, another big one, ready? Hard as you can. *Good*. All right, take a minute to breathe if you need to. You're doing just fine."

Why would she take a minute? Why would she want any time at all? All she wanted was for the pain to be over. Robin drew in a long breath through the sweat-soaked cotton of Cyril's shirt, lifted her head, and roared. Even after her breath was gone she could feel it wasn't over, and she kept pushing with every ounce of strength she had and—

"Here he comes! There's his head! He's out!"

The rest of the little body slithered out, and Robin collapsed into Cyril's pillowy bulk. It was over. Over. Finally. And for the first time in months, she could breathe—*really* breathe. She rolled her head to one side and sucked in a gallon of oxygen, felt it flood her lungs and radiate energy throughout her body. She was her own person, herself, once again.

And then panic.

"Where is he?" She struggled to rise, but she couldn't sit up because she was still dripping blood and who knew what else. "Is he okay?"

Cyril put his hands under her arms and lifted, inching himself off the edge of the bed. A nurse came with a clean sheet and Robin let herself be guided onto her back, absorbent padding stuffed between her legs.

She didn't care about any of that. The other end of her body was suddenly distant and irrelevant. "Is he—is he okay? Where is he?" A couple of nurses and a doctor were huddled around the baby warmer in the corner. Robin grabbed Cyril's hand. He had to be okay. He had to live. "I need to see him."

Cyril ducked his head a little to the right to see between the nurses. "Just—I think they're just checking him out."

She pressed her forehead against the back of his hand. "He has to be okay. He has to." After all of this, if it were to end in death, again, she couldn't bear it. Everything would be over.

And then—finally—a little mewling cry. Robin dropped Cyril's hand

and covered her face. The baby was breathing. He was okay. She was okay. Then she looked up and shoved Cyril toward the baby heater. "Stay with him." Someone needed to be there, next to her child—someone not in scrubs.

"Okay." Cyril shuffled over. "Um."

The pediatrician looked up. "Do you want to cut the cord?"

"Um—no. I'm not—I'm not the father."

The attending physician—a petite, bespectacled woman whom Robin had earlier counted among the nurses—knelt at the end of the bed and worked her latex-gloved hand up into Robin's vaginal canal. With her fingertips, she scraped around Robin's uterus, using her free hand to knead the outside of her abdomen. Robin clenched her teeth, but sighed with relief when the placenta slid out. "Doesn't look like you tore," the doctor said. "Should be a quick recovery."

The pediatrician turned around, bearing the baby—*her baby*—wrapped loosely in the ubiquitous hospital swaddling cloth.

"Oh," Robin breathed, as the doctor set the tiny creature in her arms. He was beautiful. So tiny, so perfect. Not Tavis, not her, not anyone—just his own perfect self. His skin was dark and his fingers were still a little blue, but coloring fast. She gazed at him, waiting for that rush of maternal affection, the one where everything else disappeared except for his beautiful little face.

It didn't come. He was a baby, a beautiful baby, but he didn't feel... somehow he didn't feel uniquely *hers*. He was no more perfect than any other newborn.

She brought him close, and as his cheek touched the bare skin of her neck he turned his head toward her, his tiny mouth opening in a perfect *O*. Robin pulled her gown away, exposing her right breast, and lowered him into place. She wasn't one to breastfeed in public, but here, in this moment, self-consciousness seemed entirely beside the point. He continued to root, mewling again, so she took her breast in one hand and popped it, gently, into his mouth. He latched. Just like that. She felt, weirdly, as if she were watching him suckle at someone else's breast.

Relief. That was what she felt. He was alive. That was good. She, too, would continue to live.

The pediatrician put a finger out to brush his little cheek. "A little early, but very healthy. Six pounds, five ounces, nineteen inches long."

"Jesus." Cyril's voice cut through the post-delivery hush. "Isn't anybody gonna tell her?"

Robin's heart stopped cold. What was wrong? Did he have Down Syndrome? FAS? She'd gotten blackout drunk twice after Tav's death, and the OB had said it was unlikely to matter at that early stage of the pregnancy, but what if she'd been wrong? He looked normal, to her, but with newborns it was always hard to tell. She couldn't deal with anything else right now. The baby was out, he was alive. Nothing else. No more.

The doctor smiled, apologetically. "Ultrasounds are not completely reliable. 'He' is a she."

"What?" Robin laughed with incredulous relief. "Are you serious?" She pulled back the blanket and spread the scrawny chicken legs. "Oh my—oh my goodness. How—?"

"Sometimes the umbilical cord gets in the way, and... well..." She shrugged. "You get what you get."

Robin looked at the baby again. She had fallen asleep nursing, her mouth still open slightly. *She.* Her brain struggled to reorganize itself around the change of pronouns. *She.*

"I'm so thirsty," Robin realized.

"We'll get you some water right now." The OB gestured to one of the nurses, who nodded and left. Briefly, she conferred with the pediatrician before they both bowed out, promising to check in later.

Cyril stood alone in the middle of the delivery room floor. He glanced at the curtain, then looked at the floor and cleared his throat. "I'll go."

"No." Robin had not for an instant forgotten that he was a disgusting, horrible human being who had no right to speak to her, ever again. Let alone witness the birth of her child. But Trinity was home with Seth, who was—she hoped—sound asleep, and her mother was away.

The first night after Seth had been born, they'd swaddled him and put him in the bassinet. Without warning, he'd spit up a bunch of amniotic fluid and started choking on it. Robin had been unable to reach him from the bed, and if Tavis hadn't been there—

"No," she said again. "You don't get to just *leave*."

A nurse tapped at the door and entered with two giant plastic carafes of ice water. "One for you too," she said, handing the second to Cyril. Both had straws stuck in the top, but Robin seized hers by the handle and gulped straight from the lip.

"Look at that," the nurse said, leaning in to admire the newborn as she worked a stethoscope out from under her collar. The baby was resting, quietly awake, in the crook of Robin's arm. The little eyes, shiny with antibiotic ointment, stared raptly at Robin's face. "She adores you."

Cyril sipped from his straw a few times, and then just continued to stand there in the middle of the floor as the nurse checked Robin's vitals.

Robin waved at the couch by the window. "Sit down."

He nodded, silently, and shuffled around the end of the bed. He put the carafe on top of a cabinet and let himself down on the crappy convertible couch, leaning back with a labored sigh. The seat wasn't deep enough to support his center of gravity, and he had to shift sideways, struggling to pull one knee up beneath his belly. The front of his shirt was wet, either with her spit or tears, and his left pant leg was smeared with some sort of bodily fluid. He brushed at the streaks of blood on his arms.

She ignored him until the nurse left, then decided to ignore him some more. The baby was rooting again, so she pulled the gown down and let him—*her*—have a go at her other breast. In her peripheral vision, she saw Cyril shift his gaze to the window. As if modesty suddenly mattered.

The baby was latching far better than Seth ever had. Robin didn't want to set her expectations too high, but there might be a glimmer of hope that this child would be a calm, easy ride. It was the very least the universe could offer.

When the baby passed out again, Robin laid her tummy-down between her breasts. They kept the L&D intentionally warm, now, to promote skin-to-skin contact. She fumbled for the bed controls, motored it down to a forty-five-degree angle, and closed her eyes.

"You… want me to turn off the lights?" Cyril's voice was a low rumble.

Robin didn't answer immediately. "Yeah," she said finally. "Go ahead."

He huffed and grunted himself to his feet, then spent a few minutes shuffling around to various switch plates, trying to figure out which combination turned off one section of overhead lights as well as the lamp above the bed.

Robin didn't hear him sit down again, because at that point exhaustion had overtaken her, and her consciousness melted away.

"I'M SORRY," a nurse whispered, flicking on a single dim can light just inside the door.

Robin blinked. She had no idea how long she'd slept, except that it hadn't been more than an hour or so. The nurse was one she hadn't seen before.

"Sorry," the woman whispered again. "I just need to check you and the baby."

"I know." She glanced at Cyril. His head lolled to the left a little, couched on the pillow of his own neck. He was snoring. She let the nurse take her temperature and blood pressure and help her change the pads down below. She also accepted the Tylenol but declined the harder drugs. Her pain level was surprisingly low.

The nurse slipped a stethoscope under the baby, listened to her heartbeat, and poked and prodded her a little more. "Everything's just fine," she said. "We'll let you both rest for now, but in a few hours we'll need to take her for her shots and a blood draw."

Robin nodded, and the nurse ducked under the curtain and out the door.

Suddenly, she remembered her mom. Glennis was out of cell phone range, but there had to be a landline at the camp. Her mom would want to know ASAP. What time was it? Robin looked around the room, but didn't see a clock. She still didn't have her phone. "Hey," she said. "What time is it?"

Cyril didn't move.

"Hey. Asshole." She reached for the rolling cart next to her bed, grabbed the crumpled paper cup they'd given her the Tylenol in, and lobbed it at his face.

He jerked and sucked in a long breath.

"What time is it?"

He blinked, blearily, rubbed his eyes, and managed at last to focus somewhere above her head. "Three."

"Oh." Robin considered borrowing his phone to text, but—no, even if it went through, she didn't want to deliver the news like that. "My mom's gonna be so surprised." And disappointed to have missed the event. But a granddaughter—that would make up for it. Robin had already passed on all her Legos and action figures, but Glennis had boxes of carefully preserved dress-up clothes and rag dolls stacked in the rafters of her garage.

Robin fumbled for her water and finished it off. "I'm starving."

It hadn't been a request, but Cyril struggled to his feet again and lumbered out the door.

The baby was still out cold. Robin shifted, adjusted the pillow behind her neck, and reclined the bed a little more. She closed her eyes, but even as tired as she was, sleep wasn't going to come. She could hear nurses in the corridor, walking back and forth, and beeping from some machine out in the hall. Muffled cries from the room next door. She wished one of the nurses would appear and take the baby for her shots.

Robin looked down at the tiny face half-buried in her right breast. Tried to see herself in the O-shaped mouth, the upturned upper lip, the dark wavy hair. "I love you," she said, almost experimentally, and realized only then that she hadn't said it before. *Should* have said it before now.

She had spent eight months trying to pretend this wasn't happening. And now... what if that was a switch she couldn't turn back on?

The door clacked open and she looked up, expecting a nurse to duck around the privacy curtain. Then Cyril yanked the cloth aside, muttering a curse. He dropped a brown cafeteria tray on the cart next to her bed. "Kitchen's not open until five. Nurses' station had this."

"Oh." He'd collected four Jell-O cups, three juice boxes, two spoons, and a plastic bowl of broth. She pried the lid off the broth and dipped a finger in; it was lukewarm.

He took one of the Jell-O cups and a spoon and reinstalled himself on the couch.

Robin picked up the bowl with one hand and sipped, careful not to spill on her daughter's head. It wasn't exactly food, but it satisfied her stomach for the time being.

"Trinity texted," Cyril informed her. "Earlier." He put the empty Jell-O cup and spoon on the cabinet next to his water. "She'll bring Seth when he wakes up in the morning. I can take him after that, if that's…"

"Okay."

He was silent for another moment, and then cleared his throat. "Look. I—"

"Do you think this is really something I want to talk about right after the birth of my daughter?"

He closed his mouth. Shook his head. "No. Sorry. I—I'm sorry."

The baby stirred, letting out a faint whimper. Robin guided her toward her right breast this time, but the baby's latch was only momentary. She broke away and let out an angry little bleat. Robin stroked her cheek, then thought to check the diaper. The room was too dark to tell whether the yellow indicator line had turned blue, but the diaper felt a little puffy. "Go flag down a nurse," Robin told Cyril. She could have used the intercom on the side of the bed, but it wasn't an emergency or even particularly urgent. Cyril could hang out in the hall until a nurse had a spare moment. "I think she needs a diaper change."

Cyril let out a rumble of irritation, but he got to his feet and flicked the light on above the bed. He put a hand on the cart with the baby bassinet, leaned over, and yanked out the bottom drawer. He pulled out a couple of itty bitty diapers and slapped them down in the bassinet. "I'll do it."

Robin squinted in the light. "Seriously?"

"How hard can it be?" He came to the side of the bed and thrust out his hands, palms up.

Abruptly, Robin's self-consciousness returned. She eased the baby off her breast and covered up—as much as was possible with a thin hospital gown, in any case. "Just remember to support—"

"Her head, I know." He scooped the baby out of Robin's hands. For a moment he held her suspended in the air, one hand cradling the curve of her skull. Then she kicked out one scrawny leg, and he smiled and tucked her, with surprising tenderness, into the crook of his elbow. He glanced at Robin. "I'm not a fucking idiot."

Robin shrugged and watched as he set her down in the bassinet. Her arms and legs jerked and her face screwed up into a pre-wail. "Sh-sh-sh," he said. "Hold on." He hummed twinkle-twinkle, then began to sing in a low, husky voice. Her face relaxed and her eyes roamed. Quickly, he ripped the diaper tabs open and pulled it out from under her rear.

"Leave the diaper in the bassinet," Robin said. "The nurses will want to know she peed."

Cyril nodded, still singing, and inched the back of the new diaper under her rear. He folded the front up and then pulled it down again. There was a dip in the paper material to accommodate the umbilical cord, but Robin's little girl was small enough that it overlapped anyway. He folded the top edge forward, then shook his head and folded it inward, twice, before pulling the tabs tight. Someone had left a swaddling cloth draped over the back of the bassinet, and he picked it up. "Okay, what I don't know is the wrapping thing."

"It doesn't—"

"Just tell me what to do."

She rolled her eyes. "Fine. Fold the corner over. Not that much—yeah. That goes under her head." Robin waited as he got it positioned beneath the baby. "Okay, pull the left side over her shoulder, pretty tight, and tuck it under her ribs on the right. Like between her arm and—yeah."

As Cyril bent over the infant, her little eyes focused on his face. He met her gaze and made a little tut-tut noise before sticking out his tongue. She was too little to giggle, but she *stared.* "Okay?" he said. "Now what?"

"The, uh, the bottom comes up and gets tucked into the same—" Her voice broke. "God damn it. How—" She shook her head. "How is it that you can be an absolute disgusting excuse for a human being, and yet—"

And yet he wrapped the last corner of the blanket around her daughter, turning her into a tight little baby burrito. He lifted her out of the bassinet, still supporting her head, and tucked her back into his elbow. "Thought you didn't want to talk about it," he rumbled.

"I don't." She pressed her fingers against her nose. "God. Fuck. I…"

"Say it," he said. "Just say whatever you need to say."

"It should have been him," she blurted. "Here. With me. Not you." And then she was crying. "It should have been him."

"I know," he rumbled.

"God damnit." She reached for him, blindly, but her fingertips only brushed the cotton hem of his shirt. "Just—come here."

He shuffled to the side of the bed and she put her face in his shirt and wept.

"I wish." She sobbed. "I wish *you* were dead."

He just stood there, holding her sleeping baby as she cried.

Finally, she took a couple of deep, slow breaths and pushed him away. She wiped her eyes on the coarse white bed sheet before holding her hands out for the baby. He handed over the little bundle, hiked his pants up, and turned back toward the couch.

"I need to ask you something, Cyril."

He turned half-toward her, waiting.

"You, and Tavis…" It was a suspicion that had been creeping up on her for a while now. Because writing emails to stop her from offing herself only worked for one letter, or two. Not twenty-five or thirty. "Were you… in love with him?"

Whatever Cyril had expected her to ask, it clearly wasn't that. If it were possible, his face turned a shade whiter. "What?" he said at last, quietly.

Robin had just given birth to a child. She wasn't afraid of anything or anyone, least of all words. "You heard me. Were you in love with my husband?"

Cyril's mouth opened slightly. "No," he sputtered. "I—I mean, he was like a brother, but not like—not like *that.*"

"Are you sure?" All the time they spent together. The bond she never could quite understand. The way Cyril had let himself go, completely, after their wedding. And the letters—they had kept Tavis alive, or at least the illusion of him. Perhaps Cyril had written those words as much for himself as Robin.

"Look," he said, and closed his eyes. "I don't see people as people. I see them as... obstacles. To be circumvented. Or... manipulated." He opened his eyes again, and looked down at the baby in her arms. When he spoke again, his voice was low whisper. "I know that's fucked up. Love is not a feeling. Or a word. It's an action. And that kind of love—the love you are talking about—is... Well." He shook his head. "It's not something I'm capable of performing." He tried to lift his eyes, briefly, and failed. "Does that answer your question?"

She looked at him, standing there in his rumpled shirt on the scuffed linoleum floor, blood-streaked arms dangling limp at his sides. "Yeah," she whispered. "I think it does."

"Yeah. Well." He ran a hand over the stubble peppering his face and reached for the arm of the couch. "I'm gonna try and get some sleep."

"Wait."

He looked down at the floor and blew out a heavy, wet breath. Then he nodded and turned to face her.

Robin set the tight little baby burrito back in Cyril's uncertain arms.

He looked at the infant face for a long moment, unmoving. She was drifting back to sleep now, her mouth twitching at the corner.

"She looks so tiny," Robin whispered. "Next to you."

His mouth twitched up on one side. "Everyone—"

"Looks tiny next to you, yes, yes."

"Sorry. God. I'm sorry." He closed his eyes and shook his head. "You—giving birth, I—" His voice broke. He looked at the wall and bit his upper lip, hard.

She had heard of men getting emotional at a delivery, but Cyril was the last man on earth Robin would have expected it from. "Hey, um... it's okay."

"No. It's not. It's—unequivocally not." He shook his head. Tried to speak again, looked at the ceiling, and shook his head again. "I... I'm not even going to ask for forgiveness. Not from you. But if you would let me, I will try—" he swallowed. "I will try—very hard—to be a friend."

She waited, quietly, until he mastered himself, then reached out and adjusted the blanket around her daughter's chin. "Sonora, meet Uncle

Cyril. He was your Daddy's best friend."

27

THE HOSPITAL AWAKENED AT FIVE. A new shift of doctors and nurses stopped by to introduce themselves and take her stats, then whisked the baby down the hall for her shots, a bath, and a blood draw. Cleaning crews came through, and someone else from housekeeping took breakfast orders and promised food ASAP.

With Seth, Robin had gotten an epidural and a catheter and she'd rested in bed for twenty-four hours. This time the carafe of water went straight through her system.

"I really don't want to ask you this," Robin said. "But I need to use the bathroom."

Cyril glanced up from his phone. "Not like I haven't seen your tits and ass already."

"Wow, that helps."

He shrugged and shoved himself forward. "All the shit kinda takes the sexiness out of it. I'm not sure how husbands can still want to fuck after seeing—"

"Hey," she warned.

"Jesus, I'm joking. Pretty sure any man with a brain would gladly hit that ass—"

"Oh my *God*, you are foul." But Robin was laughing. Because he was so obviously trying to make her mad. Perhaps it was giving him too much credit to think he was doing it specifically to make her feel less self-conscious, but that was the result. She popped the bedrail down and smacked his arm before letting him help her up. "Oh," she moaned immediately, clutching the rubbery flesh of her stomach. "Oh my God, my guts are falling out."

"Are you okay? Should I call—"

Robin laughed again, this time at his concern. "No." She'd half expected him to reply with a joke about baby heads and vaginal canals. She hobbled toward the bathroom door. "This is just what having a baby feels like, unfortunately."

"Why the hell would you do this more than once?" He opened the door with his free hand and edged himself out of her way.

"Love."

"Clearly a synonym for insanity."

Robin shifted from Cyril's arm to the rail on the bathroom wall. "That's about the size of it." She nodded toward the bag of supplies the nurse had hung inside the bathroom door. "Can you just, like, put that on the floor by toilet?"

He did as asked, then backed out and swung the door shut until it was only open about an inch. "I promise I won't look."

"Trust me, you don't want to." Robin eased herself onto the toilet and waited as blood and coagulated tissue drained out of her. It wouldn't stop for at least a few days, but when the flow tapered to a slow drip she hooked the handle of the bag with one finger and pulled out the squirt bottle. She filled it with warm water from the sink—which was thankfully within reach of the toilet—and rinsed herself as best as she could. Not that it made much difference, but it felt good to get rid of some of the crusted blood. Then she sprayed herself with the topical anesthetic and worked herself back into the mesh shorts that weren't supposed to be underwear, really, so much as something to hold the giant sanitary pads in place. The ice pack she'd been using was warm and limp, so she tossed it and popped a new one before tucking it into the pad. The whole thing felt like wearing a diaper packed with rocks.

By the time she got to her feet again, she was feeling weirdly shaky, and was thankful to have Cyril to lean on as she hobbled back to bed. "Breakfast came," he informed her, even as she looked up and saw the tray.

Getting back into bed again was more painful than she'd anticipated, and Cyril retrieved two cushions from the couch so she could recline comfortably on her side. Then he opened all the plastic-wrapped items on her tray, adjusted the height of the table, and positioned it in front of her.

"Thanks," she said. And meant it. Lack of sleep was starting to catch up with her, and she felt weirdly out-of-body as she ate lumpy oatmeal and sipped orange-flavored water.

Cyril was standing at the end of the bed, eating from his own tray, when a chorus of honks sounded outside. He went to the window and pulled back the gauze drape.

"Somebody get rear ended?"

He grunted a negative. "They found us. Well. Me."

"The news people?"

"Yeah. Sorry."

"Not your fault. I mean, it kind of is. But I don't…" Robin tossed her fork onto the tray and made a noise of disgust. She was still hungry, but it would have to wait. The entire room was rocking gently. "I… am gonna try and sleep now."

Cyril put down his oatmeal, drew the blackout curtain, and turned out the lights.

"Robin."

Her sleep had not been so deep that she was surprised by Cyril's voice. She cleared her throat, wiped her eyes, and reached for the orange juice, although already she was dreading the prospect of another trip to the bathroom. "I was dreaming about him." His words; his voice, not quite audible, in her ear. A kind of half-lucid daydream.

On the couch, Cyril was silent a moment, apparently not sure how to respond to that. "Trinity's on her way over," he said finally. "With Seth. I told her to come in the back."

"Okay." That was good, she guessed. She was so tired she was having a hard time registering any kind of emotion. She blinked and then realized that Cyril was holding her daughter. "Oh… they brought her back."

"She's doing that thing with her mouth. I think she's hungry."

"Okay." Robin motored the bed up a bit, groaning as it placed more pressure on her nether regions. She shifted onto one butt cheek and held out an arm.

The bassinet was next to Cyril, and he put the baby in it before getting up from the couch. She wailed in protest, the first forceful sound she had made. "Hold your horses, kid," he grunted, scooping her up again.

Robin accepted the little bundle and sighed with relief when Sonora latched on, strong. Her milk must be coming in.

"That's kind of amazing," Cyril noted. "When you think about it."

Robin looked down at her daughter, sucking with gusto. "I don't feel anything."

"Really? Because that looks like it would hurt."

She almost let it go. Then she shook her head. "No. I mean... I don't *feel* anything." There was, suddenly, a lump in her throat. "For her."

"Oh," he said.

It was a terrible admission. She didn't know what she expected him to say—to be shocked, or indifferent, or perhaps mostly just a witness. With Tavis, some critical part of her heart had also died. "When I had Seth, I was so in love I couldn't sleep for twenty-four hours. I literally stayed up all night because I couldn't stop staring at his face."

"Do you need anything else?"

"Um... what?"

He pointed at the couch, now two cushions barer. "I'm gonna sit down. Do you need anything?"

"Oh. Um, no, I guess not."

He dropped back into the couch and settled himself with a few grunts before pulling out his phone. "Give yourself a fucking break."

"For not caring about my own child?"

"What do you want me to say, that you're a terrible mother? Because you're not. You lost your goddamn husband. Hell," he added, tossing a hand toward the baby, "even if you never feel a single thing for that kid, you'll still feed her and diaper her and hug and kiss her every bit as much as you do Seth. That's what matters."

Robin felt a tear slide down her cheek. This was all ridiculous and would probably pass in a week or two, but.... "What if she *knows*?"

Cyril let the phone drop. He let out an elaborate sigh and then, finally, looked her straight in the eye. "You love her," he said. "You just don't know it yet. Jesus. You are so high on hormones."

Two hours later, Trinity arrived with a bag of clothes and Seth in tow. "I don't think they spotted us," she said. "Robin. Thank—"

"*Cereal!*"

Cyril snorted himself awake half a second before Seth did a cannonball into his stomach. "Oh—God," he wheezed, still managing to catch Seth before he tumbled head-first onto the floor. "Jesus. Hey, kid."

Seth threw his arms around Cyril's neck as far as he could reach, shut his eyes tight, and squeezed. "I love you," he whispered.

Cyril looked at Robin over Seth's curls. They hadn't discussed this. But the fact that she hadn't woken him or told him to get out spoke for itself. He didn't say anything, either, but she saw the thanks in his eyes.

"Hey bud," Robin said, when Seth finally seemed to be finished celebrating Cyril, "come meet the baby."

Seth looked from Cyril to Robin, clearly worried that Cyril would disappear as soon as he let go. Cyril plopped him on the ground and gave him a shove. "Go on, kid. Say hello."

Seth put his hands on the bed railing and peered over. Robin held Sonora out, then unwrapped the swaddling far enough for one little hand to wiggle out. Seth reached over the railing, extended one finger, and poked his sister in the face. She wrinkled her nose and opened an eye.

"I have a surprise for you," Robin said.

Seth looked up, suddenly very alert.

"This... is not your brother, buddy. It's your sister."

Trinity, who had visibly restrained herself from interrupting this family moment, put her hands over her mouth and squealed.

"Well, buddy?" Robin prompted. "What do you think?"

Seth looked from her to the baby and back again. Then he shrugged. "Can we go home?"

28

GLENNIS CUT HER RETREAT SHORT the instant she got the news, arrived just as Robin was being discharged, and moved into Robin's office-guest-room for two whole weeks. The thing with babies, though, was this: it wasn't until a month in that they started cluster feeding and screaming bloody murder at four in the morning. Only then did sleep deprivation begin to wear Robin down to the point of putting the cereal in the fridge and the milk in the cupboard and her keys on top of the bookshelf. (Why *there?*) Only then did she neglect to drink the requisite five gallons of water every twenty-four hours; only then did the slight dehydration snowball into mastitis; only then was she already up at four AM, massaging her breasts in a scalding hot shower, when the baby decided it was time for her morning screamfest.

Only then did she accept Cyril's standing offer to come entertain her four-year-old for the evening, and the meals from church were gone so all she could manage for dinner was spaghetti, which was fine, who cared, except that after she'd started boiling the noodles she opened the fridge and realized that the jar of sauce she thought was three quarters full was not any quarters full, and she decided to make boxed mac and cheese instead or maybe frozen corn dogs but she couldn't figure out whether she was supposed to turn on the oven first or get the baking sheet out or what, so she ended up standing over the sink, crying hot silent tears, and even then all she could think of was how this was just going to make her even more dehydrated and when on earth was she going to find time to drink another gallon of water? And then the baby started crying again and she decided life was pretty much over.

"Hey."

Somehow she hadn't heard Cyril coming in from the living room. He took the wooden spoon from her hand and set it on the counter. She sniffed and wiped her eyes, but she couldn't think of anything to say, so she didn't.

"Look at me." He studied her bloated, tear-streaked face for a moment. "You need sleep."

The complete obviousness of that statement, combined with the utter impossibility of it ever happening again, prompted her to burst into loud sobs. The baby, hearing her, ratcheted up her cries another notch. The baby didn't care if she cried. All the baby wanted was milk. Or not milk. Who knew what the hell else. And then Seth, poor Seth, who deserved more than a mother who—

Cyril put a hand on the counter and leaned over, letting out a grunt of effort as he tried to reach the car seat handle. He missed on the first attempt, but managed on the second. He lifted the seat onto the counter, fiddled with the handle a moment before figuring out how to flip it back, and plucked Sonora out. She blinked at him for half a second, dangling in the air between his hands, and then ratcheted her wail up another couple of notches.

He put her over one shoulder and patted her back, to no effect whatsoever. "Go upstairs," he told Robin. "Go to bed."

"But she—"

"You were feeding her when I arrived."

Robin put her hands over her eyes, as if that could stop the wailing. "So?" As far as Sonora was concerned, any increment of time longer than twelve seconds was *forever*.

"So that was like twenty minutes ago. She's not going to starve." He put his free hand on her back and shoved her out of the kitchen, one step at a time. "Go. To. Bed."

Robin stumbled through the living room, where Seth was watching television. Again. Poor kid had probably watched more TV in the past two months than he had in the rest of his life combined. She bent to put her arms around him and kissed his little face, and he was so absorbed in *My Little Pony* that he didn't even react. She was failing him, and her daughter was still screaming, and—

"Jesus Christ," Cyril snapped. "Would you just *go?*"

HER PHONE WAS RINGING. Her breasts were rock hard and throbbing. God. What time was it? Who was calling at—one in the morning? Cyril? Robin blinked at the phone. Somewhere in the house, Sonora was screaming. Didn't he have the kids—oh God, what had happened?

Even as she answered, she was rolling out of bed. "What is it? What's wrong?"

"Calm down. She needs to be fed. I'm not sure I can get up the—oh."

Robin lurched down the stairs and into the living room. Cyril had wedged himself into the rocker-recliner in the corner. Sonora lay cradled in the depression formed by the top of his stomach and his man-boobs, kicking her feet out, right-left-right, in the little dance that meant *I am incredibly angry*. Which she almost always was.

Cyril started to pick her up, but Robin reached over and plucked the baby out of his hands. She dropped onto the couch, yanked her tank top down, and plugged her right nipple into Sonora's scream. *Suck*, Robin willed. *Suck, damn it.*

Sonora latched. Silence. "Oh," Robin sighed, sinking back into the cushions. The pain drained away in a rush of oxytocin. "Oh, fuck yes." Now if the baby would just keep feeding until she could switch to the left side, too. It was so much better than pumping. She glanced down at the breast in question and saw that her shirt was wet, since it had apparently decided it needed to let down milk too. More clothing changes, more laundry, more everything.

It was another minute before she remembered Cyril. He was still sitting in the rocking chair, fiddling with something on his phone. "Thank you," she said. "For the sleep, I mean."

His eyes flickered to her, her breasts, and quickly away. "Sorry it wasn't longer."

"It can't be, at this point." Even if she pumped in advance, she'd still have to get up to pump again. "But that was the longest I've slept since she was born." Four hours. A fucking miracle. How on earth was she going to survive six more months of this?

He shrugged. Then he gripped the arms of the chair and heaved himself forward. It took him two tries, but he got to his feet and shuffled toward the kitchen. He cleared his throat noisily.

"Where are you going?"

"To take a piss."

Robin looked down at her daughter's face, milk puddling at one corner of her very satisfied little mouth. Palpating her breast revealed that it had deflated significantly, so she stuck her pinky finger into Sonora's mouth to break the seal and quickly swapped boobs before she had a chance to scream. All she was to this kid was a giant bag of milk and feeding her felt *so good*.

There was a loud thud from the back of the house, and then she heard the office toilet flush. Hopefully Cyril hadn't just broken the seat. His footsteps plodded back into the kitchen, and she heard a clink of silverware on ceramic. Helping himself, apparently.

Robin was starving. She wanted to call out and ask him to get her some of whatever he was having, but she didn't want to startle Sonora now that she was past the desperation phase of the feed. With her belly half full, she'd be more than happy to forgo the rest of the feed in favor of some more screaming, and then she'd be starving again in an hour. Robin wanted to cram every single possible last fraction of an ounce into that little belly while she had the chance. Sonora wasn't underweight, at least for her adjusted age, but she was still skinny. Babies didn't sleep until they got fat.

Cyril appeared in the doorway, holding a bowl. Robin held a finger to her lips and he nodded understanding. He shuffled across the room, used a leg to push one end of the coffee table toward her, and set the bowl down on top. It contained spaghetti with what looked like ground beef in a cheese sauce.

"What is this?" she whispered.

He motioned to the bowl. "You had parmesan and butter, so I made some Alfredo. And added the leftover taco meat."

She raised her eyebrows in exaggerated surprise.

"What?" He shrugged. "Just because I don't cook doesn't mean I can't." He shuffled back to the rocking chair, lowered himself into it, and returned to a game on his cell phone. When, a few minutes later, Sonora popped off Robin's breast and looked around, alert, he put the phone down and held out his hands. "I'll burp her."

"Um... okay." Robin pulled her shirt straps up and passed Sonora over. The instant her hands were free she grabbed the bowl of noodles and shoveled. "Maybe it's because I'm starving, but this is really good."

"A stick of butter'll make pretty much anything good."

"Granted." She stopped halfway through the bowl to pee—the toilet was not broken—and pour herself a super-sized glass of milk. Half of it was gone by the time she sat back down on the couch in the living room. As she polished off the rest of the food, Cyril switched Sonora from one shoulder to the other and continued patting her back in firm, rhythmic thumps. Robin frowned. "How do you even know what to do?"

He nodded to his phone. "Youtube." As if to punctuate, Sonora let out a loud belch.

Robin laughed. "Wow. Okay." She gathered the dishes and took them into the kitchen, then stopped into the laundry room to change her shirt and start a load. Now that the food was hitting her stomach she was starting to feel sleepy again. Maybe if she was quick, she could get Sonora down and get another couple hours before Seth woke up. She went back into the living room and held her hands out for the baby.

"Fuck no," Cyril said. "Go back to bed."

She just stared at him. "Are you kidding?" she said finally. "You've been here for like eight hours."

"And you're here twenty-four-seven. I stay up all night to play MMOs. I can handle a baby."

"I—are you serious?" He was serious. "I, um... well, I'm not going to say no to that."

She got halfway up the stairs before turning around.

"No." Robin shook her head. "No, this is—" This was not him. Even if he was sorry about being sick and disgusting enough to write those letters, and regardless of whatever feelings he may or may not have had for her husband—Cyril did not waste time on guilt. Or at least he didn't admit it to anyone if he did. "Tell me why you're doing this."

He was rubbing Sonora's back now, with three fingers, and as she watched the motion slowed. He let her slide gently down until she had come to rest on his stomach. She was out cold.

"I made a deal," he said.

"What, with the devil?"

"The prosecutor."

"Oh." Robin pulled out the piano bench and sat. That meant... no trial. No testifying. No twenty-four-hour news coverage. Which was an absolute relief. "But... I thought you wanted to fight it."

"Changed my mind." His eyebrows jumped a little as he said it, giving the phrase a sarcastic twist.

Really? Just like that? "Are you doing this for us? Seth and me?"

He shrugged. "Nah. Just... didn't want to do more damage than I already have."

"Good." Robin didn't need him fighting her battles or making her decisions, but she'd sure as hell take this. "So—you can tell me, then."

He cocked on eyebrow.

"What you did."

"Oh." He shifted and cleared his throat. Sonora stirred a little, then went back to drooling on his chest. "Yeah. It's not a big..." He shook his head. "Tavis had more than enough to prove those two assholes were murdered. Interviews and schedules and whatever else. I showed him how to keep everything secure and not get himself red flagged. That was enough to fuck those guys, sure, but it was obvious they were just being used. If Tavis had gone public—which he wanted to, because he honestly thought people would care—his command would have thrown those two Marines under the bus and wash their hands of the whole thing. The end. So..." He rolled his eyes upward and shrugged. "I told Tav to make me a list. People's names, types of documents that might be helpful, email addresses. I'd already spent plenty of time testing Cooke's system, so I knew where all its vulnerable points were, and it was the perfect, uh... backdoor to get me past the Marines' security. I'm not saying it was easy—took me a few months to finesse what I needed out of a couple of techs—but I got enough to stage a serious hack."

"That was when the FBI cleaned your house out?"

"Not too long after, yeah." He snorted. "Like taking my machines was going to stop me. I've spent the last couple of months hacking... well, everything. And everyone."

"And then you dumped it all."

"Not *all* of it. Just... enough." He looked smug. "I could do a lot more damage, especially if this goes to trial, and the administration knows it. They're more than happy to make this about the kid. Takes the spotlight off them. They get what they want, I get what I want."

"That was your goal," she realized. Not infamy. Not chaos. Not anarchy, or whatever the hell it was that Anonymous and their ilk stood for. All this time, Cyril's agenda had been the same as Tav's. "You did this to save Shafik."

"That's what all this military shit is supposed to be about, right? Saving someone else's kids." He shrugged. "Mission accomplished."

Cyril had done as much as Tavis to make that happen. Maybe more. "You made them care."

"Nobody ever said I wasn't good at what I do."

And now he was going to prison. "So you're just... giving up? I mean, isn't there a possibility you could get off?"

He snorted. "They've got plenty to hang me on, and they're ready to do it. This way... at least it's on my terms."

"Which are what?"

"Ten years in a minimum-security prison. Not sure where, yet." He scratched his belly. "Lawyer's making sure I'll be accommodated. They'll find somewhere to stuff me, though."

"Wow," she said. "Ten years. That's..."

"Less than the thirty they wanted."

"Oh, God."

He shrugged. "My lawyer says once I'm in, he can work on getting it reduced to five. Maybe."

"Still." Seth would be... nine, at the very least. Would he even remember Cyril? "At least it won't be all over the news." Robin licked her lips. "And what about... what about his death?"

Cyril was silent for a moment. He looked dark. "Nothing," he said.

"Couldn't find a thing. But if it did happen like Walker suspected—if they found out what he was doing—they'd know better than to leave any kind of trail. Tavis was the one on the ground, IRL. I don't... have that access." He shrugged. "We'll probably never know."

Robin breathed carefully. She'd known that it would be this way, on some level, but she had hoped—deep down—that all of this would expose the truth about Tav's death. But nobody was closer to this than Cyril, and hearing it from him...

"I tried," he rumbled. "I really... tried."

"I believe you."

They sat in awkward silence for another moment. Then Robin put her hands on her knees and stood. "Well. If you're serious about staying up with that little monster, I'm absolutely going to take advantage of you."

He nodded, and she started up the stairs. Then she turned and came back down.

"Hold on," she said. "If you—if you made a deal, how come you're not in jail?"

"Lawyer's still negotiating. The whole thing is pretty complicated. But yeah, they'll set a date for self-surrender when they figure out where they're sending me. Probably in a month or two."

Two months. It had all seemed so distant and improbable. They'd taken months to charge him and make an arrest, and the trial had been pending for another couple of months. And now—ten years. An entire decade of his life, gone. She'd felt that Cyril deserved what he got, but— God. Ten years. Because he'd accessed some classified information. Because he'd used it to save a little boy. Because, whatever his flaws, he'd wanted to do right by Tav.

Robin swallowed. "I'm sorry."

Cyril shrugged. "Get some sleep."

SHE WOKE NATURALLY. It felt like the first time in years. It felt like a miracle. The sun was up. She was rested. She could hear Seth running around downstairs, laughing. And she smelled food.

Cyril was in the kitchen, Sonora propped in the crook of his arm, watching with a kind of bleary baby confusion as he ladled pancake batter onto the cast iron griddle.

"Mommy!" Seth streaked by, then did an about-face and rocketed into her arms. She winced as he slammed into her breasts, but straightened as he locked his legs around her waist. "Peoples been knocking!"

"They saw my car in the driveway," Cyril growled.

Robin shrugged. "Doesn't matter, they come knocking every other day anyway." This was what their lives were going to be until Cyril went to jail, and probably for a long while afterward. Prisoners in their own homes. She set Seth down and leaned over Cyril's arm for a peek at the baby. "You're a natural."

The instant Sonora got a whiff of her scent, she started screaming. Cyril jiggled her, to no avail. "She's either happy or furious. No in between."

"Just like her brother." Robin scooped Sonora out of his arms and took her into the living room to feed while Cyril and Seth had pancakes in the dining room. As she finished up, she heard Seth giggling. She juggled Sonora from one arm to the other to get her robe back on, then propped her against one shoulder and followed her son's voice into the dining room. "What's up, buddy?"

His giggles had become uncontrollable, and all he could do was point at Cyril, who was sitting with his back to the kitchen doorway.

Robin circled the table. He was asleep. Sitting up at the table, with a fork still in his hand. His head lolled to the left. "Oh, gosh. Okay, finish your breakfast, bud. I'll take care of him."

She retrieved the baby bouncer from the living room and buckled Sonora in. She was alert, and seemed content, at least for the moment, to ogle the owl and snail dangling from the arch over the seat. Robin angled the bouncer so she'd have a view of Seth at the table.

Then she slid the fork out of Cyril's hand and cleared his plate, which still contained three quarters of a pancake. Robin worried about startling him—what if he toppled over? But he was already starting to list to the left, so... She put a hand on his shoulder.

He snorted faintly.

Seth giggled. "He won't wake up!"

"He's been up with the baby all night, bud." She gave his shoulder a gentle squeeze, and then patted him with a little more force. "Cyril. *Cyril.*"

He snorted again and jerked forward suddenly. "Whu—"

"It's okay. You dozed off."

He blinked and shook his head, as if coming up out of deep water. "Uh. Sorry."

"Come on." Robin wedged her hand under his elbow, offering some small measure of support as he rose. The chair tipped backward, but she caught it before it fell over. "Your turn to sleep."

"Yeah. Guess so." He rubbed his eyes, then looked around until he found Seth. "Be good, kid. I'll see you later." He turned toward the foyer.

"Nope. You just fell asleep sitting up. You are not driving anywhere. This way." Robin turned him around, gave him a shove toward the back of the house.

He muttered some incomprehensible protest, but allowed himself to be steered through the kitchen, past the laundry room, and into the office. Robin swept the cushions off the sofa and hauled out the bed. Even after laundering, the sheets still smelled like her mother's perfume. She pulled the pillows out of the closet and tossed them into place. "There."

Cyril looked down and mumbled something, still incomprehensible.

"What?"

He made a vague gesture toward the bed and then rubbed his face. "Low."

"Oh," she said, understanding. "Um." Offering an arm to lean on wasn't going to help, but she grabbed the chair from her desk and bumped the lever on the bottom until the seat popped up as far as it would go. "Here," she said, pushing it to the side of the bed. "Sit down. You can kinda—"

He nodded and sagged into the chair. She hit the lever again and it sank down, not quite as low as the bed, but low enough for him to sort of roll onto the mattress. He grabbed an arm of the couch and managed to rock himself into the center of the bed. It groaned, but held.

"Blanket?"

He shook his head. But, she realized, he was going to suffocate under his own weight if he wasn't propped up. "Hold on." Robin ran back into the living room and collected a few more pillows from the couch. She helped position them under his shoulder and head, then grabbed the bottom of his shirt and pulled it down over his belly. "Okay?"

He cleared the phlegm from his throat. "Just wait 'til I try to get up again."

Cyril was being sarcastic, but the concern was a valid one. Robin frowned, then leaned over and patted his pockets. She pulled out his phone and pressed it into his hand. "Call if you need anything."

"Sorry," he mumbled.

She stopped, hand on the door jamb. "For what?"

He gestured to himself.

Robin sighed. "Cyril." She let her arm drop and came back to the bed. She put her hand on his belly and let it rest there, feeling him breathe. It was probably the baby hormones, but something deep inside of her suddenly wanted to care for this profoundly dysfunctional human being. "My kid loves you. All of you."

He didn't move. But he wasn't asleep.

She sucked in a breath. "As for me, well... Heck, any time you wanna stay up all night with my screaming baby and cook breakfast, you're more than welcome to this crappy sofa-bed. Any time at all."

Which was, as it turned out, more or less how Cyril moved in.

Part Four
Summer

29

ROBIN LET HERSELF IN the back door, smiling as she was greeted with the faint sound of Seth's laughter.

"Sh-sh-sh-*shhh*. Don't tell your mom."

Her smile disappeared. She unbuckled her tool belt, dropped it on the kitchen counter, and strode into the living room. Cyril was on the couch, Sonora propped up on his stomach. "Tell me *what?*"

Seth rolled onto his back, kicking his feet up in the air and slapping his hands over his mouth to cover his giggles.

Cyril rolled his eyes. "It's nothing—"

"Tell. Me. What?" Nobody kept secrets from her about her children. Especially not Cyril.

He cast a glance at Seth. "Fine. Tell her."

Seth rolled off the couch and landed on all fours before hopping to his feet. "Nora laughed!"

Robin looked at Cyril, and then down at Sonora, who was gnawing intently on a rubber giraffe. "Why is that...?"

"Forget it. Just thought you might wanna..." The giraffe slipped out of her saliva-slimed fingers; Cyril caught it midair and held it as she struggled for a better grip. "You know. Be the one to experience it first."

"Oh. No." She shook her head. "It doesn't bother me." She'd never needed to have all the milestones to herself. Though the fact that Cyril possessed enough empathy to imagine she might was a surprise.

"Okay!" Seth crowed. "I believe you!"

Robin cocked an eyebrow. "What does that mean?"

"Do it!" Seth prompted, throwing himself against Cyril's knee. "Do it again!"

Cyril let out a sigh. "Okay, okay." He seemed reluctant, almost a little... embarrassed? He picked Sonora up, dangling her by her armpits so her toes just brushed his shirt. Then he cleared his throat and sang, in a pretty passable Harry Belafonte: "My girl's name is Sonora; I tell you friends, I adore her. And when she dances, oh—"

"O-KAY!" Seth shouted. "I BE-LIVE-YOU!"

"Dude." Cyril gave him a friendly scowl. "Wait for your cue."

"Oh."

He cleared his throat again. "And when she dances, oh brother! She's a hurricane in all kinds of weather." He tossed Sonora up about three inches—gently, and not far enough to break contact with his fingers. But her lips pulled back to show her toothless gums and she let out a stuttering little chortle. "Jump in the line, rock your body in time." Cyril nodded to Seth, who completely missed the cue. He sighed. "Kid."

"O-KAY! I BE-LIVE-YOU!"

Cyril gave her another little jiggle. "Jump in the line—"

"O-KAY! I BE-LIVE-YOU!"

Robin laughed. "Sorry, I'm afraid he got his sense of rhythm from me and Grandma. Now—let me see this cutie." She scooped Sonora out of Cyril's hands and gave her an Eskimo kiss. "Are you a smiley girl? Are you Mommy's smiley girl?" Sonora kicked happily, but didn't laugh again. "You like music, don't you? Did you like that song?"

"O-KAY!" Seth shouted, "I BE—"

"Kid—give it a rest. Just for one minute, huh?"

Robin lowered Sonora to her chest and looked down at Seth. "How about you go... outside?"

Seth gaped. "*Really?*"

While there wasn't *always* a journalist camped outside the house, the unpredictability of their presence meant that the back yard hadn't been a safe place for Seth to play in weeks. He'd been able to get some outside time at Marta's and with Glennis, thank goodness, but he was still going stir-crazy. Which was why Robin had spent the last week building an eight-foot tall fence. "Yep. Really. I just finished."

"I can go out? *By myself?*"

Robin waved him toward the door. "Go for it."

Seth streaked out of the room, whooping with glee.

It hurt her heart to think that such a small thing—a fenced-in square of pavement and grass—felt like freedom to her four-year-old. But it wouldn't be like that forever. It couldn't. She glanced at Cyril, and they both knew what she was thinking: it would get better after he was gone.

But then he'd be gone.

Robin propped Sonora over one shoulder. "Coming?"

Cyril waved her away. "I'll start on dinner."

She shrugged and started after Seth. Then she hesitated—and turned back. "Nah, come on out with us. Dinner can wait." She offered her free hand.

Cyril nearly said something rude; she could tell. But he clamped his lips together and nodded, ignoring her hand as he leaned onto the arm of the couch and rocked himself to the edge. "I can..." He grunted and exhaled as he got to his feet. "I can take the baby if you want."

Robin shook her head. "I've got her." And for once she wasn't fussing or looking for milk. "Babies are kind of nice when they're not screaming." She led the way through the kitchen and out onto the little back porch—a landing with steps, really—and squeezed to one side to make room for Cyril.

Seth was jetting around with a broken piece of railing from the old fence, which she'd somehow missed. Did it still have a nail...? No. Not exactly safe, but not a potential trip to the ER, either. Good enough.

"Nice." Cyril shaded his eyes with one hand and surveyed the new fence: eight feet tall and solid redwood, no gaps. "Nobody's getting over that thing."

She pointed to the stumps of the old fence posts, which she'd chainsawed off at roughly ground level. "I still need to dig those out, but I can do that whenever. Thanks, by the way. I'd never have gotten this done without you here watching the kids." Not even Tavis would've hung around holding Sonora all night, every night, for weeks. Of course, Tavis wouldn't have slept in until noon every day, either.

Seth ran past the deck, screeched to a halt, and back-stepped a couple of paces. "Again!"

Cyril let out a sigh that was half a growl. "Later, kid, okay? Give it a rest."

"Aww, *maaaan!*"

Robin elbowed him in the gut. "Oh, come on. Humor him." She grinned. "You do it so well."

Cyril didn't answer, and Robin turned Sonora around to watch Seth as he went back to playing swords or whatever it was. Abruptly, Cyril sucked in a breath and belted out, "Daaaaay-O! Me say daaaay-O!"

Seth spun, hands on hips, and glared. "No! Wrong! That's wrong!"

Robing laughed. "Shh! Buddy, give him a break."

Cyril kept going. He didn't have all the lyrics memorized, but he filled in whatever he was missing with "blah blah," which Seth found utterly hilarious. He was laughing so hard Robin couldn't help but laugh, and she could see Cyril struggling to keep a straight face. She sat Sonora on the railing and bounced her along with the music, which got a little hiccough-giggle out of her as well. When he came to the end, finishing off with a deep, dramatic vibrato, Robin made Sonora's little hands clap. "Yay, Uncle Cyril, yay!"

He made a flourish with one hand and a slight bow. Then he harrumphed, loudly, and muttered something that ended with "dinner" before turning to go inside.

Robin stayed outside to do bubbles and sidewalk chalk with Seth until Sonora started getting fussy. "All right, baby girl, all right." Seth was engrossed in scribbling "robot guys," so she left him and went inside, where Cyril was doing something at the stove that already smelled quite good. Courtesy of his mother, he had hundreds of comfort-food recipes filed somewhere in the back of his brain—and having a personal chef was a luxury to which Robin was very quickly becoming accustomed. "I got some more asparagus," she said. "If that works as a side."

He grunted a negative. "It's going in the quiche."

"Oh. Yum. I gotta feed this thing, but let me know if you need help."

He grunted again.

She took Sonora to the living room rocker, flipping on the TV as she sat down. Well; not TV, exactly. Cyril had ordered a bunch of equipment and now instead of cable they had Netflix and Amazon Prime and some other stuff. It was a heck of a lot cheaper, anyway. She turned the sound way down and put on one of those trial-by-fire restaurant shows. Robin hated cooking, but it was fun to see Gordon Ramsay chew out amateurs. Sonora sucked enthusiastically, gazing up at her with those adoring eyes.

Robin yawned. She could live like this, she realized. Sleeping most of the night, working half the day; Cyril in the kitchen, stirring the pot, laughing with the kids. Awkward television viewing every other night. It wasn't the best of all possible worlds—it wasn't Tavis—but it wasn't the worst, either. Certainly better than doing it all on her own.

But not even second-best would last forever.

After a while, Seth's footsteps tripped in through the back door and into the kitchen. There was perhaps half a second of silence before he shouted, "*Again!*"

CYRIL USUALLY RANG her cell around two in the morning. Robin would pull on her bathrobe and fumble blearily downstairs to the living room, where he'd be standing with Sonora, waiting to pass her off so he could get a few minutes to pee and get some water or have a snack or whatever. When she finished, he'd take her back and Robin would stumble back up to bed.

So of course, on the one night Sonora didn't start screaming bloody murder, Robin was up worrying. Was Cyril sleeping through her cries? Had she died of SIDS even though Robin moved the entire infant-safe crib into the office two weeks ago? The usual. At three, she gave up, grabbed her robe, and went downstairs. No crying. Well, that ruled out one possibility.

There was a light on somewhere, and she followed the glow into the dining room. Cyril was seated with his back to her—shirtless—in front of a spread of leftovers. He held the quiche from dinner in one hand, a fork in the other. He glanced up as she came around the side of the table, put down the pie dish, and took a long swig of milk. "Sound asleep," he said. "Checked twice."

Robin sat down across from him, not bothering to disguise her sigh of relief.

Cyril pushed a bag of dinner rolls toward her.

What the hell. She leaned forward, grabbed the bag, and undid the twist-tie. Cyril went back to the quiche. They'd altogether eaten about half at dinnertime, and now he'd pretty well polished off the rest.

Robin buttered a roll and ate it. "You don't have to hide this, you know." Even with him doing most of the cooking, she'd have to be an idiot not to realize the food was disappearing at a rate that was hard to reconcile with what they ate at the table.

He motioned for the rolls; she passed the bag back and he took one out, sliced it in half, and filled it with spiral cut ham and mustard. "I'm not hiding it from *you*."

"Oh." She watched him eat the roll in three quick, savage bites. "You really do love him, don't you."

He cut himself another slice of ham.

A thin wail sounded from the back of the house. Robin sighed and pushed back her chair. As she rounded the table, she put a hand on Cyril's shoulder. "Thank you."

Sonora was nearly two hours overdue for her nightly feeding—which was fantastic, since it suggested a full nights' sleep might be somewhere in the future—but she was also *furious*. Robin flicked the desk lamp on to its dimmest setting and reached for a diaper. Sonora usually nodded off while she was nursing at night, and if she still had a wet diaper Cyril would have to deal with the fallout an hour or two later. And he deserved a little sleep, too.

Diaper change accomplished, Robin grabbed a pillow from the bed and plopped herself into the desk chair. Sonora was so worked up it took her a while to notice the boob in her face, but when she did, she latched so hard Robin sucked in a hiss of pain. Not two minutes later, she felt herself slide inexorably into a kind of trance-like level of relaxation. She propped her heels up on the end of the fold-out bed. It was so hard not to fall asleep nursing, at night.

The floorboards creaked in the hall as Cyril lumbered through the laundry room and into the bathroom. Robin could hear him shifting around. The toilet flushed. Water ran—brushing his teeth, maybe?

"Hey," she loud-whispered, when the door opened and the bathroom fan clicked off.

The bedroom door swung in a little. "Yeah?"

"Can you grab me a burp cloth from the dryer? Or a shirt, if you see one." As usual, she'd leaked right through the breast pad and down the front of her tank top.

Cyril grunted and plodded away. He came back with both items, and, shuffling around the sofa-bed, held them out.

"Thanks." Robin tossed the shirt over the end of the crib and stuffed the clean burp rag into her bra. It would do. She glanced up as Cyril was edging back out the door. "Hey, don't let me kick you out. I'll try and stick her in the crib when I'm done."

He looked at her and then at the bed and shrugged. Robin realized, belatedly, that she was sitting the chair he'd been using to get into the bed, but Cyril grabbed the sofa-arm, worked a knee up onto the mattress, and half-rolled onto his side. The feet of the fold-out jumped, landing again with a thud. The room was filled with labored breathing and screeching springs as he struggled to center himself, punching pillows into place under arms and back. Horizontal, his mass spread and pooled; when he shifted, the movement went through him like ripples in liquid. A curious demonstration of physics.

Sonora pulled away from Robin's left nipple, so she pulled the burp cloth out and switched her to the right. As she did she reached out and switched the desk lamp off.

All was quiet, except for the wheeze of air as Cyril struggled to catch his wind. After a while, even that slowed. Robin watched his stomach rise and fall with each breath, in almost-synchronicity with Sonora's suckling. The room was dark, but not quite dark enough that Robin didn't feel like she was sitting there staring at Cyril staring at her. He wasn't asleep.

He cleared his throat. "So do you love her yet?" His voice was a low rumble.

"Um." She had tried not to think about that much. Tried, mostly, not to beat herself up about what she did or didn't feel. "I don't know. I feel..."

She still didn't feel anything like what she'd experienced with Seth.

But maybe you just didn't get that same kind of rush, the second time around. You already knew what parenthood was. It wasn't a revelation; it was just more of the same.

Robin looked down at the baby, who was gazing at her with that rapt, wide-eyed stare of adoration as she sucked. "You know what's different, with her? I mean—everything. But—what I didn't really expect."

Cyril was silent. Waiting. Listening.

"With Seth, it's so... one-sided. I love him with everything I've got, but to him, I'm mostly just a necessary evil. He needs me to do things he can't do himself—but from day one, he was always focused on that goal. Independence. He could barely even nurse, as a baby, because he was always looking somewhere else. Reaching for that next step. I know he'll never even begin to comprehend what I feel for him. And honestly? It doesn't even matter. I don't care if he loves me as much as I love him. I'm not hurt or insulted. I just *love* him. No strings." Robin put her hand on Sonora's little head, so round and perfect, and fingered a few strands of fuzzy baby hair. "But with her... It's not like I wouldn't die for her. I would. But..." She hesitated, not sure she could even get her mouth around the words. "When I look at her, I feel like *she's* the one in love with *me*." And... maybe that was okay. Maybe it was God, or the universe, giving her what she needed most. "I just... I guess I wish I could give that back. I wish it was there. Naturally."

"Have you tried?"

"Tried what?"

"Having... feelings? Shit, never mind. What the fuck do I know."

Robin sighed. "Tavis would probably have written me something deep and insightful about the whole thing." She regretted the words the instant they left her mouth—and they hung there, in the center of the room, like dead weight.

"I'm sorry," Cyril said.

"It's not your—"

"For not being him."

CYRIL SNORED like a buzz saw. Robin's father had snored like that, and sitting there listening to the regular snort-wheeze, snort-wheeze was oddly comforting. Sonora seemed to agree—she was dead asleep when Robin put her back in the crib.

She stood there for a moment, hands on the bedrail, looking at her daughter in the dark. She'd gazed at Seth like this every night, in his infancy, and yet how often had she done the same with this little one? Passing her off to Cyril was a relief. She was a mom of two now, she was busy, and soon she'd be doing this all on her own. Time enough. And yet...

Truthfully, it was hard to look. Because with Sonora's infant beauty came the memory of all Robin had lost. The knowledge that Tavis would never come up behind her, put his hand on her shoulder, and whisper a soft word of encouragement in her ear. Never again would a sleepless night end with a warm note on her pillow.

But just this once, she made herself look. "I love you," she whispered. And again: "I love you." And something inside of her, something she had been holding very close, broke.

And the love was there. All of it. The endless, overwhelming, matchless one-way love of motherhood lived, inside of her. It was deep, but it was there. Silent tears streaked her face.

It was there.

30

THREE AND A HALF MONTHS, as it ended up being, passed in the blink of an eye.

She was sitting on the couch, watching a home improvement show while Sonora took her evening feed, when Cyril lumbered down the stairs. Robin glanced up. "Asleep?"

Cyril shook his head. "Will be soon, though."

"Thanks." She patted the cushion next to her on the couch and he sat, giving off a hint of Old Spice as he shifted to get comfortable. Robin had none-too-subtly stocked the guest bathroom with toiletries, and he had, without comment, begun using them. Old Spice had been her father's favored scent, and now every time Cyril came into the room she got a whiff of bittersweet nostalgia.

They watched, silent, until the commercial came on. She hit the mute button, pulled her tank back into place, and handed Sonora over to Cyril so he could burp her while she drank a glass of water.

"Friday," he said.

She looked at him, and understood. "How long have you known?"

"'Bout a month." Sonora complained and he shifted her to the opposite shoulder. "Didn't want it hanging over your head."

"Where...?"

"Taft. It's north of here, by Bakersfield—"

"I know where it is. They can... accommodate you?"

He shrugged. "It's a minimum-security prison. The, uh, easiest, I guess, in terms of prison."

"It's still prison."

"Yeah."

"But that's—I mean, it's close. Close enough to visit."

"If you want."

Suddenly there was a lump in her throat. She set the glass of water down. "Seth—Seth is going to be—"

"He's going to be *fine*," Cyril said, sharply. As if it had to be true. "He's a good kid. He has his mom. His grandma. Plenty of support at church. He doesn't need—"

"You," Robin interrupted. "Are you going to be fine?"

"No." He snorted lightly. "But I never was."

"Oh, God. Cyril." She traced the faint lines her nails had etched, months ago, in his flesh. It didn't seem like enough. She scooted close, until her body pressed against his belly, and rested her head on his shoulder. Cyril shifted slightly and then, when she didn't move away, circled her shoulders with one arm. His touch was heavy and warm.

The home improvement show came back on.

31

SETH FOLLOWED CYRIL out of the playroom looking sober, but there was no evidence of tears. He hadn't grasped the finality of his father's death, a little over a year ago, and although he'd matured considerably in the intervening months Robin still wondered whether he understood what "Cyril being gone" would mean. She had, after all, kept them apart those few months—and then, along with Sonora, Cyril had re-entered their lives. Perhaps Seth thought it was going to be like that. A short separation followed by a joyful reunion.

Ten years. Cyril would be nothing but a distant memory, if even that.

Robin glanced at her mom. "You know how to reheat the milk—"

Glennis put a hand on her shoulder and squeezed. "I did it with you and with Seth, sweetie. She'll be fine." She put out her other arm for Seth, as he came near, and he curled himself around her leg. "Both of them will. You—take your time." Then she glanced at Cyril. Not with affection, but no longer with animosity, either. "Take care of yourself."

He nodded.

Robin hugged her mother, kissed the kids, and followed Cyril out into the morning sun.

He didn't have a bag. There was no reason to take one; everything that was his would be confiscated the moment he self-surrendered. Robin had looked over the prison handbook online, and they even had rules about personal photographs: only one snapshot could be on display, in a frame that had to be purchased in prison. He'd left a small pile of belongings in Robin's keeping, which she'd stuck in a tub in the garage next to Tav's things. The rest... well, there hadn't been much else, other than food and electronics, the latter of which the FBI had already taken. He'd sold his car, and a rental company would be overseeing the house and granny unit. Robin had charge of his bank account—specifically, she was tasked with sending him a certified money order each month that would be deposited into a prison account with which he could use buy "commissary." There was a limit on how much prisoners could accumulate in the account each month, so it couldn't just be a one-time thing.

She was backing out of the drive when Seth flew out the front door, his face a mess of tears and snot. "Oh, no."

Cyril spilled out the cab before she had even fully stopped. He knelt, half-falling, planting one knee on the lawn with a heavy *oomph*, and caught Seth up in his arms. "It's okay, buddy," he rumbled, petting the head of curls. "You're gonna be okay."

"I'm just going to miss you," Seth sobbed. "So, so much!"

"I know," Cyril said. "I know."

Robin put the truck in park and climbed out over the passenger side. They had agreed not to talk about prison with Seth—not until they knew what the situation was, not until Robin had figured out whether it would be okay to expose her son. But she couldn't be silent. "We'll visit, buddy," she said, patting his back. "I promise. Okay? I promise. You guys can play games, or—I dunno. I'll figure out something. Okay? This is not the end." Cyril was going to prison. But he wasn't dead.

Seth continued to sob until, finally, Glennis came and gently pried him out of Cyril's arms. She could barely lift him, he was so big now, but with Robin's help she hefted him onto one hip and carried him inside, his face pressed tight against her neck.

Robin helped Cyril up—or rather held one arm while he slung the other over the open cab door and hauled himself to his feet. "Thanks," he muttered, and rocked himself back into the passenger seat.

They drove two and a half hours in silence. Robin imagined Cyril's thoughts were largely the same as hers: Was he going to be okay? Would they make him work? What if he got picked on? What if someone hurt him? At the very least, he was going to be hungry. Very, very hungry. Robin couldn't even begin to understand Cyril's screwed up psyche, but she knew food was an emotional crutch for him. If he didn't have that, how was he going to cope, mentally? It would be hard enough to cut him off at home, in a familiar environment, but in a tiny shared cell...?

Taft appeared on a freeway sign. Five miles.

Robin reached out to crank up the AC another notch. The further inland they went, the hotter it got. "I'm thinking of going north," she said.

She felt him look at her.

"Your boss, Cooke, he... he offered to put me up while I remodel his house. If I do it during the summer, his wife can take care of the kids. They seem like nice people, and I just..." She glanced at him. "I thought maybe it would be good. To get away."

He grunted. "Yeah. Sounds good."

"So if you don't hear from me for a while—"

"I'll survive."

The exit off I-5 to the prison came before the town. Robin glanced at the clock on the dash. "Do you want to grab some lunch first? You have plenty of time."

He shook his head.

"Are you sure—?"

His stare was fixed on the road. "Let's just get this over with."

But walking through those doors was not the end—not for him. For him it was only the beginning.

Still, she put on her blinker and took the exit. Wishing she had thought to pack some food. Something to share, together, before...

The farmland passed quickly, and soon the tires were crunching over tarmac littered with gravel. Long wire fences appeared on the right. A double row of them, topped with coils of barbed wire. Everything was dry, nothing but bare yellow dirt and brown scrub brush. Robin slowed, and they passed a sign that looked like nothing so much as a cinderblock tombstone.

TAFT CORRECTIONAL INSTITUTION

And then she was turning into a parking lot. There were a few other cars, most of them dusty and old. It was so hot out the tarmac shimmered in the sun, but a couple of women loitered outside the entryway of the main building, cigarettes in hand.

Robin concentrated on parking. Not right in front, although there were plenty of spaces. There were a few trees around the building but none on the lot, so no hope of shade. She picked a spot about two rows away from the path that led to the front doors.

"Well." Cyril popped the door open, admitting a wave of sauna-like heat. "Bye."

"Wait." She put her hand on his shoulder.

"For what?"

"I…" She swallowed. "I'm going to miss your cooking."

His mouth quirked up, on the right. "You'll be fine."

"I know. But… still."

"Yeah. Well." He pulled away and rocked himself out of the truck, exhaling as he lumbered into the blistering sun. "See you in a decade."

Robin hopped out of the cab and ran around to the passenger side. She grabbed his arm. "Jesus, Cyril. Just—wait. Okay? You've got the rest of the day to walk through those doors." What the hell did he think was waiting for him, inside?

"Look, I suck at good-bye."

"You did pretty good with Seth."

"What, you want a hug?" He jerked his arm away and started across the parking lot.

"Yeah," she said to his back. "As a matter of fact. I do."

That brought him up short. He turned to look at her, brow furrowed. "Uh… okay?"

"Well, not if you're gonna make it all weird." Before it could get any more awkward, she put her head down and wrapped her arms around his circumference.

It was like the first time, in the doctor's office after the ultrasound. For a moment he didn't move, and then his arms folded around her in a weighty, slightly pungent cocoon. Their clothes were already moist with sweat, and she didn't care. He wasn't her father, but there was something in Cyril that *felt* like him, in a way she couldn't quite explain. Robin closed her eyes and tried to solidify this embrace in her memory, because it was going to have to last her a long time.

"I'm going to miss," she whispered. "You."

He let her go.

She couldn't quite look him in the eye.

"Uh…" He scratched at the stubble on the side of his face. Drops of perspiration were beading on his forehead. "You okay?"

Didn't he get it?

Even after weighing in all the shitty, fucked up things he'd done— and written—he'd still managed, somehow, to be good and kind. He had taken her to dinner and baked her a cake. He'd spent endless evenings entertaining Seth and Sonora, and had, quite literally, sacrificed his own freedom for a little boy on the other side of the world who would never even know his name.

All this time, he'd forced her to keep her guard up, to protect herself. Her kids. And now—now she didn't have to. He couldn't hurt her any more.

And the truth was, she didn't want him to be gone.

"Oh, chica," he said, his voice low. "Don't." He touched a finger to her cheek. "Not for me."

She wiped her eyes with the backs of her hands and swallowed. "I need your help."

"I'm… about to walk into prison. Make it quick?"

She wiped her eyes once more and shielded her face from the sun. The only place available to sit was an iron park bench, right out in the sun. They could get back in the cab, but it would be an oven without the AC on, and she was already low on gas as it was. "Oh. I know." She went around back of the truck, using her key to unlock the camper shell, and popped the tailgate down. The upper window was tinted, and when she pushed it up it offered a bit of shade. She glanced at Cyril, who had followed, hanging a few steps behind. She put a knee up on the tailgate and pushed her toolbox out of the way, back into the bed. "Here. Just for a couple of minutes."

He eyed the tailgate warily. "I don't think you want me to—"

"Damn it, Cyril, just sit down." This was hard enough without him being an ass. "It's rated for five hundred pounds. It'll hold." She went back to the driver's side to retrieve her purse, bracing an arm against the headrest as the entire cab tilted backward. The tailgate protested with a low, worrisome creak.

"Fucking—told you—so," he gasped, when she came back around. He was red-faced and huffing, propping himself against the frame with one arm as he used the other to try and heave his bulk backward.

"It's fine." Robin grabbed his right foot with both hands, centered it on her torso, and shoved. Together, they managed to work his leg up far enough to shift his center of gravity off the tailgate.

She climbed up into the bed opposite him, folding her legs crisscross-applesauce to fit between his, and rummaged in her purse. "Here." She handed him a water bottle, yanking his shirt back down while she was at it. "Hot as hell out here." It felt kind of good, in a way, deep in her bones.

"Not gonna be any cooler in there." But he drank, reserving about a third of the bottle to pass back to her.

"Thanks."

They looked out over barbed wire fence and yellow dirt. There was nothing for miles.

"So," Cyril said, when he'd gotten his wind. "How long you planning on us sitting here?"

Robin sucked in a breath and let it out, slowly. "Until I get the courage to do this." She reached into her purse, thumbed past the partially-crumpled paper Cyril had written his front porch speech on, and pulled out Tav's letter.

Cyril looked at the envelope in her outstretched hand. "Nope."

"Cyril, please." Was he going to make her beg? Now? "You knew him. Do this with me." She wasn't doing it for Cyril. Or because of Cyril. This was, finally, for her. It was time. She forced a smile. "Don't make me wait ten years."

He glanced forward, through the front of the cab and, beyond, the open prison doors.

"Look at me." She waited until his eyes came around—to her knees, her shoulders, and, finally, her face. "Please."

"God," he snarled. "Fucking doe eyes."

"I'll take that as a yes." Robin slipped a finger under the edge of the envelope, where she'd already ripped it a little. And suddenly her hands were shaking so badly she couldn't get it open. "Can you—I'm sorry. Can you open—"

"Yeah." He plucked the envelope out of her fingers. "Why the fuck not."

She watched as he tore the edge with one firm gesture. Saw the blue ink, in Tav's lanky scrawl. Cyril tugged at the folded paper, but she leaned forward and put her hands over his, stopping him before it could slide out. "Swear to me," she whispered, her voice suddenly hoarse. "Swear to me that this is his."

He looked at her. Met her eyes, just barely. He nodded. "I swear."

"And you don't know what it says?"

"The usual bullshit, I assume."

"Jesus, Cyril—"

He put a hand up. "I don't fucking know what it says. He gave it to me a couple days before he deployed, I never touched it. Now, you wanna read the damn thing or not?"

She nodded.

He pulled it out. Unfolded the single sheet, carefully, and placed it in her shaking hands.

Robin leaned back against the side of the camper shell and held the paper out to catch the sun.

Hey, Robbie.

And then it was all a watery blur. "I can't," she choked. "I can't." She had been running from it for so long, but here it was, still waiting. And in another moment it would be over. The end.

"Hey. No." Cyril reached for her, but she was too far. "Come over here." He shoved her toolbox further into the truck bed, making room.

She choked back the tears long enough to clamber over his leg, awkwardly, and wedge herself against his side. She hugged her knees to her chin.

Cyril draped an arm around her shoulders. The back of the camper was broiler-hot, but they were both sweating so much already that the skin-to-skin contact wasn't any worse. She buried her face in his belly and cried.

"Look at me," he said.

Eventually, she did.

"You can do this."

"I know. I know. But." She swallowed, and, finally, held out the letter. "I don't want to do it alone."

He looked down. Away. Elsewhere. "You don't want me to—" He shook his head. "You don't want me."

She'd told herself Tavis leaving the letter with Cyril was a poorly-executed joke, but he was never so careless, not when he wrote. "There was a reason he left this with you, Cyril," she whispered. "And you know it."

He sucked in a breath and let it out in a kind of low, uncertain growl.

Robin pressed the letter into his hands, and he didn't push her away.

But he didn't look at it, either. He cleared his throat with a loud harrumph. Shifted his bulk and plucked at the armpits of his shirt. Was he, too, trying not to cry?

She put her hand on his wrist. His palm opened, and she slipped her fingers inside. She bowed her head, summoning Tavis in her mind's eye: quirking that crooked smile as he sat down, pen in hand, and began to write.

The paper rattled. "Dear Robbie." Cyril's voice was gruff. "I kind of suck at this but I will give it my best shot. If you are reading this, I'm dead. So. I'm sorry." The way he spat the words out, quick and sharp, made it sound choppy, not like Tavis at all. Somehow, that made it a little easier to hear. "But I'm also—"

Abruptly, his voice broke off.

Robin lifted her head. Cyril's eyes flicked back and forth, scanning down the page. "What?"

"I can't do this." He shoved the paper at her chest.

She didn't take it. He couldn't stop. Not now that he'd started. She needed to hear it all. Every word. She put her hand back in his, and squeezed. "Yes. You can."

"You don't—"

"Read the goddamn letter, Cyril."

He looked at her with an icy intensity she'd never seen before. She held his gaze, and the moment stretched. She would not bend.

And then he lifted the paper, spitting out the words in a low, husky monotone. "But I'm also kind of not. Dead. And I don't mean that like a metaphor. Or whatever. Do you remember back when we first met? I mean, I know you do, you watch it on YouTube all the time. Anyway, I read you that note. About falling from the moon. Except here is the thing. I didn't write that letter."

"No," Robin said.

"I didn't write any of the letters."

She jerked her hand out of Cyril's grasp. "No." This was a joke. This was Cyril, lying. Again. She tumbled backward, away from him, into the furthest corner of the cab, barking her lower back against her tool box. This was some sort of crazy, who knew what the hell kind of messed up game—

"You're smart, Robbie," Cyril hissed, his eyes still fixed on the page. He hadn't looked at her. Hadn't moved. "So I am pretty sure you can guess who did."

She lunged forward, snatching the letter before any more lies could tumble from his lips, and clambered over his leg and out of the truck. She started to run, but there was nowhere to go. Her knees buckled, and she dropped to the pavement in the shade of the cab, praying the words on the page were not identical to the ones that had come out of Cyril's mouth.

But they were.

This is my fault. Okay? I asked him. Because I wanted to impress you so bad, and he's so good at putting stuff in words. I didn't even think it would work. But it did, and then—I was scared of losing you, when I deployed. So I'd just tell him what I wanted to say, and he'd make it sound really good. Sometimes he'd suggest stuff to add, but it was still me. My feelings. You know? That's how it was, at first. That's how I told myself it was okay.

Then I came back. And we—you know. That first time, in your dorm room? When you pulled the letter out of your bra and asked me to read it aloud? Swear to God, Robbie, that was the first time I ever saw those words. And then you pulled out a whole box of them, and you had more than I remembered. Way more.

I was so pissed. I'm not even kidding. I went straight to his apartment and punched him in the face. I knocked out one of his molars. He's still missing it.

I swore that was the end. That if you wanted a letter, I'd write it myself. But I tried and it just—it was so stupid. I couldn't even show you. The whole thing would be over, and I just... I couldn't lose you. You are my life. You are the only reason I do the things I do.

Honest to God, I didn't realize he loved you until after the wedding.

He hid it so well. It was always just a joke to him. A game. Like everything else. I don't know, maybe he even believes his own lies. Hell, I didn't want to see it, either. But after the wedding, he got really depressed. For a long time. I'm not sure he ever came out of it. Remember that night you got so mad, because I didn't come home from his place until four in the morning? We weren't gaming. He swallowed an entire bottle of pills. I spent the night in the ER, praying he would live. Because if he died—

Everyone thinks I'm a hero, Robin. God. I'm not. I'm not.

That's why I have to do this. I'm a coward, and a liar, and a—whatever else. But I'm done lying. If I can do this thing... if I can save someone, Robin, I'll be the hero you believe I am. I'll burn this damn letter and tell you myself, face to face, and if you leave—well. I'll be loved for myself, or not at all.

But if I don't. If you're reading this... God. If I'm dead, I want you to know that Cyril loves you.

If he says he doesn't, he's lying. He loves you more than life. More than himself. And if I'm being honest—he loves you more than me.

Every word he ever wrote was true.

A sound escaped her. A kind of throaty, inarticulate moan.

At her back, the wheel shifted. The tailgate creaked.

Robin stared at the words on the page. The only words, it seemed, that Tavis had ever truly composed. She put a hand out, brushing them with her fingertips. As if her living skin had the power to wipe clean this posthumous confession. "Who... who were you?" Her husband. Her lover.

The father of her child. Children. And yet not.

"He was," Cyril rumbled, "exactly what he seemed."

Patriot. Devoted husband and father. Soldier. Athlete. Hometown hero.

"That was the man everyone else saw," Robin whispered. She stared at the silver band circling the fourth finger of her outstretched hand. And then she closed her fingers on the page. "Poor," she choked. "You poor, stupid boy." How could she love him now? How could she hate him? He was dead. He was a lie. He was... a work of fiction.

And here, beside her—

"You." She stood, forcing herself to look at Cyril. His red, bloated face; shirt soaked with sweat. Hands dangling at his sides. Breath like a wet bellows. "All this time." She held the letter up, crumpled in her palm. "Your words. Your soul."

He fixed his eyes on her hand. The letter clutched inside. "His blood."

"You—you're the one who let it come to that." Though she wasn't sure she wanted it, she stuffed the letter into her back pocket. There was no sense to this, no rhyme or reason that would put everything to rights. But she asked anyway. "Why? Why did you never say? When we started dating—"

He snorted. "Fat kid with a smart mouth? I never had a chance. Why take it from Tav?"

"And my—my potential refusal justified deception? That's not love, Cyril, it's ownership."

He shrugged and turned away, stepping out of the shade of the truck and into the sun. "I tried," he said finally, in a voice so low she barely heard. "A thousand and one times, I tried—"

She followed, close on his heels. "But you never *did.* God, Cyril. If not in college, or when we got married, or when Seth—" She choked. Oh God, Seth. How could she even—? Robin shook her head. "Why not when Tav *died?* For God's sake, Cyril, you had a million chances. Why did you never *say?*"

"After he died?" He turned back, flinging out a hand. "Sacrificed himself for his goddamn country? God, how could I? You had perfection.

You'd never forgive me for taking that away."

"Perfection? Perfection is a fucking *gravestone*."

"What does it matter? I was never going to change—"

"Who asked you to? You never even give me the chance!"

"Jesus. What fantasy world are you living in? Love's not some magical potion. I'm not going to stop eating pizza or clean up my language or become socially acceptable. How long—honestly, how long do you think it would have lasted, before I stopped using my mouth to apologize for being *me* and started using it to hurt you? I'm not going to change. Not for you, not for anybody. Not for love." He sucked in a couple of ragged breaths. "And I don't care how much of a fucking saint you are." He lifted his arms. "You don't want me like this."

For a moment she just stood there, mouth open in disbelief. "You," she sputtered at last. "You—eloquent—fucking—liar. Maybe that's what you told yourself, at first. Maybe it was even true, once. But after all this time? You know me. You *know* me. And you say that to my face?" She held her hands out, palms up. "You know I could have loved this. All of it. All of you."

He swatted the air with a hand. Looked, for a moment, as if he would offer a rebuttal. But in the end, he just turned and shuffled toward the prison doors.

Robin could hear him wheezing by the time he reached the sidewalk path, and he stopped at the picnic table to rest, leaning his backside against the edge.

This was what he expected. What he wanted, even. For her to lash out and disappear, leaving him to rot in this pit. Alone. Justice served.

She couldn't leave it at that. She wanted to. But she couldn't.

Robin jogged across the lot. Stopped in front of him, hands on hips, close enough to feel his hot, heavy breath upon her face. Considered slapping him.

But it was too hot for fury. Her tears had run dry.

"What a waste," she exhaled. "All this time, Cyril. All the time we could have had." She put her hand on his face. Felt the sweat and stubble against her palm. "And now I lose the man I loved, not once, but twice."

He wouldn't look at her, still.

"Tell me, before you go. Tell me you love me."

He turned his head to the side, trying to shake her touch. "Tavis. Tavis loved you."

"Maybe he did, in his own way. But it wasn't his words that captured my heart." She let her hand drop to his stomach, pressing her fingers into his flesh, trying but failing to reach solid bone. "Say it, you goddamn coward. Say it to my face."

He swallowed, thickly. "No."

"Why not? I don't get it, Cyril. You're not afraid of rejection. You glory in it. All this time—" She stopped. Took a step back. And it hit her. "Oh my God."

His eyes flickered up. And then away.

"That's it, isn't it," she whispered, knowing—feeling—with certainty that she spoke truth. "All this time. You were afraid I'd say *yes.*"

She put a foot onto the bench beside him and boosted herself up, making herself all of four inches taller than the top of his head. "Turn around."

He pushed himself off from the table, tried to move away.

Robin grabbed his shirt. "Turn around, asshole."

He did.

She bent forward, close. Put her lips—

"No." He shoved her away. Hard.

"What? Isn't this what you wanted? To run your hands up and down my body, to memorize every curve and—"

"Stop."

She grabbed his hand and pressed it to her waist. "I'm here. Go ahead."

He jerked free. "I." Swallowed. Made a vague, helpless gesture toward her body. "I don't—I *cannot* spend the next ten years thinking—hoping you might be here when I get out."

Robin didn't pity him. She might have, once. Not now.

When she put her hand on his face again, he did not push her away. She rested her forehead against his, forcing him to look her in the eye.

"You know what?" She wrapped an arm around his neck. Slid her other hand over his shoulder and down the curve of his side. And pressed her lips to his. He tasted like salt and Old Spice.

At first he was wooden; unresponsive. But she waited, and felt him, at last, surrender with a breathy shudder. His hands brushed her hips, and then his arms enveloped her with that firm, familiar weight. And for a moment—just one moment, deep inside—she let herself feel the gallop of his living heart.

He gasped for breath. "Robin—"

She pulled back—just far enough so that when she spoke, her lips brushed his. "You," she whispered, "do not get to make that choice." She hopped down from the bench, checked to make sure her keys were in her pocket, and headed for the truck. She tossed the words over one shoulder: "I do."

"Please," he called. His voice was ragged. "Please. Let me write."

Epilogue

ROBIN HEARD GLENNIS and the kids in the playroom, but she turned right, through the living room, and went upstairs. In the bedroom, purse slung crossways over her body, she knelt next to the bed and pulled out the boxes of letters, stacking them until the pile was a good three feet high. She carried the stack downstairs, through the kitchen, and into the back yard.

The fire pit was small, but she made it work.

She dragged the purse over her head, dropped it on the Adirondack chair, and dug through the collection of receipts and other miscellaneous papers. The book of matches was still there, buried in the very bottom. Her fingers were steady as she flipped up the white-feather logo and tore out the second match.

"Honey?" Glennis stood in the doorway to the kitchen, using a hand to shield her eyes. "What are you *doing?*"

"Celebrating my liberty."

Robin watched the letters burn.

Acknowledgements

AS MUCH AS *SURVIVING CYRIL* is the story about a complicated romantic relationship, it is also a book about parents and children. It is fitting, then, that my first and most heartfelt thanks must go to my parents, John and Linda Biggers, and to my in-laws, Jan and Vince Caro. This book would not have happened without these wonderful people—not only because two of them are literally responsible for my existence, but also because each of them sacrificed time, energy, and a lot of long car rides to care for my children while I locked myself in the office and wrote. Accomplishing anything in the company of two rambunctious little boys is a challenge, and writing a novel sometimes felt downright impossible. But here it is, thanks to you.

Second on my list is my agent, Jim McCarthy, who performed the role of midwife in birthing this literary baby. Though *Surviving Cyril* didn't sell traditionally, it wasn't for lack of trying. This is a fickle business, and not all books are born the same way. Thanks for being in it for the long haul.

It will be obvious to anyone who has ever read or watched *Cyrano de Bergerac* that I owe a huge literary debt to playwright Edmund Rostand. If literature is defined as a conversation across time, my hope is that this novel continues the discussion that *Cyrano* began. Another rather large tip of the hat goes to actor Steve Martin, whose comedic interpretation of Rostand's masterpiece, *Roxanne*, was a huge influence during my formative years.

Special mention goes to *Des Moines Register* columnist Daniel P. Finney, whose incredibly vulnerable series on recovering from morbid obesity provided insight into Cyril's character that I could not have gained elsewhere.

I am fortunate to have a host of writerly friends, many of whom read portions of this manuscript at various points along its journey to completion. Most of you operate under a variety of pseudonyms, and rather than risk terribly misnaming or completely forgetting someone, I'll simply say: Thank you. You know who you are.

Last, but not least, I offer my love and gratitude to Kelson Hootman. If he doesn't know why, he certainly should.

Discussion Questions

THE FOLLOWING PAGES CONTAIN two sets of discussion questions. The first set is intended for use in any group discussion of *Surviving Cyril*. The second set of questions is designed for us in a comparative discussion between *Cyrano de Bergerac* and *Surviving Cyril*.

Discussion questions for *Surviving Cyril*

1. In Chapter 1, Robin has just been widowed. How does her grief affect how she acts and reacts to those around her?

2. Who is the most important person in Robin's life? Why? How does this compare with who (or what) other major characters prioritize? What does each character's primary motivation say about his or her outlook on life?

3. What role do parents play in the narrative? How do their actions and behaviors influence their children?

4. In what ways does Robin fulfill traditional female gender roles? In what ways does she break with tradition? How does her conformity/nonconformity impact her relationships with others?

5. What does Tavis have in common with Robin's father? How about Cyril and her father?

6. Why is Cyril so good with Seth—and so bad with everyone else?

7. What role does Cyril's obesity play in the narrative? If he were to lose a significant amount of weight, would that change anything?

8. Later in the narrative, Robin realizes her grief has blinded her to the struggles of others. What are some things she fails to notice or empathize with? Is she truly alone in her grief or not?

9. At one point, Seth asks if Cyril is a "bad guy." How would you answer this question?

10. Deep down, do you think Robin knew—or at least suspected—the truth about the letters?

11. How does knowing Cyril wrote the letters change your reading of the book? Looking back, what were some details (such as Tav's knack for memorization) that might have tipped you off? Which scenes or passages read completely differently, knowing what you know now? Does it change your view of Cyril?

12. Identify some of the moments where Robin or Cyril could have avoided a great deal of pain "if only" they had chosen to say or do something slightly different. Are there any "if only" moments in your own life? What might you have done differently?

13. Is Tavis a hero? How about Cyril? What will Robin tell her children about both men?

14. Ten years from now... with Robin be waiting?

15. What letter(s) didn't Robin burn?

Comparative discussion:
Cyrano de Bergerac and *Surviving Cyril*

1. Identify some of the scenes, thematic elements, and symbolism shared between *Cyrano de Bergerac* and *Surviving Cyril*.

2. Compare the three central characters: Roxanne/Robin, Cyrano/Cyril, and Christian/Tavis.

3. How does Cyril's profession and personality compare with Cyrano's? What is Cyril's "long nose?"

4. How does the addition of a child impact Robin as well as the overall narrative?

5. Compare the relationship between Cyrano and Christian with that of Cyril and Tavis.

6. Most of *Cyrano de Bergerac* is devoted to Cyrano and Christian's relationship/deception before skipping 15 years to the "reveal." *Surviving Cyril* spends most of the narrative in that "gap" period. Why might Hootman have made this choice?

7. How does telling the story from Roxanne/Robin's point of view change the narrative? Does she view the deception differently than Cyrano/Cyril?

8. Does Hootman's retelling change your view of *Cyrano de Bergerac?* What insights into the original story have you gained?

9.   *Cyrano de Bergerac* combines elements of comedy and tragedy. Steve Martin's 1987 comedy, *Roxanne*, is a comedic retelling of the story. Would you consider Surviving Cyril to be a tragedy, a comedy, or something else?

10. *Cyrano de Bergerac* ends with the death of Cyrano. In *Surviving Cyril,* Cyril goes to prison. How does this detail change the narrative? (If you've seen *Roxanne*, discuss the effect of that ending as well.)

CPSIA information can be obtained
at www.ICGtesting.com
Printed in the USA
LVOW12s0925090717
540729LV00003B/517/P

9 780998 807003